PRAISE FOR KRISTÍN MARJA BALDURSDÓTTIR

"Kristín Marja's novel isn't just a well-written story about the life of a female artist in the last century—it relates to today. *Karitas Untitled* is the story of a woman trapped in a tangible tug-of-war. And it's powerfully told."

—Melkorka Óskarsdóttir, *Fréttablaðið* newspaper, Iceland

"Karitas's story is graced with precisely all the qualities you would expect to find in a great, award-winning book."

—*Kristianstadsbladet* newspaper, Sweden

"A wonderful story that, like any great novel, grabs you for the duration of the story and then follows you long after the book, sadly, is over."

—Kathrine Lilleør, *Berlingske* newspaper, Denmark

"Let it be said at once: Baldursdóttir's novel about the fate of women at the beginning of the twentieth century is magnificent. One laps up the story as if it were the milk that is fundamental for survival in remote Iceland . . . Like the fat Icelandic herring that are salted into barrels, so the history of Icelandic women is set in layers—remembered, retold, sketched, and written by a dedicated descendant."

—Tine Maria Winther, *Politiken* newspaper, Denmark

"Kristín Marja Baldursdóttir's novel *Karitas Untitled* is not just the poignant story of a young woman but also a portrait of that transitional period in Icelandic history that led to modernization."

—Fríða Björk Ingvarsdóttir, *Morgunblaðið* newspaper, Iceland

Karitas
Untitled

Karitas Untitled

Kristín Marja Baldursdóttir

Translated by Philip Roughton

AMAZON **CROSSING**

Text copyright © 2004 by Kristín Marja Baldursdóttir
Translation copyright © 2022 by Philip Roughton
All rights reserved.

Previously published as *Karitas án titils* by Forlagið in Iceland in 2004. Translated from Icelandic by Philip Roughton. First published in English by Amazon Crossing in 2022.

Published by Amazon Crossing, Seattle

www.apub.com

Amazon, the Amazon logo, and Amazon Crossing are trademarks of Amazon.com, Inc., or its affiliates.

ISBN-13: 9781542027076 (hardcover)
ISBN-10: 1542027071 (hardcover)

ISBN-13: 9781542027083 (paperback)
ISBN-10: 154202708X (paperback)

Cover design by Emily Mahon

Cover image: *North Wind, Iona* (*The Bather*), by Francis Campbell Boileau Cadell (1883–1937). Private collection/Bridgeman Images.

Printed in the United States of America

First edition

To Soffía Eydís, Hildur Erla, and Hulda Elsa Björgvinsdóttir

This book was written in memory of my paternal grandmother, Guðný Sæmundsdóttir, who raised me; my mother, Hulda Elsa Gestsdóttir; my maternal grandmother, Kristín Jónsdóttir; and my great-grandmothers, Sigríður Ólafsdóttir and Karitas Guðnadóttir.

Special thanks go to Hrafnhildur Schram, art historian, for providing assistance and information about Icelandic women artists of the past, as well as Bogga Sigfúsdóttir from Skagafjörður, Elsa Jónsdóttir from Borgarfjörður Eystri, and Erna S. Jónsdóttir, who worked as a hired hand in Öræfi, for her knowledge and stories of the people and history in that district. Moreover, I would like to thank Arngrímur Viðar Ásgeirsson from Borgarfjörður Eystri and Guðrún Bergsdóttir in the Öræfi district for their assistance and cordiality.

I

Karitas

Untitled 1915

Pencil drawing

"Take this child from me. I'm about to lose my wits."

The maid stares wide-eyed into space.

My sister and I exchange glances. She stops in the middle of her hymn.

Our mother walks slowly over to the maid and lifts our sleeping brother from her lap before the maid adds her usual refrain: "Down again I needs must go."

She gets to her feet and crosses the room in a stately manner, knitting needles in hand, but suddenly twitches, throws her hand over her mouth, and tries to stifle her cries as she dashes to the stairs and down. Our mother positions herself at the top of the stairs as if to prevent us from leaving, but she doesn't need to—we're under strict instructions to stay inside during the maid's hysterical fits. We've never seen what she gets up to out in the farmyard, but the ruckus she makes when she yowls, wails, and curses the steep mountains can always be heard inside.

From outside comes a prolonged howl.

My sister starts in again on her hymn, attempting to drown out the noise.

Our mother hurries out. I follow her. Just this once—I simply have to see what it means to lose one's wits. I go down, paying no heed to my sisters' reproachful looks. Our mother is standing in the farmyard by the southernmost building, looking up at the gables. I duck, slink to the well, and crouch down.

The four gables loom against the dark-blue sky and white moon.

Straddling one of the gables, arms outstretched, is the maid, wailing. She smacks her splayed legs against the gable as if trying to spur a nag, gesticulates and claps her hands as she jabbers and curses, throws out her arms, tilts back her head and howls. Is like a cross on the house.

Woman cross on a house.

The performance repeats itself. The maid curses as she sits astride the gable, holds her arms out stiffly, and howls.

From inside the farmhouse comes the sound of a high-flown hymn.

The moon laughs, but the mountains are silent.

My brothers come walking up in the moonlight, each with bundles of cod heads in both hands. They stop abruptly in the farmyard, stare thunderstruck.

"She's lost her knitting needle," says our mother.

The clothesline sang in the icy air as the sisters touched it. The aprons that they had hung to dry had snuggled together in the cold and transformed into a tangled, frozen clump. A sea wind had lashed the aprons during the night, and the sisters tried to work out its methods. Had it blown first from the north, then from the east, before finishing its winding with a prolonged southern blast—or done the reverse? They glanced all around, as if expecting to see the wind rush by with a head and tail, but it had made its way over the precipitous mountain well before dawn, leaving behind frost that growled beneath their feet.

The maid came out into the farmyard in search of the knitting needle that she'd lost during her last fit, saw the garments on the line, and said, after poking at them with a moan, "You'll be tangled like aprons all your lives, my lambs." She bleated into the icy morning air as she looked around for her needle. The girls' mother joined them in the yard. Spoke not a single word as she examined the aprons. Simply pressed her wool shawl to her bosom and screwed up her eyes, as people do in bone-chilling cold. Looking half-frozen, she shifted her attention from the aprons to bay, short, broad, and brimming with surf, peered hard at the open ocean as if wanting to conjure their father up from its depths, then turned halfway and stared gloomily up at the snow-covered mountain that could, whenever it pleased, unburden itself only to bury men and beasts. Finally, with her back to the sea, she let her eyes run up the valley to the heath where the evil spirit dwelled. After turning full circle, she said dryly, "We're moving north in the spring."

In the mornings, the sea was medium blue. The bay like a china plate with a white stripe around the rim. At first, the sisters thought it was the winds to the west that had made up their mother's mind. Those cold winds from high in the sky that circle over the farms hunkered in the valley, dive, tear, and shred, batter men and beasts, whip the sea into a frenzied, malignant monster that devours young men. Young, beautiful fathers who set sail before sunrise, beaming with optimism, but fail to return after sunset as promised. Karitas often woke just as her papa was leaving. He would notice her awake in her bed, bring her a slice of bread sprinkled with brown sugar; she would munch it while the others in the family room slept. He gave her her first sketchbook, which he had bought in Ísafjörður, said that she was so good at drawing, had probably gotten it from him. He drew so beautifully, her papa, and he showed her how. Then one morning, he left and didn't return in the evening.

It also crossed the sisters' minds that their mother might finally have had enough of the maid and those fits of hers. The poor woman always had bad days between Candlemas in February and the Feast of the Cross in May, because it was at that time, many decades ago, that the mountain sent white death over the valley. But despite the derangement that had set in after the avalanche swallowed her children, she was easy enough to get along with between fits, and was a real workhorse. As it turned out, the decision to move had nothing to do with her—which came to light when the brothers asked their mother straight-out why they had to go.

"So that you can attend the Comprehensive School in Akureyri," she said. "I've heard that town is lush with greenery."

They'd often heard her talk about the benefits of schooling, how important it was to be well-read and educated. She herself had wanted to study midwifery, which would have involved moving to Reykjavík or Copenhagen, but somehow nothing came of the idea, even though her father had been reasonably well-off and could perhaps have paid for her studies. "I expect it was Papa who kept her here in the west," said Halldóra. "He was such a beautiful man; I'm sure she didn't want to lose him to someone else." The itinerant teacher had told their mother that she simply had to send her eldest son, Ólafur, to school, and that Páll, the next eldest, was no slouch when it came to his lessons, either. Yet the man never mentioned the three sisters, despite their being older than the brothers and reading with no less enthusiasm. Their mother, on the other hand, had been planning on getting them into school from the start. She said: "The times are changing. Down south, women go to school—even to the Learned School. They publish newspapers, hold seats on the city council, and have their own union. They'll probably even end up as legislators in the capital."

But the maid didn't want to move with them to the north.

"I'm not budging. In the west I was born, and in the west I shall die. I'm not abandoning this bay while my children lie beneath its grassy valley, waiting for their mama." She kept harping on their mother's mad idea of charging over mountain and moor with six children in tow, and as winter drew to a close, little else was discussed in the valley but the widow's sad decision to take her six children and march off into the unknown. People shuddered at the thought. When to this was added her determination to get the entire group of children into school, people sat shaking their heads, and began asking each other earnestly whether it wasn't perhaps Steinunn Ólafsdóttir herself who was mad, and not that poor maid of hers. And the maid whom no one else had wanted to employ now enjoyed the full sympathy of her neighbors and was offered a place at three farms in the valley. The fisherman who had taken the widow's elder sons with him to sea was the only one who ventured to ask her how she, a penniless widow, planned to support six children in town. "I expect I'll use the knitting machine," she replied slowly.

Ólafur and Páll were thrilled to be going to Akureyri to study and immediately began trying to sell their worldly possessions, such as their pocketknives and whetstones, whereas each of the sisters reacted differently. Karitas was like a reef subject to the tides, either standing tall and firm or immersed in bottomless fantasies, paying no mind to the bustle. Bjarghildur, who was convinced she was her mother's favorite and was considered by many to be a miniature version of her, prepared for the move resolutely and prudently, backing her mother's plan in word and deed. But the eldest daughter, on whom the widow relied most, seemed distracted. A boy farther up the valley, Sumarliði, had become the object of her adoration. When, four years ago, the great avalanche wrecked two farms and buried a third, this Sumarliði had saved lives through sheer, dogged persistence. After several days of shoveling, the rescuers had pulled out four bodies and wanted to stop, considering it out of the question for any others to have survived, but the young man wouldn't hear of it. On his last legs from the cold and lack of sleep, Sumarliði had adamantly refused, and when the exhausted men witnessed his determination, they had no other choice than to take up their shovels again. With the icy silence of the mountain at their backs, they kept digging until they finally reached a roof. The part of the farmhouse where the residents had been when the avalanche fell hadn't collapsed, and five people, among them a couple with an eight-week-old child, saw the light of day once more. They were all safe and sound, and later, the woman said that the most difficult moment of her life had been when she heard the rescuers stop shoveling. The couple rewarded Sumarliði with a gold watch for saving their lives, and word of his heroism spread throughout the fjord.

When Halldóra saw Sumarliði lift his shovel again, she told herself softly, though just loud enough for her blue-nosed sisters standing next to her to hear, "This man or none." She was fifteen years old at the time. Her younger sisters were eleven and thirteen, and hadn't yet started their periods. Still, they understood what she meant. On the other hand, it proved difficult to get the hero to understand the girl's wishes, despite numerous attempts being made to sharpen his awareness. For four whole years, Halldóra would make trips up the valley under the pretext of visiting Sumarliði's sister, who was exceptionally dull and consequently very wearisome, and would cast him warm glances and laugh at his jokes every time the young folk gathered. But it all came to nothing; the man was completely unmoved. The younger sisters found this terribly puzzling, considering how pretty Halldóra was, how fine-figured. They'd even pitched in to help straighten out their sister's love life, stopping Sumarliði on the road and pointing out that Halldóra was at home, if he might like to take a little walk with her. But he just gave a manly laugh and said that they certainly were a piece of work. When nothing could be done to persuade the young man, Halldóra became like most other girls whose hearts weigh heavy with love: one minute upbeat and hopeful, and the next, taciturn and downcast.

Thus, the upcoming move hardly worked to lift her spirits; far from it. As preparations were being made, she moped around the farmhouse, sluggishly doing what she was asked. But the siblings all knew the reason for her glumness, and because nothing is as hard for a soul to bear as a forlorn heart, they tried to be patient with her, even shielding her when necessary, despite none of them ever having been lovesick. Yet they all knew how much she hurt. Shortly before their move, Halldóra's last spark of hope was extinguished when Sumarliði sailed south with another man to fetch a boat—and did not stop to say goodbye.

The farm and most of its belongings were sold—livestock, buildings, utensils, and tools—and then they had to pack whatever was going north with them. Everything had to fit in a single horse-drawn cart, and Karitas noticed her mother clench her teeth more than once as she sorted their things and arranged them in trunks: clothing, blankets, and linen, as well as the cups and saucers, the apple-puff pan, the iron, and other essential items. She had planned to give the maid the waffle iron as a parting gift, but Bjarghildur wouldn't hear of it after all the gossip the woman had started. As far as she was concerned, the maid could show up to her next job empty-handed. It would serve her right. But Bjarghildur didn't tell her mother this in so many words; instead, she acted dejected and said, quite piteously, "Not only do we have to move north, we also won't be getting any waffles on holidays!" It sufficed. The waffle iron went into the trunk.

Karitas

Untitled 1915

Pencil drawing

The morning is misty gray.

The colors of the sea, the mountain, and the valley have dulled, as if the thin strip of fog painted over a picture in haste before fleeing the bitter cold that crept into the bay in the small hours.

Over the heath, still white with snow despite it being Whitsuntide, goes a cart, pulled by sturdy workhorses. Men from the valley escort the widow to her ship.

She rides straight-backed, with Halldóra next to her, shoulders slumped. The two elder brothers follow the cart, listening to its every creak.

Among the trunks, knitting machine, and sacks huddle we two younger sisters, bundled in wool. Our youngest brother rests in the arms of Bjarghildur, who hums to him, while I sit scrunched between two trunks, watching the shoreline recede.

A horse-drawn cart on a white heath.

Anxiety at the trip over the heath has kept me from sleeping for many nights. I know that an evil spirit dwells here, luring travelers and dragging them to a deep bowl hidden among the steep, landslide-ridden slopes. I look bitterly at my siblings, who have never sensed the presence of trolls and monsters as I have, let alone perceived ghosts, and I regret not having stayed behind like the maid.

Over the white heath hangs a fog that is waiting to swallow us.

All around me in the cold stillness, I hear whispering.

The hold's hatches and the opening to the staircase had both been shut after the sea worsened, and the sour smell of vomit hung over the prostrate passengers. The families had prepared makeshift beds on the floor, while two women not in the death grip of seasickness propped themselves on their elbows and entertained each other with birthing stories. Steinunn was speaking.

"Karitas came from the sea, but Bjarghildur from the ground like any old potato plant. I was home digging up potatoes when I began having contractions, and everyone else was out in the fields. At first, I ignored the disturbance because the potatoes needed harvesting no less than the hay, and I was convinced I had enough time as it had taken three days to bring my eldest daughter into the world. But when the pangs intensified and I thought I had better go inside, it was too late: all I could do was squat there in the potato patch and let nature take its course. Two years later, when I had my third daughter, it was the same story, but that time, I was down at the beach gathering seaweed when the contractions began. From my previous experience, I knew how things would go, so I went behind a big rock where I would have sand beneath my feet, but as I was delivering, the tide began coming in, and it was only by the grace of God that the child wasn't swept away. After two births in nature, I didn't dare venture far from the farmhouse the next times I was due, and because of that, it was soft bedclothes that received my three boys, not sea and soil."

It was evident from the other passenger's expression that she wasn't certain whether Steinunn was telling her what really happened, or a dream. Still, it being an excellent story, she decided not to ask, although she did peer at the sisters as if trying to guess which had come from where and which had come into the world the ordinary way. They lay sprawled over each other like kits in their den, deathly pale and helpless from nausea, but their brothers, apart from the youngest, sleeping in his mother's lap, were no longer susceptible to seasickness and had stayed on deck with the crew.

Steinunn's fellow passenger had no such stories of her own, having delivered all of her children indoors, but in order not to be outdone by the widow, she resorted to relating some unusual delivery stories that she'd heard. After chatting long enough to reach the point when conversants begin sharing their personal circumstances and plans, Steinunn told the woman briefly about her desire to provide her children with educations. The woman, astonished at Steinunn's daring, rocked on her mattress and asked whether it wasn't madness for the widow to rush off into the unknown with six children and an empty purse. Steinunn replied that in this case, having no money made no difference.

"In Iceland, no one who works dies."

Her fellow passenger agreed, but said that she, poor commoner that she was, could never have imagined sending her children to school, and in any case, it was too late now, since they'd all grown up and moved away. Yet she couldn't resist mentioning one of her sons, who was a highly distinguished person, "and a deckhand on the *Gullfoss* itself, neither more nor less, the new ship that arrived in the spring. On board, they dance and sing, I'm told; the ship is so big and steady that there's hardly any rolling out on the open sea. The cabins are all first class, and when the ship glides into the ports of Europe, all of the passengers, most of whom are higher-ups, gather on deck and wave at the crowd waiting on the quay." Steinunn, who'd had to settle for a place in the ship's hold to spare expenditure and had little desire to hear about the luxuries of the upper class, thought for a moment before replying that she doubted that people waited on the quay in foreign lands—"at least not the men, because as far as I know, all of Europe is at war, and they're most likely on the battlefield, and although I don't doubt the magnificence of the ship, I can hardly imagine that women on the Continent have any more time than we do for loitering on the quay, even if a ship docks." At this reminder of the war being fought on the Continent, Steinunn's fellow passenger grew anxious about her son and didn't hear it when Karitas asked quietly whether she had any idea what it cost to sail aboard such a fine ship. When no answer came, Karitas gave Bjarghildur a little nudge and whispered in her ear: "Do you think we'll ever sail overseas aboard such a ship?" Bjarghildur responded crustily to the irritating whispering, waved Karitas off, and exhaled weakly, "Leave me alone; I have no home." Karitas saw that there was little to be gained from her in the state she was in and turned to Halldóra to ask the same thing, but stopped when she saw her sister's expression. It didn't result from nausea alone, that much she knew, and she stroked her sister's arm to express affection and sympathy. Her sister just lay there, curled up and miserable on her makeshift bed, although the suffering on her face did nothing to spoil her comeliness. She resembled an image of the Savior on the cross.

Gloom settled over the hold; they were out on the deep, and the rolling intensified. The vomiting worsened, the little ones wet themselves, and the sisters held their noses, tried to breathe through their mouths. Then they felt the ship slow down; the engines hiccuped and stopped. People propped themselves on their elbows and stared at the hatches. For several moments, neither a cough nor a groan was heard.

"Ice," someone then groaned from one corner. "Damned ice."

The hatches were torn open.

Freezing sea air streamed into the hold.

Karitas

Untitled 1915

Pencil drawing

Glaring white light floods the deck.

Dark-clad passengers stand deathly still, hunched, squeezing their eyes shut and opening them in turn. Finally, the view clears.

The ship is lying at the edge of an ice sheet that stretches as far northward as the eye can see.

The scowling, thickly bearded captain comes and stands before the group, his legs spread and his hands behind his back, and announces to the passengers that they cannot proceed northward past Horn; the country's old enemy was blocking the route, as everyone could see, but before the ship turned back for Ísafjörður, they should all gather for a short devotional this cold Whitsunday. The deck officers hand him a hymnbook and Bible. He takes off his captain's hat.

The passengers, tousled from their sojourn in the hold, glance at each other.

Beneath the still, clear sky, the word of God is read and hymns are sung.

A devotional on deck.

Our mother stands there with her children, her expression melancholy. Halldóra and I clasp our hands over our stomachs and try to hum along for appearance's sake, but Bjarghildur is truly cheered by the word of God. At the hymn's second verse, she steps forward boldly, expands her chest with a deep breath, gazes with sparkling eyes at the expanse of ice, and sings so loudly that you can see down her throat.

She leads the singing, earning her the notice and admiration of her fellow passengers. The captain praises the power of the young lady's voice. Bjarghildur beams.

The ship turns back for Ísafjörður.

Our mother brings us along to coffee with acquaintances of hers in town. When they hear how the sea ice has hindered her journey to freedom and schooling, they declare, in a slightly moralizing tone: "Is your wild-goose chase with the children finished, then?"

We hear our mother's terse, cold reply:

"I'll just go the long way around."

Sailing southward and eastward around the country took so long that the sisters lost their land legs. Little time was lost docking; the old steamer stopped in only three ports, and it wasn't until the last one out east that the passengers from the west got the chance to go ashore. The siblings were disappointed not to get to see the capital. It was late when they sailed into Reykjavík harbor, and there was no crowd to greet them. A few men on duty saw to mooring the ship, while several souls on their way east waited on the quay, motionless in the fine rain. The siblings stood clustered at the railing, staring flabbergasted at the throng of buildings in the capital until the crew cast off, and the ship continued at full steam. On the way south, the weather had been decent enough for the passengers to remain on deck during the day; they only had to endure the hold overnight, but now the waves began rising, causing the sisters to lose their will to live once more and stay below. Approaching the harbor in the Westman Islands, the ship was reasonably steady, so they crawled up on deck to get a breath of fresh air and gazed torpidly at the seabirds screeching on the cliffs. "Looks bountiful enough here, plenty of birds and fishes," screeched Karitas above the noise of the fulmars, attempting to lighten her own mood and that of her sisters, but their only response was to retch and fumble their way back down into the hold. However, as they sailed eastward along the south coast, with its white glaciers and black sand, the sea began to settle and their bodies to return to normal. The sisters stuck their heads up out of the hold, their faces deathly pale, and held themselves nearly straight-backed despite their shakiness. Apart from the chill in the air and cool southern breeze, the weather was fair as could be, and passengers emerged one by one onto the deck, filled with the hopefulness of Icelanders in the sun. The sea was smooth and beautifully blue, and in the midst of all the mildness, Steinunn grew so sleepy that she could barely hold up her head. Before succumbing to her longing to return below and lie down, she explained apologetically to her children that her drowsiness was caused by sailing counterclockwise.

The sisters sat down on a coil of rope on deck and began combing each other's hair with long, slow strokes. The sea air danced in their locks, and they squinted in the sunshine. When it came to braiding, Halldóra was first, since she was the eldest. The others sat her between them, divided her hair in two, and braided it nimbly. After tying the braids up, they switched seats, the next eldest replacing the eldest. When Karitas sat in the middle, she turned the conversation to their future in the greenery to the north. "What do you suppose will become of us in the north?" Halldóra braided her youngest sister's hair so tightly it made her scalp ache. "As if it matters what becomes of us. Things could hardly get any worse. We're like vagrants; our home has been broken up, we've been dragged away from friends and all the places we knew. Maybe I'll just enter a convent." "You'll have to go abroad to do that," said Karitas curtly, turning her head, which was turned forcefully back. "Mama said we've been promised lodging with the man giving us jobs," said Bjarghildur, newly braided and refreshed and eager to steer the conversation onto more-hopeful paths. But the eldest sister was snappish: "One room, with access to a measly little kitchen. All seven of us are supposed to spend the winter cramped up in there, I ask? Frozen by a relentless draft, no doubt. I've heard that those wooden hovels are leagues behind turf farms when it comes to warmth. How are they even heated, might I ask? A coal stove in the corner of the kitchen can hardly do the job, besides the fact that an eternal norther blows on Akureyri, with no mountains to block it, as in the west. We'll die of cold before the year is out." The younger sisters had no reply. They hadn't known she was capable of such bitterness, their Halldóra, who was always so warmhearted and resourceful—and they blamed the change on the lack of initiative of the hero in the bay at home. Karitas, however, couldn't help but think about the wind out west; the mountains certainly hadn't sheltered the aprons from it, that much was certain. But she didn't dare mention this, as matters stood, and instead asked innocently, in order to soften her sister's mood, "Do you suppose it's warm overseas?"

Their mother slept soundly as they sailed past the Eastfjords, which opened one after another in dazzling sunshine. At the mouth of Seyðisfjörður, they undertook to wake her, which was no easy task, and sailing up the fjord, so mesmerizingly calm, deep, and blue, had a strange effect on some of the travelers. Which wasn't surprising at all; it was like sailing into Divinity itself. No one could say a word; they just stared silently at the mountains and landmarks, and when a church came into view on a small spit to starboard, those coming home swallowed hard to try to hide their emotions. Karitas watched them in secret and found their reactions normal; this was their fjord, but when she saw her eldest sister's rapt expression, saw the luster in her eyes as she stared into the blue, she felt uneasy. It was as if Halldóra had disappeared into another world, and Karitas had to nudge her twice before she snapped out of it. She looked distractedly at her sister, "I'll be staying here." It never occurred to Karitas that she might be serious; she'd heard people praise the beauty of mountains and fjords before without it really meaning anything. But that wasn't the case here, and neither before nor since did anyone understand what had gotten into Halldóra.

On the quay, the atmosphere was different than in the south; the people were lively and held their heads high. They greeted the passengers as if they were neighbors, asked about the weather and important personages in the capital, and pointed out where the travelers could get fresh milk and pastries. With solid ground underfoot, the siblings were extremely light of step, as was their mother, who was perking up after her long sleep. As a result, none of them paid much attention to the changed look in their eldest sister's face and eyes as she regarded the buildings and townspeople. They and their shipmates sat on a slope that overlooked the gleaming fjord, enjoying their pastries and gulping down milk. Then Halldóra stood up, wiped her mouth, and announced bluntly that she was going to stay in Seyðisfjörður and needed to pop back aboard to fetch her things. Her braids didn't move as she walked in a stately manner back down to the quay. Her family stopped eating. They had only just managed to ask each other what was going on when Halldóra reappeared with her bundle. Steinunn didn't want to make a fuss in front of the other travelers, all watching with bated breath, so she told the other children to wait quietly while she herself got to her feet and went to meet her daughter. She stood there talking to Halldóra for quite some time. Finally, they both returned, sat down on the slope, and continued to eat as if nothing had happened. But when it came time for the ship to depart, it became clear that Halldóra had gotten her way. She began saying her goodbyes to her brothers and sisters, who looked at each other in bewilderment. "Halldóra will be staying here," said Steinunn. "She'll find a good job." Karitas was baffled, but Bjarghildur looked gravely at her sister and asked how she was planning to feed herself. "It will be taken care of," the mother answered for her daughter; she had heard that many people were on the lookout for housemaids.

Tears welled in the brothers' eyes, and the youngest began crying as they said goodbye to their favorite sister. Halldóra hugged them one by one, kissed them, and asked God to keep them, then swung her bundle over her shoulder and walked away. As if it had always been her plan. They stared at her silently, motionless. She had walked some distance down the road when Bjarghildur's head cleared. First, she snorted, and then tore off her shawl, turned up her nose, stamped her feet, and finally said, "For shame!" The family members stared at her, their souls still numb from this unexpected parting and not knowing quite how they should take this eccentricity. They stood stock-still as Bjarghildur ran off after Halldóra. She caught up with her sister, circled her, waved her arms, wagged her index finger at her, and finally slapped her. Time stood still for several moments, and then Bjarghildur strode back to them, swinging her arms dramatically. Halldóra followed close behind. Stiff-shouldered.

The ship was being untied when the family reboarded it. Steinunn held her eldest daughter's shoulders and made sure that she didn't stumble, and folk remarked that the girl must be seriously ill, so drained did she look. Once they were out at sea, Karitas whispered anxiously in her sister's ear, "What exactly did you say to her?" but Bjarghildur only retorted haughtily that it was none of her business. That was that. Bjarghildur furrowed her brow and said no more. Halldóra sat there stone-faced. Karitas didn't dare ask her.

The cold intensified as they sailed farther north, and sharp cracks sounded from the steamer's tired planks. People sat huddled in the hold; men blew into their palms, and women pulled their woolen shawls tighter about them. The eldest daughter still stared blankly. She hadn't said a word since they left Seyðisfjörður, and acted as if Bjarghildur were a north wind that had to be avoided. Their destination drew nearer.

The brothers relayed word from the captain that they would reach the mouth of Eyjafjörður by noon, but there was no need to tell Steinunn that it was a short distance to their destination; she had long since gathered her children and their belongings. She hung her head and nodded again and again, as if making mental calculations or going over past events it would be best to have at the ready in the coming days. Then she pulled her large, thick woolen shawl over her shoulders, looked over her flock, and said curtly, "Put on your mittens, too. It's getting colder."

The sea ice sailed with them into the promised fjord. The mountainsides were flecked with white, and over them hung a gray veil. The biting breeze slipped down their necklines and under their skirts. Icebergs floated aimlessly on the harbor basin, called "the Puddle," and started in alarm and scattered when the ship stormed mercilessly past them. The woman who was going to provide her children with an education in this northern town known for its abundant greenery paled when she came up from the hold and looked around. The children followed and took deep breaths of cold air when they saw their new home decked out in ice. "Isn't it June?" snapped Bjarghildur. "Where are all the trees, Mama, and the flowers?" asked the youngest child. The elder brothers, who, due to their intelligence, bore the responsibility for the widow's feeling obligated to provide them an education, could barely hide their disappointment when they saw the frosty town, even though the houses along the shore, some two- and three-storied, were no less stately than those in the south, and spat over the railing. It was Karitas who tried once more to lighten the family's mood, saying cheerfully as the ship docked: "Well, Mama, we've gone the whole way around."

They found lodging in a fish warehouse.

There were big piles of saltfish on the lower floor, and the stench was so strong it burned their nostrils. On the upper floor were rooms with bunks for the girls who worked cleaning fish, and there they lugged their trunks. Steinunn was so disappointed not to have gotten the housing she had been promised that she froze for several long moments on the threshold of the room to which they were shown. Had Ólafur, who remembered that his education was within reach, not tried to lighten the mood by speaking up, it was unclear what her next reaction might have been. "In any case, we're lucky to have this until we find something better," he said in a loud, manly voice, and at that, the family went in.

Two bunks, four beds. As usual, they slept two to a bed, except that Halldóra now got her own. They felt they owed Halldóra something, though they weren't certain wherein the debt lay; they simply wanted to do all they could to see the warmth return to her eyes. The rooms came with access to a kitchen, and when the fish girls congregated to eat, there was little elbow room, and even less when the family from the west joined them. But the girls welcomed them warmly. They were given pats on the shoulders and hot coffee, and this kindness helped Steinunn to regain her bearings. She invited the children to come along and have a look at the town while she went to meet the shipowner.

The family from the Westfjords ambled on sea legs through the streets of the northern town, looking in every direction as if on the run from the law. They couldn't begin to find the words to describe what they saw: the tall, elegant wooden houses that lined the shore all the way out to the spit made them feel both confused and out of place. The brothers pulled out their handkerchiefs as they regarded the Comprehensive School, which towered like a palace on its hill above the town. Everywhere they looked, there were shops: Thomsen and Hansen, Jónsson and Björnsson, a soap shop, butcher shop, bakery. They had no idea how to comport themselves in the midst of all this splendor and stepped on each other's toes and into puddles; they saw banks and a hospital, a factory and a freezing plant, and at the quay, whole mountains of empty herring barrels. One or two things were beyond their comprehension at first, such as the poles with nine cross-bars standing alongside the streets, but after some deliberation, they guessed that these were so-called telephone poles. A small house stand-ing in the middle of a square with a sign saying "Cigars and Tobaccos" awoke in them the suspicion that Icelandic wasn't even spoken here. "French," muttered Páll. "English," corrected Ólafur. "It's Danish, you numbskulls," said Bjarghildur, tired of their ignorance. But when an automobile suddenly roared past them, they were thunderstruck, and little Pétur burst into tears.

They fled back to the fish warehouse.

That first evening, they gathered around the small table in their room and ate bread with anchovies, which their mother had bought at Jónsson's or Björnsson's, and when they had all eaten their fill, they were informed of the plan of action in their new home. "Tomorrow morning, we're all going to work," said Steinunn. "The boys at the freezing plant, while the rest of us wash fish at the lot. Karitas will stay here. She will do the cooking and the laundry and keep an eye on Pétur." The last time they'd all sat together around a small table was just after the children's father had died. Now, no one was dead, but it was still as if a small nameless flower were withering away. They had no foothold; they sat together in their cubbyhole as if shackled there. They couldn't even hop out into the yard. Karitas longed to be able to take the air, as she had back home in the bay; wave her arms, dance with the birds and be happy, and she suddenly felt like an old woman who couldn't remember why she was there, of all places. But her mother remembered. She cleared her throat, reached for a box lying at her feet, took some rock candy from it, and offered it to them. Then she brought out a Bible. "We won't be knitting tonight—but which do you want to hear, stories from the Old or the New Testament?" Being unaccustomed to having a choice of Bible reading, the children looked at each other in surprise. "The Old," they muttered. They found life more epic in that part of the Bible. "Jacob or Moses?" Steinunn continued, sticking a piece of rock candy in her mouth. "Moses," said the brothers, who found the parting of the Red Sea captivating. "I've told you that story so often," said Steinunn. "I think I'll tell you of when Jacob's daughter falls into the clutches of Hamor's son." She hurriedly munched her candy, leafed through the Bible, found the right chapter, and read the first verse. Then she let the book sink into her lap, stared out the window at the bright summer evening, and continued the story. This wasn't unusual at all, because she knew the Bible practically by heart. But as the story progressed, astonished expressions appeared on the faces of the elder sisters, who were no less well-read than their mother in the books of Moses, although they never flaunted it, and Bjarghildur opened and closed her mouth in silent indignation. Halldóra smirked. Tucked under her duvet after the story was over, Karitas realized that the narrative had undergone considerable changes in their mother's telling and that Jacob's daughter had behaved most peculiarly. Hamor's son had raped the girl; their mother hadn't changed that, but what came afterward was much more colorful than normal. The heroines of the old Icelandic *Njáll's Saga* had stepped into the book of Genesis.

Tucked into their bunks, the children tried to breathe normally so as not to worry their mother, but anxiety kept them from sleeping well into the night, and when the cold, northern daylight pushed its way through the thin curtains, they sprang awake, feeling slightly addled. With rather much ado, they prepared themselves for their first day of work in this town; items that had been plain to see in their open trunks just last evening were now impossible to find. In the kitchen, skirts swished and plates and mugs clattered, but somehow they all managed to slurp down the ink-black coffee before heading downstairs at six o'clock. Karitas and little Pétur, left alone upstairs, looked at each other worriedly. Now that Karitas was responsible for the housework, she ordered her little brother to make the beds while she gathered up socks and other clothing that needed rinsing out after their great sea voyage.

Karitas

Untitled 1915

Pencil drawing

Water is boiling in a large pot on a coal stove.

I pour the hot water into an enamel laundry tub, drop underwear into it, take some soft soap in my hand, squish and press it between my fingers, rub it into the underwear, dunk both my arms in the water, and relish the warmth.

I look out the window.

East of the house is a rowboat on dry land.

Twelve women stand around it in the morning breeze, scrubbing cod with ice-cold water.

A man is standing at the boat's prow. He has his hands in his pockets.

The women hunched over the boat are bundled up in long skirts and coarse jerseys, with headscarves pulled down around their faces. I have to peer at them for a long time before I recognize my mother and sisters, standing there side by side. They are cold; their hands are red and blue. Their skirts are dripping wet. They scrub away.

Women wash fish.

Upon seeing them, I knuckle down on the laundry, scrub rub rinse, underwear socks jerseys. I wring the garments until my fingers and upper arms ache, then lay the wrung laundry in the tub and grab the bag of clothespins.

There are tattered clotheslines on the north side of the house.

I put the tub down and stand on tiptoe to reach the clothesline. I can see the rowboat and the twelve women a short distance away. As I am busying myself hanging up the laundry, I sense someone behind me. I turn to look.

Standing there is a little boy. His eyes are particularly beautiful, and I can't pretend that I don't see him. "What are you staring at?" I ask, but not in an unfriendly tone even though I'm tired and still groggy. He doesn't answer, but just stares at me. Then he bends down, grabs a clothespin, and hands it to me. He hands me one clothespin after another. Then runs away before I can ask him his name.

The midnight sun gazed at itself in the windowpanes, but the ice that drifted in the harbor entrance acted as if the time of year were irrelevant, showing no signs of leaving, though it was already July. But the fish girls were on a tear; they were done washing and spreading saltfish out to dry, and were now doing piecework with their arms and sometimes even heads down in the herring barrels. Stories were told of the fun at the salting lot, but Karitas wasn't allowed to take part in the salting, despite her pleas to her mother to let her join in. She was needed at home, said Steinunn, who found it unthinkable that no one should be there to take care of the housework for such a large household. In between bringing coffee and lunches down to her family at the herring lot, Karitas did heavy loads of laundry and baked rye bread, even though there were two fine bakeries in town. "Save money," said her mother many times a week, hoarding every króna like a dragon does gold.

When the herring salting began, the town came alive, bustling with so much activity that newcomers had the impression of being in a big city. The quay was chaotic: men rolled barrels, sharpened knives, and ran shouting and calling amid the herring girls, who couldn't keep up with the salting, no matter how frantically they worked. Boys struggled with wheelbarrows and tossed the herring into the tubs, while the boat owners strutted around with hats on their heads and cigars in the corner of their mouths. The piles of herring grew higher, and the barrel stacks became unclimbable mountains. The Puddle was filled with as many herring boats as steamships, which made unfamiliar noises. The town itself saw no less action: workmen dug ditches for water pipes and toiled away, spreading gravel onto the streets, which were one big muddy morass from the thaws and rain; horse-drawn carts clattered this way and that; housewives lugged water buckets or scurried between the houses and shops; children played in every alley. While hurrying to and from the herring lot, Karitas counted over forty shops. Sometimes, after bringing those down at the lot food and coffee, she took little Pétur by the hand and let him marvel at all the splendorous things on display. She herself could have lingered endlessly in front of the soap shop. A fresh, wonderful scent wafted out to the sidewalk, and every time someone went in or out, she stood in front of the door, closed her eyes, and drank in the fragrance. The soaps and essences in the windows were from all corners of the world and in all colors of the rainbow; she saw lemon and almond essence, Marseille soap, and even Italian washing powder. She wondered what it would be like to do the laundry with Italian washing powder. Her thoughts flew southward over the sea, and she tried to imagine how Italian women washed their clothing; did they use washboards and scrub brushes as she did? But little Pétur wasn't interested and pulled her back north to Iceland, led her away when he had had enough of the soap. His mind was on the shop where the friendly merchant was inclined to weigh out an eyrir's worth of figs and dates for poorer children. It wasn't just the bustle at the harbor and the steamships that gave the town its big-city air, but also the names of the shops—"Hamburg" and "Edinburgh" and "Paris"—indicating that this place was home to men of the world who wore Danish shoes.

One balmy summer day, when Karitas couldn't find Pétur anywhere and went out looking for him, she saw those cosmopolitans, as her mother called the worldly people in leather shoes. She heard children near an elegant house at the foot of the slope and headed toward the sound, and before she knew it, found herself at the fence of a delightful garden, where finely dressed people sat at a cloth-covered table in the sunshine and sipped tea and coffee with their little fingers in the air. She stared spellbound at the grandeur, and every tiny detail stuck in her mind. The white tablecloth, the flowery cups, the silver pitcher, the liqueur glasses, and the cigar box. The men were wearing vests, and the women white blouses with dark silk bows around their necks. Every single one was wearing Danish shoes. Lace-up leather shoes. Those in the garden didn't see her as she stood there behind a tree, kneading a leaf between her fingers as if in a trance. But someone's gaze rested on her from a different direction. The little boy with the beautiful eyes was standing behind her, staring as before. "What are you doing here?" she hissed softly, breaking a branch in startled surprise. He stuck his hand in his pocket and, without a word, pulled from it a tin soldier, which he then handed to her before running away. She hid the tin soldier in her apron pocket for many days, taking it out once in a while and pondering who this voiceless tyke might be. Then she forgot about him, but not the images from the garden. She didn't, however, mention the genteel gathering to the others at home, despite longing to describe the cloth-covered table and the leather shoes. She said only: "You were right, Mama, this is a very lush town."

It was often late in the day before the salting girls took off their oilskin skirts. Despite the soreness in all their joints, the sisters ascended to the loft of the fish warehouse with their heads held high when their shift was done, especially Bjarghildur, who felt superior to Karitas now, being a working woman who contributed to the family's livelihood, while her younger sister pottered about making porridge. She felt that Karitas had it too easy, and to express her indignation and superiority, she adopted the habit of giving her sister a good kick in the shin after lying down to sleep in the bunk they shared. On the other hand, the brothers, who shoveled herring out of the boats and were paid a higher wage than the salting girls because they were men, or counted as such in some respects, didn't put on any airs but thanked Karitas with a kiss for washing their socks. And although the sisters didn't say as much, they were no less grateful for this service than their mother and brothers, especially since it was questionable whether they were capable of doing laundry themselves anymore, considering the state of their hands. The skin on them was red and raw from the stomach contents of the herring, the wetness and brine, against which their canvas gloves offered no protection, and once the red blotches had formed, the skin began to peel off, allowing the salt to soak in deeply. Although Steinunn daubed their hands with udder balm, they couldn't heal up overnight. After the sisters' first few shifts, they whimpered with pain in their bunks. Still, they wouldn't hear of giving up, and despite the terrible sores and the stench in their clothes and hair, they weren't exactly unhappy—due both to the liveliness of the herring lot and their prospects for profit. The herring were a windfall that no woman in her right mind could forgo.

When the boats had to stop fishing for a few days to allow the salting girls' hands to heal, Steinunn counted her money. The children had never seen a single króna of their wages; it was their mother who picked them up on payday, but they livened up when she explained how the money would be spent. She sat at the table, stacking krónur and aurar in the evening sun, and the siblings leaned their heads on the edges of their bunks and followed the counting closely. After she had counted and perched the stacks behind a notebook that lay open in front of her, Steinunn stared pensively out the window and said, "We need to save a great deal before autumn. I've got to get us a better place to live, buy beds and maybe a table and chairs, and be able to pay for notebooks. And I'll have leather shoes made for you."

The siblings' hearts skipped a beat, and they turned this way and that in their bunks, their minds racing. "If we're diligent and frugal, it should work, but we mustn't waste any money. Not a króna. But if there's something that you desperately need," she said, directing her words at the elder children without looking straight at them, "you can try asking me." Then, from the bunk of the eldest sister, who hadn't been able to wash her face before going to bed due to the sores on her hands, came this: "I need money for soap."

Early the next morning, the widow set out for the shoemaker's with her flock of children in a line behind her. The siblings walked solemnly, as if the street were the aisle of a church and they were about to encounter the Divinity itself, and they didn't even dare to clear their throats, so great was their fear that their mother would change her mind if anything disturbed her determined steps. This was one of the greatest moments of their lives. It had never crossed their minds that they might one day own leather shoes, and they could picture how this would change their lives and their position in society. Their sheepskin shoes, as soft and light as they could be on a mowed hayfield, swelled when wet and then shrank when they dried and became so stiff that sores formed on their toes. Not to mention how uncomfortable it was to have wet feet every time it rained. In leather shoes, they would be able to walk with dry feet through snow and slush; maybe their noses would stop dripping as well, but even more important, they could look other children in the eye without feeling ashamed.

The shoemaker sighed heavily when he saw the group. He had hardly gotten a proper night's sleep the last few months due to his enormous workload. "You make shoes, don't you?" Steinunn asked politely after entering the shop, even though the answer was obvious, since the walls were barely visible through all the leather and soles. The shoemaker said that he couldn't deny it, and sullenly carried on with his work as if he expected them to leave when they saw how busy he was. "Would you be so kind as to measure my children's feet?" asked Steinunn, not giving an inch. "You can start with the girls." The shoemaker inhaled sharply and whirled around with his hands raised, intending to give the widow a piece of his mind, but then met the gaze of three fair-haired maidens who stared at him as if he were the Creator Himself. He had no chance. Without a word, he grabbed his measuring tools and ordered them to sit down on the stool and remove their shoes. Then he knelt impassively before them and measured their pretty feet with expert care, giving himself plenty of time for each foot. He was much quicker measuring the brothers' feet, and when he was done, he stood up straight, looked haughtily at the widow, and barked: "And you, too, perhaps?" Steinunn just shook her head. When they said goodbye, however, he was the most genial of men. His sincere admiration of the maidens had not been diminished in any way by his measuring of their feet, and he said that the six pairs of shoes would be ready by autumn. When Steinunn offered to pay a deposit, it was he who shook his head.

Unattached girls with gentle bearings drew the attention of young men, even if they wore only undyed woolen clothing. Boys running errands in a southerly direction turned right round and headed north if the sisters were going that way. For Halldóra, this attention was nothing new, even if her chosen one had spurned her, which was why she was unimpressed with the "young men's silliness," as she called it. Bjarghildur, on the other hand, was exuberant and quivered with excitement when boys gave her appreciative looks. Both sisters, though, made sure to look down demurely if they were given the eye, especially if their mother was around. Bjarghildur longed to whisper about the boys with her older sister, but her attempts fell flat, as she might have expected. Halldóra was vindictive, although none of them knew whence that came, as there was no vindictiveness on either side of the family—but her relatives had grown used to many months of sulking on her part once she felt offended. She had by no means forgotten her sister's intervention in Seyðisfjörður. Bjarghildur could just deal with it herself. To her younger sister, Bjarghildur had nothing to say on such matters, and in any case, Karitas aroused no longing in the hearts of curious boys, as childlike and skinny as she was. Even so, she did have an admirer no less than her sisters, even if he was just a little chap. She was constantly running into the tot; wherever her errands took her, he was sure to pop up and offer her one thing or another, most recently dates. "I'll be darned! The little fellow is after you," Bjarghildur teased, which did nothing but irritate Karitas. "He's my friend, and his name is Dengsi," said little Pétur proudly, although his sisters didn't condescend to listen to him. Steinunn, however, asked: "What are his mother's and father's names?" That, Pétur didn't know, but he could tell them Dengsi's papa owned a large shop where you could buy harmoniums and tobacco pipes and plenty of dates, and Steinunn left it at that.

Even if Halldóra was reluctant to discuss young men's merits with her sister, there was more than enough whispering and giggling among the fish girls in the loft when the topic was men, which was some compensation for Bjarghildur. The warehouse loft was filled with banter from morning to night during the "sores break," as the girls called the pauses in the herring fishing, and even if their hands were out of action, there was no end to their wit when it came to stories and verses. The brothers liked to mingle with the girls in the kitchen, and the girls treated them kindly. Fussed over them, pampered them, admired the shapes of their heads, patted and fondled them—they being the only men in the house, after all. Ólafur and Páll were in seventh heaven, neither having ever received so much female attention, and then, when the herring girls had bad days due to their sores, the pampering was reciprocated. The brothers went to work washing the girls' socks and jerseys, and the girls fed them treats and sang so loudly for them that Steinunn felt it best to shush them, for decency's sake. They always did as she said. She was the oldest of them all; the girls respected her and found most of what she said quite reasonable. She was also the only woman there who had the right to vote, and when it came time for them to rest their vocal cords after all the singing, they sat down and earnestly discussed women's rights. They certainly didn't share all the same opinions, but the one thing they agreed on was the newly won right to vote. Despite it extending only to those aged forty and above, this was a great victory for the women of Iceland.

"Now, like the men, we get to have a say in what happens with our country."

"And with the fish, woman!"

"Soon it'll be considered completely natural for women to become members of parliament, not to mention get an education. We'll become doctors, lawyers, and priests."

"Oh, now you're just fantasizing!"

"And in the end, we'll earn the same wages as men."

"Well, I'll be darned!"

"The nineteenth of June was a great day for liberty."

"Pish, I don't know about that. I was reading one of the Reykjavík newspapers, and it said that women will have to start keeping up with the country's political debates now, read all the political articles and suchlike, attend meetings, and give speeches, and they'll have to do all of it in between milking the cows, doing the housework, cooking, taking care of the kids, spinning and sewing."

"Where did you say you read that?"

"In one of the newspapers from Reykjavík."

"Did it really say that?"

"As I'm sitting here."

But then it was as if Steinunn could no longer stay still; she became touchy, asked what time it was, and began looking around for the boys. She found them outside, and ordered them to come in and wash their sisters' clothes.

Spiders dangled from the eaves and spun for their lives; summer had come late, and soon it would be autumn. Karitas spun her own webs with the same diligence. In between the cooking and laundry, she dashed all over town on an eternal quest for food for her family, and by late summer, she had ingratiated herself with some farmers and fishermen, and had even been promised space in the freezing plant where she could store meat during the coming winter. "Unbelievable how she manages to blather her way into those men's good graces," Halldóra said flabbergastedly—and unusually, being so taciturn, in the main. But Bjarghildur stopped kicking her sister's shin so much. Steinunn was pleased with her daughter's resourcefulness, realizing better than others just what an accomplishment it was to get hold of milk in a place where the better-offs took precedence among the farmers. The town's shortage of milk had become a matter of concern to thinking people, and women had begun to suckle their infants well into their second year to avoid having to stuff them with potatoes and salty food, which their sensitive digestive systems handled badly. But Karitas was in the good graces of a farmer up past the top of the slope, and the family got milk every other day. It went onto their porridge and into Pétur. They smiled with delight every time they raised their porridge spoons to their mouths and tasted the milk, smacked their lips to savor it, and many times during their daily grind, they thought about the precious drops awaiting them when their shifts were over. So Karitas undertook the walk up the slope with determination, though it took its toll in a pounding heart and shortness of breath, especially if there were many chores needing doing and time was of the essence, but on the other hand, the trip back down was light and easy, particularly when one zigzagged right and left. Karitas often found it the best part of the day, and she stopped to catch her breath at the little ledges here and there on the slope.

It was the same with fish as the milk. There was no shortage of salted lamb or sausages, but getting fresh fish was another matter, and not in the purview of everyone. The catches were all salted or sold;

wholesalers bought them for export. But Karitas always got fish for her pot. She knew not only the farmer above the slope, but also the owner of a small fishing boat down at the quay—a man with many children of his own. How she had managed to endear herself to these men, she couldn't rightly remember, although she did recall having told them stories about folk and elves in the Westfjords and promising them machine-knitted jerseys for their children in the winter, once her mama was done with the herring salting. Steinunn was speechless. She had no explanation for her youngest daughter's enterprise and pluck other than the southern blood that had entered the family's veins via foreign fishermen in the century past. Apparently, they were talkative and bold, those southern men, and since it was endlessly sunny where they came from, they had reason enough to chatter away. But how on earth had Karitas come up with the idea of securing a promise for storage space for meat at the freezing plant? "What meat, might I ask? And how am I supposed to start knitting for those children? I can't set up the knitting machine in such a cramped space." This she said mainly to herself, but Karitas caught her words and stared for several long moments at the knitting machine that sat unpacked among the fish stacks on the lower floor.

She started looking around for new lodging.

The shipowner had half promised her mother other accommodations beginning in the autumn, but based on the previous experience of the promises of this honorable man, Karitas didn't think his words worth trusting, and began making inquiries of her own. It seemed most obvious to her to ask the merchants' housemaids when she saw them on the street, because they heard everything that happened in town, indoors and out, and had a good overview of the townspeople's living arrangements. But they only shrugged their shoulders after staring long enough at their own toes. There was a great shortage of housing; the girls in the warehouse loft really ought to have known that. But it wasn't out of the question that the family could move to one of the sheds at the shore where the poor folk lived, that is, if someone down there kicked the bucket. Karitas was deeply offended and resolved to have no further exchanges with the maids, and instead turn to those with influence. But to march into a higher-up's office and ask for housing seemed a bit far-fetched. She racked her brain for days.

One morning as she was wringing out the laundry, she suddenly saw how she might gain access to one of them. She began looking out for the boy with beautiful eyes who sometimes brought her dates without a word, and one day she caught hold of him. "Does your papa own the house you live in?" He stared at her in anguish, because she had never spoken to him except to ask what he was staring at or what he wanted, but then he nodded his head uncertainly. "Does he own any other houses in town?" she went on relentlessly, without releasing her grip on his jersey, and he glanced around furtively for several long moments but finally pointed northward, at a small house on the road leading up out of the town. "Exactly," said Karitas, without taking her eyes off the house nestled at the bottom of the slope. She could see that it would suit her family quite well, but it was a different matter whether the current occupants or the owner would agree. "Take me to your papa," she ordered, driving him before her like a sheep. The merchant's office was next to his shop, and they walked straight in. The man was standing there talking loudly on the telephone. For a moment, Karitas forgot why she was there, so captivated she was by this action, having never seen anyone use a telephone before. When the call ended, she had to swallow several times and moisten her lips, so disconcerting had it been, but finally, after the merchant impatiently asked several times what they were doing in his office, she regained her composure and blurted out: "How lucky you are to have a telephone! You can speak to kings and priests without ever leaving your office, and can tell them what goods they should buy in your wonderful shop!" "We'll leave kings out of this," he grunted, chuckling softly as he plunked himself down in the chair behind the desk. He was still worked up from his call and was about to ask again what they wanted, but Karitas beat him to the punch and told him about an old woman in Seyðisfjörður who had been terrified of telephones, thinking that their ringing was made by the devil himself: "When we were sailing around the country and stopped in Seyðisfjörður for pastries, a woman traveling with us told a story about how she had once worked as a maid for a merchant there who had a telephone, and his old nurse was so frightened of the device that she hit it with a broomstick every time it rang. Finally, she broke it, and the merchant didn't dare get himself another telephone until his nurse became bedridden and could no longer hold a broom!"

The father and son laughed heartily at the difficulties of the merchant from the Eastfjords, but then the northerner opened his mouth once more to ask why they had come, because every moment was precious at the height of the fishing season. Karitas cut him off again and said they'd made quite a voyage indeed that Pentecost: "But the captain didn't let the heavy seas upset him; he just steamed east and then north at full speed, making my stomach turn upside down. Mama liked it just fine because she was in a hurry to get to the north and start working, but still, as bad luck would have it, when we arrived at last in that freezing northerly, the fishery wretch had already rented out the place we were supposed to live in. And imagine it: now we're stuck, the seven of us, cramped in a cubbyhole at the fish warehouse, and what will happen in the autumn when the salting is finished and Mama has to start knitting to feed us, she can't set up her knitting machine in that cramped space, it's absolutely out of the question, so I was just wondering whether you might have any spare housing for the machine and us, such as, for example, that house there on the slope, where Mama should have no trouble at all knitting both underwear and jerseys for your family?"

The merchant, having long since stopped laughing, stared at her in stunned silence. When he had assured himself that she was truly finished speaking, he said, "Well now." He then added distractedly that he had actually been thinking of letting a teacher who was coming north in the autumn have the place when the carpenter in it moved out. "Oh! So, it will be free, then!" exclaimed Karitas exuberantly. "It's only two small rooms and a kitchen, with an attic you can hardly stand upright in, and another family lives in the northern part of the house," he muttered, not yet having recomposed himself. "Two rooms and a kitchen!" repeated Karitas, gasping, "that's exactly what Mama needs. Goodness, she'll be happy. Oh, what a gem you are, Mr. Merchant!" In a dither, he rubbed his eyes, and then said curtly: "Do you think your mama is capable of paying the rent?" "I assure you she is," snorted Karitas. "A widow who can pick up and sail through ice and storms with six children in order to provide them with an education ought to be able to scrape together enough aurar for rent." The merchant was still at a loss for words. Then, after a brief silence, he said that she should send her mama to him the next morning. Throwing a grouchy look at his son, who hadn't opened his mouth except to laugh, he added, "Don't be hanging around here all the time, boy."

Karitas gripped her skirt and curtsied.

Karitas

Untitled 1915

Pencil drawing

The morning sun colors the fjord and the town.

A strange light over the fjord. Pale and misty in the early morn, colorful and frolicsome at midday, deep and serene at dusk.

Like a wealthy lady, the mountain on the other side of the fjord changes outfits several times a day: a light-blue morning gown, a dark-blue day dress, purple evening wear.

When I arrived in the spring, it wore a white hat on its head.

I sit atop the milk can on the slope and look at the mountain and the fjord.

I roll my head, entranced and contented, to absorb the expanse into my memory so that I can store it and evoke it in the evenings, when the confined space of our small room fetters me.

Then I see the woman with the hat.

She is standing farther down the slope, her back to me. The blades of grass reach to the hollows of her knees and toy with her velvety skirt.

In her left hand, she holds a small trowel, and she moves her right hand quickly over a picture propped in front of her on three long pieces of wood.

A woman paints a picture.

A morning picture of the fjord and town in the sunlight.

An exact copy, a photograph in color.

The slender brush in her hand gives life to the clouds; it is as if they move in the picture, and a strange smell is carried on the breeze, as if it has sprung from the clouds.

An old woman appears in the doorway of a house at the foot of the slope, and I wait with bated breath for her to appear in the picture.

The woman in the hat pretends not to see the old woman, but suddenly stops moving her right hand, yanks it in, steps backward, and turns halfway, so that only her profile can be seen.

She doesn't spot me atop my milk can on the slope.

Then she coughs in the quiet.

I start in alarm, get up quickly, and set off for home, but my feet catch on my skirt. I pull at it hastily, and the milk can, reveling in its freedom, rushes off down the slope. It rolls along, opens, and leaves behind a little white stream that runs happily through the grass.

"The milk can got tangled in my skirt, it was all the woman's fault," she sniveled to her mother down at the quay, so upset about losing the milk that she couldn't give a clear account of either the accident or what led up to it. Seeing her daughter's despair, Steinunn refrained from scolding her, especially after the great favor she did the family a few days before, but instead, tried to console her child as she gutted herring, saying it wouldn't kill them to go without milk for two days. Karitas, however, was inconsolable; with sagging shoulders and tears in her eyes, she walked back up the quay. But in the kitchen that evening, her mother wanted to know who that woman was. No one would get away with mistreating her children. It was best to clear this up, considering the flap the siblings were in over the lack of milk. Little Pétur was crying with his face stuck in the milk can's opening, and Bjarghildur, exhausted and cranky, became belligerent, shaking her sister and barraging her with insults. The brothers found Bjarghildur's outburst over-the-top and tore her vigorously away from her victim. This only made her more furious, and she turned to attack them, using her elbows as weapons. Steinunn was at a loss. She tried sharpening her voice and looks, but to no avail; the youngsters' blood boiled, and they made such a ruckus that the fish girls left their rooms and gathered, pale and frightened, in the kitchen. It was unclear how the fight would have turned out had not Halldóra suddenly emerged from the family room, where she had allowed herself a little nap. She walked into the kitchen in a dignified manner, calmly lifted a full water bucket from the floor, and, with a quick movement, doused the combatants. She then ordered them, soaked and alarmed, to sit down on the bench. No one said a word. Steinunn wiped her forehead, and the fish girls shook water off their skirts.

"No one behaves this way toward a girl who has found lodging for a family of seven," Halldóra said in a deep, low voice. They looked at each other, having completely forgotten that fact, and then looked incriminatingly at Bjarghildur, who was still breathing rapidly because of the anger that swelled in her breast and found no outlet. Bjarghildur tried to blow it out through her nose and pursed lips. "She could just have told the truth, that she lost hold of the milk can through sheer blasted clumsiness! She didn't have to make up lies about some woman in a hat!"

As everyone slowly regained their composure following this flare-up, they felt it most sensible to make the best of this for the good of all, to forget about the brawl and the soaking and turn to the one around whom this all revolved, loitering miserably in the corner. "Tell us about the woman you saw," the fish girls said softly, and began wiping water off the floor. The mother and her daughters echoed the request as they rustled up food for the entire group.

"I just saw her, she was standing on the slope, painting a picture on a wooden stand," stammered Karitas, her head bowed. "I was sitting on the milk can, and when she coughed, it startled me so much that the can toppled." "See? She just sits lollygagging on milk cans when she's supposed to be working!" yelled Bjarghildur. The others shushed her gruffly but said, after giving it some thought, that it must have been extraordinary seeing a full-grown woman playing around with planks and pictures on a hillside while all normal people were working down at the quay. "And it was a woman, you say?" "Yes, it was a woman." "Are you sure?" "I could tell by her breasts, which I saw from the side."

The brothers perked up their ears and asked for more details. Karitas described the woman's appearance and actions as precisely as she could, and then one of the fish girls clapped a hand to her chest as if she had discovered a new angle to this matter and looked inquiringly at the others. "Could she have been what they call an artist?"

The others shook their heads slowly, and even Halldóra stared wearily. No, they'd never heard of a woman being an artist. They had, however, heard stories about men who painted pictures like that, but they were mainly overseas.

"Fancy seeing a ghost in the middle of the day!" Bjarghildur exclaimed sarcastically, unable to restrain herself, and the girls fell silent, unable to come up with any explanation for this woman's behavior—if it was a woman at all. "Does your girl have second sight?" whispered one of the fish girls to Steinunn, who was sunk too deep in her own thoughts to answer. Although the others didn't say it out loud, they all believed that Karitas had either seen a ghost or that her imagination had run away with her along with the milk. But they just ate in silence, and the fish girls talked about the lovely evening weather before returning to their rooms.

Karitas couldn't get the woman out of her head; she saw how she moved, smelled her, heard her cough, but she never saw her again. Every day she panted her way up the slope, whether it was a milk day or not, and looked for the woman with the picture, waited for her in the same place that she had sat on the can, but the woman never showed herself. Gradually, Karitas, too, became convinced the woman had existed only in her imagination.

"She was a vision," she said to the milk can.

Karitas

Untitled 1915

Pencil drawing

The bedclothes still smell of sweetgrass.

My sister and I hold the duvet to our noses to feel the departed summer breeze.

We are both lying on our sides. Bjarghildur lets one leg rest on my hip and warms my throat and the nape of my neck, front and back, with her hot, heavy breaths.

The rain holds the house in its embrace, the windowpanes weep.

The light in the oil lamp tries hard to keep calm, yawns and stretches to conceal its unease.

I sweat beneath the duvet, I want to throw it off me, stretch my legs, but I am trapped in my sister's arms. As sleep approaches slowly, like a beggarwoman coming down from the heaths, the slightest movement can startle her. The bed is narrow, but Bjarghildur needs rest after standing all day. To avoid irritating her, I'll endure this confinement, and let the light of the oil lamp lead my thoughts along the ceiling and walls and out the weeping windowpanes.

The wall clock has difficulty keeping time after lying idly in a footlocker all summer. As it ticks, I look out the bedroom door and watch my mother, who is sitting alone, sewing.

A woman sews in the evening.

The others are already in bed. The brothers are nestled beneath the sloping roof of the attic, where you can hardly stand upright. The odd sniff or cough can be heard from above. Halldóra is sitting in her nightdress on the edge of her bed in the front room with my mother, rubbing ointment into her hands. Her bare feet are swollen, but she pays them no attention. She focuses entirely on her hands as she daubs each finger with ointment and strokes it as if squeezing on a tight ring. After this prolonged, tiring procedure, and covered in ointment, she lifts the duvet, lies down, sighs, and turns toward the wall. She has the bed to herself.

On the other side of the table in the middle of the room, little Pétur lies sprawled in his bed, sleeping securely and openmouthed, knowing that sometime later in the evening, his mama will crawl under the duvet to him. She is still sitting at her knitting machine in the corner, busily sewing everything together, lapels and back pieces, sleeves and collars. Now and then, she moves the lamp on the small table beside her to get a better view of the garments.

Light and shadows cavort, transform her facial features, erase the lines around her mouth, soften the wrinkles around her eyes, make her bright and young, and then darken her face, draw a deep vertical line on her forehead between her eyes, paint brown circles under them, thin her lips, sharpen her features.

"Are you still awake, Karitas?"

"I'm boiling hot."

"That's good to hear. I wouldn't want you to be cold."

"Bjarghildur has her leg on me."

"Let her sleep; maids need rest. They never get to sit down. When I was young and worked on a farm, I was often so tired when I finally got to bed that I wanted to die. In the evenings, after slaving away all day in the meadows raking and bundling hay, I had to help the male farmhands out of their wet shoes and socks, practically undress them, dry their feet, and then feed them. They were worse than small children. Then they leaned back and relaxed, while I had to mend their shoes and stitch up the holes in their socks and other clothing well into the night. If I wasn't quick enough, I had them all on my back: the farmhands, the farmer, and the housewife. I myself went around in dirty rags because I never had time to see to my own needs. I don't remember smiling once that whole time. The demands made on us girls were enormous. I told my mother about it, and she never again sent me to work as a day laborer. It was the injustice that really burned me up. Raking and binding hay was much harder than mowing, yet we were paid only half as much as the men—besides having to attend to them."

"Do you think that poor Bjarghildur has to undress the merchant in the evenings?"

"I pray to Almighty God that she never does! No, times have changed, dear child. This new era will bring women brighter days. We can get educations, and we can vote. Who would have believed such a thing when I was growing up? Your sisters are certainly unenviable, even if maids no longer have to pull men's rags off them. They have to bake and cook, scour the floors, do laundry, mangle and iron, mend and sew, and must never look up or take the slightest break. But they're going to save up money to enroll in the Women's College next year."

"But they're paid such terribly low wages. They'll have to save up all their lives."

"I wouldn't say that. But we really must find you some work so that you can save up for your own schooling. Whether at the Women's College or the Comprehensive School."

"There are so few girls at the Comprehensive School—just daughters of wealthy folk."

"How well I know it. But while you wait, you must be diligent in reading Ólafur's homework so you'll be prepared to go straight into second or third grade when the time comes. What did Ólafur learn at comprehensive school today, and what homework did he have?"

"They learned about the old heroes. Warriors and athletes. The teacher loves talking about them, Ólafur says, and it's what the boys want, too. The girls get no say, because they're too few in number and too shy. The boys all want to be able to swim like Kjartan in *Laxdæla Saga* and leap like Gunnar in *Njáll's Saga*. He could apparently leap his own height."

"That's because he was short. But didn't they read about Guðrún Ósvífursdóttir and Hallgerður Langbrók, too?"

"Not much. They were too wicked, I suppose. And Hallgerður was always in her pantry, anyway."

Their own pantry was like a beautiful girl impatiently awaiting her future. The winter provisions had been laid in: a barrel of salted lamb and another of whey-cured meats stood next to a sack of potatoes; sugar, coffee, grain, and flour adorned the shelves, along with butter and cheese. "The only thing missing is the root vegetables, which I'll grow next summer once I've got my vegetable patch going," said Steinunn on one of her constant trips in and out of the pantry. "I'll have rutabagas, carrots, turnips, and rhubarb." Each time, she shut the door behind her to keep the warmth from the coal stove in the kitchen from slipping into the coolness of the pantry, but she herself never grew cold, even when she spent a long time inside it rearranging tins and bags and wiping invisible dust off the white-painted shelves.

"In spite of the hardships in this country, my children have always had enough to eat," she said, and just to be on the safe side, she rewrapped the butter. What bothered her most were the two empty bottom shelves. Steinunn wondered whether she should perhaps boil meat for canning, as she had done out west, but wasn't sure if she could take time away from her knitting to do so. Orders for knitted underwear and sweaters streamed in, some the result of Karitas's ill-considered promises, others of their own accord. Mindful of her obligations, she reemerged reluctantly into the warmth. Although the pantry was a match for any in the best of households and the coal cellar had been filled to the hatch, the money they'd earned in the summer was running low and needed supplementing. But before resuming her knitting, Steinunn turned on the faucet in the kitchen. She always did so when she came out of the pantry. Turned the faucet on and off several times. Stared, entranced and fascinated, at the clear, ice-cold water as it ran into the sink. "No. No time for dawdling," she said, then took a pot, filled it with water, plunked it down on the coal stove, and lit the fire. The stove sighed blissfully as it simmered liver sausage and sent its steam languorously into the pitch-black evening.

The town was shrouded in such darkness that those out and about could barely see their hands in front of their faces without a lantern. The two maids, waddling home exhausted after their day's work, carried small lanterns that dangled at their sides. When Karitas peered into the darkness and saw two little lights approaching the house, she went and stood in the open doorway, and the aroma of the freshly cooked sausage wafted past her to the sisters' nostrils.

"Don't let out the heat!" cried her mother, who stood guard over both warmth and cold.

The weary sisters sat down with their brothers at the table in the front room, and although they had been given a bite to eat by the merchants' wives while cooking dinner for them, they dug into the liver sausage, particularly Bjarghildur, who had the appetite of a large man.

"I could eat an entire mare and more," she said, gobbling down the food. But the nourishment didn't make it down to her feet, which were freezing after hours of standing on the wet stone floor of the laundry room in the basement of the merchant's house, so Karitas was given the task of filling a washbasin with hot water so that her sister could soak her feet before bedtime. Halldóra, however, examined her hands in the glow of the table lamp and applied the evening's first layer of ointment.

The sisters also poked their noses into their brothers' education as the boys pored over their homework: they criticized the boys' hand-writing, which they found awful, and ordered the younger ones, who were in primary school, to leave more space between their arithmetic problems so that the page didn't look like a big black blotch. Karitas had the sense to do Ólafur's homework exercises before her sisters came home, in order to escape the fault-finding. Bjarghildur could be very cutting, resentful as she was of how her sister got to stay at home and read her brothers' books. "She's only two years younger than me, but gets to hang around at home and study," she whined, forgetting that the plan was to send her to the Women's College next year if they had enough money. Seemingly uninterested in this talk of schooling, Halldóra merely watched her younger sister attentively as she drew on a sheet of paper. "Try drawing me," she said suddenly and provocatively, and Karitas was thrilled. She selected a decent sheet of paper and con-centrated so hard that her eyes hurt. The result was quite good, and Halldóra nodded appreciatively. Ólafur said boastfully, as if he deserved credit for Karitas's talent, that she drew all the pictures for his geography and botany homework and that the teacher was always praising him for them. Bjarghildur said, "Wouldn't you be better off going to a photog-rapher than having caricatures of yourself drawn?" No one had thought of that before. But of course, it was time they had a portrait made, said the head of the family. This idea was given an enthusiastic reception, not least by the illustrator herself, who saw an opportunity for them to don their Sunday aprons, finally. "Should we wear our bodices?" Bjarghildur asked, as if the question of the photograph were already decided. Steinunn looked doubtful. "I don't know what a photograph costs, but it certainly isn't free. Most likely, we would have to make jackets for the boys, which requires money, time, and probably some knowledge of men's tailoring." Halldóra, looking thoughtfully at her hands, said, "I start work tomorrow at a sewing workshop, so it shouldn't be a problem for me to sew something for the boys."

You could have heard a pin drop.

The siblings couldn't recall ever having seen their mother sit down at the table, least of all if anyone was eating, but now she pulled up a stool and demanded an explanation with her eyes. Halldóra explained that she'd secured a job at the sewing workshop before quitting her job as a maid. "The old biddy really got my goat with her constant grumbling and criticizing everything I did. Tonight, I politely bade her farewell and said that she could send my wages here. The pay at the workshop is twice as high." Steinunn looked at her daughter for several long moments before saying, "You're really something." She said no more about it, but was light of step as she walked back into the pantry. The sisters were tucked up in bed, with Bjarghildur's leg draped over Karitas's hip, before they brought up the matter of their elder sister's entrepreneurial spirit. They whispered back and forth beneath the duvet in which the summer wind still lingered. Bjarghildur admired Halldóra's savvy at having gotten herself another job before quitting as a maid, while Karitas harped enthusiastically on Halldóra's wording: "'The old biddy really got my goat.' Did you hear what she called the merchant's wife? The merchant's wife, no less. 'The old biddy'! Did you hear that, Bjarghildur?"

"Don't whisper so loudly in my ear. Do you think I'm deaf? But it's just like her to have kept this quiet. She keeps everything to herself!"

By keeping quiet, revealing nothing, Halldóra ensured that no one could change her plans. When it dawned on others what she was up to, it was already too late. She also used silence as a weapon to get her way. She never said plainly what she wanted, but just hinted at her wishes while the others mollycoddled her, as if it were their fault that she had lost her husband-to-be, let alone hadn't gotten to settle in Seyðisfjörður. Of course, their mother was to blame for their move to Akureyri, and it was no mystery to anyone who had thwarted her wish to stay in the Eastfjords, but Karitas, who'd never had anything to do with her eldest sister's affairs, still felt guilty and tried to do all she could to please her. The brothers, on the other hand, took no notice of Halldóra's unspoken wishes. If anyone wanted anything from them, they would have to say it clearly and forthrightly. "Pity that I don't have a sewing machine," she said distractedly one evening. "I can never get to the machines at the workshop to sew jackets for the boys, never mind cut them out—we're always so busy there. But if I had a sewing machine, I could bring the patterns home and make them here."

"It's a shame that we don't have a sewing machine," her mother agreed. "And it would cost a pretty penny to hire a seamstress." "Yes, a dratted shame," repeated the daughter. "The only way might be to buy a hand-cranked one on installment from the merchant. But then, of course, we would have to know someone. I doubt that they would entrust newcomers with such a costly item."

Their mother agreed. This was a dratted difficulty, and they racked their brains over possible paths to a solution, which all, however, seemed closed. For some inexplicable reason, Karitas felt it was her duty to resolve this, even though neither her mother nor sister had even so much as glanced in her direction during their conversation. Within a week, she had gotten her sister Halldóra a sewing machine on very favorable terms. The merchant's son had, as usual, accompanied her to his father's office.

Every evening after that, Halldóra sewed until shortly before midnight, taking over the table in the front room. The brothers wrote in their exercise books on the floor, and did so cheerfully, seeing as how all this fuss was being made for them. But even though Halldóra had earned a reputation for incredible prowess with a needle shortly after her confirmation—"She'll be famous all over Iceland for her needlework, that girl," people out west had liked to say—it was evident from her fits and starts and frowns that the jackets weren't an easy task. The boys had to try on the jackets-to-be every half an hour, and if they were already in bed, they were immediately dragged to the front room, sleeping or not. The sewing machine itself was the subject of due attention and admiration from everyone, both the family members and the women who came by to have Steinunn knit something for them, and it could be said that the machine lent the home a certain luster as it stood there on the table in the living room, gleaming black with gold ornamentations. They all had to run their hands over it at least once a day. They never asked how Karitas had managed to finagle the machine out of the merchant—she wouldn't have remembered, anyway.

The snow settled on the roof, and they slept to the humming of the sewing machine, the clicking of the knitting machine, and the unsteady ticking of the wall clock.

But it was just like Halldóra to keep quiet, as they soon found out again. One day, they learned that she had gone to see the doctor. It was little Pétur who announced this, draining the family's cheeks of color. When the eldest daughter came home from the sewing workshop, Steinunn waved her into the kitchen, where she asked in a low voice what she had been doing at the doctor's. "Nothing in particular," said Halldóra, walking into the living room as she answered, making it clear that anyone who wanted to could hear why she had been to see the doctor. "I just needed a medical certificate to send to Reykjavík along with my application. I'm going to attend the Midwifery College in the autumn."

For the second time, Halldóra's ambitions left them speechless, and this time, the widow was so upset that she had to brew coffee, despite it not being coffee time. Her dream of providing all of her children with an education was now within sight, and not only that dream, but also her own youthful dream of becoming a midwife could come true through Halldóra. She was ecstatic. "You will be a good midwife, my dear, but it will cost you many sleepless nights," she said in a slightly hoarse voice. Optimism and pride reigned in the house that evening, a kind of inner mirth that broke out in silly jokes, and the siblings got to clown around even though it was late, because their mother was distracted and kept discovering urgent business to attend to in the pantry. But over the next few nights, Bjarghildur had trouble sleeping. She tossed and turned and flailed.

"Everyone's going to school but me," she said sleepily and bitterly each morning.

Karitas reminded her that she was in the same boat, but her sister wouldn't listen. "We'll find a way to get you into the Women's College," said Steinunn, perfectly undisturbed, "but I can't say if it will happen in the autumn. The cost of living is so terribly high, and female students at the Women's College don't get financial support from the government like those at the Midwifery College."

"Wasn't it just like her to choose a school she doesn't have to pay for!" Bjarghildur spat with undiminished bitterness. To underscore her lamentable position in the household and in society, she tortured her family with stories about the lifestyle of the merchant family for whom she worked and suggested that her ancestors' ineptitude was the cause of her being a miserable housemaid. "If my ancestors had had the pluck to open a shop, I would be learning to play the organ like the merchant's daughter, whose clothes I wash, yes, and would probably be on my way south, to that fine women's college."

This lament of hers rang sour in the widow's ears. "Shame on you, Bjarghildur. You come from solid Westfjords stock."

Steinunn didn't take her daughter's grumbling much to heart, but it seemed to have roused her to deeper consideration of her ancestors and their accomplishments or shortcomings, depending on perspective, because, for the next few days, she brought them up quite often. It was as if she were trying to make clear to herself the bonds that linked ancestors and descendants, whether the former's deeds would influence her children's future or whether she herself would be capable of steering their lives as she willed, regardless of blood ties. As she knitted on the late-winter mornings, she had plenty of time for reflection, but kept her thoughts within her home's four walls, apart from when the neighbor woman at the other end of the house had something to discuss with her. Then, as if inadvertently, she would sometimes comment on the moods of her marriageable daughters and immediately receive a sympathetic response, because the neighbor woman had had her nine children in eleven years and knew exactly why one might want to discuss the temperaments of young people, especially girls. Some afternoons, it would start raining out of the blue, at which the neighbor woman would knock lightly on Steinunn's door and ask if she should take the laundry in off the line for her as she gathered her own, which Steinunn, of course, would accept, saying that she had been so lost in thought over her knitting that she hadn't even noticed that it had started pouring yet again. As they folded the damp laundry, the two women chatted about the weather and the recent increases in the price of soap, which were, of course, the fault of the war—"as if we should be the ones to suffer for it, here in the north, when they're battering the daylights out of each other out there in the world"—and then the neighbor woman accepted Steinunn's offer of a cup of coffee, just a drop, and as they stood there sipping their coffee, they examined the knitwear carefully and fingered the jackets Halldóra was sewing. Their conversations turned to the children's schooling. Steinunn touched on Bjarghildur's sulkiness—how she, due to the poverty and ineptitude of her ancestors, was being cheated out of the chance to attend the Women's College. She felt comfortable bringing these things up with her neighbor, for even though Jenný was twelve years younger than herself, she was a straightforward and reliable person. In addition, she was particularly even-tempered, which was best shown by her contentment with her cramped abode: two small rooms, a tiny kitchen, and an attic almost too small to stand upright in, just like their own; this woman who was married to the town's foremost carpenter and should therefore have rightly lived in a two-story house with a good basement—"but my Guðmundur simply doesn't have time to build us a house, as busy as he is building up the town, and every time he's about to begin on our house, there's a fire somewhere, because most of the new houses are constructed from Norwegian waste wood and go up in flames at the slightest spark, and then, as you might expect, he's called on to build a new one, while our house is put on hold." But she was never dissatisfied with her Guðmundur, and they had one child after another, despite the fact that the man was hardly ever there, even at night. The worst thing about it was—as she confided in Steinunn when she spoke about childbearing, which she did often—that for each child born, she lost a tooth. "I'll end up toothless if he doesn't stop," she said, running her tongue over the teeth that were left.

Even if all those children had taken the neighbor's teeth, they were of great benefit to women who owned knitting machines. Not only did Steinunn knit everything that could possibly be knitted for the children at the other end of the house, she was also paid for every single garment as soon as it was finished. Carpenters were in no trouble with money. Steinunn, on the other hand, had little of it, and therefore couldn't help but open up to her neighbor, who paid all her debts and was scrupulous and honest. Steinunn had not had any expectation of a solution being found to the problem of Bjarghildur's schooling, but Jenný knew a woman who knew another woman, and that woman was quite familiar with women's colleges, especially the one in Reykjavík, so she would definitely speak to the woman she knew and find out if anything could be done. And only two days passed before she stopped in again with the laundry from off the clotheslines, with the message that she had spoken to the woman she knew and that woman had spoken with the woman familiar with the Women's College in Reykjavík, and she had called there and said that the matron had said that the girl from the north was more than welcome there, but that she had to send in an application and be able to pay the school fees.

There was the rub. So, they dove into calculations and speculations at every opportunity, in the kitchen, out at the clotheslines, and by the wall of the house, all to determine how Bjarghildur could scrape together as much money as possible before the autumn. In the end, and with Jenný's help, Steinunn was fairly sure she had secured her two jobs for the summer. The merchant's wife's maid learned of these plans only when her mother handed her paper and pen one evening and said, "Here. You can write your application for admission to the Women's College in Reykjavík."

Bjarghildur was overcome with joy. All that night, she talked and sang in her sleep. After the application was sent south, she slept like a stone all night, on the same side, without moving, to the great relief of her bedmates, because Bjarghildur always spoke so clearly whenever she did so in her sleep. Steinunn, however, tossed and ran her mind over the morass of difficulties now facing her in connection with her daughters' schooling. Not only had she obliged herself to pay the school fees, but her eldest daughter's sewing machine was still largely unpaid, and there was little hope that the future midwife could pay off the debt before she went south. "I'll pay off the sewing machine before I leave," said Halldóra, shrugging off her mother's objections as she sewed, "but what's worse is having Bjarghildur tagging along to Reykjavík."

In the photograph taken after Easter, in cold weather and snow showers, the elder brothers were wearing their new jackets, like adult gentlemen, and the youngest wore a shirt and vest. The mother was wearing the Icelandic national costume, and the younger sisters, their dress bodices and aprons. Halldóra was wearing a Danish outfit that she herself had made, despite owning a costly Icelandic national costume, practically brand new. "Oh, those national costumes make you look old," she said, refusing to dress in the pride of Icelandic women. The younger sisters were highly offended and complained as vehemently as they could about Halldóra's stunt, but deep inside, they smarted at seeing how well her leather shoes went with her Danish skirt. Fortunately, the photo only reached up to the family's knees, meaning that their leather shoes were never seen, however much they stood out. Before the family portrait, Páll's confirmation photo was taken, as Steinunn wished to kill two birds with one stone. All of the fuss over the confirmation and the photo session turned the house upside down, although as far as anyone could tell, that was entirely to the housewife's liking. For the first time since the move, she welcomed guests to her home—the family from the other end of the house and two fish girls from Dalvík who had stayed on in town—and treated everyone to coffee and waffles. The house was packed with guests. The confirmation child was given two books and a pen and couldn't fall asleep that night for sheer joy. When it was all over and the photographer presented them with the portraits, they were filled with pride and looked at the photographs for days. Of course, they missed having their father in the big photograph and became wistful when they tried to imagine how it would have looked had he been sitting there next to their mother, handsome and blond— "Papa was so good-looking"—and bickered a bit about which of them resembled him most, but although his absence saddened them, they still felt as if the portrait proved what a fine, handsome family they were.

"We must stand together," Steinunn said firmly when the photograph had been framed and hung on the wall, "and always remember to support each other in life's struggle. It is our duty to stand together, that is how families in Iceland have been able to thrive, and that is why nature could not squeeze the life out of us. We fight, we Icelanders, we fight."

Karitas

Untitled 1916

Pencil drawing

The evening sun is on its way to bed.

Its rays color the slope above the house red.

Halldóra sits high up on the slope, so far from the house that we can't see her eyes. The position of her head and legs suggests sadness. Our mother shades her eyes with her hand and looks up.

"Bring her some berry pudding," she says to Bjarghildur.

Bjarghildur lifts her skirt and makes her way with the bowl of pudding up the slope to her sister.

They sit there together for a while.

"Go up there and find out what's going on," our mother tells Páll. He obeys, goes up the slope, but quickly returns with the empty bowl and says that Bjarghildur ate the pudding she brought for her sister, and now they were both sitting up there whining. Our mother scoops a new portion of pudding onto the plate, asks him to bring it to Halldóra and make sure that she eats it herself, but he stubbornly refuses to participate in such nonsense and goes to get ready for bed. It falls to me to climb the slope. I sit down next to my sisters, who are both teary-eyed and using their skirts as handkerchiefs.

Three sisters on a slope.

I ask what it is that's making them cry. Bjarghildur grabs the plate of red pudding and says that there's nothing peculiar about people shedding tears; it would be strange otherwise, and I should surely be able to see that myself, and she takes a hefty spoonful of the pudding. And soon afterward, another. She devours the pudding with gusto, while Halldóra stares torpidly into space.

Bjarghildur hands me the empty bowl.

"Just think, she lost the best catch in the Westfjords. There is no hope that he will ever wander north to this windy craphole, despite our having been forced to, just so those stupid boys could go to school. But what's the point of marrying sailors, anyway? The sea swallows them all."

"I wouldn't want that for my children," whispers Halldóra.

All three of us realize how hard we've had it, and tears well in our eyes. Still, we've come through every ordeal. Fatherless, we've fought by our mother's side, endured the maid's madness, witnessed our household broken up, lain in a stinking cargo hold for days, vomited our guts out, slept a whole summer in the loft of a saltfish warehouse, suffered "herring sores" and exhaustion, lost the best husband-to-be in the Westfjords, and we're still standing as straight as cliffs in an icy sea. We've never winced, never whined, but now the time has come, and who knows what future awaits the three of us. Will we ever have good husbands and children like ordinary women? Is it our innate destiny to sacrifice ourselves? As we have already done. In obedience to our mother.

"We did our best to make her life easier," we whimper.

We cry bitterly until midnight.

When the wagtail began traipsing around the patch of earth that was to be turned into a root-vegetable garden as soon as the ground thawed, everything went awry. Not that the bird had anything to do with the havoc, but rather, it was the spring air that came with it. It cleared away the lethargy that lay like a skin over the soul. Suddenly everyone had errands to run: old people began moving about, tottered around the corner to empty their chamber pots, housewives set about airing duvets, and men streamed down to the quay. The smacks raced the motorboats to the fishing banks, and ships arrived more frequently.

Karitas was fetching fish for supper from her friend, the small-boat owner with the big family, when she spotted the approaching fishing boat, or rather, the folk from the Westfjords standing aboard it, their faces windbeaten. One of them was the hero from back home. He still radiated vigor. When she saw him, Karitas gasped. As she watched them and pondered her best course of action, she threaded a string through the mouth of her haddock. She decided to deliver the news to Bjarghildur first and let her decide how to handle it; that way, she herself would be least responsible. But this was big news, and Karitas set off running with the gaping haddock dangling at her side to the merchant's house where Bjarghildur worked. She hammered at its back door until the surly maid tore it open and asked if she was losing her mind. Karitas blurted out that he had just sailed in, Halldóra's Sumarliði. Bjarghildur practically leaped in excitement, teetered on the threshold, grabbed her cheeks, and slapped them with her palms as if to bring some order to the chaos in her head. "And was he alive? Was everything all right with him?" she whispered, wide-eyed. "Yes," Karitas whispered back, although there wasn't another soul in sight. "As strapping as ever." "What shall we do, what shall we do?" Bjarghildur muttered to herself, looking in all directions over the head of her sister, who stared up at her, confident that she would receive robust instructions. "Run up to the sewing workshop, break the news gently to her, then come back here as quickly as you can and tell me what she said, and if you don't come straight back, you'll have me to reckon with," she said, raising her voice as if she were admonishing a small child. Karitas ran off with her haddock. She had to wait a little while as someone went to fetch Halldóra from the sewing workshop. Finally, she came out with a tape measure around her neck and looked at the haddock in her sister's hands. "Aren't you supposed to take that home? The haddock?" "Yes, yes, of course, but first I was supposed to bring it here, or, I was supposed to come here, not the haddock, of course, it's supposed to go home, the haddock, it's going home as soon as I'm done here—Sumarliði is down at the quay!"

Halldóra looked for a moment into her sister's eyes, then pulled the tape measure from around her neck and began to wind it up, slowly, looking at the sky as if she wanted to check whether it was going to rain, and when the measuring tape was in a small roll, she looked at her sister, smiled, and said, "Take that haddock home."

"All she said was that I should take the haddock home," panted Karitas when Bjarghildur tore open the back door. Bjarghildur wasn't gentle: "You're lying. She must have said something more, you just can't remember." "No, she just smiled and said, 'Take that haddock home.'" "Smiled? How?" "Just like this," said Karitas, grimacing with her teeth clenched to show her sister the smile, which, however, did not in the least resemble the smile under discussion.

"Not all smiles are the same, dear. A smile isn't just a smile," said Bjarghildur irritably as her breast rose and fell. "Take that haddock home," she ordered, and then slammed the door in her face.

The arrival of the hero from the west touched Steinunn as well, which surprised Karitas, as up until now, her mother had shown little sentimentality regarding her daughters' future husbands. "Sumarliði? Is he down at the quay?" she exclaimed, and Karitas could see that she was slightly befuddled.

She took the haddock from Karitas and slung it onto the kitchen table. Suddenly it was as if she couldn't quite remember what she had been meaning to do before taking the fish, which was unlike her, a woman who was always so businesslike when it came to her work. She shifted utensils, opened boxes and cans, went into the pantry and stood there for a while without touching anything, came back out, looked Karitas up and down with a deliberative gaze, and then asked abruptly, "Was he on his own?" "No, there were three of them." "Well then, this haddock won't be enough for dinner." She went back into the pantry, turned around a few times, shuffled things on the shelves. "And either you'll have to run back down and try to get another one, or I'll make chowder and have bread and good porridge with it. Don't just stand there idly, girl. Grab a rag and get to work."

There was no less bustle now than before the confirmation reception. Shortly before dinner, when the women of the town had finished all the housework apart from cooking and calm was descending over their homes, Karitas was stuck polishing and scrubbing, arranging and tidying, while her mother stood over pots and pans and turned the kitchen upside down, as if a visit from the king were imminent. Not a single soul, however, had given notice of their coming. The fuss astonished Karitas, but she dared not express that or point out to her mother that the three travelers might have come to town on other business than to visit unmarried girls from the Westfjords. The brothers were no less dumbfounded by the flurry of activity, but had no more courage than their sisters to express their surprise.

By seven o'clock, the house was as serene as could be. The furnishings glistened and smelled of polish, the housewife had put on a clean apron, and the aroma of fish chowder and porridge wafted out through the open windows. But there was no sign of visitors from the west. The siblings shot each other sidelong glances. Steinunn hovered by the window, but suddenly, her shoulders tensed, she turned on her heel, grabbed the dinner plates, stormed with them into the front room, and began hastily setting the table. There was a knock on the door.

"Oh, Sumarliði, is that you, here? What brings you to these parts? Are you on your own?"

They couldn't clearly hear his answer, but they did catch something about a seven-ton fishing boat, a drift net, and the shipping of saltfish, and they also heard mention of business. Then they heard their mother invite the dear man inside to have a bite to eat—they had just been sitting down to dinner, and why on earth hadn't he brought his companions with him; there was certainly plenty of food in the house.

And there he stood in the doorway of the front room, broad-jawed and manly, looking over the group of siblings. The anticipation in his eyes faded when he saw who was at the table. He looked around, and Karitas knew exactly for whom, and it seemed her mother did as well, for she said quickly, "They'll be here any minute, the elder sisters. Bjarghildur is working as a maid for a merchant's wife and Halldóra at a very fine sewing workshop here in town, but sit down here now with us, for goodness' sake; you must be hungry after your journey. How was it? Did you run into sea ice off Horn?"

He was clearly relieved to hear that the sisters were still living at home, despite being away just then, and he sat down next to the brothers, who had been gaping in speechless admiration of his manliness. He said that they had avoided the ice by sailing in the wake of the coastal steamer as far as Húnaflói Bay. They had, however, seen icebergs. "And since I was here, I felt that I ought to come say hello to you." "That was nice of you, Sumarliði," said Steinunn. She served him such a huge helping of chowder that her sons stiffened. "But what is the news from home?" He said that there was little news to tell, but related the most important of it, mainly concerning the fishing industry. "And how has it gone for you here in the north?" "Quite well, thank you," replied the mistress of the house as she stood there eating. "The winter was fairly cold, of course, but luckily, we've had plenty of coal, and although many of the houses here are difficult to heat, most of them being built of cheap Norwegian waste wood, this house is a good one, though small, as it's built of Icelandic driftwood, and we've managed really well to keep it warm inside." He looked around at the clean-scrubbed floors, the tidy beds, the knitting machine, the sewing machine that had been positioned on top of a crocheted cloth on a small table, and at the housewife's apron, before saying in an appreciative tone: "You have certainly made a pretty home for your children here, Steinunn." "Oh, I wouldn't say that," she replied modestly, before going into the kitchen and briskly opening the faucet.

"And how are you all doing, then?" he asked, turning at last to the siblings, who had been waiting impatiently for the hero's attention. He had barely spoken the words before Ólafur proclaimed, "I'm in the Comprehensive School."

"You don't say!" He looked at the younger brothers. "And you're in primary school, naturally?"

They nodded bashfully. Karitas tried to remain inconspicuous. "I'm starting comprehensive school in the autumn," said the newly confirmed boy in an unusually deep voice. "You don't say! Everyone's in school. So, I'll have good news to tell of you when I return to the west." Steinunn reentered the living room with a triumphant gleam in her eye.

He ate heartily, despite seeming to be on the lookout, glancing constantly in the direction of the windows and doors, and had begun eating his porridge when footsteps were heard on the gravel outside. A shiver passed through the house. "Halldóra is here!" said Steinunn loudly, because, in the last few minutes, she had been gripped by an unusual cheerfulness that made it difficult for her to keep her voice under control, and she rushed toward the door to meet the girl. But it was the merchant's wife's maid who stepped into the front room, her hair brushed neatly and her face sleek from a vigorous washing with soap, lighthearted and beaming as if she had been dancing a polka all day. "Oh, Sumarliði," Bjarghildur said jubilantly, "how nice to see you! I had no idea that folk from the Westfjords were in town. Is it really you? You have truly caught me by surprise!" It was evident from his stiff movements when he stood up to greet her that the young lady wasn't the person he had been waiting for, but her cordial greeting and obvious admiration perked him up.

The conversation at the table now became very lively. The housewife was in high spirits, and the younger siblings chattered away at the guest when they got a word in past Bjarghildur, who did more than her fair share in keeping up the merriment—though the others were certainly no slackers. But as the minutes passed with no sign of Halldóra, the lively mood subsided somewhat, and they began listening more intently in the hope of again hearing footsteps in the gravel outside. "I can't understand what's keeping Halldóra," Steinunn said worriedly. "Could she have gone to the cinema?" asked the guest, making it abundantly clear that he hadn't come to greet old neighbors from the Westfjords out of courtesy, but to see the household's eldest daughter. "Halldóra never goes to the cinema," Steinunn replied haughtily. She was dead set against idleness and the frivolous pursuit of leisure.

As the clock passed nine, he stood up, thanked them for the sumptuous treats and enjoyable evening, shook each of their hands in farewell, said that he would look in again before he departed, and walked out. The sisters looked at each other resignedly. Light of step and humming, Steinunn cleared the table.

Then Halldóra came home. They met on the gravel.

Although the sisters would certainly have liked to slip out and follow along with their meeting, it was impossible; their mother signaled them silently to stay inside. So instead, they sat at the window facing the future vegetable garden, because the young people apparently meant to converse where the wagtail had been traipsing. The bright spring evening was still, so still that every word carried in through the open window.

He rooted in the dirt with his foot as he told her about the seven-ton boat, his parents and phlegmatic sister, while she circled him with her hands clasped behind her back and listened politely, nodding now and then. The two maintained a sensible distance from each other, and it didn't appear to be going anywhere in particular—until finally, as if out of nowhere, he reached out, grabbed her by the arm, and drew her to him. In a low voice, he said something that none of those inside could make out, and Halldóra smiled. They stood close together, and a long time passed. But in a single moment, all hopes crumbled to nothing. Halldóra moved away from the hero, placed her hands behind her back once more, took a few steps toward the window as if wanting to be overheard, and asked, "Why have you come to see me only now, Sumarliði?" He appeared not to know what to say in reply, and then there was silence, apart from the sounds of him clicking his tongue and mumbling alternately "Well" and "You see." Finally, he said loudly and tenaciously, "Time just got away from me." For several long moments, she stared at him—she was tall and so slender about the waist that it could be spanned with two hands—and then said in a clear voice, "I will never marry you, Sumarliði."

Karitas

Untitled 1916

Pencil drawing

Our black Sunday skirts brush the snowdrifts.

We hike up our skirts and try to step in old footprints until we come out onto the street where the snow has been trampled down. Then we let our skirts drop, speed up, walk side by side. Our skirts swing lightly right and left, in an even, gentle rhythm.

We're wearing long, black skirts, my mother and I.

Black-clad women on their way from church.

The winter sun and the glare from the snow cut into our eyes, so we look down to keep from seeing dark spots. We focus on our carefully polished leather shoes, which peek out regularly from beneath our skirts. Neither of us says a word. I would never dream of breaking the silence; I know that my mother needs to think over the priest's sermon and reflect on the newly concluded service in its entirety.

On the Puddle, boys are showing off their skating skills. My mother holds her hand over her eyes to shield them from the piercing light and peers out at the ice. "Am I seeing right? Are those your brothers out there?"

"It appears so. Weren't they going to go skating after mass?"

"It must be them. But we need to hurry home."

She walks so fast that I have to make an effort to keep up with her.

"For what has man for all his labor, and for the striving of his heart with which he has toiled under the sun?" she says out of nowhere.

I don't know whether she's quoting the priest, seeing as how I sometimes forget his words straightaway, or whether this is a philosophical question I am expected to answer.

"It's hard to say," I reply, deciding that it's best to answer. "But at least it gives people something to do and keeps them from being bored."

My mother smiles.

"I saw Madam Eugenía greet you at church, Karitas. How did that come about?"

"Yes, we met at the home of the merchant's wife, and I am to go and see her soon."

"Oh?"

"Yes. What do you know about Madam Eugenía, Mama?"

"From what I have heard, she studied drawing in Copenhagen around the turn of the century. I had no idea until this past winter that women ever studied such things, but then she married a government official and turned to embroidery. Apparently, she is extraordinarily skilled in the hand crafts. Was she asking if you would do her laundry?"

"No, she wants me to do something much finer."

"And what might that be?"

"I happened to be doing the laundry down in the basement when the parlor maid came and said that the mistress wanted to see me. I thought that she was going to scold me for using too much Italian washing powder, which foams so well, but luckily, that wasn't the case. But I was shown into the parlor, and there sat the mistress, along with Madam Eugenía."

"Oh?"

"They were drinking tea."

"Hopefully, you curtsied politely when you went in."

"Indeed I did—right down to the floor! And then the mistress said: 'Well, this is she, our Karitas. Her sister worked as a maid here last year, and proved to be exceptionally diligent. Their mother came here from the west a year and a half ago, a widow with six children, and she put them in school. The eldest daughter is studying to be a midwife, and the one who was with me is now attending the Women's College, both in Reykjavík. The elder boys are at the Comprehensive School, and the younger is in primary school.' And then she asked me if I wanted to go to school, too. I said that I hope to, and then she said that you are an exemplary woman, pious and of fine character."

"You know that you will be going to the Women's College, too, Karitas, even if you must wait a bit."

"Yes, yes. But in any case, we started talking about the drawings I did with the merchant's daughter when she was ill at home last autumn and I was asked to help her pass the time. The mistress had them on the table and said that Madam Eugenía had been looking at them."

"How were they dressed?"

"In the drawings?"

"No, Madam Eugenía and the mistress."

"Madam Eugenía was wearing Danish clothing, a dress with black piping, whereas the mistress, well, wait a second, how was the mistress dressed? I think she was wearing a white blouse with a black bow around her neck."

"What did the madam want with you?"

"Well, Madam Eugenía asked where I had learned to draw such women, and I said that I copied pictures that I'd seen in the French and English fashion magazines belonging to the mistress's daughter."

"What did she want with you?"

"Oh, then they both smiled, and Madam Eugenía asked if I drew other things as well, and I said that I drew ships and mountains and people and that sort of mingle-mangle, and then she wanted to know how long I'd been drawing, and I told her that I'd been drawing ever since Papa gave me my first sketchbook, back home in the west."

"Karitas, what did the madam want with you?"

"Madam Eugenía wants to teach me drawing. She said that I was obviously talented, and that it would be a true pleasure to instruct me."

"And how much do you have to pay?"

"Pay? For what?"

"For the lessons, of course. You could hardly have imagined that she would teach you for free. Nothing is free, Karitas."

Karitas

Untitled 1916

Pencil drawing

"Sit down by the window, next to the flowers, Miss Karitas.

"Turn your left side to the light. I am glad that you came on time. I don't tolerate unpunctuality. You may place your sketchbook on the table in front of you this time, but then you must accustom yourself to holding it when you draw—you may need to do sketches out in nature or wherever else you might be, and you will use this pencil. Here is an eraser, which you must try to use as little as possible, and now I will place before you the vase that you shall draw, a beautiful vase, pattern-less, and now I will leave you in peace for a while, and you show me what you are capable of.

"This isn't bad at all, Miss Karitas. The contours are rather good. The vase is slightly skewed, but why didn't you use the entire sheet? Why is the vase in the upper-left corner, and so tiny?

"You wanted to save paper? I see. But it's also easier to draw a vase that is only four centimeters than a vase that is twenty centimeters, isn't it? Now we shall try again, and this time you must use the whole sheet. Goodness, how it's snowing! I noticed it cloud up earlier. The light will be better once it stops.

"Are you still at it? Well now, this vase is a bit sightlier than the first, despite it being seriously lopsided. But where is the light that falls on the vase, Miss Karitas, and where is the shadow on its right side? Yes, you're bewildered, I see. What happened to the light and the shadow? Now we shall study the light, Karitas, and shade the vase, even if it is lopsided. I'm going to sit down here beside you."

Women at a flower window.

The tone of her voice is captivating as she finds faults, criticizes, corrects, improves, instructs. I'm overcome with shyness, cannot utter a word, feel as if I'm in another world. I sit at the window and draw for the entire three hours of the lesson, don't move from my seat, don't speak, concentrate on the vase, draw it again and again, countless vases.

"Would you like a cup of tea?" I'm asked, and I start in alarm and hiccup as I say, "Yes, please."

Madam Eugenía has the parlor maid bring us tea on a tray, and when I lift the teacup to my lips with my pinky finger aloft, I know that this is how I want my life to be. To sit at a window and draw in peace and quiet, and to have someone bring me tea.

I wrestle with light and shadow. Madam Eugenía sits with her embroidery and thinks. Never looks up except when a horse-drawn cart clatters past the house. Then she turns her head slowly toward the window, looks into the light, straight-backed and still, slips away from the world.

The needle sticks deep into her fingertip. Her eyes seek out the shadow again; she sucks the blood off her finger.

"More shading," she says, avoiding looking into the light.

The vase kept Karitas from sleeping. Its form assumed the strangest shapes, black, crooked; sometimes faces appeared in it, their eyes opened wide. In one dream, it shattered, and the shards flew into her face. When she was awake, it appeared in the washtub; she shaped it using the foam and the sheets, before slapping them onto the washboard. "Are your drawing lessons with Madam Eugenía going well?" asked the merchant's wife, standing far enough away so as not to be splashed. "Yes, I think so," Karitas stammered, rubbing the sheets vigorously against the washboard, because she couldn't remember if she had been procrastinating or talking to herself when the mistress appeared.

"Art is flourishing in the halls of our house, I have heard," said Madam Eugenía's husband when Karitas bumped into him at the street corner. She had never before seen the official in person, and she was flustered. "Is your drawing going well?" he asked, with a warm smile on his chubby face. "Yes, I think so," Karitas replied, curtsying. "Brilliant, brilliant, I know that my wife is enjoying the teaching; it helps her pass the time in these darkest days of winter. She hasn't painted since she was in Copenhagen. She takes more pleasure in needlework now. But she was a first-rate artist, and it is a boon for a man to marry an artistic woman. She creates a beautiful home for her husband, and I have no doubt that you will do the same later in life, Miss. Good day to you," he said, doffing his hat with a smile as he entered the halls of art.

Her mother wanted only to know how much Madam Eugenía intended to charge for the lessons. She had limited interest in the art of drawing, and, in fact, felt it to be a waste of time to draw the same vase innumerable times. "She hasn't said anything about payment?" "No, but she wants me to give my pictures titles, and I don't know what to call the picture of the vase. Maybe just *Vase*? No, she didn't say a word about payment." Karitas had pondered ways of asking Madam Eugenía what the instruction cost. If, for example, she was offered tea, she could just sort of ask politely, as she took a sip, what the madam's usual fee was for such lessons, but there was always something about Madam Eugenía's demeanor that prevented her from doing so. In the end, when she had begun to fear her mother more than the madam, she plucked up her courage. She had sat down at the window, taken her pencil in hand, and cleared her throat a few times when Madam Eugenía, who had been meandering about the parlor as if she were looking for something, turned quite abruptly toward her.

"What do you intend to draw now, young lady?"

"Just the vase," stammered Karitas, so surprised by the madam's behavior that she forgot all about questioning her.

"You've finished drawing the vase; we're not drawing any more vases," said Madam Eugenía loudly and triumphantly, and before Karitas could react to this sudden turnaround, the madam grabbed the vase with both hands and smashed it with all her might against the edge of the table. The fragments were flung all over the floor. Karitas covered her face with her hands. Madam Eugenía stood straight as an arrow beside the table and stared hard at her pupil. Karitas let her hands sink, and just to say something that might be considered appropriate in these particular circumstances, she asked in a low voice: "Wasn't it terribly expensive?"

"Horrendously," Madam Eugenía whispered, bringing her face so close to Karitas's that she could see the little yellow ring around the madam's pupils. "How much do my lessons cost?" Karitas asked flusteredly, unable to understand afterward why she had blurted out such a question at so delicate a moment. "Do I need money?" Madam Eugenía asked in return, sounding quite surprised.

Karitas had no answer to that.

"I don't need money, but you," she said, lifting Karitas's chin, "could be a little more communicative."

Karitas had never before been accused of reticence, and she was so stunned that she couldn't say a single word in return, no matter how she tried. By the time her tongue finally loosened again, the parlor maid had already come and swept up the fragments and left again with her broom, and the madam had found what she'd been looking for before sacrificing the vase. Karitas kneaded the corner of her apron as she began telling the madam about her sisters, who were in school in the south, though they saw very little of each other despite both being in the capital, which was because Halldóra had had to sell her sewing machine to pay for Bjarghildur's school fees because their mother hadn't had enough money, and even though they had all worked as hard as they possibly could salting herring in the summer, it had only just been enough, because their mother had also needed money for their household, of course. But she got no farther with her story, because the madam interrupted her: "Can you people up there on the slope ever think of anything besides money?"

After the vase, Madam Eugenía thought that they should deal with the face. She sat down opposite Karitas and told her to start by drawing hers, so that she could see what she was capable of. Their talk of money had upset Karitas so much that she couldn't concentrate, and as a result, she did a far worse job than when she drew her sister Halldóra. What was she supposed to talk to Madam Eugenía about?

The madam's face was oval, her forehead high, her eyes deep-set under her straight eyebrows, her nose straight, her mouth round and pouty. Her chin had a tiny cleft, her hair was brown and set up in a bun, her neck was long, her shoulders straight and slender. Karitas tried as hard as she could to come up with something to talk about, and Madam Eugenía waited. "You're very comely," she finally said, resignedly, finding herself unable to talk about her own monotonous life: her family, her siblings' schooling, the laundry. Everything she said would be colored by money.

"Beauty is the curse of women," said Madam Eugenía.

Karitas floundered for a moment, unsure of the best way to respond to philosophical statements, but she freed herself from this predicament by steering the conversation in a more practical direction. "My sister Halldóra is also very comely," she began, forgetting that she wasn't going to talk about her family, "but she refused the most promising match in the Westfjords because he waited so long to propose to her. She'd been pining for months because he didn't propose to her before she traveled north, and had even sat up on the slope crying her eyes out for an entire evening, and Bjarghildur cried with her. My sisters are terrible cryba-bies, despite being pretty. We once compared our faces in a mirror, and we saw that Halldóra had the most beautiful eyes, Bjarghildur the best nose, and I the prettiest mouth. If we put ourselves together, we would make a beautiful woman. So, you might say that Halldóra always has her eyes open, Bjarghildur follows her nose, and I've got quite a mouth on me."

To her surprise, the madam laughed heartily, and Karitas looked happily at her. It had been a long time since she'd seen a woman laugh; in general, the women around her did not laugh often, least of all the gentlewomen, and she found herself quite enjoying the feeling of mak-ing another person laugh.

"You're a clever one, little Karitas, as I already knew."

She wiped away her tears of laughter with her middle finger and gave her a long, thoughtful look.

"Karitas, you need to go out into the world. You need to become acquainted with wise and well-read people, the arts and their masters. You need to see flowering chestnut trees in bright sunshine, let trains rush you through fields and forests, see castles, horse-drawn carriages, and singing swans on ponds, experience the bustling life of big cities, smell the wonderful aromas wafting from restaurants, wave to the fish-wives in the harbors."

"Do they smell strongly?"

"Do who smell? Do you mean the fishwives? No, Karitas, they don't smell at all. But the smell of the fish in Copenhagen was different than here at home. It promised delicious meals, fried in butter and almonds—our mouths watered at the thought."

"Were they happy?"

"The fishwives? You're still thinking about them? Yes, they waved back at us and tried to lure us to them. But we lived in a boarding house, so we didn't need to buy fish."

"Madam Eugenía doesn't need money," Karitas reported to her mother.

"What does she need, then?" Steinunn asked, taking a break from shoveling snow. "Everyone needs something, the high as well as the low. But perhaps inflation hasn't touched her; she probably doesn't have the faintest idea of how much the price of rye flour has gone up, of butter, mutton, fish." "In Copenhagen, women don't work cleaning fish; they only sell it," said Karitas in a scornful tone that was meant for herself, because on her way home, it had dawned on her how silly it had been of her to discuss fishwives with such a woman of the world, instead of agreeing with her when she mentioned the arts and singing swans. What must Madam Eugenía think of her and her family?

"Finish shoveling for me, Karitas, I need to go and get dinner ready."

Karitas took the shovel, but hadn't yet begun when the neighbor's kitchen window opened slowly. "What's her house like on the inside?" whispered Jený, sticking her head out. She glanced furtively at the stairs at the other end of the house, and when she was certain that the housewife had gone in, she cleared her throat and waited expectantly for an answer. Karitas moved over to the window, rested both her hands on the handle of the shovel, and tried to give an honest picture of the government official's house: "It's incredibly elegant and tidy in there, everything in silk and plush, lots of paintings on the walls, polished tables, and patterned rugs on the floor. I sit by the flower window in the yellow parlor, whose walls are covered in gilded wallpaper and where the light is best. Now I'm drawing portraits. I find it hard to draw the eyes right, but I'm good at noses." Jený took a deep breath of the cold air: "And what does she do all day?"

Karitas squinted at the vegetable garden sleeping beneath its white blanket and tried to picture Madam Eugenía's activities: "She sits at her needlework and gives her maids instructions, I think." Jený said, "She has two of them, doesn't she? And no children in the house. No children who need to eat, need to be dressed, bathed, and put to bed. What sort of life does that woman lead?"

She slammed the window shut.

The merchant's wife was no less interested in the circumstances of her friend, Madam Eugenía, even if that interest was vaguer and less directly articulated. "How is the new washing powder working out? I see that it foams well?" Karitas stroked the soapy lather off her arms and tried to speak naturally, despite being startled by her mistress suddenly standing in the middle of the basement: "Yes, it's the very best washing powder that I've ever washed with in my life." "I'm glad to hear that. By the way, are things going well with Madam Eugenía?" "Yes, indeed they are. I'm drawing faces now. I'm having a hard time keeping both eyes in line, but Madam Eugenía said that that will come with practice." "I'm sure it will. Madam Eugenía is so adept, and it is quite unheard of that she should spend her time instructing others—she has enough on her plate already! But she has good help; doesn't she have two girls at the moment?" "Yes, the parlor maid and the kitchen maid. One of them has got quite a noticeable bump now!" The mistress winced, grew restless, and stepped in the wet spot on the basement floor without noticing it. "Is that so. Indeed. Then she must hire a new one when the time comes. But listen, if she asks you, then you must know that I cannot possibly lose you as my laundress, my dear Karitas, and absolutely not as long as my daughter is so ill and in constant need of clean bedclothes. Just so you know—and there is no need for us to speak of it any further."

Karitas's brothers were the only ones who showed any interest in her art itself, and in their sister's struggles with faces, and they never asked her about her teacher's circumstances, that sort of thing being entirely outside their area of interest. They were more than willing to model for her, and turned their faces and pubescent bodies every which way in order to facilitate the artist's work. Despite the asymmetrical eyes and protruding chins, which gave their portraits an enigmatic air, they liked the results very much and praised their sister to the skies. "You'll be a world-famous artist, Karitas," they said over each other, although the thought crossed her mind that they were buttering her up because they needed her talents for drawing pictures of plants in their notebooks. But the praise was nice, whether it was given out of self-interest or not, and she gladly made all sorts of illustrations of plants for them. The new sketchbook for which she had scrimped and saved filled up with faces and people in various poses.

Some evenings, she saw from her mother's expression that it would be best to keep the sketchbook under her pillow and stick to knitting. Her brothers always needed a great many socks. Although it wasn't stated out loud, but only hinted at with mumbles and murmurs, the evenings when the housewife and her daughter sat knitting as her sons did their homework were clearly most to Steinunn's liking. If the knitting was going well and the pantry was in good shape, she would happily hear stories about school life, especially about their lessons—tales of boyish pranks did not interest her at all. Sometimes she had Ólafur or Páll read aloud the latest letters from Bjarghildur and Halldóra, who always gave detailed accounts of their studies and described the teachers' words and deeds so vividly that the family in the north felt as if they had known them since childhood. The girls never wrote about the social life in the capital, and in any case, their dormitories shut their doors at ten o'clock, making evening outings out of the question, as they explained, and as Steinunn never let her sons forget when they asked permission to visit their schoolmates at the dormitory in the evening. "My children remain indoors at night," she said grouchily, and according to her timeline, night began after dinner in the winter and at midnight in the summer. Once a month, on a Saturday evening, she made an exception to her strict rules and allowed the brothers to stay at the dormitory with their friends until ten o'clock.

Karitas

A Woman Bathing 1917

Pencil drawing

The empty wooden tub stands waiting on the kitchen floor.

The light from the oil lamp flickers over the walls, on the run from the cold wind trying to force its way in through a crack in the window. Snow has piled up on the windowsill and lies against the windowpane like a white fleece.

On the coal stove, tap water simmers in two large pots.

While my mother and I wait for the water to boil, we take off little Pétur's togs. He is scrubbed with a coarse, wet washcloth until his skin turns red.

We are hardhanded, but he doesn't dare make a sound. He is told that if he wants a bath, he must be spotless beforehand, "for this is ladies' water, and ladies are clean before they get in it." But since he is here, he will be allowed to join in. We indulge in this luxury in secret, because the boys aren't at home. Had they been, there wouldn't have been enough bathwater for all of us, and we have to be sparing with the coals.

The water boils; the window is shut tightly. We lug the pots to the tub, pour the water in carefully, and mix it with ice-cold water from the faucet. Little Pétur is helped into the big wooden tub.

We let him splash about for a few minutes. Then he is pulled out, dried, dressed, put beneath his duvet, and told to behave.

Behind closed doors, the real bath begins.

Pétur can't understand why he isn't allowed to sit on the kitchen counter and watch me splash in the water. He sees only the steam creeping over the kitchen threshold, hears me whisper as I step down into and up from the tub. He is nodding off when I come to the living room in my white nightgown, my face flushed and hair dripping.

The kitchen door is ajar. Again, someone steps into the warm bath.

"Karitas, come and pour water over my hair."

Fragrant and clean, I stand behind the tub and pour lukewarm water over my mother's hair.

Holding the pitcher, I wait for a moment.

I look at her bare shoulders, soft and rounded, the wet hair floating on top of the water, the light from the lamp, which colors her skin silky white, the steam from the kettle on the pitch-black stove.

The evening-blue window with a white cross.

"You sit like a cellist when you draw."

Karitas lost her composure and became self-conscious, not because she was sitting any differently than she ought to be, but because she couldn't remember ever having seen a cellist. Nor a picture of one, or of the instrument. Hadn't someone said that it was a big violin, and should she dare to say something, move, and reveal her ignorance? That she didn't even know what a cellist was. "Perhaps," she said, smiling. That word gave no information about her knowledge or lack thereof. "But Madam Eugenía, when I draw at home, I usually do so beneath my duvet in the evening."

"What was the last thing you drew beneath your duvet?" whispered Madam Eugenía, leaning forward.

"I drew my mother in the bath," she replied, but became bashful as soon as the words crossed her lips, for she suddenly felt that it had been indecent to draw her mother under those circumstances.

"Did you draw her naked?" asked Madam Eugenía, with a gleam in her eye.

Karitas dropped her eyes, ashamedly.

"When I was studying in Copenhagen, we girls weren't allowed to draw naked people. We did it anyway; we drew each other in our rooms in the evenings. But no one knew, no one.

"So you drew your mother naked, little Karitas; well done, absolutely brilliant. Let me see the picture."

Karitas said that she couldn't.

"Yes, you can. Bring the picture with you next time."

And that she did, without understanding herself. But she wanted so badly to hear what Madam Eugenía thought of the drawing.

Madam Eugenía flipped slowly through Karitas's sketchbook, extremely slowly, until she came to the picture of her mother in the bath. Karitas was on edge. She felt as if everything were racing inside her; her heart beat faster, the blood rushed to her cheeks, and her mouth went dry. She was overwhelmed by the feeling that everything that had happened so far was worthless, that the only thing that mattered was what the woman sitting across from her would say next.

"Go. You've got to go."

That was all that Madam Eugenía said as she put down the sketchbook.

Karitas swallowed her disappointment.

"Go, where? Am I to go now?" she sighed at last.

"Go to art. It has called to you. It will be a long journey, and ogres will waylay you. When you finally reach the blue-green mountain blazing amid the others of deep blue, it will close behind you, and you will become its prisoner forever. But that imprisonment will bring you greater bliss than freedom ever could. Karitas," she then said, as if she had been speaking to someone else about the mountain and was only now turning to her. "I am going to keep your sketchbook, but you will get a new one. In it, you must draw everything under the sun and show it to me when I return."

She went to the large ornamented cabinet, opened a drawer with a key that she drew from her skirt pocket, put Karitas's sketchbook in it, and locked the drawer again. Karitas watched in anguish as the sketchbook disappeared. Then the madam opened another drawer, drew from it a brand-new sketchbook twice the size of the old one, and handed it to her without a word. Karitas accepted it halfheartedly, having nothing against getting a new sketchbook, and such a nice one at that, but pined deeply for her old one. She didn't dare object, but felt a tightness in her diaphragm just knowing that her sketchbook, with the picture of her mother in the bath, was locked in a drawer in another person's house.

"Are you going somewhere?" she asked breathlessly.

"I will be sailing overseas next week, but will hopefully return in the autumn."

Karitas looked at her in alarm. "Haven't you heard about the U-boats? The Germans have threatened to sink every single ship."

"No one is sinking me," said Madam Eugenía.

The vegetable garden threw off its white blanket.

The slope above the house cast off its dirty rags. The pantry's empty shelves, dark with soot, demanded washing with soap and water. The home was cleaned high and low; every single plank in the house was scrubbed, every dishrag washed and wrung, and finally dough was kneaded for crullers. That was the custom in the spring, and when people came home from a long journey. This time the occasion was twofold. The spring ships were on their way.

The preceding spring cleaning comprised the welcomes, but whether it was meant to be token affection for those coming home or to let the same know that the household got on excellently without them was never clear; rightly, it should have been the other way round, in the opinion of those who had remained discontentedly at home. Those who returned from pleasure trips ought to show their appreciation by taking a rag and scrub brush in hand the moment they stepped through the door. But such had never been the case in this household. Since there were so few women here, the men were compelled to participate in the drudgery of base women's work. This was why the brothers' expressions were far from happy, despite the fact that the household's elder daughters were on their way home. To ensure the completion of the cleaning and the crullers, Bjarghildur had phoned the merchant's house and asked the madam to pass the message to the laundry girl that the newly graduated sisters were due to arrive aboard the next coastal steamer.

The family had been waiting for an hour at the quay when the steamer finally docked. They were slightly startled to see how sophisticated the sisters appeared as they stood there at the railing. Halldóra was wearing a hat. Bjarghildur was wearing the Icelandic national costume and gloves. It wasn't their clothing, however, but rather their demeanor that made the greatest impression. How they turned their heads slowly to both sides, and how they raised their hands gently, as if they were made of porcelain, when they waved to those standing on the quay. The brothers found their priggishness comical and made no secret of it. Karitas, who was captivated momentarily by their elegant appearance, would probably have found it funny, too, had she not glanced at her mother, in whose eyes pride danced. Her joy was infectious and eclipsed all other emotions. The family stood on tiptoe and thrust out their chins as they waved to their conquering heroines.

Kisses were exchanged, and complete strangers congratulated both the daughters and their mother for her daughters. Their trunks were whisked up into a cart, and all seven of them walked along behind it, solemnly and a bit pretentiously, for anyone who passed by them had to know that these were educated folk.

At last, Steinunn had the whole family under one roof again. At one table. They could encircle it. She poured them coffee, stuffed them with crullers, encouraged them to eat—"and have some more, there's plenty"—whereas she herself didn't sit down for a second. Bjarghildur waved her arms and was unstoppable with her stories of people and events, and her siblings who had stayed at home laughed and giggled. Then the sisters pulled presents out of their trunks: a new silk scarf for their mama's national costume, embroidered handkerchiefs for Karitas, poetry collections and playing cards for the brothers, and all the while, Steinunn walked around the table, urging them to eat more crullers. The cake stand emptied, the coffee was finished, and fatigue began to set in. One by one, the brothers slipped out into the spring weather, but the sisters and their mother remained. The room fell silent.

"You don't owe anyone any money from this winter, do you?" "No, Mama." "Your behavior in the capital has hopefully done your family proud?" "Yes, Mama." "Let me see your diplomas."

That was what they had been waiting for all along, and were quick to find their papers among the clothing in their trunks. They had not brought shame on the family when it came to their exam grades, that much was certain. Karitas cried out with admiration time and time again, and Steinunn had difficulty hiding her delight. "It's not bad," she said, and couldn't stop fiddling with the beautifully handwritten diplomas. "Not bad at all. I expect that you were near the top of your class?" "I would think so," replied Bjarghildur complacently. "Not bad at all, no it isn't." Steinunn went over the numbers once more before putting the diplomas aside. "What's next, girls?" Halldóra looked at Bjarghildur, wanting her to answer first, so that she herself, as usual, could have the last word, but when her sister began to scratch the back of her neck, seemingly unwilling to commit herself, Halldóra cleared her throat and said modestly, while reaching for her letter of employment: "I have been hired as a midwife in the Eastfjords."

They looked at the midwife in amazement.

"Not bad at all," Steinunn said at last, and her eyes shone, though her expression remained the same. She was about to add something, but Karitas spoke first. "What about you, Bjarghildur, what are you going to do, what positions do women with diplomas from the Women's College get?" "There are, of course, many different things that I can do," Bjarghildur began, somewhat haughtily, though at the moment, she couldn't recall what they all were, and she said no more about it. Halldóra stroked her fingers slowly, one after another. The others looked down and ran their hands along the edge of the table. "She'll come up with something," Steinunn said, tapping the table's rim with her fingers. "Some have worked as teachers, others have run model homes, but what matters most is to have an education—it can never be taken away from you." Then, addressing the midwife, she asked, "But when will you start your new position, my dear?" And Halldóra, who had mastered the art of getting the last word, looked tenderly at her mother: "I sail for Seyðisfjörður tomorrow."

Karitas

Riders 1917

Pencil drawing

The hoofbeats are heard long before we discern the dust cloud.

The road leading out of town is empty; the riders cannot yet be seen.

We brush our hair in the morning sun on the gravel outside the house and listen to the sounds that carry to our ears in the silence.

We decided to walk together down to the spit, and have just passed the north corner of the house when Bjarghildur stops abruptly and stares up the road as if hypnotized.

The clattering of hooves is distinct.

"We can't keep loitering here," I say, and I start off again but look over my shoulder.

Bjarghildur stands as if spellbound in the middle of the road, her hands clasped, waiting.

The riders appear, six men, each leading a spare horse. They ride swiftly into town. The gap between them and Bjarghildur closes rapidly; the hoofbeats drown out all other sounds. I see that my sister is in danger and shout to her.

The riders have spotted the girl who stands motionless in the middle of the road. They halt their horses right at her feet.

The horses snort and neigh. The riders exhale deeply on their restless horses, waiting for a message or news that they presume the girl is about to deliver.

Bjarghildur says nothing, stares at the men who have the sun in their faces, looking from one to the other.

I can see that she isn't in command of herself, and put my arm around her to lead her away.

"Was there something the young ladies wanted to tell us?" shouts the man who appears to be leading the group.

"No, we were just out having a look at the weather," I say.

They look at each other.

"We were looking for a brooch that my sister lost," I lie.

The leader glances at his comrades and dismounts. He approaches slowly, without taking his eyes off Bjarghildur. With only one step left between them, he pulls a packet made of folded silk paper from his breast pocket and opens it. In his palm lies a shining silver brooch set with red stones.

"Is this the brooch you're looking for?"

They look at each other, their eyes ablaze.

Bjarghildur takes the brooch from his hands, pins it to her bosom, smiles.

"This is the brooch that I was looking for."

The group of riders that had come to town to sell fine horses from Skagafjörður stayed in a hotel for three days. The first evening, the same day that the brooch that had never been lost was found, there was a knock on Steinunn and her family's door, and outside stood the riders' leader, who said in a loud voice when the housewife opened the door,

"My name is Hámundur Sveinsson, a priest's son from Skagafjörður, and I have come to take Miss Bjarghildur to the cinema."

Karitas could have wept with envy.

The next day, he came somewhat early, and, without introducing himself, said, "Now, I was thinking of inviting Miss Bjarghildur to a café." And on the third and final day, he announced to the housewife, allowing himself to smile slightly as he did: "Bjarghildur and I are going to go for a ride outside of town."

The family was on edge the entire three days that Bjarghildur stayed out late. They had no idea what all the fuss was about, but suspected that there was something going on that could easily have consequences for her future, and in order to avoid being accused of interference of some sort later, they tried to curb their tormentous curiosity. Bjarghildur gave them no chance to try and fish information from her regarding the priest's son from Skagafjörður. She went down to the spit at the crack of dawn to wash and lay out saltfish to dry, and didn't come home until shortly before dinner, huffing and puffing and having no time to talk to anyone as she had to hurry to wash and tidy herself before her knight appeared. Her interaction with the family was limited to brief messages. Little Pétur usually brought a flask of hot coffee wrapped in a wool sock to her down at the spit, but on one of the days of fuss, Karitas spared him the inconvenience. She left her mistress's laundry in a tub by the clotheslines, snatched the coffee from her brother's hands, and hurried to her sister.

"For God's sake, Bjarghildur," she said in a tremulous voice, "has he kissed you?"

Bjarghildur replied that it was none of her business, and she wouldn't dream of telling her anything at all because she blathered so much. "But I was with you the first time you saw each other," Karitas whined, and her sister softened slightly.

"He hasn't kissed me, but I have kissed him. For the brooch, you see."

Steinunn didn't ask any questions. She opened the door for the young man when he knocked, and said, each time he announced his business, "If you would wait just a moment," and then called for Bjarghildur and disappeared into the pantry. The children had no idea what she felt about the young man, but once the riders from Skagafjörður were gone and salty gray mundanity had taken over again, Bjarghildur began to tiptoe around her mother. She wanted to know what her mother thought of the young man, and it was clear that her opinion meant everything to the daughter. "He makes a decent impression," said Steinunn, and that was all. Bjarghildur took this to mean that her mother liked the young man very much, and therefore determined to bring up another matter with her. She said that she was interested in hiring on to a farm in Skagafjörður; she wanted to do farmwork again. "Yes, why not?" said Steinunn, unperturbed.

Karitas, on the other hand, was upset and complained. She said that she couldn't bear to see both of her sisters disappear into the blue, for although both seemed to think that being older gave them the right to boss her around, their company was dear to her. "I have no girlfriends," she whimpered as they got ready for bed, "and now you're leaving, too, right after returning from the capital." "You'll have to find yourself a friend, my poor dear," said Bjarghildur, being surprisingly gentle with her. "How am I supposed to do that when my head's down in a washtub all day?" she sobbed, and Bjarghildur said that she had a point. The night before Bjarghildur's departure, she was nearly inconsolable and sat as if paralyzed on the edge of the bed, long after her sister had gotten under the covers. "It's not just that I'll be lonely, it's also that now all the worries and toil will land on me because I'll be the eldest here at home." Bjarghildur was of course well aware of this but didn't want to discuss it, either, and turned toward the wall, relieved to be free of that burden.

Before Bjarghildur rode to Skagafjörður, Steinunn talked to her in private in the kitchen. What the mother and daughter talked about, the youngest sister never got to know, although Bjarghildur couldn't keep from saying bitterly as she slammed the trunk lid shut, "Halldóra didn't get a lecture before she went east."

That night, after Karitas had crawled into her cold bed and stared blankly into the living room, she saw her mother cover her face with one hand and lean forward.

"Are you dizzy, Mama?"

"No, no," replied Steinunn after a moment, and she straightened up again. "It just struck me that two of my daughters have left home."

One night, Madam Eugenía returned.

Karitas didn't see her come ashore, but instead, heard the merchant's wife tell the kitchen maid that Madam Eugenía would not be coming to the planned dinner party because she was feeling under the weather. From what the mistress said, her friend had apparently returned to Iceland several days ago. Karitas waited to be summoned, firmly believing that her lessons weren't over; at least, the madam had never indicated otherwise. Hadn't she said she was just taking a short trip abroad? That was how Karitas remembered it, and for that reason, she waited and hoped. But the days passed, and no message came from Madam Eugenía.

A gloom lay over the town those autumn days. In a northerly gale and rain, salty seawater flooded the streets, giving a foretaste of a cold, wet winter. The shortage of coal kept the townspeople awake at night, and although attempts were made to use brown coal and peat, these were inadequate for heating the larger buildings. The Comprehensive School was closed due to lack of fuel, and Steinunn was stuck with two half-grown, eternally hungry schoolboys with nothing to do. After their bowl of porridge in the mornings, they were sent to look for work, and although they tore through town like a couple of roaring lions, asking everywhere for even the smallest of jobs, their efforts bore no fruit until the neighbor woman stepped in. While hanging laundry behind the house, she and Steinunn discussed the town's wretched situation, and when it came to light that the foreman of the clothing factory owed the carpenter a favor, it was decided, there at the clotheslines, that he must see to it that the boys were hired to do odd jobs for the factory. There, the looms sang as never before, because the war prevented the import of foreign textiles. The brothers became errand boys, which slightly improved the household's financial situation, but the war intensified and the cost of living rose. The pantry was in a dreary state.

But it was the coal that life revolved around, from dawn until dusk.

"We have a tough winter ahead," Steinunn said. "I dreamed it."

She could not be persuaded to tell them her dream, making them suspect that it had been chilling.

Karitas suffered from both cold and malaise. She found herself falling asleep shivering and exhausted every night, and waking with aches and pains every morning. The merchant's wife had finally raised her wage, but at the same time, piled new chores on her. Besides doing the laundry in the dank basement, she now had to scour the floors on both stories and run errands for the mistress when she needed some trifle, which was often two or three times a day. This meant Karitas was constantly on the move, if not up and down the stairs, then hither and thither in town. When she passed the government official's house, she slowed down and gazed longingly up at the flower window. She never saw Madam Eugenía in it, not for so much as a second. Yet she knew for certain that she was there. With her drawings locked in a drawer, a picture of her mother in the bath.

One afternoon, she was staring so intensely at the window that she paid no heed to where she was going and walked straight into a pole. Behind her, she heard someone burst out laughing. She wanted to ignore it, but curiosity prevailed and she turned around. The boy with the beautiful eyes was standing behind her, smiling from ear to ear, but quickly put on a serious face when he saw her thrust out her jaw. She regarded him for a moment or two. He had grown considerably and now reached up to her chin. She crossed her arms, looked at him haughtily, and waited. He rummaged through his pockets but could find nothing to give her, to his dismay. She grinned. "Well, my boy, so I get nothing today?"

He hurriedly looked away and out at the sea, as if he had spotted a ship. "How old are you now, my poor dear?" she asked, but before he could mutter an answer, she had an idea. "Listen, my friend, maybe we could go over to your father's?"

He set off without a word.

The restaurant owner from the house next door and the shipowner who lived across the street were sitting in the merchant's office, enjoying cigars and steaming-hot coffee. "This is the daughter of Steinunn Ólafsdóttir, the widow who put all of her children in school," said the merchant, clearly pleased with himself at knowing which townspeople were the parents of which children, and the men looked at Karitas, sucked on their cigars, and drank in her youth. "My son brings her to me regularly," the merchant continued, and the men nodded and looked at his son, who blinked his riveting eyes. "Take your cap off when you come inside, boy. And is everything going well in the young miss's home?"

"Yes, thank you," Karitas replied, curtsying hastily. "Everything's in good shape at home, especially since the house is built of trusty Icelandic driftwood, as the merchant knows best himself, although something went wrong with the coal stove when we were going to make porridge, the hotplates refused to heat up, but then Jenný, the neighbor who had come to pick up knitted underwear from Mama, said it came as no surprise to her that the wretched stove wouldn't heat up, being a foppish Danish tart who thought brown coal from Tjörnes was beneath her, and for that reason wouldn't condescend to work even when lit. And then Mrs. Jenný gave the stove's leg a swift kick with all her might to knock it down a notch, and just like that, it sprang into action, but Mrs. Jenný's big toe doubled in size, and now she can't put on her Danish shoes anymore, but instead, has to hobble through the slush in Icelandic sheepskin."

The men shook with laughter, making the coffee dance on the rims of their cups.

"But what can I do for the young miss today?" asked the merchant when he'd recovered. "I don't suppose you need another sewing machine?"

"No, we have little use for a sewing machine at home, now that the seamstress has moved to the Eastfjords, where she crosses fell and fjord to deliver Eastfjords infants, legitimate and illegitimate. On the other hand, the knitting machine can't keep up with the demand and runs night and day with all its clicking and clapping and doomsday clamor, because we're apparently in for a harsh winter and there's a shortage of good underwear, which is why I would like to ask if the merchant might be interested in selling long underwear of the finest wool in his shop."

Again, the men were amused, they bounced in their seats, declared this an excellent afternoon, smoked and puffed in each other's faces, until the shipowner said, "You know what, boys, the young lady is absolutely right; we'll all be drawers-less in the spring if those scoundrels overseas keep the shipping routes closed."

"I was thinking about making a trade," said Karitas. "You get a batch of underwear, and I get a sack of coal."

They swallowed their smoke and stared at her as if she'd lost her mind, so she hurriedly explained that the sack of coal was meant for the foppish Danish tart, but this time, her humor didn't find its way to their hearts, and instead, kindled a heated debate about coal. Before she could manage to put out the flames she'd lit, they began practically shouting over one another, cursing the war that was devastating the Icelandic fishing industry, bringing a recession and cold over the nation, and they stood up, puffing and blowing and spilling coffee on themselves, and began stamping back and forth through the office, their bodies so heavy and close-packed that Karitas thanked her lucky stars that she was able to slip out before being bruised up between them. Once outside, she stood there bewildered and rattled, trying to determine if a deal had been made or if it had all been in vain. Then the boy with the beautiful eyes yanked on her jersey from behind and said politely, "Miss?" She turned around.

He stared up at her face, held his index finger below his left eye, tried to open it as best he could and said that he had a speck in his eye, could she get it out? She felt sorry for him, even if she wasn't in the mood to tend to anyone or anything just then, pulled him under the office window so that the light fell on his face, took hold of his chin and peered hard into his eyes. He shut them and sighed blissfully.

"Open your eyes, boy!" she ordered, shaking him so hard that he had to grab her by the waist to keep from losing his balance. They stood there like that for a long time as their breaths combined and ascended to the sky, nestled in the clouds that had hidden behind the darkness, and then she said, "I don't see anything," and let him go. "And stop following me." She turned on her heel and stormed off into the evening, which would soon be pitch-black, but he called out before she disappeared from his sight: "You'll be getting what you asked for, Miss."

Karitas

Woman with a Music Box 1917

Pencil drawing

The drifting snow settles over the house like gossamer.

The house is still and silent, as if tucked under covers. The windows have shut their white lace eyes.

Behind the lace curtains, all is awhirl. The maids have fallen out, and their squabbling can be heard out on the street. I pluck up my courage, tear off my scarf, and rap firmly on the door.

The elderly kitchen maid opens it: "Oh, is that you, dear? Come inside, the wind's blowing right into the house."

"Might I have a word with Madam Eugenía?"

The kitchen maid says that the madam isn't in any condition to receive visitors, but then bites her lip, says that she has been a bit ill, and, after a moment's thought, adds, "Perhaps she will see you. Come into the parlor while I go and find out."

She walks ahead of me into the yellow parlor, lights an oil lamp. I look at my old seat by the flower window, which preserves the best memories of my life. I hear someone go upstairs, come back down after a short time, and go straight into the kitchen where the bickering resumes. No one comes down. The quarrel in the kitchen intensifies.

They forget all about me there in the parlor. I go into the vestibule. Hesitate, look at the stairs leading to the upper floor, lift my skirt, and tiptoe up the stairs. I come to a long corridor. The doors to the rooms on both sides are closed, except for one at the far end. Therein, a music box is playing.

I inch my way slowly down the dark corridor, peek in through the doorway.

Madam Eugenía is standing half-naked over a washbasin, holding a music box. Her hair is a mass of tangles, locks hanging loosely over her bare arms. She puts down the music box, rinses her face with both hands, dries it with a white towel.

The music box comes to the end of its lively tune.

Madam Eugenía glances toward the door. Her cheeks are sunken; there are dark rings under her eyes.

"Are you ill?" I ask.

"Are you in the habit of barging into people's bedrooms, Miss Karitas? Are you not taught good manners at home? Do you have business with me?"

"I just wanted to ask if I should come back and continue drawing," I say.

"No," she says bluntly, and the word is like a gush of cold water in my face. After a few moments, I resolve to ask if it's because I haven't paid for my lessons.

Again she says no, and I turn to leave. But then I can't help but blurt out, "May I have the picture that you are keeping in the drawer downstairs, of my mother in the bath?"

Madam Eugenía says derisively, "Should I expect to be drawn later as I'm standing here now, half-naked over the washbasin? No, you're not getting the picture of your mother, because it's in Copenhagen."

She slams the door shut.

A month before the town filled with folk from the surrounding countryside who came to buy Christmas gifts and attend parties that lasted late into the night, and a week after the fiasco at Madam Eugenía's, Karitas was overwhelmed by her emotions. Tears streamed into the washtub as she scrubbed the merchant's underpants, they ran down her cheeks in the bakery as she ordered the madam's Christmas cakes and flooded her face on her way home through the pitch darkness and bitterly cold wind. "Just look at you, child!" said Steinunn, astonished, not recalling ever having seen her daughter's eyes so red and swollen before. But the lump in Karitas's throat prevented her from saying a single comprehensible word, and it was only after she had washed her face with cold water and simmered herself some milk that she could sigh that there was in fact nothing wrong with her, she had just been doing some thinking. Steinunn, who knew that thoughts could cause people more harm than cold and other hardships, asked if someone had done her an injustice or talked down to her. No, she denied that emphatically; she had just been thinking about the future, which was bleak; she had nothing to look forward to, absolutely nothing. Her self-pity appalled Steinunn, and she brusquely pointed out to her daughter that she was still young and healthy and had her whole life ahead of her—"and I have no doubt that you will marry a good man, have many children and a beautiful home." "But that is exactly what I don't want," Karitas sobbed. "I want to go to school like my siblings; I want to learn like them; people are always going on about the widow who sent all of her children to school, but that's not true—I've never gotten to learn anything. I'm just a washerwoman who slaves away all day so that her lousy brothers can go to school."

There, she had said it, the thing that had gnawed at her heart for months, and the widow from the west was so taken aback by her daughter's bitterness that she laid aside her knitting. Karitas went on sobbing. "And on top of that, I don't even get to draw anymore, even though I enjoyed it so much, because Madam Eugenía doesn't want to see me again."

Steinunn never got a chance to answer the accusations, because just as she was about to speak her mind, there was a furious pounding on the door. Outside stood a man who looked vaguely familiar, shouting: "A sack of coal for Karitas!" And then he was off. Steinunn stared at the coal sack as if she were seeing things, but when she turned and looked at her daughter to ask for an explanation, the girl's sobbing changed into a piteous wail. "Why didn't you give the man underclothes in return for the coal? That is what I promised him!"

The small fishing boats, packed with people from the nearby communities, filled the Puddle in the days leading up to Christmas, and the merchants, dressed up and in high spirits, were delighted with the brisk business they were doing in these latest worst of times. It was as if the northerners had forgotten all about the war out in the world; they ignored the shortage of wares and bought everything that was on the shelves. Glad at heart now that there were cakes in her pantry and a decked-out Christmas table, the merchant's wife sent the laundry girl home at noon on Christmas Eve with smoked lamb and a bag of candles. But Karitas didn't have the same joy in her heart, because she missed her sisters. For the longest time, she had hoped that they would come home for Christmas, but it was unfortunately not to be; one of them had to be on hand if some little easterner had a mind to come into the world over the holidays, and the other was unwilling to leave the Skagafjörður countryside as long as the man she had set her sights on had not yet been brought into safe, marital harbor.

This was the second Christmas that the older sisters spent away, and the rest of the family found the house rather empty without them, despite trying their best to create a festive atmosphere. Páll had made a beautiful wooden Christmas tree, which they placed on the table that the sewing machine had previously adorned, and they spent many evenings cutting little bags from colored paper, which they hung on the tree's arms. "It's really starting to look nice in here," said Steinunn, who didn't seem to take the sisters' absence very badly. "Sooner or later, everyone has to spend Christmas in some other place than their parents' home."

Shortly after noon, the winter sun began to warm the house's south gable, so the siblings clustered around the kitchen window and basked in its rays as they nibbled on strips of dried fish. But then the brothers felt it a shame not to enjoy the nice weather while it lasted, and they decided to go down to the quay to see how the folk from the nearby communities had coped with getting home, and took Pétur with them. Left alone, the mother and daughter busied themselves with their chores in peace and quiet. Karitas stayed as close as possible to the window so as not to miss out on the sunlight, and watched the townspeople bustle in both directions along the street as they finished up their last errands before the start of the holiday.

Then she saw her, dressed in black and wearing a hat and gloves, heading north.

"Mama, I think it's Madam Eugenía," she said hesitantly, and her mother joined her at the window. "It looks to me like she's on her way here," said Steinunn. "I can't talk to her; she slammed the door on me last time!" cried Karitas. Steinunn laid her hand on her daughter's shoulder to calm her and looked deep into her eyes. "Women can have bad days when they spare no one, least of all those whom they care about." Before opening the door for the madam, who knocked lightly upon it as dames with hats do, she glanced searchingly over the living room to reassure herself that it was presentable to this distinguished woman from the town center.

From out on the snow-covered gravel, Madam Eugenía bade them good morning, and Steinunn bade good morning in return without moving from the doorway. "Lovely weather today," said Madam Eugenía, smiling. Steinunn agreed, without smiling. Madam Eugenía introduced herself and asked if she could have a few words, and Steinunn replied that of course she could, and finally stepped aside to allow the madam to enter. Karitas pressed herself against the kitchen window and didn't utter a peep. Madam Eugenía looked around unabashedly, inspecting the commoner's home with great interest, and then nodded and gave an appreciative look to the head of the household, who stood there on the alert, although she did have the presence of mind to ask the visitor to sit down. After taking a seat, Madam Eugenía removed her gloves, straightened her skirt, and undid the shawl that she had tied loosely over her winter coat, but left her hat on. She declined the coffee and crullers that Steinunn offered, saying that she had just eaten, but then said that she wouldn't mind having a glass of water and some raisins if the housewife was so fortunate as to have them on hand. "How are your children doing at school?" she then asked, once the raisins were brought to the table, and Steinunn said that the youngest was the only one attending at the moment; the two eldest daughters had completed their studies down south last spring, and the brothers had had to put their studies on hold because the Comprehensive School was closed due to a shortage of fuel, as everyone knew.

"Weren't you planning to have Karitas attend the Women's College in Reykjavík?" asked Madam Eugenía amicably.

"It's just as short of fuel as every other school!" cried out Karitas from the kitchen.

"Planning to and not planning to," Steinunn said quickly. "The Comprehensive School here in town was also an option. But things went as they did."

"Karitas is a very talented girl and needs to get out of the house and into a school," said Madam Eugenía, even more amicably than before.

"I know," Steinunn replied heavily. "She has a great many merits, and it is not least due to her diligence and support that we have been able to send the boys to school and maintain our home here in the north."

"I can well understand mothers' desire to provide their sons an education, as they will need to support their own families later on, but because of your daughter's talents, I would like to offer to pay for her schooling. This is why I have come to speak to you today. I will pay for her room and board and all of her school expenses, and her travel, of course," continued Madam Eugenía, when the housewife did not react.

Karitas gripped the windowsill. After a long inner struggle, Steinunn said, "It would be a significant sum."

"Money doesn't matter to me. It's getting what I want that does."

Again, there was a long silence. At last it seemed that Steinunn Ólafsdóttir had made a decision. She took a deep breath and said, "Thank you for your kind offer, but I think that I will see to it myself that my daughter goes to school in Reykjavík."

Madam Eugenía took a sip of water from her glass and practically slammed it back down on the table. "I wasn't thinking that she would go to Reykjavík, but to a foreign country. To the Royal Academy of Fine Arts in Copenhagen."

Karitas sank into a crouch.

Before setting out for their house, Madam Eugenía had undoubtedly prepared herself thoroughly for countering their objections to her regal offer and achieving her goal, yet it seemed as if the quiet, almost numb reaction, as when people are involved in an accident, came as a surprise to her. While waiting for an answer, she began to feel a bit uncertain, and pulled at one of her gloves as if it were too short for her long fingers. Karitas squatted under the kitchen window in a strange, blissful state, almost giddy; she wished that she could feel that way forever, that she could crouch there for the rest of the day and repeat those majestic words in her mind—"Academy," "Academy of Fine Arts," "Copenhagen"—and imagine the world behind them. In her mind's eye, she saw herself waving to the fishwives; she would probably buy a fish from them now and then; would they be selling haddock there, or cod? But her mother, who never let herself be taken in by palaver and fancy words and had brushed aside her surprise, yanked Karitas back to the ice-cold kitchen floor. She asked how the madam proposed to guarantee both her daughter's studies for an entire year and her return ticket, in the event of her own illness or the like, and the madam, quickly recomposing herself, said with a touch of sarcasm, seeing as how others were doubting her credibility, that it would not be just one year of studies, but five—this time flabbergasting Steinunn. Now, she could stand still no longer, and began pacing the floor with her hands behind her back, wanting guarantees down to the tiniest detail, and to be given a precise description of how every single one-eyrir coin was going to find its way from the madam's purse into her daughter's pocket. Karitas was ashamed of her pettiness and suspicion. But the madam didn't let the mother's interrogation put her off her stride, launching into a long speech about bank accounts and seeming to enjoy herself immensely as she spoke. It wasn't until Steinunn stopped abruptly in the middle of the living room and asked matter-of-factly why she was doing this that Madam Eugenía raised her eyebrows, with an impenetrable expression on her face.

"Does it look to you as if I have anything more important to do, Madam Steinunn? Besides, Karitas is a talented young woman, with a quick tongue. Due to the instruction that I have given her, she will be able to take her entrance exam as soon as she reaches Copenhagen. People there were enthusiastic about her pictures. I assume that you have seen your daughter's drawings?"

"I've seen some of them," said Steinunn.

"Perhaps you have seen her beautiful drawing of a woman bathing?"

"A woman bathing?"

Karitas sprang to her feet and gnawed her fists as she waited for what would come next.

"A woman bathing, yes. It was a striking picture."

"I haven't seen it," Steinunn said thoughtfully, "but I did see another picture, quite a pretty one, of a woman standing over a washbasin with something in her hands."

"The stove has gone out, Mama!" shouted Karitas.

Madam Eugenía said that she hadn't seen that picture, and there was a touch of gaiety in her voice when she got up and added that she would sail to Denmark at the end of the winter and take Karitas with her. "Merry Christmas, Miss Karitas!" she called into the kitchen before she left the house. The mother and daughter stood at the kitchen window and watched her walk back down the street, southward. The winter sun had lingered in order to escort her home.

"Is she going to have her baby overseas?" Steinunn asked herself.

After the New Year, the family was forced to spend most of their time in their beds.

The cold drove them to it. A glacial paw from the north had clamped its claws around the town, storming in like a wild beast with such violent blizzards and cold that the earth groaned. When it slackened, the cold settled like a white petticoat over the loins of the fjord and closed the sea lanes.

"Sea ice again," said Steinunn wearily.

The snowstorms lasted for days on end. There was no more coal, so they had to heat the house with kerosene and cook their food on a Primus stove. Every last woolen garment was used to keep their bodies warm, and despite the duvets being stuffed with high-grade Westfjords eiderdown, they weren't enough when the temperature dropped to thirty-five below. They all nestled in the living room; the elder brothers tried to keep each other warm under one duvet, and Karitas and her mother shared another bed, with Pétur between them. Most often, he lay on Karitas's chest in order to eke out more warmth, because Steinunn couldn't keep to her bed during the day. She was constantly roaming the house, tending the fire, bringing them bread or porridge, and in between, toiled away at the coffee grinder to keep herself warm. They could hardly bear the stench from the kerosene, but even worse was dragging themselves out of bed to use the chamber pot. It took such a huge effort to relieve themselves that they tried to drink as little as possible. Little Pétur crawled shivering out of bed but was dumbfounded when he pulled the chamber pot out from under it. He had never seen frozen urine before.

"Kneel down so you don't miss," Steinunn ordered. The cold made her cranky.

The storms subsided, but the frost held the town in its iron grip. The whole country was ice-cold and white. In the silence, people could clearly hear the crunching of the icebergs as they squeezed past each other out in the fjord. Folk dashed between the houses, trying to move as fast as they could, knowing that after a few minutes outside, their fingers would be stiff with cold, regardless of whether their mittens were made of wool or leather. People feared frostbite, but even more frightening was the thought of visitors from the seas to the north. It was said that the silence of the ice sheet was broken only by the roars of the polar bears. When news spread that four people had already been killed by polar bears, the women began to take measures. "If the door doesn't hold, we can run up to the attic—there's no way that they can climb those narrow stairs, that's for certain," said Steinunn. "They'll wreck the knitting machine," said Karitas from the bed. "Just let them try it," said Steinunn.

They slept badly, and not just because of the cold.

The primary school was closed and work came near to a halt due to the cold, as well as the sickness that followed in its wake. The merchant's house was deathly silent. The daughter, who had contracted one illness after another—Karitas had heard talk of pleurisy, typhoid, and tuberculosis—now lay white as snow in her bed. No one was allowed to go in to her, no one needed to draw for her. She was only eighteen years old and lay waiting to be fetched by her grandmother, who dwelled in the great beyond. Stories were told of people who had died of cold in their beds, but when the specter of starvation began to wave its shroud over children and the elderly, the women took action. They borrowed a classroom at the primary school, set up stoves there, and began to cook meals for the famished. Every day, the room filled with people, but some were so weakened by hunger that food had to be sent to their homes. Steinunn helped with the deliveries, as did Jenný. They never spoke about the misery they encountered, but when they returned home, they glanced at each other and shook their heads.

The frost relented, but the ice did not. Karitas looked in despair at the endless ice sheet and at the quays that no boat could reach. She longed to knock on Madam Eugenía's door and ask her opinion on this state of affairs, whether she thought they would be able to sail abroad in early spring or whether travel would be delayed until autumn. It mattered a great deal, because if she had to spend yet another summer washing saltfish and cleaning herring, the skin on her hands would be ruined. But she didn't like the thought of going and knocking, not least because of her mother's remarks on the madam's condition, which Karitas hoped was just conjecture. Karitas told herself that the good woman had just eaten too much in Denmark, where apparently everything was cooked in butter and baked with eggs. Steinunn seemed undisturbed, despite the fact that the journey was never discussed, but neither did she act as if it weren't pending, because at the other end of the house, where there was a sewing machine, preparations were being made more or less openly. "We need to be sure the lady is properly dressed," said Jenný as she measured Karitas's front and back. "No fewer than three dresses will do, and preferably a coat as well, because I've never seen an Icelandic knitted shawl in the foreign fashion magazines, and shouldn't she have a second pair of shoes, Steinunn?" The knitting machine sang around the clock as well, sharing the work equally.

But the ice did not yield. Stories of the white ogre haunted the townsfolk as much by day as in their incoherent dreams, in which stairs hung in midair and crooked doors gave way before white paws. One evening, heavy blows were heard on the front door. The brothers had fallen asleep, but Karitas lay drawing on a sheet of paper beneath the duvet, and her blood turned to ice. Steinunn didn't move from the knitting machine, but sat stock-still, head down. When the pounding came again, she glanced at her daughter and stood up. "Don't open it, Mama," pleaded Karitas, but Steinunn went to the door and tore it open.

No greetings or kisses were heard in the living room. The visitor came in silently and was received in silence. Snow was brushed off, coat and shoes removed. Steinunn entered the living room, holding Halldóra, pale and haggard, in her arms.

"Move over, Karitas. I need to get Halldóra into the warm bed."

Karitas

The Pharmacy 1918

Pencil drawing

The oak shelves at the pharmacy bend beneath the weight of mixtures.

Countless small drawers affixed with white labels bear mysterious inscriptions.

The mustached pharmacist attends to two young ladies. They are wearing Danish coats, fur hats, and muffs.

I enter, coughing.

The pharmacist looks up. I bid him good day. He nods. The ladies look round but can't be bothered to greet me, and turn back to their purchases.

I wait, regarding the collection of mixtures and the Danish coats.

Then little bells ring, the door opens, and in steps Madam Eugenía.

The pharmacist glances toward the door, and his face lights up in a smile. The young ladies turn to look, smiling as they do, and tilt their heads. Without prompting, they bid good day. Forgetting the young ladies, the pharmacist asks what he can do for the madam.

The madam pays him no heed, but looks me straight in the eye and says, "We sail with the next ship."

The pharmacy falls silent.

"But the sea ice?" I whisper.

"An icebreaker will clear me a path. Are you ill?"

"There's nothing wrong with me, I'm just getting some medicine for my sister Halldóra, the midwife. She returned from the Eastfjords seriously ill. She kept putting off having a doctor see her because she had no time to be sick. Every time one woman finished giving birth, the next one started, and she had to rush all over the countryside and down into the fjords in this freezing weather—the ice to the east was no worse than here—but eventually she became so exhausted that she wanted nothing more than to come home and get medical help here in the north. She has a bad case of pneumonia and is so ill that our sister Bjarghildur has ridden here from Skagafjörður, through all the heavy snow. And now she's watching over Halldóra day and night. We all are."

Those present listen to her story without moving an inch.

"What can I do for the young lady?" asks the pharmacist, softly and sincerely.

"Well, I'm supposed to be getting some cough syrup," I say, and hand him the prescription.

The trunk was on standby next to the bed in the back room, but its existence was treated as a deadly secret, despite the fact that it was gradually filling up. As was to be expected, life revolved around Halldóra's homecoming and her illness, and in Bjarghildur's opinion, the fuss about Karitas was nearly intolerable at this worst of times. Karitas wasn't even sure that she had fully realized she was going to live overseas for a long period of time, but on the other hand, it was made clear to her that people don't make trips when their next of kin lay close to death.

"Death? Do you really think it's that bad?" she whispered beneath the duvet.

"Do you think I would have ridden all the way from Skagafjörður through heavy snow if she had only caught a cold? I know my duty—unlike certain others. And by the way, those same others have always behaved like small children. Stop this chatter now; I need to get a little sleep, if it's not too much to ask."

Regarding the youngest sister's impending trip abroad, Bjarghildur had very little to say, even though both sisters had been informed quietly and directly, after a sufficient amount of time had passed, that their little sister had been invited to travel to Denmark to study. "What do you mean?" said Bjarghildur. "Can't she learn to sew here at home, like everyone else?" "She's going to study drawing," said Steinunn, leaving it to the brothers to finish her sentence.

"At the Royal Academy of Fine Arts in Copenhagen," they declared triumphantly.

Momentarily, both sisters' eyes lit up with admiration. Bjarghildur gasped, and Halldóra, terribly ill as she was, lifted her head from the pillow—ever so briefly. "Well, I never," said Bjarghildur, thrusting out her lower jaw, openmouthed, as she often did when a matter involved her or her family's prestige. "But who is going to pay for it?" she asked quickly, knitting her brows. "The madam who gave her drawing lessons last year has guaranteed her room and board for a full five years," announced Ólafur, who was attuned to his sister's moodiness and knew that she disliked a fuss being made over anyone other than herself. He enjoyed bothering her, and preferably upsetting her. As he expected, her satisfaction with the success of a family member, which could possibly mean kudos for herself, disappeared in an instant. She didn't want her porridge. She sat down on the edge of Halldóra's bed and concentrated on getting the gruel into her.

"There, now," she said gruffly every time that Halldóra managed to open her mouth.

"I always knew she was an artist," Halldóra whispered between spoonfuls.

"There are others who could have studied the arts, such as, for instance, singing and playing the organ, had they been as pushy as certain people," said Bjarghildur. "And it is of course all well and good to be able to draw, but where does she see herself finding work when she returns from all this traipsing about?"

No one could answer this question, least of all the prospective artist herself, who sat there modestly over her porridge while the others talked about her, but who still hoped, the entire time, that her mother would intervene and tell the sisters once and for all how imperative it was for Karitas to study abroad. But Steinunn didn't say a thing about it. And when Karitas told her about her expected departure date, "Yes, yes, it's fast approaching," was all she said. Not a word about whether it bothered her that Karitas was going abroad given her eldest daughter's condition, or whether she would be sorry to lose her. Or would miss her.

In the evenings, when Karitas was safely tucked in with Bjarghildur, with the latter's leg draped over her hips and her warm breaths on her neck, she was tormented by insecurity and worry. At those times, she couldn't imagine leaving her mother and siblings, her cozy home, the town where she now knew every house and every single small-boat fisherman, and then, on top of that, to be tossed about seasick and short of breath—to who knows what in Copenhagen! She didn't have the faintest idea where she was going to live or whether she would get anything decent to eat. If she got anything to eat at all, that is. And she turned gently in the narrow bed until her sister's warm breaths were in her face, and stroked her cheeks gently because she loved her so much, loved them all so much and felt ashamed at being such an awful person to even think of leaving them. Finally, she fell asleep with a weight on her chest, determined to inform Madam Eugenía first thing the next morning that she wasn't going anywhere. But as soon as it grew light and she heard the cries of the seabirds, she was again gripped by the longing to go abroad and study.

On the Sunday four days before the great voyage, she was sent for by Madam Eugenía. She was served tea at the splendid flower window where she had spent her best moments, and Madam Eugenía laid in her lap a burgundy-colored velvet purse, not much larger than an envelope, and said that she should keep all of her papers and money in it. A strange expression came over Karitas's face, since she had very little experience managing money; she handed her wages over to her mother. But then Madam Eugenía opened the burgundy purse and pulled out a bundle of Danish banknotes. Karitas burst into laughter, like an idiot. Madam Eugenía let her laugh all she wanted, whereas she herself didn't so much as smile, and then informed her of the arrangements that she had made for her stay in Copenhagen. Karitas would lodge with a friend of hers who ran a restaurant, where she was to work as a waitress over the summer and learn as much Danish as she could for the school year. Then, when school began in the autumn, she would work in the kitchen both after school on weekdays and on the weekends. And she could keep her room in the friend's house. It had been agreed. And just one other thing: she was not to go out in the evenings.

Karitas told her mother what future awaited her in Copenhagen, trying to quote Madam Eugenía precisely and saying she only hoped that the madam would keep her word on all of this. Steinunn said she had heard that that woman always kept her word. She went to the door and looked into the living room, where there was no one but Halldóra, asleep, and then shut the kitchen door. "And she is no less wealthy than her husband, if not even grander and richer. But I am glad to hear that she is going to have you work alongside your studies. I hope that it goes well, for it would be sad to think of you sitting there idly on the weekends. You're terribly little given to needlework, Karitas, but still, you must now try to take up your needles regularly. I have packed them and some yarn into your trunk. And you must try to get to church on Sunday now and then, if the restaurant lady allows it, but if she is against it, don't sulk, but instead, read your Bible whenever you have time, I put it in your trunk, and assign yourself particular scripture passages daily. Be polite and cheerful to people with whom you associate, never gossip or speak badly of others. All such talk gets passed on. And you must write me good long letters and inform me well and thoroughly of everything that happens to you. God willing, I shall be reading them in Reykjavík. I am considering moving south next year or the year after so that I can complete the boys' education. I would also like to remind you that making eyes at young men can have certain consequences, so avoid such behavior, as you have thus far. Accept neither gifts nor refreshments from them, because if you do, they will expect something in return. If men speak to you, look the other way, yet answer their questions with the fullest courtesy. And I needn't say more about not wanting you to be out after dark. But what about Madam Eugenía's condition—is she showing yet?"

Later in the evening, it dawned on Karitas that her mother had been laying down precepts for her daughter's life.

Halldóra's condition worsened over the next few days, despite Karitas's praying to the good Lord each night to make her better before she left. The doctor was sent for again. The children waited in the kitchen while he examined Halldóra and spoke quietly with Steinunn. They gathered that it was too risky to move her to the hospital—besides the fact that it was already jam-packed with patients. They had to wait and see what the next twenty-four hours would bring. It could go either way, but they were to keep a close eye on her, and then he gave Steinunn detailed instructions and left the house, showing obvious signs of fatigue from his lack of sleep.

Bjarghildur stepped close to Karitas and whispered bitterly, "And you are still determined to travel abroad, even though your sister is dying."

Karitas hid her face in her hands and began to sob. Unable to bear it, Ólafur took her in his arms, patted her on the back, and then grabbed Bjarghildur's arm tightly and asked why she could never be nice to her sister. Bjarghildur shook him off, put her hand on his chest, and pushed him so roughly that he banged into the wall. Páll and Pétur jumped in, and a violent scuffle broke out in the kitchen.

They dropped their hands when their mother appeared in the doorway. She looked gravely at her offspring. Didn't say a word, but they all knew very well what she wanted to say.

Bjarghildur refused to sleep in the same bed as Karitas on her last night and crawled into bed with Pétur. Steinunn didn't go to bed at all; she sat at Halldóra's bedside all night. Karitas lay alone in the inner room, unable to sleep. Anxiety played cruel tricks on her stomach and digestion; she had to go to the privy time and time again. Her mother understood what was going on. She didn't leave Halldóra's bed, but once as Karitas went by, she grabbed her hands, rubbed and stroked them, and said, "You'll get so cold from all this back-and-forth, Karitas." Karitas burst into tears and laid her head in her mother's lap. Her mother stroked her hair and face. They sat like that for a long time.

The brothers loaded her trunk onto a cart, put on their mittens, pulled their hats down over their ears, and told her to hurry, the ship couldn't wait for small girls like her. They tried to put on cheerful faces, but sadness shone in their eyes. Karitas kissed Halldóra, her forehead, her eyes, but Halldóra lay in a daze, her face still and white; only her hand moved reflexively when Karitas pressed it, a light grasp, as if to say goodbye.

"I'll say goodbye to you here, Karitas, and then watch you go," said Steinunn. She took her in her arms on the steps and laid her cheek against her daughter's, and they listened to each other's heartbeats. "Remember to say your prayers in the evening, and if the darkness haunts you, say the Lord's Prayer again and again until God brings you sleep."

Bjarghildur stood straight as an arrow behind her mother, her arms folded over her chest. "You have no right to leave like this when your sister is lying here deathly ill, and don't you dare try kissing me."

"Just listen to yourself!" said Steinunn.

But Bjarghildur wouldn't back down. Karitas was distraught.

The brothers pulled the cart, and Karitas followed abjectly behind, holding her little brother by the hand. She looked back again and again, hoping against hope that Bjarghildur would come running, but saw only her mother's pale and serious face behind the pane of the kitchen window.

Little Pétur squeezed her hand: "Are there animals in Copenhagen, Karitas?" "I think there are some birds," she replied distractedly. "Bjarghildur says that there are both poisonous snakes and man-eating apes there. You must be careful, Karitas." Then she could no longer hold back the tears that had been waiting to burst out ever since she woke, and, crying, she wrapped her arms around her little brother.

Ahead, they could see the ship lying alongside the quay and the blue strip of sea like a trail behind it, where the icebreaker had cleared a path for Madam Eugenía. She was nowhere to be seen, but there were a considerable number of people on the quay, and the ship was still being loaded. The brothers hastened aboard with the trunk, and then it was time to say goodbye. Karitas looked at her brothers and knew that the next time she saw them, they would be men. And her little brother a teenager, whose shoulder she might just reach up to.

"You're so awfully small and thin," Páll said suddenly, as if he had read her thoughts. "Yes, we must hope that you'll put on a bit of weight out there in Copenhagen, Karitas," said Ólafur authoritatively, and then they showered her with kisses and hugs. "And remember to send us letters, and for goodness' sake, try to enjoy life out there." She dried her tears and said that she would do so for them. She walked up the gangway, waving as she did, and they waved back and made all sorts of funny gestures with their hands until they were out of sight. Karitas had spotted Madam Eugenía standing by the railing and was about to go to her when she saw a blue-clad person coming running toward the quay.

"It's Bjarghildur!" she shouted, before dashing back down the gangway.

Bjarghildur came running up at full speed and they dashed toward each other, one beaming with joy, the other scowling, which Karitas didn't see until they met on the shore. Bjarghildur grabbed her arm tightly and said straightaway, full of rage, "If you leave your dying sister, Karitas Jónsdóttir, you will regret it forever! Do you really want to have it on your conscience that you abandoned us when we needed you most? We're a family and must stand together, and what will happen if Mama gets sick and dies? If you go, the devil will follow your every footstep, because he settles into the souls of those who betray their loved ones, thinking only of their own skin, frippery, and frills. You will be shunned, outcast, and ignored, I promise you!"

Now Karitas knew what Bjarghildur had said to Halldóra in Seyðisfjörður those years ago.

"Let go of me!" she cried, terrified by her sister's violence and the curses, but Bjarghildur tightened her grip, her face distorted with rage. "You have no right to leave, you monster! You shall come home with me this instant!" And, strong as an ox, she dragged her along the shore ridge, Karitas trying to break free by hitting her sister's arm. She looked toward the ship and saw Madam Eugenía standing at the railing; all of the passengers were aboard, the ship was about to depart, the crew was making ready to draw up the gangway. She fought tooth and nail, but Bjarghildur drew strength from her resistance and, without letting go, slapped Karitas in the face so hard that she fell, then yanked her up again by her braid and dragged her along by her hair.

Neither of them saw Steinunn approaching. She appeared suddenly on the street above them, gray-clad, bareheaded, and grim-faced, and had reached them in an instant. She separated them with one quick movement and shook Bjarghildur violently. "How dare you do this to me, fighting like a street urchin in front of all these people! Karitas is going to Denmark, do you hear me? Now clear off home!"

She hurriedly embraced Karitas, stuffed the loose braid into her collar, and said, "Run, Karitas, and don't let anyone stop you!"

People shook their heads as she returned, flushed and panting. The gangway was relowered. Madam Eugenía hadn't moved. She just stood there looking stately, gazing landward, but a smile played on her lips. She glanced sidelong at Karitas, said, "These things can happen even in the best of families, can't they?"

Karitas was in no state to answer. It wasn't Bjarghildur's seething expression that stuck in her mind, but rather, her mother's face. Her eyes. They had been red, as if from weeping. She had wept as she watched her daughter walk down to the quay. Karitas had never seen her mother weep. She thought that mothers never wept. And she remained standing there gazing after her, her youngest daughter.

Gray-clad at the shore.

II

Karitas

Aprons on a Clothesline 1923

Pencil drawing

The wind comes from all directions.

The sky is gray, the trees ragged after the winter.

The street is small and narrow, the rows of buildings like low houses of cards. Folk are waking; through the half-open windows, I hear voices, the clattering of plates, but no one looks out.

They can't hear our footsteps over the wind.

My three brothers pull my trunk on a small cart; I look delightedly from one to the other. They have grown into handsome men. I feel almost shy, but know that it's they who are embarrassed because I, the smallest in the group, am older and have just returned from abroad.

Their sister has come home after a long absence.

They tell me about the people in the capital. Unable to take my eyes off them, I listen, until one points at a light brown house and says, "That's where we live."

But I don't look at the house. I see only the fluttering white laundry on the clotheslines next to the steps.

My mother's aprons.

Three large aprons, white and trusty. The bibs hang downward; the strings thrash each other wildly.

Then my mother steps out onto the stairs.

"An atelier?"

"It's a workshop."

"I know that. The photographer in Akureyri called his workshop an atelier. And do you have money for the rent?"

"No, my money is all used up. I was thinking of getting a job salting herring up north this summer."

"They're saying that the herring hasn't shown itself yet, even though we're well into June."

"I also want to set up an exhibition of my pictures here in Reykjavík, which means that I'll need money to have frames made for them."

"Your brother Páll is so dexterous; he ought to be able to put together a few old frames for you. There's no point in talking to Ólafur. Ever since he started at the University, he hasn't had time for anything but studying law."

"I simply must set up an exhibition."

"Apparently, Bjarghildur put on an exceptionally fine handcraft exhibition with the other members of the Women's Club up north. I would never have expected that; it was always Halldóra who was skilled with her hands. You could never handle knitting needles properly, Karitas."

"I never thought that Halldóra would die."

"You don't have to scrimp on the liver sausage on your bread; I know how much you like it. Have some more cake, too. Yes, Bjarghildur has done well for herself up there in the north. After she and Hámundur got married, she took over the household from his mother, and apparently, people have rarely seen such a well-managed household as that at Þrastabakki."

"She never answered my letters."

"You didn't become acquainted with any young men in Copenhagen, did you?"

"A friend of mine sometimes invited me to restaurants and cafés. But we're just good friends, I suppose. He wanted me to go with him to Rome."

"Is there anything to see there?"

"All artists go to Rome, Mama."

"Oh, do they now? In your last letters, you didn't say a word about Madam Eugenía. What happened to her after she gave birth to the boy?"

"She went with her lover to Paris."

"People do get around, don't they?"

"But the agreed-upon payments always came regularly to me until last year, when they suddenly stopped. That's why I was so short of money the last few months and couldn't go to Rome."

"Your skirt looks rather short to me."

"That's the fashion now, Mama."

"I know that. But still, you should be careful with such things. People take a dim view of show-offs here in Iceland. Even if they have studied art at prestigious academies. And people don't care much about foreign customs, either. So you're thinking of going north to Siglufjörður? They say it's a risky place for young women. Some have come back from there a little thicker around the waist than when they went. But you need money, and you won't find much work here in Reykjavík, what with unemployment as it is. Wouldn't it make more sense if you went to work for Bjarghildur? Her home is apparently quite lively and frequented by guests, particularly after she learned to play the organ and joined a church choir. I expect you wouldn't be bored there."

"I'm going to rent a workshop and set up an exhibition, and need a fair amount of money to do so. I simply must go work in the herring. I

would like to ask you to keep one of my trunks for me this summer—
the one with my pictures."

"If you go north, stop by the churchyard."

"Would you like to see my pictures, Mama?"

"I'll have a look at them when we come home from mass."

Two pious stepsisters who had resolved to redeem the world and devote
their energies to Christ through merciful works, but who wished first to
acquire worldly wealth, were given the immediate opportunity to test
their resolve aboard the coastal steamer.

Like Karitas, they were on their way north to work in the herring,
and when they saw how terribly seasick she was, they took her under
their wing and tended to her the entire journey. They themselves had
no trouble getting out of their bunks and eating their provisions. They
emptied Karitas's bucket to keep her from retching due to the stench,
washed her face thoroughly every time she vomited, and sang hymns to
her when she felt a little better. Karitas was touched by their kindness.
They were from Snæfellsnes, both brown-eyed and around thirty years
old, and they told Karitas, when she had enough presence of mind to
listen, that they were overjoyed to have never been involved with a man
and could consequently stand face-to-face with their Redeemer pure
and undefiled, when the call came.

"My name is Helga, and this is Ásta. She was born shortly after the
New Year, like most of the children of her mother, who changed jobs
every year but left her newborn offspring behind with her mistress,
and I was born just before Christmas the same year, because as soon
as Mama took Ásta into her care, she became pregnant, despite having
believed that she would never have children. So we were gifts from God,
she said, and we hope to be able to display that through our actions
and love of our neighbors. Now we shall help you to your feet. We are
drawing near to Siglufjörður—can you hear the racket of the birds on

the shore? But Ásta never saw her blessed mother, who wandered from parish to parish like a deceased soul who cannot find eternal rest. It is said that she fell off a cliff; she disappeared one night during a raging storm and was never seen again. Stand here with us on deck and have a look at the village. Though the fog is hindering the view, you can still make out the outlines of the herring barrels on the quay. Aren't they like the mountains surrounding the fjord? But once, she loved a young man who played the violin and repaired churches, and the story goes that they had been planning to get married, but one day in late autumn he was sent by a farmer to search for sheep that hadn't returned during the roundup, and as he was searching, a violent northerly storm hit the heath and he got lost, and it's believed that he fell into a deep crevice in a cliff by the river. Look at all the people on the quay and in the village—what a crowd! They say that the village's population doubles in the summers, but Ásta's mother started acting strangely following his disappearance, getting out of bed at night because she thought she heard his violin out in the meadows, and in the end, she abandoned her parish. It's best that Ásta carries your trunk; you take the sack holding your duvet, and I'll help you down the steps so that you don't stumble. And then she roamed from farm to farm, hired on at farms with churches, thinking the young man might turn up at one of them to do repair work, but because of her beauty, the farmhands couldn't leave her be, and, as distracted as she was, she never understood their advances until it was too late. There's no salting being done, the herring hasn't come yet, but her soul found no peace, and after her child was born, she laid it in her mistress's lap and asked her to look after it while she went looking for the young man—she had heard his violin and knew that he was nearby. Let me see the name of the man whom you're supposed to meet. Ásta and I will take you to him before we go see our own contact. And then she never came back to fetch her children, and one stormy night in the east, people heard her get out of bed and go downstairs in the dark but never come back up again, and when the storm let up the next day, she was nowhere to be found. They searched for her for a few days before giving up, thinking that she had fallen off a cliff. But now we're going to say goodbye, thank you for the company and God be with you."

The barrack stood by the sea. Karitas reported to the office on the second floor, and after the clerk had growled and complained about the lack of herring, he sent her up to the third floor, third room on the left, where the herring girls lodged, and told her that she would be called for as soon as the herring arrived. In that room, which was painted blue, she saw two bunks; the upper one was empty, but in the lower one, a young woman sat cross-legged, smoking a cigarette with a holder as if she were seated in an elegant salon. Her hair was cut short and she wore a skirt that reached just down to her calves.

"Good afternoon," she said in a deep voice. "May I offer you a Teofani?" She held out the open pack of cigarettes to Karitas.

"Well, why not," Karitas replied after a moment's thought, despite the fact that she had never gotten the hang of using tobacco. But this young woman reminded her of the world from which she had only recently parted, and in which she would have loved to stay longer, and she wanted to befriend her to help keep her memories alive. So she put down her trunk and the sack holding her duvet and let the young woman light her cigarette, and then sat down on the bunk opposite her. There they sat for a while, smoking in silence and wearing slightly mischievous expressions, but through the cloud of smoke, a connection developed between them, the basis for a closer acquaintance. They puffed smoke at each other until the girl said, "My name is Pía and I'm from Reykjavík, but where are you from?"

Karitas opened her mouth to answer but hesitated, because she suddenly didn't know where she was from. She wasn't from Akureyri; it had been five years since she left that place. Nor was she from Copenhagen, that much was certain, and even less from Reykjavík, even though her mother lived there, because she'd stayed with her for only two nights.

She was going to say, "I'm from the west," but then she got another idea. "My name is Karitas, and I've come from abroad." Then she fainted. When she came to, her first thought was that she was still seasick, out on the wide sea, because the stepsisters' Christian faces still hung over her and she needed to throw up.

"How could she have thought of smoking on an empty stomach?" said Helga. "I am half-inclined to say that it serves her right, but now things should start looking up because Ásta has made gruel that we are going to get into her, and then we will put a cover on her duvet and let her take a little nap. But what great luck it was that the men referred me and Ásta to this place, after all; we'll take the upper bunks, and can look after her."

The herring were obstinate. The speculators shook their heads nervously; they had been raking in herring here since the turn of the century—where had they gone, what was happening in the deep, were they sleeping, those cursed things? The boats searched day and night, and the salting girls who had come north with little money to their names began to feel uneasy. Over the first few days, they had been certain of having work aplenty and good earnings, but now things were looking bleak, because when young women have few other pastimes than strolling and promenading from shop to shop, their wallets are quick to empty. The village was so full of people that it resembled a big city; the general stores were so crowded that there was hardly any elbow room, and inside the taverns, which were low-ceilinged wooden buildings, people could barely breathe due to the close quarters and tobacco smoke, in addition to the odors of train oil and fishermen's oilskins.

Karitas's barrack was filled with herring girls, many of whom had traveled great distances and were itching to get to work. While waiting for the herring, they exchanged news and stories, gathered in the kitchen like a noisy seabird colony, and downed coffee until they felt queasy. The two stepsisters set out to find worthy projects in this Gomorrah, as they called it. They wouldn't venture into the taverns where men had consumed too much of the bitter drink and knocked each other's teeth out in their idleness, but instead, waited for the sinners over in the Norwegian infirmary, where they were allowed to help in emergencies—and for which they never demanded any pay. They were so busy that they were rarely in their own room, and besides, they loathed Pía's smoking, which they saw as a symbol of the frivolous way of life of the young women of the capital. Her hairstyle and attire shocked them, and although Karitas's appearance was similar, they clearly considered her to be an entirely different breed of person. "Be careful," they said seriously, before rushing out of the room with skirts aflutter—they hadn't yet switched to the fashionable short skirts—and Karitas took their warning to mean that she shouldn't let the girl from the capital corrupt her.

Often, they lay in their bunks in silence; Pía smoked and read while Karitas thought. She knew nothing about Pía, because in Denmark she had learned not to be too inquisitive at the start of an acquaintance. Pía seemed to appreciate that. She asked nothing about Karitas's personal circumstances; probably in order not to be questioned in return. When they talked, it was about the upcoming herring salting. Pía was a little bit worried, not knowing the procedures, so Karitas described precisely what happened to the herring from the time it landed in the girls' hands until it lay gutted and salted at the bottom of the barrel. They also talked about the other folk in the barrack and made good-natured jokes about the eccentric ones. One evening, as they were on the verge of nodding off after growing tired of hanging around idly, Pía dryly asked the stepsisters, who had finished mumbling their prayers, whether they had ever considered becoming missionaries.

There was a brief silence while the two women in the upper bunks made up their minds as to whether they should answer this sarcastic question, but then Helga replied impulsively that it was their goal to attend a missionary school in Norway; first, though, they had to earn money for the trip. After passing on this important information, she said that the time had come for the two of them in the lower bunks to reveal their own plans for the future, and asked their reasons for saving up money. Since Pía remained silent as a stone, Karitas felt that she really ought to answer, especially as the sisters had confided in her. So she told them that, after five years of studying in Copenhagen, she was penniless, and now needed money to set up a workshop.

"Yet another seamstress," Pía remarked languidly.

"I attended the Royal Academy of Fine Arts," Karitas said brusquely.

"Then you must be very skilled with your hands," said the sisters in chorus. "Are you able to do French embroidery, as well?" Karitas sensed that this was neither the time nor the place to talk about art, let alone put her knowledge on display, so she politely asked Pía if they might hear about her plans, whether she was thinking perhaps of becoming a gentlewoman in Reykjavík. Pía sat up. "I'm saving money for a trip around Iceland. I'm going to take a good look at the plants in the lava fields, the insects on the seashore, the trout in the lakes, the birds on the cliffs, the foxes on the high heaths, and the trolls in the mountains." Then she lay back down and turned toward the wall. However, her words didn't satisfy the others' curiosity, but roused the unrest that slumbers in the soul on summer evenings when the sun has wrung out the drizzle and settled comfortably in its red dress over the fjord. They wanted to hear more about the fox that slinks over the heaths, see schools of trout come swimming, listen to the whimbrel trilling in the lonely quiet; they longed to go out into the summer night. Then the sisters sat down at Pía's bedside and started jabbering, each with her own story to tell of contests with animals out in the wild—even beach fleas under the rocks on the seashore got the equivalent of an entire chapter.

Once the roommates' hearts had united through nature, they also told each other about their mothers and learned that Pía's was a Danish dame who drank her cod-liver oil from a silver dram cup. She had burst into tears when her daughter informed her of her decision to explore the uninhabited expanses of that draconian land, where birds of prey glided over fiery volcanoes. It was unladylike and would damage her reputation. No one wanted a wife who had traipsed all over the wilderness in men's breeches, and she would see to it that her daughter didn't receive a single króna for the journey. But the daughter had just looked at her mother placidly and replied, "Well, if that's what you want, Mama, I'll just go salt herring in Siglufjörður and earn the money there." To which, the mother said, "Good Lord, I think I'm going to pass out." And she passed out.

They looked admiringly at the heroine, though she hadn't yet earned a single penny, and felt enthusiastic and happy; it was as if the air were charged with daring and pluck. The sun was up and about again after its midnight nap, and from out on the fjord came the jaunty clonking of the herring boats.

They were allowed out into the summer night.

The door to the barrack was yanked open; the foreman pounded on the door of every room. "Herring!"

They tucked their locks beneath their headscarves, every single little hair that wanted to be free, ran their hands down their ankle-length oil skirts, pulled up their woolen socks in their knee-high boots, stuffed their hands into thin rubber gloves, pulled pairs of shabby mittens over them, and yawned in each other's faces, ready for action. "Experienced girls fill four barrels an hour, but the best manage six," said Karitas, who knew the ins-and-outs of this business from her salting years in Akureyri, while the beginners from the countryside and capital, who had never come near herring, felt a chill, even though the sun was shining. Whether this chill was due to nerves and anxiety or lack of sleep, they didn't know, but they didn't regret the time they had spent together earlier that night; it had brought them closer.

"Salt over here, boys!" thundered Karitas. "And then bring another barrel, right away!" As if she were salting at the pace of three, and mustn't lose a single moment.

Karitas

Herring Barrels 1923

Watercolor

The sun shines in the middle of the night.

The heavily laden boats cruise up the fjord, heading for the herring lots where the girls stand armed with clippers.

The herring is landed, tossed into the crates where it wriggles and glistens like treasure in the *Arabian Nights*. Paying no heed to the death throes, we clamp our fingers around them and cut their throats with ice-cold resolve.

The lots are packed with people, men and adolescents get in each other's way, hollering, yelling. As if a riot has broken out.

The seagulls go mad.

We try to outdo each other, sweat, tear off our pullovers.

"He's looking at you," says Pía.

I give her an inquiring look.

"Up there," she says, nodding her head at the prow of a herring boat.

"I don't see anyone," I say, and ask what he looks like.

"Handsome," says Pía.

I feel a tingle. To think, a handsome man was looking at me! I feel a bit sad to have missed it.

"He's still looking at you," says Pía.

"Where?" I ask, losing hold of a herring.

"There by the cart next to the barrel stack. You missed him; he's gone behind the barrels."

The herring barrels are stacked into unclimbable mountains all around us; I see no man, am starting to get annoyed. I haven't slept, am tired and hungry. I ask Pía to stop clowning around, to concentrate on her work. She won't get paid staring at the men.

"He's still looking," says Pía.

"Where?" I yell in her face.

"Right in front of you," Pía mutters through her teeth.

I look up, straight into sea-green eyes.

And he certainly is handsome. Tall, muscular, yet slim, with auburn hair and dark eyebrows. He is wearing a blue sailor sweater, one hand in his pocket, the other holding a cigar, his posture relaxed. But his gaze, that heavenly gaze.

I see him in sunshine in the middle of the night. Hear music in my head when he looks at me.

After twenty-four hours of gutting and salting herring, they staggered back to the barrack, praying to God to send foul weather even if it cost them their earnings, flung themselves onto their bunks, fell asleep while undressing. Herring danced before Karitas's eyes, the barrels, the washing tubs, the shapes, the people, the throng, and that man, over and over again that man. She stamped the images in her mind so that she could sketch them later, sometime when she was alone and her hands were supple again. They were so sore, red from the herring's corrosive stomach contents. She was worried about her hands, and the smell had dug itself into the bone.

The girls whimpered like puppies when they were roused after three hours of sleep, lurched down to the herring lot, couldn't remember what day of the week it was. Their vigor was gone, but still, they tried to buck up, grit their teeth, work toughness in, as the older women said. Gave the barrel a quick kick as soon as sleep tried to sneak up on them, so hard that it hurt. Their heads ached, but still, they made fun of each other, let fly with words that were unseemly for proper girls, burst with laughter in between gutting herring with pursed lips. During their fourth shift, in a cold drizzle, when they felt as if they hadn't slept since they were infants and the drudgery had made them sullen and irritable, Ásta, who usually said little, started to sing. She began quietly, nasally humming a melody that no one recognized, but then words trickled out of her, a line or two of songs that they knew, and finally she sang a whole song, raising her voice as the others fell silent and listened. It was easier to work with her singing in their ears; they hoped that she would sing until the end of the shift.

"Stop that damned singing," said the quay foreman, who considered it his duty to perk the workers up with regular scoldings, because then they would quickly give him what for, which could be highly entertaining. But today, they didn't talk back, just shushed him; they were listening to the singing. They longed for music. Preferably played by an entire orchestra. A mazurka or schottische. Or a waltz. In Copenhagen, there had been dancing. A waltz on a mirror-smooth floor in a great hall where the lights shone in glittering crystal chandeliers and the musicians wore tailcoats.

At last, there was dancing in the far north.

The dance hall was the herring lot, the chandeliers the midnight sun, the tailcoats were of Icelandic wool.

The herring girls had slept for twelve hours straight, so soundly that those who were up and about near the barrack feared that they had left this world, so frightful was the silence. But soon they heard twittering and whispering from the bunks, giggling, bursts of laughter: "How rich we must be now, after all this salting! I simply must wash my hair, who borrowed my soap, where's the blouse I hung in the closet, I'm dying of hunger, does anyone have any rye bread, who said they have powder, wasn't someone going to make coffee, shouldn't we heat the curling iron?" They did each other up, loaned each other this and that little thing that could make the difference in their overall appearance, but the stepsisters vacillated. They longed to dance, but would it be pleasing to God and beneficial to their reputations if they let themselves be seen in the arms of a man? Besides the fact that some of the men tended to be importunate, say no more, but on the other hand, they had a duty to mingle with others, just as their Savior had done, walking among the humble and poor.

"It's probably best for us to stay at home," said Helga heavily, "and besides, our old skirts are completely out of fashion."

"No one will ask us to dance, in any case," said normally taciturn Ásta. "We're such scarecrows."

They looked at the fashionable dames, with their hair cut short and wearing skirts that barely covered their calves, and leaned back despondently against their pillows.

"We'll dance with each other, my lambkins," said Pía. "You're welcome to borrow my skirts if you can squeeze yourselves into them."

And that is what they did.

The evening was warm; their cardigans would do. To get to the lot, they had to elbow their way through the crowd packed as close as a barrelful of herring, gleeful and brimming with anticipation; the bright summer night was ahead, music, liquor, and beautiful girls; energy streamed through their veins like burning lava. Mazurka, schottische, and polka they danced with each other, with other girls as well as with men, folk from the village, folk from the neighboring communities, from the south, the Eastfjords, the Westfjords, they put up with it when the men pressed too close against their breasts, so close they thought they felt every part of their bodies, in addition to their panting breaths.

And when Karitas sat down on a barrel to catch her breath, she saw him again. Dancing a quick-paced dance with a pretty girl, as if he'd been here the whole time, panting, his forehead dripping with sweat. Yet she hadn't seen him before. She had looked but hadn't spotted him. He was taller than other men, and therefore, she should have been able to see him. And he saw her. She was sure of it, although she tried to look in a different direction. He looked over at her after every turn but didn't come to ask her to dance, danced with all of them but her, which was fine, too, she had no time for such nonsense, she had more important things to think about, it would be best if she just went home, where she could do a few sketches in peace before the dancing girls came home. And it didn't look as if that would be anytime soon. Pía was arm in arm with a Norwegian, and the future missionaries were engaged in a lively conversation with some students from the capital, who, despite the admonitory looks from their interlocutors, were passing around a flask. Surely, it was best to go home before the men got so drunk they started brawling. Karitas sauntered halfheartedly in the direction of the barrack, wondering if she was just old and tired—her feet were tired, anyway, her toes pinched in her prim dress shoes, sore and aching, so she bent down, took off her shoes, stood there in her silk stockings, and tried to work out how long it would take her to get home.

Then she was lifted off her feet.

She was so startled that she couldn't utter a sound, and her shoes dropped from her hands.

It was him, that man.

She looked in his eyes, caught a faint whiff of liquor and tobacco, shaving soap, and herring, and felt as if she were shackled by his arms. He bent down, holding her tightly as he squatted to allow her to pick up her shoes. Then he straightened up, and they looked each other in the eye before he began to walk in rhythm to the music from the herring lot.

He's going to carry me home because he saw that I couldn't walk any farther, she thought, and was excited to see how this adventure would end. But the man took a different route, past the barrack, along the street, and up the slope. She said nothing, despite her nerves; she didn't want to give him the satisfaction. The man could just as well speak up and explain his actions. If he could speak, that is.

He set her down next to a large rock that had tumbled from the mountain in ancient times and was on its way to the sea, but had been stopped by the country's hidden guardian spirits.

When he let go of her, he said: "You're light as a feather."

"How glad I am to hear you speak; I thought you might be mute," she said. "And what am I doing here, might I ask?"

He took off his jacket—the night was mild, he was sweaty—and spread it out on the grass. "Please sit." She sat down on his jacket, he sat beside her, their shoulders touched, and they saw the mountains opposite them reflected in the fjord. She longed to say something; her words fought with each other inside her, but she didn't give in; he should say something, this man, now that he'd carried her up the slope. But he seemed far from interested in starting a conversation. Finally, he looked at her, held out his arm, laid it over her shoulders, and held her close. As if they had been engaged for a long time. She felt his warmth, which was pleasant indeed, but at the same time, a tiny bit of anxiety crept up on her; what would he do next? Should she act as if it were nothing, or let him know that this game on the slope must end soon? It was late. But then he said, "We're going to sea tonight."

"Oh," was all she said.

"But I don't think we'll find any herring. It's gone for now. It may well come again, but not this summer, Karitas."

"How do you know my name?"

"I asked around, of course. You've just returned from Copenhagen, where you studied dressmaking, didn't you?"

"Yes, I've just come back," she answered quickly, and because his hand brushed her side and came alarmingly close to her hips, a contextless stream of words poured from her, pushing and shoving each other as she tried to line them up: "Once, my sisters and I were sitting up on a hillside, crying together, it was a beautiful spring evening, but a bit cold, as I recall, and Bjarghildur ate all the red pudding that was meant for our dear Halldóra. Óli brought one bowl and I another, and she ate both. She always had such an appetite, did Bjarghildur," she said, looking deep into his eyes to convey to him how significant that had been.

"Why were you crying?" he asked, having no interest in Bjarghildur's appetite.

"Oh, because Halldóra had refused Sumarliði, even though she never said so."

"And will you refuse Sigmar?"

"What Sigmar?" she asked suspiciously.

"This one," he said, turning and gently pushing her onto her back.

She let him kiss her for several moments. It could hardly do me any harm, she thought. But he was like other men, not made solely to kiss. The Creator had given him a more comprehensive task, and there was nothing to suggest that he was going to shirk it. The man was worked up, that was clear. No one could miss it. Oh my God, what have I gotten myself into? she thought, before hitting him in the head as hard as she could. But it was like swatting away a fly, so she tore at his hair, knowing that boys have sensitive scalps, and screamed, "Are you out of your mind?"

He stopped, panting as if he'd been running. "Forgive me, I just lost control."

She felt as if she'd heard those words before.

"I'll go get us something to drink," he said as if it were the next item on a longer agenda, "and you wait here; don't budge," and he dashed off down the slope. She watched him as she sat there, trying to regain her composure. He looked back to make sure that she wasn't going anywhere, and then he disappeared into the bustling crowd. Should I go or stay? she thought, wedging her feet into her tight shoes. If I go, I'll lose him and may not ever see him again; he'll find another. But if I stay, it could have dire consequences. For just a moment, she drank in the scent of his jacket, and then made her way down the slope. The dance was still in full swing on the lot; the blood rushed in the veins of tipsy revelers. She looked for him, hoping to see him or that he would see her, but had a hard time telling people apart from a distance. She waited a moment at the seashore, feeling it better to tell him that his jacket was still up on the slope, but upon seeing no sign of him, she pulled her cardigan closer to her breast and pushed her shoulders up to her ears. Her hand was on the door handle of the barrack when, for a second time, she was yanked abruptly off her feet. He was angry. And had a bloody mouth.

"What happened to you?" she stammered.

"I had to give a few fellows from the south a working over. But I've brought a lemonade for you and a drop of brennivín for me. Let's go back up the slope."

She tried to break free from his grasp.

"Don't be afraid, I promise I won't do anything," he said, "not tonight."

The nights passed, and the herring had fallen fast asleep again.

In the barrack, the stepsisters lay praying, each in her own bunk with hands folded together, and when their murmuring came to an end, Pía asked Karitas if she could draw them and sell the pictures as icons. "Sit down here on my bunk and read that Bible of yours together," she ordered. "Karitas is an artist, educated at the Royal Academy, and is going to draw an immortal picture of you." The stepsisters obeyed and clambered down from the upper bunks, but only because this had to do with the Bible. Without taking their eyes off the artist—"Didn't you say you were a seamstress?"—they sat down on the lower bunk, slightly drowsy. The Bible was thrust into their hands. "Tilt your heads a little closer to each other!" which they did earnestly, "Now, look pious," which they also did gladly, "and both of you hold on to the Bible, just like that, yes, that's lovely," said Pía.

"I've drawn a lot of women, a lot of girls in various poses," Karitas said as she worked, "but we girls were never allowed to draw nude models, even though it would have been so important for our training to get the chance to study the human physique, a person's shoulders, neck, upper arms, chest, loins, thighs, yes, and all the rest of it. We had to draw from plaster statues."

"Let's go, Ásta," whispered Helga, red in the face, and she grabbed her stepsister by the hand and tried to drag her out. Pía was able to save the picture by apologizing for Karitas's manner of speaking, saying that it was common for artists to talk about the human body as if it were any old landscape; she reprimanded Karitas for thinking out loud and pushed the stepsisters back into their seats. Then she said that she was going to the kitchen to smoke. It was there that Karitas drew her later, sitting at the table with a cup of coffee in front of her, next to it a checkered cloth, her eyes half-closed, a cigarette in the corner of her mouth—and she was madly keen on being given the picture. She also kept the one of the sisters, sitting on her bunk, holding the Bible on their knees. They themselves didn't want it, saying they'd never seen such a grotesquerie: crooked shoulders, oversized noses, coal-black, disheveled hair, their faces so strangely square. It wasn't them, and the Bible, the very Bible, looked clunky and deformed. What an exaggeration, calling herself an artist and not even being able to draw!

"I'm going to sell these pictures later, and get gold and silver for them," said Pía.

Suddenly, he was standing in the barrack's kitchen in his blue sailor sweater, the fisherman who searched for the silver of the sea, and asked if Karitas was one of the girls who slept there. The girls in the kitchen were unable to answer right away, because the man was so handsome that they got chills down their spines, and instead, stared at him in silence until Pía had recovered enough to point him to Karitas. She lay scantily dressed in her bunk, sketching away unsuspectingly, but was quick to pull the duvet up to her chin when a man in all his glory suddenly filled the doorway. After looking at her for several moments, he got straight to the point and asked if she would go out for a walk with him.

It being broad daylight, she thought it would be perfectly harmless.

They strolled through the village, and he told her that he was from the east. He hadn't mentioned this to her when they were sitting on the slope, so she asked whether he had known her sister, the midwife. He said that no midwife had ever come to his home; he had been living alone ever since his mother departed this world. He owned a small house by the sea but was rarely at home; the sea called to him all year round.

He wanted to know more about her, and she went on for some time about her family. When she explained to him, with great humility, that she hadn't in fact studied dressmaking in Copenhagen but drawing, he was extremely surprised. "Are you telling me that you're an artist?" he asked, to which she replied that that was exactly what she was telling him. He looked at her with his green eyes, which were precisely the same color as the sea below them, and said that she would have to prove it. She said that was no problem, and asked him to wait on the quay while she ran to the barrack to get her sketchbook.

She drew a ship for him, refraining from experimenting with form.

"You're damned good," he said admiringly, unable to take his eyes off the picture. Encouraged by his praise, she blurted out that she'd never gotten to draw a naked man, which was detrimental to her development as an artist. "Imagine if Bernini had never seen a naked man!" she exclaimed, laughing acridly. He agreed wholeheartedly. "Yes, or Einar Jónsson," and was no less shocked than she by such reactionism. His understanding of art surprised her. Not having expected him to know anything, she was exuberant—and then he said straightforwardly, "You can draw me naked if it will help you in your art."

She was flustered, her heart began pounding, she babbled something about sculptures that she'd seen, walked nervously around him on the quay, talking incessantly as she did, until he stopped her by gripping her arm tightly. She accepted his offer. For art. For her future as an artist.

He led her to a room in the house of a friend of his and locked the door behind them.

Nervousness coursed through her as she stood there in the locked room with him, making her feel a bit faint. He spoke not a word, but just ran his eyes up and down her body as if it were he who was planning to draw her and not the other way around. She sat down on a chair by the window and opened her sketchbook. Cleared her throat, crossed her legs, took her pencils from her dress pocket and made a few strokes with them, testing their tips expertly, stuck all but one back in her pocket, cleared her throat again, straightened her back, and put on a neutral expression.

He undressed slowly.

First, he removed his shirt. She looked quickly out the window, and then back at the paper. Then he removed his shoes and socks, followed by his trousers. She stared out the window, acted as if she noticed something through it. When she turned her head to look, he was lying stark naked on the bed, beautifully formed. He let the bulky upper part of his body rest on his right elbow, rested his left hand on his left leg, which he had pulled in, stretched out his right leg, and looked at her provocatively.

She began working. She blinked rapidly, looked alternately up and down; her pencil trembled. Then she stopped seeing him; she saw only his body. His bone structure, the contours of his muscles. She drew and drew, working almost frenziedly.

Until something happened over which he had no control. She saw it happen. At first, she froze, and then her ears began to buzz, her blood to boil. She dropped her sketchbook on the floor. He got up, took her by both of her hands, and pulled her over and onto the bed with him. The sketchbook lay there on the floor for a long time.

The roommates lay in their respective bunks, listening to the seabirds crying for herring that would not show itself. The murmur of the other herring girls carried to their room from the kitchen, a sound that they found pleasant to hear. The stepsisters took turns blowing their noses; they had caught colds. "You up there," said Pía, "can't you call on Christ and ask him to send us a few fish? I'll soon be out of money for tobacco."

"Yes, and ask him to make sure they're fat so we fill the barrels faster," Karitas added.

"You should be ashamed, you two. You don't know what awaits when you take the Lord's name in vain. I don't think it's healthy for us, Ásta, to stay much longer in this den of iniquity. If the herring doesn't show itself in the next few days, we're off."

"To where?" whispered Ásta.

"That I do not know, my dear Ásta. God's ways are inscrutable, but He will lead us to the light."

She had barely uttered the last word before one of the herring girls stepped in and handed Karitas a letter that had come in the mail. Her roommates asked her, for God's sake, to read it aloud to them to help pass the time. "That is, if there's nothing sad in it, Karitas."

The two in the upper bunks took Bjarghildur's letter as a godsend.

"Dear sister," began the letter, "everything is fine here at Þrastabakki, and the hay harvest is better than average." Then came a long explanation as to why she had never answered the letters her sister had sent from Copenhagen; she had been so busy that she simply hadn't had time. And even though she was now scribbling these few lines, she should actually be out in the cowshed with Hámundur, because their best dairy cow, Flekka, would be calving at any moment. "Now I'm sitting here by the dresser in the drawing room, enjoying a piece of the cake that I baked in the new stove that Hámundur brought home the other day. I got the recipe at the last meeting of the Women's Club, which will soon be making preparations for its autumn activities. This time we'll be embroidering a new altar cloth for our church and collecting donations for a new organ—an idea that a few of us in the choir came up with. The hay harvest went very well, as I mentioned before—it certainly kept all of our hands full. There are usually six of us here in this household. Besides me, Hámundur, and his mother, there are also the farmhand and the two indigents, but the three maids we had this summer will be leaving in the autumn, which is very inconvenient for me, as the slaughter is around the corner and we always have a great many guests. Hámundur has become the parish administrator, as you may know, and he and his party colleagues hold long meetings here. They must be well catered to, obviously. Mama tells me that you are in need of money, so it crossed my mind to offer you work until Christmas, and even longer, if you would like. Hámundur and I have always paid our help well. It is good to be here—the farm is large, the surrounding countryside is beautiful, and Sauðárkrókur is just a stone's throw away. Now, write to me and let me know whether or not you can come. If you know of any other girls who could imagine working for us this autumn, they are most welcome."

"I would rather go to the moon," said Karitas.

"He has sent us the light," Helga whispered.

They bathed in the autumn sun in Bjarghildur's farmyard, looking at the faded marigolds in the flower garden as she rattled off the farm's history from the time of Iceland's settlement to the present day, pointing this way and that until Karitas could no longer restrain herself and declared that they were all about to wet their pants after their long journey. Much against her will, Bjarghildur paused her lecture and told them to slip around the corner of the farmhouse and face the east, but then determinedly picked up the thread again after they'd relieved themselves, explaining to them the changes that had been made to the old turf farm, telling them all about the construction of the fourth of the gable houses, which was made of concrete and incorporated the three main rooms, as well as the extension to the back of the two middle houses, where there was now a kitchen as good as any on the best farms. Then she invited them in, where the guided tour continued, and they plodded dead tired and thirsty on her heels from one room to the next, until Karitas asked if the girls could possibly have a sip of water before they fainted.

Bjarghildur led them into the kitchen, where they were finally allowed to sit down, and after she had brought them milk, serving Pía first because Karitas had introduced her as a consul's daughter from Reykjavík, she finally asked openly and unassumingly, in the manner of the mistress of an estate, if they had any news to tell of Akureyri. When Karitas said that they had only stopped long enough to visit Halldóra's grave, Bjarghildur put on a mournful face and recounted her elder sister's death in detail—"for which Karitas was not present, because she needed to go traipsing overseas"—and the guests shed tears into their milk glasses, exactly as she intended. Pía, who noticed Karitas's pain, got up and said that the housewife needn't go to any trouble for Karitas or herself; they were on their way south and would be leaving first thing in the morning, but on the other hand, she had now gotten first-rate maids in the stepsisters, who would be staying.

"You can't leave right away," said Bjarghildur, in an entirely different tone. "I am in desperate need of people for the autumn work. I have to slaughter a hundred and twenty lambs, clean the stomachs and intestines, stuff them and sew them up to make liver sausage and blood pudding, and then get it all stored in whey, boil down meat for canning, and before I can do all that, I need to gather rhubarb and pick bilberries and crowberries up on the mountain and currants from the bushes in order to make jams and jellies, and also make sheep-sorrel juice and wine from arctic thyme and rhubarb, and then I need to grind yarrow for tea, dig up potatoes, rutabagas, and carrots, all of which must be done along with the other chores, such as milking the cows and sheep and feeding the chickens, churning butter and making skyr, washing all the laundry and rinsing it down in the stream, carrying the coal in and the ashes out, and on top of that, there's the breadmaking and all the other baking, the knitting, and embroidering the altar cloth for the church—and you really expect me to do all of that with only two maids?"

The others were flabbergasted and scratched their heads uneasily, until Pía said that it could very well be interesting to take part in the winemaking; she had never done such a thing before, but when it was over, they would definitely be going south, wouldn't they, Karitas?

Karitas turned up her nose. When they arrived, Bjarghildur had only kissed her fleetingly and not said a word about her studies and homecoming, or even asked how she was doing, despite the fact that they hadn't seen each other for more than five years. By contrast, she had fawned over the other girls as if she hadn't had visitors for months on end. So Karitas just shrugged her shoulders sulkily, as if she couldn't care less about any of them. But the stepsisters' faces shone with excitement and anticipation for the impending autumn tasks. "Might there be some smaller chores that we can start on now?" Helga asked, tilting her head with a smile, and Bjarghildur, still trembling at the thought of the entrails of a hundred and twenty lambs that awaited her, said that she could go soak the saltfish down in the stream.

The farm's residents trickled into the kitchen and secretively took the measure of the girls. The farmhand, Stjáni, who had gone to fetch them in Sauðárkrókur, the two indigents, Ína and Mummi, both in their twenties, whom Bjarghildur had taken in and whose upkeep was paid by the parish, and the mother-in-law, Þórunn, the old priest's widow. The householder himself was nowhere to be seen; he'd had to go up the valley to oversee an auction. Those present said little, except for the old priest's widow, who asked whether the madam would be setting the table for her guests in the middle room and using the fine tableware. Bjarghildur said that she had been on her way to doing so, but had first wanted to get the guests settled and bring in their trunks, which were still out in the farmyard, and in any case, they weren't guests but her maids, which her mother-in-law should have been able to deduce.

"The old lady is growing senile," she whispered to them as they left the kitchen. To start with, the stepsisters were to sleep in the outermost room of the old farmhouse—"farthest from the farmhand, who is a skirt chaser"—but it could be cold there in the wintertime, in which case, they would be moved in with the old priest's widow. Pía was given the room that had been occupied by a daughter of the farm's previous owner, upstairs above the main entrance, the prettiest room, clad in light-blue wallpaper with little pink flowers; nothing else would suit a consul's daughter, and Pía winked at Karitas, who had a suspicion that a certain person intended to partake of tobacco there undisturbed. But the sister, whom the housewife hadn't seen in over five years, was shown to the old widow's room, the innermost one in the concrete house, "so you can keep warm; the stove is in the middle room and heats both the inner room and the front one, where Hámundur and I sleep." Karitas, who would rather have had her own room so that she could draw in peace, said nothing, understanding that by means of this arrangement, her sister was showing her affection. Then they went to the middle room and had coffee and cakes, like distinguished guests, and the priest's widow, who was in her element when the fine tableware was used and she was wearing her national costume, carried the conversation as was her wont in her heyday, when it was she who held the keys to the pantry. She looked at the young women approvingly, rocked in her seat, and fingered Karitas's skirt. "Such fine fabric, did you get this from Briem? Is it silk or taffeta?"

"Neither, I think. I had it made when I was living in Copenhagen."

"Well, I'll be. So the young lady speaks Danish!" the widow exclaimed, sprinkling words from that language into the things that she said. "Were you at the Kunstflidskolen with my daughter Þuríður? That is where she studied, and earned a certificate for her diligence and skill."

"Þuríður was in Copenhagen long before Karitas, Þórunn," Bjarghildur said loudly, as if she were speaking to a deaf person or wanted to change the subject. But the priest's widow was just getting started. "I also speak Danish, if you would prefer to use it, and here in my room, I have many volumes of *Illustreret Tidende* and the *Journal for Toilette- og Damehaandarbejde.*"

"Those magazines are from the turn of the century, and everything in them went out of fashion long ago, Þórunn," said Bjarghildur.

"They also tell all about the royal family," the old lady continued. "You are by all means welcome to have a look at them, seeing as how you know Danish."

She took no interest in the other girls—she was certain that they didn't speak Danish, not like she and Karitas did. While the young women discussed their relatives and acquaintances, checking to see if they shared any, the old widow spoke incessantly to Karitas, leaning close as if everything she said were between the two of them only, and whispering quickly and purposefully. Although Karitas often found it difficult to make out what she said, the gist was descriptions of various worthies who had gained invaluable life experience while studying on Danish soil.

Bjarghildur was sorry not to have met Pía in Reykjavík the winter that she attended the Women's College; the daughters of gentlefolk had been so prominent in the life of the city, but Pía said that she had probably been with her relatives on Funen that winter. On the other hand, she was able to tell news and stories of the Reykjavík bourgeoisie, which

Bjarghildur found quite a windfall. The stepsisters were unassertive in the main, behaving as if they were in Heaven; they sat there genially and modestly, answered politely when someone addressed them, stuck to the old habit of letting one speak for the both of them—causing all of the others to fall silent when Ásta finally opened her mouth and asked softly, "Is there a church on this farm?"

Inspired by this inquiry, the housewife dove into telling the history of the farm's church, which had been blown off its foundations in a huge storm many years ago, but was rebuilt and was now served by a priest in that parish, after the old priest, her father-in-law, was called to join their ancestors, and then she told them all about her work with the church choir and the Women's Club, adding, with an affected laugh, that she had, for the last few years, been taking organ lessons in Sauðárkrókur, and occasionally took it upon herself to play at mass when the organist was prevented from doing so. And to entertain them for a moment, that is, before they began to work in earnest, she went and sat at the organ in the corner. "This is a bridal chair, embroidered by my mother-in-law," she said, running her hand over it before she sat down and began to play her favorite hymns. After the first, she began singing one hymn after another so spiritedly that the stepsisters reflexively folded their hands in prayer. It was then that the householder rode into the farmyard, but the madam's voice was so sonorous and the accompaniment so powerful that they neither heard nor saw him until he stood in the doorway and filled it completely, authoritative in his parish-administrator's cap, smiling, the very picture of health.

"This is quite a haul!" he joked as he looked over the group, and then greeted his wife by patting her lightly on the shoulder without taking his eyes off the other women. "And which of you is Karitas, then?" he asked, but without waiting for an answer, he went to her, kissed her on both cheeks, and said, "It's high time that I got to meet the artist. Bjarghildur has told us so much about your achievements—making it known all over the parish and priding herself on having a sister studying at the Royal Academy in Copenhagen."

Karitas was moved by the warm reception. She couldn't remember anyone, apart from her brothers, having expressed admiration for her artistic education; even her mother had kept her delight with her daughter bottled up, for the most part. The man didn't kiss the other girls, but shook their hands so vigorously that it hurt, and welcomed them all heartily: "My Bjarghildur can certainly use the reinforcement in the season ahead." Then he touched his mother's shoulder to let her know since she had stood up, that she could sit back down.

From the very start, he won all of their hearts.

At dawn the next morning, they were sent up the mountain with buckets, with the indigent Ína in tow. She carried their coffee flasks in wool socks, and crullers in a cloth tied together at the corners. Bjarghildur asked them to keep an eye on her; she had a tendency to disappear, she said aloud, but to Karitas, she whispered, "Ína is mad about men, and if she gets wind of a road-construction crew, she's gone." Karitas whispered this information to Helga and Ásta, who kept Ína under their strict supervision, knowing all too well about women who had the tendency to disappear. On the way up the mountain, where the berries awaited them in blue and black clusters, Karitas asked them what had become of the farmhand who was Ásta's father; had he stayed on at the farm after her mother disappeared? Helga replied that their mother had sent him to her sister in Hornafjörður as soon as she found out that the maid was with child. "He was never told that he was the father of the child and still doesn't know, and may simply be dead," she added, throwing herself down on some crowberry heather. As the sun colored the district yellow and purple, they worked hard at picking berries, enjoying the freedom of the mountainside, and Ína peered down into the heather and gathered spiders in her apron pocket.

And the spiders crawled eagerly, wildly, about the mountain, as if searching for mates, and shoved their way into the farmhouse where fifteen kilos of sliced, juicy rhubarb was soaking in a tub.

"Fifteen hundred grams of good raisins, rinsed and cut in two, are added," Bjarghildur told Pía, who had been slicing rhubarb since six o'clock that morning, "because the raisins speed up the fermentation, and since the brew takes on the flavor of the fermenting agent used, this turns out more like grape wine than any other homemade wine. Wine made from arctic thyme or dog sorrel is nowhere near as good as rhubarb wine." Then she emphasized to Pía how important it was that she stir it and take responsibility for it while she herself went to help with the sheep sorting. Pía asked when all that wine was going to be drunk, and Bjarghildur, still feeling quite stressed about the workload of the season ahead, replied brusquely that the wine wouldn't be drunk, per se; it would just be stored in bottles down in the pantry. Every household worth its salt had wine in its cellar; that, she must surely understand. "Sometimes Hámundur brings a drop or two with him to his meetings to give to his party colleagues who can't do without it, but in this home, no wine is drunk, and everyone also knows my dislike for this societal scourge. But I have always reaped praise for my wine, and I would like to continue doing so."

"And how long before you can try it?" asked Pía.

"My dearest, after the sugar is added, it has to stand untouched for five to six months."

"I'll be gone by then," said Pía, sounding disappointed.

"It should be possible to give the young lady a little taste of the wine from last year," said the old priest's widow, who was always present for the winemaking and was an expert on the matter, having been instructed in the art by a Danish woman and carrying the recipe in her head. Then Bjarghildur strutted with Pía down to the pantry, despite having no time to do so, to show her the produce of last year and the year before that, but once they arrived, Pía saw, to her great surprise and disappointment, only a few dusty bottles on a shelf. "Oh, well, Hámundur must have taken some of it," Bjarghildur said hastily. She apparently didn't want to talk any more about the wine, much less offer Pía a taste of an older vintage, but couldn't refrain from telling Pía in confidence that the pantry was the only thing in the home with which she wasn't happy. She dreamed of a pantry right off the kitchen, as she had seen in the homes of wealthier people in Akureyri. "Having the pantry beneath the kitchen, even if it is big and spacious, is very inconvenient, but that is how it was when I arrived. But this much I can tell you, and it must remain between the two of us: I am determined to have a pantry just off the kitchen, and I know that Hámundur will build it for me. He is such a great craftsman. As you can see, he has led the water from the stream into the kitchen—there are not many farms that have running water—and now he dreams of building a small water-driven electric generator here, and when it is ready, I will be the first housewife in the parish with electricity." She stood there silently for several long moments in order to give Pía a chance to let these great tidings sink in, and Pía sighed and expressed her admiration for the home and its master and mistress, still hoping to be allowed to taste an older wine vintage. "But as you can see," Bjarghildur said, pointing to some large barrels lined up along the cellar wall, "everything is ready for the slaughter. Now it is just a matter of getting the jam and wine down here before I leave for the sheep sorting. And then we need to make an enormous number of crullers, because I am going to sell coffee and crullers at the corral, like last year—and I made a great deal of money from it, too. So now, we need to roll up our sleeves and get to it," she said loudly, before striding up the stairs.

When the berry pickers returned with full buckets, everyone dove straight in. Tubs covered the tables and kitchen floor; the berries needed to be cleaned and rinsed and put in the stewpot, and all the women took part, including the old priest's widow and the indigent Ína, who had lost all of the spiders she'd put in her apron pocket and stood there crying bitterly into the jam jars. Still needing doing were the milking, cooking the meat for the evening meal, making gravy from northern dock leaves, and kneading the dough for the next day's bread.

Late that evening, Karitas told Pía, "I'm leaving for Reykjavík." The two of them lay together upstairs in the light-blue room of the former farmer's daughter, sneaking a smoke, but Pía asked her to hold out, for goodness' sake, until the winemaking was finished. "It's so important to me to learn how it's done." But after retiring to her own bed in the old widow's room, Karitas lay awake, tossing and turning and sighing, unable to understand the course that her life was taking. She ought to have been down south, in an atelier, painting. And painting and painting.

"Why do you look so unhappy?" asked her sister the next day, her cheeks bright red from all the autumn work needing doing.

"I simply must go to Reykjavík, Bjarghildur. I need to work."

"Aren't you working now? Didn't I say I would pay you?"

"I need to paint."

"Paint? You call that working? Have you lost your mind, or what? How could anyone imagine spending time scrawling and coloring in the middle of the autumn work, when so much is at stake? What would become of progress in this country and the future of the Icelanders if everyone thought like you? And I must say that it hurts me very much to think that you wouldn't lend your sister a hand with her household when it's most needed, after having gotten to promenade around the streets of Copenhagen for five years and eaten for free! Are you going to snub your loved ones yet again?"

The sleepless nights continued. Nor did it help that every time Karitas felt she was finally drifting off, between midnight and three in the morning, she heard the old lady start moving. She got up mumbling from her bed, tottered to the kitchen, where she stayed for some time, and then came back in and lay down, grumbling. "Tsk, tsk," she whispered into the inky darkness, "it just isn't working for them." The fourth night was bright with moonlight, and Karitas gave in and followed the old woman out. She saw her standing leaning her cheek against the door of the front room, where the young couple slept. "Is there something wrong?" whispered Karitas. "Tsk, tsk, it just isn't working, now they're both snoring," snorted the old woman.

Bjarghildur regretted her sharpness with her sister, and said one day, "Don't worry, Karitas, you can paint once I've gone to help sort the sheep. There will be a short break before the slaughter begins. Hámundur said that it would be a wonderful idea to have you paint a nice picture of the farm. But first we must fry a few hundred crullers. Then, after he has ridden up to the highlands for the sheep drive, you can sleep in my bed. We can whisper together under the duvet, just as we did in the old days."

Karitas wasn't sure that she wanted to lie under the duvet with her sister, but in order to avoid a fuss, she agreed, and one night they lay down together in Bjarghildur's bed, after determining which of them had the bigger belly beneath her nightclothes. Due to the nutritiousness of the food in the countryside, Bjarghildur won, and Karitas told her sister that the old woman was keeping tabs on her and Hámundur's love life. "She's been doing so the entire four years that we've been married," said Bjarghildur, "awaiting the heir who won't show himself, but I have gone to see the doctor, and there is nothing wrong with me." Karitas said that it would all work out if they just relaxed. "I'm afraid of it all getting a little too relaxed before we have that baby," said Bjarghildur. "I recall it being love at first sight that day when Hámundur rode into town," Karitas said.

"Not all is gold that glitters," sighed Bjarghildur as she put her left leg over Karitas's hip. "There were others besides him who had their eyes on me, and mine on them, but I chose Hámundur. I could see that he had a future ahead of him. He was so popular and generous. He proposed to me again and again, but I hesitated, because when another man, whose name I will not mention, touched me, I felt a stream of energy pass through me. But that man never proposed to me, and besides, he was far too stingy. One evening while I was working as a maid here in the parish, Hámundur came dashing into the farmyard on the parish's best horse, dismounted, and said so loudly that everyone out in the farmyard heard it, 'If you intend to marry me, Bjarghildur, the time has come. Here you have a horse and saddle, and if you wish me to be your husband, you must return both to me at Þrastabakki tomorrow morning.' I did so, and got a Danish riding habit of tweed, to boot."

"What became of the other man?"

"He's a scholar. Lives here in the parish. But where are your suitors, Karitas?"

"I'm falling asleep, Bjarghildur."

"The girls said you met a handsome man while working in the herring."

"Oh, Bjarghildur, it's so complicated. He was too handsome. I wouldn't have been able to paint with him around. I tried it once, was allowed to draw him, but it went all wrong."

"Wrong? How?"

"I was thrown off balance. He confused me."

"Is he really that handsome?"

"He is as beautiful as a spring glistening in the morning sun in winter, as a waterfall singing in the evening sun in summer. In his presence, women are struck speechless. I never said goodbye."

"Are you out of your mind? You left without saying goodbye to him?"

"Oh, move your leg, it's so heavy."

"You take fifteen kilos of light rock candy and half a kilo of brown sugar and melt them in a pot over low heat," said Bjarghildur as she climbed up into the saddle, clearly relishing the admiration of her household members, both those who were going with her to help with the sheep sorting and those staying behind to see to the chores at home. "You leave it until it turns a light brown color, then add half a liter of hot water; it's for giving the wine color." She straightened her hat, which matched her riding habit, and had Ína hand her her gloves. "Then pour that into the barrel, dissolve twenty grams of fish glue and put it in as well, and for God's sake make sure that nothing goes to waste." With an aristocratic expression, she looked over the district while slipping on the gloves. "And then you must stir the contents of the barrel to speed up the fermentation, and don't forget to milk the cows and feed the chickens—don't let me down, now—and look after Þórunn, she's inclined to sleepwalking, and isn't everything in place on the horses now, the tent, the blankets, the coffee, the crullers, cups and pitchers? Then mount up, we're leaving."

The girls who were to look after the farm and the fermentation watched as she rode down the path on her best saddlehorse, accompanied by her retinue, the stepsisters and the indigents, sitting straight-backed like an English peeress in a long skirt and tailored jacket, with a matching hat and gloves. Pía said, "She's beautiful, your sister, but not particularly fashionable."

Now that the housewife was gone, they felt free as birds—including the old priest's widow, who was in high spirits and chattered away, insisting that Danish be spoken in the home now that the Icelanders were gone, and they spoke Danish to her all day because of how fun it could be to speak gutturally now and then. She took out her Danish magazines, plopped them on the kitchen table, and invited them to have a look, and they had to make her understand, as tactfully as possible, that they had work to do even though the housewife wasn't home. Eventually, they were able to persuade her to grind the dried yarrow from which Bjarghildur made tea for use against urinary tract infections, and she busied herself with that for a good part of the day. Pía turned to the winemaking, but Karitas went out into the farmyard with her sketchbook and sat down on the old hayfield wall, whence she had a view of all the gables smiling in the gentle autumn weather. Hámundur wanted a real painting, as Bjarghildur had put it, but since Karitas had left her paints in Reykjavík, he'd have to settle for a good pencil drawing—"but it has to be a proper picture, like the ones in Þórunn's magazines."

Although she had been instructed to draw a picture that could pass for a photograph and would be a far cry from the type of artistic creation that lay closest to her heart, Karitas enjoyed being able finally to sit down with her sketchbook and pencil. In the stillness, she listened to the chuckling of the stream and the clucking of the chickens, which strutted around the farmyard in the gentle breeze. She put them in the picture. Then she felt that they looked too lonely and added the dog, even though it wasn't there at the moment. But it barked for more life, she felt, so she placed Bjarghildur's saddlehorse a little south of the farm, near the workshop, along with a few more horses, and in order to bring balance to the picture, she had a few cows stand mooing to the north. Then she felt as if she couldn't give preference to the farm animals over the master and mistress of the house, so she added them both, and had the old lady and the hired help join them. She left herself out, but was seriously considering including Pía when she heard a whisper behind her: "Put the children in, too, dear."

She hadn't heard Þórunn come, and it gave her a little start, but she asked what children she was talking about.

"The children, the children, all ten of the children that Hámundur intends to have."

Karitas felt it would be going too far to draw ten children, but to be rid of the old woman buzzing around her like a fly, and to bring even more life to the picture, she drew two children, making one chase after the dog and the other after the chickens. When the picture was finished, it was in the spirit of Bruegel, animated and lush.

Inside the house, no less hard work had been done: the sugar mixture had been poured into the barrel, the tea leaves put in a cookie tin, flatbread and whey cookies baked, and both Þórunn and Pía were red-cheeked and cheery. Karitas thought they seemed unusually jovial, and when she sniffed the air, she smelled not only the aroma of freshly baked bread, but also another, more rank smell. Pía declared she hadn't felt comfortable making wine that she'd never tasted in its finished form, so the priest's widow had urged her emphatically to sample last year's vintage, which she did, and then the two of them together, and she simply had to tell it like it was, that whoever made wine like this could easily compete with the best winemakers in Denmark and England, maybe even in America. Karitas wasn't thrilled with this state of affairs and asked the old woman to lie down for a bit and led her to her bed, before telling Pía to put on a sweater and get ready for a good long walk.

The day had begun to decline by the time they set off, and Karitas wanted to walk briskly in order to get the foul stuff out of Pía before it grew dark, but they'd only made it as far as the church when Pía began to complain about soreness in her ankle. She had to sit down on a rock for a moment, but since there was no rock nearby, she limped into the churchyard, plunked herself down on a gravestone that she liked, pulled out a dusty bottle of last year's vintage, and drawled, "Get yourself on over here to me, girlfriend. Let's guzzle this down and sing a little for those on the other side."

By the time they hoisted themselves onto their feet again to head home, darkness had fallen, and the deceased were up and about.

The sheep flocked up the valley like a white sheet of snow and, as they drew nearer to the farm, resembled a glacier tongue advancing at full speed. "A majestic sight," said the old priest's widow, who had been sitting all day on a crooked chair in the farmyard, waiting for this grand moment. "Horrifying," said Pía. "Will they be here all winter?" "The chits will all be slaughtered," the old woman replied gently. "I think it's time to head south," muttered Pía, holding her stomach. She still felt nauseated, despite her health having improved somewhat over the course of the evening, whereas for Karitas, it was just the opposite; her day had begun with retching and vomiting in an ordinary manner, but she had now reached the stage when folk lack the strength even to drag themselves away from the scene of their vomiting. She lay on a patch of rutabagas in the vegetable garden, with the chickens strutting around her as she retched. There was no more vomit inside her to bring up, but she felt that at any moment, she would heave out her liver and lungs.

"What's wrong with Karitas?" Bjarghildur asked testily as she dismounted and saw that her sister wasn't among the spectators, and Pía said that the blessed girl had come down with some sort of stomach ailment; she'd been vomiting and felt wretched, and at the moment, she was attempting to get some fresh rutabaga inside her to see if that might stop the vomiting, though Pía herself doubted it. To her relief, the priest's widow said nothing about what they'd gotten up to, whether it was because she thought it most sensible or had simply forgotten it all, and therefore, it was assumed that Karitas had come down with the flu. Helga harped on to the housewife about Karitas's poor health as she carried the young woman to her bed, washed her face, and forced her to eat a few spoonfuls of gruel. Despite the affectionate care, however, Karitas didn't improve; nausea harried her both the next day and the day after that, and she glared at Pía, saying, "I think you nearly managed to kill me with that swill." But Pía was surly. She had talked about them fleeing to the capital before the great slaughter began, but now she didn't like the idea of leaving before Karitas had recovered fully. They had both drunk the same thing that evening, but she hadn't gotten ill, at least not in any way worth mentioning.

Hámundur brought the gimmers and ram lambs that weren't to be slaughtered into the sheep shed, herded the others over to Sauðárkrókur for slaughter, brought back offal, stomachs, and intestines and stored them, and was preparing to slaughter the sheep whose meat would be salted and canned, and still Karitas showed no signs of improvement. She didn't have a fever, but often felt weak. They tried giving her the task of cleaning the stomachs down at the river, "so that she could at least be outside in the fresh air," but she couldn't avoid inhaling their stench as she did so, which made her vomit again and again. Nor could she sew the clean stomachs; the suffocating smell slipped into her nostrils. She couldn't stir the blood even after the flour, oatmeal, and suet had been added, or boil the blood pudding and liver sausages at the open hearth in the old kitchen, even though the smell of freshly cooked liver sausage is so wonderful. Finally, she was asked to dig up potatoes along with the indigent Mummi, who didn't find her to be of much help, mainly sitting in the middle of the potato patch, as she did, and staring listlessly down the valley.

"It can't go on like this, with her in such a state," Hámundur said worriedly to Bjarghildur, and she agreed completely, but neither of them had time to ride over to Sauðárkrókur with her to see a doctor. At this most busy time of the year, the household depended for its livelihood on everything being done in good time. The offal couldn't wait any longer out in the storehouse; they had to deal with it and get it into whey while it was still fresh, and the meat needed salting and the sheepskins processing. The couple shared these tasks between them: he with his farmhand handling the salt meat and the sheepskins, and she with all her maids, apart from Karitas, dealing with the offal. They worked like mad in the kitchen night and day, sewing, chopping, stirring, and simmering, with splotches of blood all over their arms and bits of chopped liver on their foreheads, and most zealous of all were Bjarghildur and Pía; it was as if they had been seized by a strange bloodthirstiness. They went berserk on the sausage production, found an outlet for urges that they couldn't put their fingers on.

They were working on the last stomachs when Mummi came in and said he thought that the woman digging up potatoes was dead. They all rushed out and found Karitas lying unconscious on top of the plants.

A doctor was fetched from Sauðárkrókur.

After giving Karitas a thorough examination in the room of the old widow, who begged to be allowed to be present but was refused, the doctor patted Karitas's cheek and told her that she must be more diligent in eating—it was crucial in her condition—and that the birth would take place in the spring, probably late May. Then he strode off to the kitchen, where the women were standing in their bloody aprons, asked for strong coffee, and told the women, bless their hearts, to try to get some nourishment into the girl. Dry bread in the morning would be best to start with, but as the pregnancy advanced and her nausea disappeared, they should definitely try to feed her some of the liver sausages that they were currently stuffing.

After the doctor had gone, they all slumped onto the bench in the kitchen and didn't say a word. Hámundur and the farmhand, who had heard the news, plodded in and stood there silently. After a few moments, Bjarghildur asked how this could have happened, looking sharply at Pía and the stepsisters as if they were responsible.

"I suppose it happened in the ordinary way," said Pía.

"God knows that I had nothing to do with it," said Helga.

"He had such beautiful shoulders," said the normally taciturn Ásta.

The parish administrator, who felt that they had sufficient grounds for an investigation into the identity of the person responsible, cleared his throat and asked the questions that he normally did in cases involving parish dependents, but made little headway, for each time that he opened his mouth, Bjarghildur groaned: "Unmarried and pregnant, what an embarrassment to the family, to think that this should happen to me, dear God, what would our mother say to that," until the parish administrator raised his voice and said, "My dear Bjarghildur, am I not attempting to discover who this man is, in order to put this situation to rights?" Bjarghildur lost control, slapped the table with an empty stomach that she'd been holding, and said that none of them had the faintest idea how devastating this was for the family, and she was so agitated that they didn't dare contradict her for fear that it would upset her even more. Then she stormed out and slammed the door behind her, and shortly afterward, Mummi came in and told them in a tremulous voice that she had come tearing over to him as he stood there digging up potatoes, had torn the shovel out of his hands, brandished it at him, ordered him to clear off back to the house, and attacked the garden furiously.

"Well, I'll be," said the old priest's widow, but her son said nothing. Finally, he asked for a cup of strong coffee.

Karitas didn't get out of bed, feeling as if there were no reason to do so. Her life was over, so it didn't matter anymore whether she was in bed or up and about. So she lay there thinking about how it would be best to die and where she should be buried, which could be a problem, since she felt as if she belonged nowhere, but when she tried to focus on her pending funeral, her thoughts began to wander, and practical details gained the upper hand; suddenly, she remembered the electric stove in the restaurant in Copenhagen, and began to think about how great a difference it would make for housewives such as Bjarghildur to have such an apparatus. About the little herald of spring in her belly, or the man who had created it, she thought nothing at all. She didn't even have to try to avoid such thoughts; they simply never entered her head. In connection with the electric stove, she began thinking about the pots the girls in Denmark had used, how thick the bottoms had been. No one interrupted her musings. Everyone kept a low profile now that the housewife was in such a mood, and were even a bit angry at the sister for causing this uncomfortable situation. Some members of the household started feeling insecure about their next meal, not to mention their futures. So they left Karitas alone, but waited for Bjarghildur to read her the riot act and put an end to this. She could be forgiven later. But Bjarghildur dug away at the potato patch with the energy of three men, hardly ever straightening up; the potato leaves flew in one direction and the potatoes in another, and she didn't answer Hámundur when he called out to her at dinnertime and asked if she was going to come in and have warm blood pudding with them. Feeling as if Karitas had been on her own for long enough, Pía brought her a plate of liver sausage and rutabaga mash and told her to force it down so that the baby wouldn't come out the size of a wren.

"This baby will never be born," said Karitas. "I'll be dead before then."

"Come on now, open your mouth. I'll feed you. When did he do it?"

"Oh, don't talk about him."

"You have to tell him. For the child's sake."

"He'll never know. I'll be dead first. I'll die anyway if I'm not allowed to paint. No one can paint with a baby in her arms. Madam Eugenía often said the same. She said that if I intended to become a famous artist, I would have to sacrifice everything. I should never let it cross my mind to have children. And now this. Oh, Pía, this liver sausage is making me feel sick."

"Are you going to go south with me, or will you stay here?"

"Neither, Pía. I'm just going to die."

"Suit yourself, Karitas."

Next, the stepsisters came in to pray for Karitas's sinful soul. They sat down at her bedside and rattled off one prayer after another, as if they would never stop; it had been a long time since they had prayed aloud or with such passion. They enjoyed it to the fullest, and would probably have sat there until after midnight had not the old widow herself told them to quit yapping and leave so she could go to bed. Once they were alone, she stroked Karitas's cheek, handed her a stack of *Illustreret Tidende* magazines, and said that looking through them would help ease her mind. "And don't you worry about this, my poppet, it will all work out, as usual, and you can be sure that the child will bring you great joy. That is always the case with children whom no one wishes for; they become either lawyers or the country's greatest craftswomen. Shame that it happened to you and not your sister."

Bjarghildur dug potatoes furiously until late in the evening, not stopping until her husband marched out to her, tore the shovel from her hands, pressed her to him, covered her face and neck with kisses, unbuttoned her blouse, groped her breasts, and then carried her to their bed.

The next morning, the housewife's prized saddlehorse was gone. Pía had left under cover of night, taking the most necessary things from her trunk and packing them in a sack, saddled the horse and dashed down the valley in pitch darkness. Not a single star was out. And the dog didn't bark once. Bjarghildur lost it once more. She went rushing around the farmyard, shrieking and shoving away anyone who tried to calm her down, and it wasn't until her husband and the farmhand both mounted up and rode off to search for the girl that she simmered down. But she said that she would stay out in the farmyard until she saw her horse again, and there she sat, rocking back and forth beneath a blanket that the stepsisters managed to toss over her shoulders, refusing even to look at the porridge that was brought to her. All the fuss led Karitas to crawl out of bed and go to the kitchen; she was unconcerned about the horse's disappearance but shocked at Pía's scandalous behavior. "How is it possible to leave just like that, without saying goodbye to people, and here I thought we were friends, and she didn't even give me her address. I don't know where she lives or what her full name is," she whined, looking reproachfully at Helga. "Why didn't you ever ask her?" Helga replied grouchily, exhausted with these unbalanced sisters and longing to see the light in her life, and Karitas plunked down onto the bench at the kitchen table. There was the rub—why had she never asked, why did she never ask people anything, why did she let everyone pass by without asking them who they were or where they were going?

"Her name is Filippía Gabríela Gamalíelsdóttir, and she lives on Laugavegur Street," said Ásta. She had asked.

They returned with the horse a little after noon, having rushed back from Sauðárkrókur due to the housewife's agitated state, and said that the horse hadn't been hard to find. It had stood tethered outside the hotel, waiting for them, but the woman, on the other hand, they hadn't found. Apparently, she had left by boat that morning, and no one knew where she had gone. "But here you have your horse, Bjarghildur," said Hámundur, looking sternly at his wife. He and the farmhand barely managed to catch their breath or finish eating their lunch before it was discovered that Ína had also disappeared. They searched the farmhouse, the sheep sheds up at the winter pastures, the church, and all over the place, and when they couldn't find her anywhere, they realized that she must have gone out on yet another one of her hunts for a man. The farmhand guessed that Karitas's newly discovered condition had lit a fire inside her and then Pía's disappearance had upset her, but out of respect for his boss, he didn't want to mention the third possible cause, which he himself found most probable and mentioned to the stepsisters— namely, the passionate caresses the husband had showered on his wife in the potato patch the night before, and which everyone had witnessed. The men had no other choice but to resaddle the horses and ride down the valley toward Hofsós, where a road crew was reportedly working. As he put on his administrator's cap and rode off for the second time, Hámundur looked none too pleased.

It was well past midnight when they returned home with Ína, who was raving mad and scratched like a cat in heat, and Bjarghildur had to lie on top of her in her bed and stay there until morning. The housewife had barely slept a wink when she went to do the milking. But Ína's ponderous body had found little rest and her mind was clearly still in tatters, because as the household was eating breakfast early that morning, she threw everything that belonged to her in the cesspit east of the farm, her clothes and shoes, her comb, mirror, and knitting needles, and was still throwing things away when Mummi found her. He shouted to Hámundur, who rushed over, but Ína, who habitually threw her belongings into the cesspit if she was disturbed during one of her amorous escapades, lashed out and screamed when he and the farmhand tried to talk sense into her. When she was in such a state, there was nothing to do but put her in a canvas sack, tie a string around the opening, and roll her down the slope below the farmhouse, which was what they did. They stood over her and said that they weren't going to open the sack until she calmed down; it was entirely up to her. After screaming, wailing, shouting, and kicking the madness out of herself down in the sack, she finally calmed down and whimpered that she promised to be good if they would open it. And she kept her promise. Hámundur led her into the kitchen, gentle as a lamb; he held her by the arm and asked wearily if the women on the farm hadn't had enough of all the fuss. Personally, he felt it was more than enough; he needed to tend to his administrative and political work, if they would be so kind as to give him peace to do so. Bjarghildur answered somewhat brusquely, as if she didn't care much for his admonitions, that he should just do as he pleased, and then she took Ína, patted and cuddled her, sat her down on the bench, fetched a comb, and tidied her disheveled, ragged hair. "Dearest Ína," she said, "the autumn work is almost done. It has taken a toll on all of us, the jam making, the sausage making, the potatoes; it's incredible how it all comes at once, but now it's over, dear, now we can start knitting."

"Doesn't the meat still have to be boiled down for canning?" Helga grumbled peevishly, and it was as if it suddenly dawned on Bjarghildur that the stepsisters were the only ones who hadn't been any trouble whatsoever. They'd gone about their chores diligently and conscientiously, without complaint, had always been pleasant and peaceful without ever receiving praise or encouragement, let alone a pat on the back or a hug. "Come with me to the church," Bjarghildur said shrewdly. "I need to practice a few hymns before the next mass. Karitas and Þórunn can take care of the rest of the meat."

Although Karitas knew that nothing could delight the stepsisters more than praying and singing pious hymns in the house of God, which they certainly deserved to do, she didn't take over their chores once they were gone. She ignored the canning and instead moved her things from the old widow's room up to the room where Pía had slept. She went and got some raisins, which were kept in a sack on the other side of the stairs, and then sat for a long time on the bed, ate, inhaled the faint smell of cigarettes, and stared at the little pink flowers on the light-blue wallpaper. "What do you think I should do?" she asked the flowers, but they said nothing, as flowers always do, yet she was certain that the answer would come to her in time; she just needed to be a little patient.

She saw the three women come out of the church, the stepsisters light-footed after having lifted their souls to heaven, Bjarghildur holding her head high, though she didn't look up at her small window—for then she would have caught sight of her. She saw Helga go to the cowshed, Ína walk down to the stream with a bucket in hand, Mummi stroll out to the vegetable garden, the farmhand disappear into the storehouse, and Hámundur ride into the farmyard, while she herself didn't move from her bed. She heard them chatting over dinner down in the kitchen, but she wasn't the slightest bit hungry. If Bjarghildur wanted her to come down, she could come up and get her. The sky turned blue-black, she listened to the animals' nocturnes before sleep, the sky turned pitch-black, she lit the lamp, the flowers on the wallpaper yellowed. The voices inside the house grew quiet, the women whispered, buzzed like dying flies, while the stream above the farmhouse now spoke loud and clear. No one came up to see her. She was alone beneath the sloping roof. She pulled out her sketchbook, brandished her pencil, drew a picture of a big-bellied woman floating in the air with a mass of spiders above her, gaping fish below. The woman had to be careful not to fly too high so as not to end up in the spiderweb, and not too low so as not to fall prey to the fish, and her face was so anguished that Karitas shed a tear over her fate; the tears fell on the woman's face and her terror grew. But then Karitas had to pee.

"Down again I needs must go," she said, like her childhood maid out west, then slipped downstairs and out into the farmyard, inching her way along the wall to the farmhouse's eastern corner, where she squatted down.

Then she saw light in the church.

For a moment, she also thought she heard organ music, dissonant. Though done relieving herself, she couldn't bring herself to go back inside. She felt as if the church were calling to her, yet she couldn't budge; her fear of the dark held her captive. She stood as if nailed to the corner of the farmhouse, staring at the church, wishing that the dog would come barking out into the silence. A gleam shone from one of the farmhouse windows onto the farmyard. She saw a laundry stick standing near the front door, inched her way tremblingly toward it, grabbed it, swung it around her, hit out at the darkness until she had gathered enough courage, and then headed for the light in the church. She held the stick before her with both hands so that she could thrash any imps and ghosts that got in her way as she crossed the hayfield, noticed none but stumbled over a tussock. The faint light in the church fell on the hoarfrosted grass; the lychgate to the churchyard was open. She approached the church door, heard the organ playing rambunctiously once more. "Ghosts don't play the organ," she told herself in a tremulous voice, then opened the door very slowly and slipped inside. She stood in the shadows near the rear pews and looked at her sister in astonishment. Bjarghildur played the prelude to the end, jerking her shoulders as she did. She jumped up, gesticulated wildly, her long blond hair hanging loose; closed her eyes, her face white as porcelain, stood on her toes, her movements supple, stretched, her body slender as a twig, turned round and round, danced like a ballerina in front of the altar rail. Then she opened her eyes abruptly, stood motionless, turned slowly toward the church door. Her face darkened when she saw her sister. Karitas approached apologetically, knowing how embarrassing it could be to be caught in a strange state of mind. She was going to express her admiration for the dancing but stopped when she saw Bjarghildur's expression, and asked, "Did you think I was a ghost?"

"Icelandic women do not fear revenants," her sister replied, thrusting her chin forward to emphasize this fact, and no less, to acknowledge the nation's exceptional women since the time of its settlement.

Karitas then asked what she was doing here in the church this night, and Bjarghildur said that she had been fulfilling her duties as the caretaker of the house of God and its reserve organist. For those delightful duties, she had no other time, seeing as how the chores were so time-consuming in such a progressive home, as her sister must have noticed; but on the other hand, she might ask, with leave, what Karitas had been doing following her out here.

Karitas said that she'd had to slip out to relieve herself, because she hadn't found a chamber pot under the bed—it hadn't been her plan to discuss chamber pots with her sister there in the church, though one might certainly find fault with the mistress of such a large farm for not providing chamber pots for anyone and everyone, considering how far it was to the privy and how difficult to get to in pitch darkness—but when she had seen the light in the church, she had drawn the conclusion that it was probably the housewife who was there, and it was as good an opportunity as any to have a word with her, since she herself didn't come to see her hired help even if they were blood relations—"and I am going to Reykjavík, if you care to know."

After looking at Karitas for a few moments, Bjarghildur said, "Aha," turned back to the organ, played a lullaby and hummed along with it. "So she's going to Reykjavík, yes indeed, unmarried and pregnant, penniless and impoverished. Won't our mother be so terribly pleased after all that she took upon herself to raise her children, provide them with an education, and instill in them good Christian morals so that they would do their country and its people proud." The last notes, she pounded on the organ, as if punishing it for bad behavior.

"Maybe I'll just go west," Karitas said resignedly, because naturally, it didn't matter if she went south, west, east, or just stayed in the north; the misfortune in her belly would always accompany her.

"Let the children come to me," said Bjarghildur, pointing with a gentle gesture toward the altarpiece, an inept rendering of the Savior by a joiner in the area, showing Christ sitting surrounded by fair-haired boys in sheepskin shoes—"and I will take His words in my mouth and say, my dear sister, let your child remain here with me in the country-side, let it run free in God's green nature, grow up on an Icelandic farm, where a healthy lifestyle and patriotic ambition are paramount."

Karitas looked at her sister in amazement.

"Yes, it is a good offer," said Bjarghildur.

"It's an offer I cannot accept," Karitas said.

"Of course you can, Karitas, and it will be a true pleasure for Hámundur and me to raise your child. Here on the farm it will have all that it needs: loving parents, clothing and food, an academic as well as a practical education, Bible reading and prayers. Here it will grow to be someone, a true Icelander."

"I won't accept your offer."

"Won't, won't, why the blazes wouldn't you, Karitas? Haven't you gotten everything? Weren't you sent abroad to study at a distinguished art academy because you're good at scribbling pictures on paper? Was I sent abroad because I'm good at singing? Wasn't I the best singer in the whole parish, didn't I sing best, was I sent abroad? And then you get a child handed to you on a silver platter, just like that, without even having to ask for it, while I, who have never shirked my duties, have always done my country and people proud, stood steady as a rock by my mother and siblings, took on indigents, supported the religious life of the parish and promoted culture and progress, have I gotten a child, despite having prayed and tried for four years? Have I? Is that justice, Karitas? Karitas, be charitable, be just; allow me to take care of your child."

"You're asking too much, Bjarghildur."

"Be reasonable, Karitas! Don't you see your own situation? You're alone and have nothing. And what about your art? Aren't you going to become a great artist, paint pictures all over the country, hold exhibitions, become famous, travel abroad? Karitas, a woman with such talent as yours cannot become a washerwoman with a child to support or an insignificant housewife on a croft down south by the sea. You have a duty to cultivate your art and make it known, elevate the reputation of the Icelandic nation, show the world that we are a people of strong Nordic stock, great farmers, poets, and artists. You must have peace to follow your calling; let me have your child."

"I can't do that, Bjarghildur."

"Karitas, I am your sister. We're built of the same stuff, the same blood, the same spirit; sisters, Karitas, sisters. For God's sake, dear sister, give me your child."

Her sister's despair touched Karitas deeply. So she said, to comfort her, "If I have two, I shall give you one of them."

In the afternoons, the wind often turned, bringing good, dry weather, and they would take the opportunity to hang out the washing. Karitas saw to the laundry; unlike the cooking, it didn't make her feel nauseated. She was standing at the clotheslines with the clothespin bag tied to her apron string when she remembered the boy with the beautiful eyes in Akureyri. At their first meeting, he had handed her a clothespin. Now, he must have been the same age as she was when he handed her the clothespin, and she asked the wind, which was turning to the north, if she would ever see him again, and felt regret for never having drawn him. She put her hand in the bag, grabbed a clothespin, and rubbed it between her fingers while thinking of all the people who had disappeared from her life: the fair-eyed boy, Halldóra and Madam Eugenía, her fellow students at the Academy, Pía and Sigmar, and she tried to recall which of them she had drawn, because she suddenly felt as if it were crucial: that only the faces she had put down on paper would she see again. Then a face appeared between the white sheets that flapped belligerently on the clotheslines. It was Hámundur; she hadn't seen him coming. He said, "Karitas, I don't know what has happened between you and your sister, but I would like you to know that as far as I am concerned, you are welcome to stay here as long as you please. But on the other hand, I would just like to mention, so that it doesn't come as a surprise to you, that I have let the father of your child know about your condition, because it is my belief and conviction that fathers have the right to know of their children's existence."

She stared at him wide-eyed, and he hurried to add that it had actually been Pía who put him on the track of the father, and that Sigmar had been grateful to learn finally of her whereabouts, the girl who had not said goodbye to him but given him so much joy on summer evenings.

"He said that he had looked for you in all the fjords."

"And what is he going to do now?" asked Karitas, tidying her hair.

"That, we don't know," said Hámundur.

Aside from hanging the laundry and twisting dough into crullers, Karitas was given so little to do that it appalled the stepsisters, because even though they were the only ones being paid to do the household chores, Karitas got free food and lodging, and should have been able to lend a hand despite her condition. "It's not as if she's the first woman in Iceland to be pregnant." But they were careful not to let their grumbling reach the ears of the housewife, who was particularly light-footed these days, having regained her former energy following the slaughter and begun organizing the winter activities with the Women's Club and the choir, even presenting her household with the idea of holding a get-together at the farm, with accordion music and a dance—"for an admission fee, of course." She went humming between the farm buildings, from the kitchen out to the storehouse, from there to the cowshed and into the workshop, and ended her tour in the stable with her favorite horse, with whom she chatted loudly. Her footsteps echoed with expectation and anticipation. On the other hand, apathy followed her sister's every step.

Then the weather turned cold, windy, and snowy, making the step-sisters shiver under their duvet in the white room. Next, a blizzard hit, with severe frost, and they took their duvet to the old widow's innermost room, and then there was a minor thaw and they moved back again, and one mild, windless Sunday, the members of the Women's Club, twelve in number like the apostles, came marching up to hold their sched-uled meeting. Some had walked ten kilometers across slushy slopes and through hollows full of water, and were wet to their thighs, but they showed no signs of fatigue. After the stepsisters helped them out of their wet clothes in the old hearth-kitchen, they were invited into the middle room, but no sooner had they sat down and pulled on their dry socks than it began snowing so heavily that the room darkened. But they just laughed loudly and told Bjarghildur that her pantry shelves would start looking sparse if she were stuck with them for days. Bjarghildur said that as far as she was concerned, they could stay until spring, so well-stocked was the farm's pantry, and they were treated to coffee and the crullers that Karitas had been twisting all day. Bjarghildur introduced her little sister, "a graduate of the Royal Academy, who intends to take her first steps as a trained artist here at Þrastabakki. Oh, yes, I forgot to tell you, Karitas, Mama is going to send your oil paints and brushes, and Hámundur is building you an easel." She looked over the group and added, "Hámundur is so dexterous." They smiled warmly at Karitas, but couldn't refrain from taking peeks at her belly. Someone had let the cat out of the bag on the last trip to Sauðárkrókur.

The meeting chairwoman yielded the floor to the club's presi-dent, who spoke about the poor children in the parish. The stepsisters brought in more coffee, and the treasurer went over the club's bills. Karitas looked at the different-colored cardigans that filled the room. As the secretary suggested that a committee be appointed to organize a raffle, Karitas envisioned cardigans out on clotheslines, flapping in a strong wind, and the women had just finished selecting the commit-tee members and were helping themselves to one more cruller when a racket was heard from outside the front door. Like someone stomping his feet to shake off water or snow. Hámundur appeared in the doorway of the middle room and looked over the comely group of women, who did not let him disturb their agenda but instead continued to talk animatedly. He set eyes on his wife and sister-in-law, smiled meaningfully, and said, "We have a visitor." Then he stepped aside.

He entered the room, the visitor, and the women stopped talking at once. Some of them ran their hands through their hair. Others blushed and rubbed their necks. But none could take their eyes off him.

He himself didn't say a word.

"Well, I'll be," said the old priest's widow at last.

Rightly, Bjarghildur should have sprung to her feet to tend to the newly arrived guest, but she was like the other meeting-goers, utterly captivated by his handsomeness, and could neither imagine what connection he had to her home nor fulfill her obvious duties as a hostess. When the man showed no inclination to greet the group, but instead, just stared hard at Karitas, who cowered next to the organ, it dawned on the housewife who he was, and she stood up, greeted the man amiably as if he had been there many times before, took the liberty of introducing him to the group, and glanced reproachfully at her sister. At last, Karitas got to her feet and went over to him.

She looked up into his face, he looked down into her face, they drank in each other's faces, and no one in the room said a word.

"Gather your things, you're coming with me," he said. Then he walked out as if the matter were settled.

A hectic unrest spread through the room. The women sighed as if they'd been holding their breath the whole time, some got to their feet without knowing why, the old widow began clearing off the tables, and the sisters bumped into each other. It was Hámundur who took charge, telling the guests that they should just keep calm; he wouldn't let anyone or anything out into the storm, strong as it was, patted his wife on the shoulder, and pulled Karitas with him out of the room.

By then, Sigmar had reached the front door. He stood there with his hands in his pockets, looking out into the wildly blowing snow. Karitas tugged at his arm, and still without a single word, having spoken none since he came, she signaled to him to follow and brought him upstairs to the small room once occupied by the farmer's daughter. He sat down on her bed and looked around, at the trunk opposite the bed and at the light-blue wallpaper with the pink flowers. Finally he opened his mouth and said that he had never before seen flowers on walls, that wasn't how it was in the east, where he came from, and he couldn't recall having seen such a thing in homes in the north, either, but the pink flowers were pretty and suited her well, as dainty as she was, and then he said, "I'm tired; we should lie down for a bit." And he lay down, pulled her to him, and positioned her between him and the wall. They turned to each other, with only a hand's breadth between them, and looked into each other's eyes without speaking, but listened intently to the snowstorm turn into sleet. Then he placed his index finger in the middle of her forehead and ran it down along her nose, lips, neck, chest as if he were dividing her into two, ended at her belly, and pressed it lightly with a questioning look.

"In May," she said.

"How could you leave without saying goodbye to me?" he asked.

"I was afraid that if I said goodbye to you, we would do what we did again. I didn't know at the time that this had already happened."

"Why shouldn't we have done it again?" he asked.

"I didn't want to become tied to anyone. I'm an artist. You don't have to marry me even though I carry your child under my belt. I can stay here if I like. Why have you come?"

"I have come to take what belongs to me. You are mine."

She couldn't help but admire his self-confidence.

He took her hand, raised it to his lips, closed his eyes. "You have taken up residence in my mind, and I feel as if I will never be able to expel you from there."

She raised her hand instinctively and ran her fingers over his forehead, hairline, eyebrows. She found the idea of being stuck in a man's mind captivating, and he opened his eyes. She waited for the question that, through time, women have most often been asked by men in love; she felt as if its moment had come, but he only asked her to continue stroking his head and said, "See if you can put me to sleep."

They both fell asleep, though that had not exactly been their intention. The sleet made their heads heavy, and they woke confused and thirsty in pitch darkness, neither having any idea what time it was. Karitas lit the oil lamp and asked Sigmar to come with her, but he said that he didn't want to go downstairs until the women had gone, but that she, on the other hand, could bring him a pitcher of water if she really wanted to. The Women's Club, however, showed no signs of dispersing. Another strong storm had blown in as if out of nowhere, and Hámundur had gone to put together hay mattresses for the guests. In the kitchen, the women had chatted over salted lamb and potatoes—Bjarghildur had boiled potfuls of them—and were now enjoying coffee and rock candy, and when Karitas showed up, she saw no signs whatsoever of them being restless. When she came in, they craned their necks to see if she'd brought her companion, then went on chatting when they saw she had not, but Bjarghildur, who had a great deal to do and seemed, furthermore, to be upset about something, signaled to Karitas to come with her down to the pantry. There, she stood before her holding the lamp up high, giving the fully stocked shelves—resembling those of a general store—a deep, warm, earthen hue. Light and shadows created sharp contrasts amid the bottles, jars, and boxes, while a white plate of salted lamb and potatoes became a living still life. The aroma of the leftover food hung in the air.

Bjarghildur said that she wanted to make it clear to Karitas once and for all that the two of them would not be sleeping together under her roof as long as they were unmarried. Karitas wanted to tell her that they had in fact just woken up, but she couldn't get a word in edgewise as Bjarghildur went on with her sermon on Christian morality. She spoke so rapidly that she hardly even knew what she was saying, but finally, she asked breathlessly, "Are you going to leave with this man, Karitas?"

Karitas said that she hadn't yet made up her mind about that; she had just come downstairs to fetch water. When she started to list the man's good qualities, without really knowing why, Bjarghildur interrupted and asked brusquely, "Karitas, what does this man have to offer you?" Karitas didn't answer, climbed the narrow staircase, grabbed an empty pitcher from the kitchen table, filled it with water from the faucet without so much as looking at the assembly, and was halfway back up the stairs to the attic when Bjarghildur grabbed her skirt and practically hissed, "Aren't you going to bring the man anything to eat?" It hadn't occurred to Karitas. She waited on the stairs while her sister went to fetch the plate of salted lamb.

"What do you have to offer me?" she asked, handing him the food.

"A grassy valley, a beautiful fjord, and Iceland's most colorful mountains."

"I have no interest in the landscape."

"A small house with a nice living room."

"I can't imagine being a housewife."

His first two offers having been rejected, he thought things over carefully, and was just about to make his third offer when the door to the farmer's daughter's room was thrown open, and there in the doorway stood the housewife, with bed linens and pillows in her arms. "We have decided who will sleep where," she said. "We women will divide ourselves up among the rooms downstairs. Helga and Ásta will share your bed, Karitas, and the men will all sleep in the same room. Sigmar, you'll share the farmhand's bed. Here's a pillow for you."

He stood up, having to bend down so as not to bump his head against the sloping ceiling, thrust the plate of salted lamb into Bjarghildur's hands, pushed her out the door, said in a deep voice, "I'm staying here," and shut the door in her face. Then he sat down on the edge of the bed and began removing his clothes. She sat on the foot-locker opposite him and watched in astonishment, and after he took off his shirt, he said, "My third offer is me. You may draw me all day long."

Having slept so well in the late afternoon, they enjoyed the night to the fullest, telling each other stories in the gleam of the oil lamp and exploring each other's naked bodies.

In the morning, when the storm subsided, they gathered up Karitas's belongings.

Hámundur saddled their horses for them. He alone stood with them as they prepared to depart, and kissed his sister-in-law numerous times, asking God and good spirits to be with her. He grasped Sigmar's hand firmly, shook it for several long moments without a word, and then watched as they rode out of the farmyard.

They stared at her in silence, five red-haired women, all alike, having lined themselves up in a corner of the sitting room as if to be photo-graphed, two sitting, three standing, none of them so much as blinking. Karitas, who was slowly regaining her composure following her sea voyage, dared not make a sound; she still wasn't sure whether they were of flesh and blood, or were elf women. They hadn't been in the sitting room when she was carried into it to rest; she had just closed her eyes, and when she opened them again, there they were. As soon as she saw them, she recalled something she and her sisters had overheard her grandma say during one of her visits, that she had been so surprised at the appearance of the elf women. They weren't all dark of countenance, as people had thought; some had red hair and fair skin. And that was all that she said on that subject. But on their way to the Eastfjords, Sigmar had told her, in an attempt to distract her between her fits of vomiting, that in his village in Borgarfjörður, where they would be making their home, there was a great city of elves. One of the largest in the country.

For this reason, Karitas did not feel terribly confident, lying there on the divan.

Nausea still plagued her, and her dizziness hadn't completely abated. She closed her eyes, heard the sound of the surf. The house stood on a bank above a rocky beach; that much she had seen, despite having been so ill when they came ashore. For a fleeting moment, she had seen the village spread out irregularly along a single road running alongside the shore. She had no idea where Sigmar's house was, nor had she been in any condition to ask. She thought twice before venturing to open her eyes. They were still there. I would draw them if I had my sketchbook, she thought, and make all the faces alike, but stretch them to slightly different lengths, and then she noticed that their expressions were gloomy, if not hostile, which made her uneasy. She got to her feet with great difficulty, looked apologetically at them, said that she had to go look for Sigmar, even though she knew it was pointless to talk to elves, and she staggered past them and down the hallway to the kitchen at the other end of the house. There sat an older man and woman, and Sigmar with them.

"Well, so you're up, dear," said the woman, who seemed to be in her fifties and lighthearted, though a little gruff. She pushed Karitas down onto a chair and said she would warm some milk for her, and Karitas felt relieved to be back among ordinary people. She didn't say a word about the elf women, having also heard her grandmother say that those who saw things that were hidden from others should keep quiet about them.

"Is the wind picking up?" the man asked. "It's changing direction," said Sigmar. "Are you going home tonight?" asked the man, looking out the window. "That was the plan," said Sigmar. The two men looked neither at Karitas nor each other as they talked. "You'd better take some peat and kerosene with you," said the man. Sigmar said nothing. "Are you feeling better, you poor dear?" the woman asked, and Karitas replied that she thought so. "Then it's best that we get going," Sigmar said, without looking at any of them.

They walked along the pitted road, avoiding the mud puddles; he carried her trunk and his bag, she carried her pouch and a canvas sack in which the woman had put saltfish and seal blubber "to tide you over until morning." They walked slowly; he didn't want to hurry while she was still recovering from their voyage east. But she felt as if she would never be well again. Not with that in her belly. It had begun to grow dark; a snow cloud lay over the surrounding white mountains. Snow lay in the hollows up the valley and had decorated the village, settled here and there around the houses, as if the white laundry flapping on clotheslines had fallen to the ground.

"The weather has been nice and dry today," said Karitas. "The women will have to bring the washing in soon," she continued in a slightly worried tone, "because if they don't, it will get all wet again. Do you have running water?" she then asked abruptly. "No, but there's a well on the next farm over," he replied. "On the next farm over?" she yelled. "But didn't you say that your house was in the village itself?" He seemed in no hurry to answer. "It's a short distance away, just here behind the cliffs." "Can we see it from here?" she asked anxiously. "No, it's down at the seashore," he said. "We can't see the village from there, but on the other hand, we have a view of the entire mountain range and the elf city." She shuddered. "And the other farm you mentioned," she asked sullenly, "where is it?" "It's farther up, next to a small cluster of lava formations, a short stretch from our house, and that's where you'll go to fetch our water." "Me?" she exclaimed loudly. "Is it I who must fetch our water?" He stopped, looked around, they had come a little way outside of the village, and he bent down and kissed her. "Are you tired? I can carry you if you want." "I'm not tired at all," she said wearily, turning her head away. "I just haven't fully recovered from my seasickness." They came to a small wooden house snuggled next to the outcrop of lava rocks, and she clutched quickly at her chest, but breathed a sigh of relief when he said it was not his. This was the home of Kára, who milked his cow and fed the sheep. "You have a cow and sheep?" she asked, as if hit by a bolt from the blue. "We all do," he replied brusquely. "And there's the well; this is where you'll fetch the water."

Then his house came into view down at the seashore, near the estuary. She stopped and grabbed her head. "A turf-and-stone farmhouse," she said hopelessly.

"A house," he said firmly.

The house was long and had a turf roof, one wooden gable facing west, the other facing east, a small window in the middle of the south wall, and visible on the north wall, which faced the sea, was a vestibule. "North of the house I have a sheep shed, a workshop, and a storehouse, all under one roof," he said, pointing. "It's the most beautiful location in the entire fjord; the only catch is the blasted water—I don't know what to do about it." "It looks to me like you'd get the waves right over you when the wind is blowing inland," she said, looking at the large rocks the surf had left behind on the northmost point of the shore.

The door was unlocked, and they walked into the darkness.

Inside, the air was damp, and it smelled bad. "It needs airing out in here," she muttered, and stayed close as he fiddled with the oil lamp, daring to look neither right nor left, certain the place would be full of elves or ghosts. But when he held the lamp up high and the light spread warmly and amiably, she looked around in surprise. They were standing in the kitchen in the middle of the house, with doors open to rooms on both sides. "Here to the left is where we sleep," he said, letting her peek into the room, which had two beds, a dresser, and a cabinet. "And here is where we'll draw," he said, holding the lamp to reveal the room on the right, which was well supplied with furniture, including a divan, a round table, four chairs with embroidered seats, a fine sideboard, and a small bookshelf. Karitas was so stunned by the furnishings that she couldn't say a word. Sigmar noticed and explained with pride: "I gave the house an overhaul after Mama died, threw out all the old junk and bought everything new at an auction in Akureyri after the fishing season last year; even the dinnerware that you see there in the sideboard. The beds are also brand new. Don't you think it would be a good idea to try them out now?"

"We need to light the stove," she sighed.

They lit the coal stove and settled in. He moved their beds together, saying that they would be warmer that way, then went and got two pails of water, explaining that he wanted to spare her that burden for the first couple of days, and then they boiled the saltfish in a dented pot. He pulled out the seal blubber, which had taken on a green tinge from being stored in salt, cut it meticulously into small pieces, clearly salivating as he did, stuck the pieces in his mouth along with bits of the fish, closed his eyes for a second, and then asked if she would like some. No, she didn't think so. Just watching him cut the green blubber was enough to make her lose what little appetite she had. They sat at the kitchen table and didn't say much; he ate and she averted her eyes. Then they heated water, and he said he'd rinse off the dishes while she made the beds. In the dresser, she found three duvet covers embroidered with blue flowers, but didn't ask him if they had been there before or if he had bought them at auction along with the rest. His duvet lay rolled up at the foot of one of the beds, and as she was covering it, she wondered where he might have slept before coming north to her. She took out the duvet cover from her trunk, and when she had covered both duvets and laid them side by side on the beds, she saw that they looked quite similar; the embroidery on both was blue. She felt certain that his mother had embroidered his duvet cover, just as her mother had hers, and she called to the kitchen and asked how old he had been when he lost his mother.

"Twenty," he said. "She drowned while fishing."

"Fishing?" she repeated.

"Yes, she used to fish, and was actually thought quite good at it," he replied, and she asked nothing more, as this information gave her food for thought. She unpacked her brown travel trunk, whose contents she had tried to keep in order since leaving Siglufjörður, and hung up her skirts and the two dresses she'd had with her while working in the herring. But when her eyes fell on the waists, it struck her that her belly would soon be expanding, and that she owned neither a dress nor a skirt that she could then fit into. She would have to sew new clothes for herself, and how on earth would she do that? She had no sewing machine. Karitas sat down on the bed to think, but the more she thought, the more miserable her situation and her future looked. Finally, she began sobbing. Sigmar hurried to her, took her in his arms, and asked if she was in any pain.

"No," she whimpered. "I have no sewing machine."

"Sewing machine?" he exclaimed. "Are you crying because you have no sewing machine?" He stared at her in disbelief, causing her sobbing to turn into bitter weeping. She wept over her recklessness and her frivolity, her condition and her poverty; she wept so uncontrollably that it startled him. He laid her down on the bed, then lay down next to her, held her tightly in his arms, and kissed away her salty tears. She cried until her eyes burned, but couldn't stop because he was so caring and tender, and only calmed down when he said, "How small and delicate you are. Weren't you the smallest of your sisters?" She felt compelled to explain her and her sisters' heights, which were in accordance with their ages, and which her brother Ólafur had made fun of—and then stories of her youth, from when she was an unspoiled, innocent girl, poured from her. She forgot all about the sewing machine.

As she let her fingers play with his hair and forehead, instinctively needing to fiddle with something as she told him her stories, he let his fingers wander over her body, as if he were checking whether everything was in place, and then he lit a fire in her blood no less than in his own. So well did the coal stove warm the kitchen that they didn't need a duvet, even as they stripped off their clothes.

Karitas

Milk Jug 1923

Pencil drawing

It's late in the morning.

The light creeps drowsily into the east window, lazy in darkest midwinter.

I'm alone in the room. I listen, hear nothing but the cries of the seabirds. I feel abandoned. I jump out of bed, run out into the farmyard in my nightgown.

The sea fills my view, as far as the eye can see.

The fjord is short, the mountains low on both sides, the columnar basalt to my right is weeping, there is drizzle in the air, which is still but biting cold.

I shiver in my nightgown, go back in, and shut the door behind me.

Then I see the blue jug on the kitchen table.

Bathing in the morning light. The window frames it.

It's full of milk. I grab it with both hands, guzzle the milk, gulp it down until I'm out of breath. The white liquid runs through every one of my veins and nerves; I feel myself filling with energy, close my eyes with delight. When I open them again, the elf city appears before me.

A black, rocky hill on a snow-white field.

I hadn't seen it in last evening's twilight, hadn't realized its size. It rises like a mountain in the middle of nowhere, like a pyramid in the desert, missing only the pointed top. I hold the jug of milk, look from it to the rocky hill and back, and wonder who brought it to me.

Sigmar had rowed out to fish before dawn, as was his habit, which Karitas didn't know that morning, for how should she know anything about his habits when she knew neither his family nor his past, and the last thing she would have imagined was his rowing out to sea the very first morning without mentioning it to her beforehand. After draining the milk jug, she sat there on the bed for a long time, not knowing what to do with herself. It wasn't until she looked out the sitting room's west window that it occurred to her to knock on the door of the woman who milked his cow and ask if she had seen him. While she was dressing, her mind began to clear a little, and it dawned on her where the milk in the blue jug had come from. Men didn't usually do the milking; at least they hadn't where she came from. And the elves out west hadn't brought people milk, but rather, vice versa, and the same surely applied to elves in the Eastfjords, as well.

The south-facing door to the small wooden house stood wide-open. Karitas didn't see the woman anywhere, just four cats that had lined up like royal bodyguards. She approached the door, stood at a suitable distance, and first called out, "Hi ho, is anyone home?" But when no one answered, she moved closer, knocked on the open door, and called out, "Hi ho," again. But the only answer she received was a meow, so she decided to go inside; it even crossed her mind that something might have happened to the woman. The house consisted of a single room in which its occupant slept and cooked, and wherever Karitas looked, there were cats. Black, yellow, striped and white, on the bed, the footlocker, the table, the chairs, the stove, the cupboard, the floor, on the windowsills. She couldn't count them all. They looked at her suspiciously. She felt a bit unsettled, having never seen anything like it, and was just about to leave when the woman came in.

On her shoulder sat a black cat. As if nothing were more self-evident than finding a stranger standing in the middle of her room, she said, "Yes, I had to go over to the Co-op for coffee and sugar, and now I'll make us some coffee if you wait a bit." This she said in a tone neither friendly nor hostile, just quite natural, perhaps a touch dry if one were splitting hairs, and Karitas simply nodded. She was speechless; never before had she seen a cat perched on someone's shoulder. "I just wanted to ask if you had seen Sigmar," she stammered at last, while the woman, whose name was Kára, if she remembered correctly, busied herself with the coffee. Kára turned from the stove, rubbed her chin, and said, "I don't remember," with the cat still sitting on her shoulder, and then looked down at the floor as if she were trying to recall. She was of medium height, slender and gray haired, her chin a little prominent, her face wrinkled. She must have been rather old.

"Thank you for the milk," said Karitas, after waiting silently for several long moments, and Kára turned away from the stove, shook the cat off her shoulder, and said, "What milk?" The cats meowed in chorus at that obviously familiar word, "milk." Karitas didn't dare try to push them off the chairs so that she could sit down, and their housemother made no attempt to shoo them away, so she drank her coffee standing. The coffee was refreshing, making her want to chat with the woman and ask her this and that, but it appeared as if the latter wasn't so inclined; she gulped down her steaming-hot coffee, wiped her mouth with her apron, and was out the door before Karitas managed to turn around. When she stepped outside again, Karitas saw no sign of Kára; the cats were still at their posts, but it was as if the rocks had swallowed the woman. Confused and distracted, Karitas trotted back across the farmyard.

Sigmar had rowed out to sea before dawn and found nothing strange about it. "Don't we want fresh fish for our pot?" he asked, knitting his brows when she chided him for not having let her know. She had nothing against fresh fish, she murmured, but she had been so worried about him. Then it was as if she had struck a wonderfully gentle string in his heart, for he asked again and again with radiant eyes whether she had really been worried about him, and when she replied sharply that of course she had, he took her in his arms. As if no one in the world had ever been worried about him before. He covered her with kisses until he could no longer restrain himself and pulled her over to the bed. "Can you never think of anything else?" she asked angrily, for at that moment, she wanted the fish more than him, and he replied: "No, God knows, I can't think of anything else."

Later, after enjoying both the fish and her, he allowed her to draw him. To distract and entertain him as he stood there naked like a Greek god—imagining how uncomfortable it had to be to stand for so long in one position—she chatted with him, asking whether he didn't find it hard rowing out to sea in an open boat in pitch darkness.

"We here in Borgarfjörður see well in the dark," he said, scratching his groin. "And anyway, it was milking time when I left. Kára was milking the cow and feeding the sheep." "She said she couldn't remember if she had seen you," Karitas said. "Kára never remembers anything, except for looking after the animals. Remind me to bring her some fish when we go down to the Co-op."

"The Co-op?" she exclaimed.

"Yes, the Co-op. Did you think we'd be eating nothing but fish?"

"Well, no, of course not," she said, a little ashamed of her indifference when it came to the housekeeping. She focused on the drawing, asking no more questions in order to avoid thinking about the inconveniences of everyday life. They said nothing until he began growing bored; he had started fiddling with his trousers, which were lying on a chair next to him, and then asked if it had been fun in Copenhagen.

"It was drudgery," she said. "I was in the kitchen doing dishes every single day. It's worse than washing saltfish in a stiff north wind. The old woman never gave me time off; I was lucky just to attend my classes at the Academy. I rarely got to go on a picnic with my schoolmates, and only once attended a dance."

"I'm certainly glad to hear that," he said.

They went to the village to buy flour and oatmeal, coffee and sugar. Before setting off for home, she complained that she had nothing to wear. Her skirt was painfully tight at the waist, her coat could hardly be buttoned anymore. She was a little irritated, feeling as if he hardly cared about her condition. "We're stopping by Högna's anyway, to bring her some fish and pick up rutabagas, so we'll ask her to sew you a few garments. She has a sewing machine," he said, as if that settled the matter. "Who is Högna?" she asked testily, since he spoke as if she had known all of the villagers since childhood, as he had. "The woman we had coffee with after our voyage here. My late mother's maid," he answered impatiently. Karitas wasn't pleased with this idea; she didn't want to go to the house where she hadn't been entirely self-composed, and had hallucinated, besides.

A cold wind was blowing from the north, and breakers crashed over the shore. She tied her headscarf tighter under her chin, pulled it down over her face. He pressed his peaked cap down over his eyes, bowed his head, and trudged onward with the handcart in tow. He reached Kára's house before her, and she saw him grab one of the bunches of fish from the cart and hand it in through the half-open door, where it was received wordlessly. With the salty air in their nostrils, they walked on past the lava rocks until they came to the pitted road. As they passed the church, whose rear gable faced them, Karitas said: "It's turned the wrong direction. Churches should face east and west, not north and south." "Yes," he said. "The church was supposed to be built on top of the elf city, but they didn't want that, the folk there. The elf queen herself appeared to one of the committee members in a dream and asked that the church be built where it stands now, with the door to the south, presumably so that she could see from the elf city who was going to church. But the altarpiece is beautiful, you should have a look at it." He stopped abruptly, peered at her in the wind, and said: "Would you like to get married?" "I don't know," she replied embarrassedly, before walking on. She couldn't tell whether it was a proposal or just a suggestion for a practical arrangement.

Children played in the road, adults were out and about among the houses. Karitas looked around attentively, but few people took notice of her; women with headscarves over their eyes seldom attract attention. When they entered the Co-op, she took off her headscarf and shook her hair loose, as women in Copenhagen do when they enter a store, but recoiled shyly when she noticed the men's eyes on her. They all stopped talking as she and Sigmar walked in. Some hung around the counter, others sat on it, and all gawked as if they hadn't seen a woman for ages. "Weren't we going to buy oatmeal?" said Sigmar loudly after greeting the men. "Yes," she said softly, trying to hide behind him. "Weren't we going to buy raisins?" "Yes," she whispered, taking a deep breath. Once they were back outside, she breathed a sigh of relief, and as he arranged the goods in their cart, she asked him gruffly why the men had stared at her like that. As if it were his fault. Which it was, in a certain respect; presumably, they'd been staring at her belly. "You're so beautiful," he finally replied, after making her wait. "That's why they stare." "Oh," she said. "Is that so." Then she smoothed down her hair, but didn't put her headscarf back on. "But where are all the women in this village?" she asked, in a slightly softer tone. "Do you think they have time to hang around blathering in the Co-op all day?" he answered, sounding indignant. "They have better things to do."

They came to Högna's handsome one-story wooden house. Sigmar grabbed the other bunch of fish from the cart, and she saw the childish anticipation in his face when he said: "Now we'll have steaming-hot coffee and freshly baked bread." He was halfway up the steps when he noticed that she wasn't following, but was standing next to the cart, fiddling awkwardly with the sacks. "I'm feeling queasy," she said, stroking her stomach as he looked at her questioningly. "I think I'd better stay out here in the fresh air until I feel a little better." "Won't you be cold?" he asked, but his concern for her well-being was not going to stand in the way of the coffee that he'd been looking forward to, and he strode up the steps and went in.

Karitas stood at the south gable, where, somewhat sheltered from the north wind, she gazed at the hazy gray mountains and wondered at people's eternal bent for viewing their homes in a beautiful light. Hadn't he said, when he was trying to persuade her to go out east with him, that these were the most beautiful mountains in the country? But she couldn't see anything beautiful about these mountains, any more than any other mountains. Mountains simply bored her. She felt like a prisoner with all these mountains surrounding her. And she was a prisoner, after all; a prisoner of her own body, her hands tied by what was inside of her. She should have been in Reykjavík, painting in an atelier, like other artists who had spent five long years in rigorous studies. This was all the damned herring's fault; if only it had shown itself, she wouldn't have had time to draw him and consequently end up in this state. She would have had money in her pocket and not needed to rely on others. She wouldn't have to be here among elves and trolls, surrounded by misty gray mountains.

The corners of her eyes were moist when he finally came back out, his cheeks flushed after his coffee drinking. Yet they had walked quite some distance before he asked if she was going to tell him why she was crying. "I'm not crying," she said tearfully, because she didn't want to tell him that she was crying over her lack of freedom. Instead, to sound like other women in the same situation, she added: "I'm just worried how this will all go. The baby is to be born in May, and I don't have any clothes for it to wear. And I don't have the money to buy the things we'll need."

"You have nothing to worry about," he said. "We'll just hire someone to take care of the baby. Högna said she would make clothes for you, and it should be no trouble at all for her to make something for the little one at the same time. You just buy the fabric and other things that you need from the Co-op. Of course I'll give you the money right away, I have plenty, at least more than many others." The rest of the way home, he went on and on about this wealth of his that she had never seen, and she found it so amusing to hear him talk for so long at once that she forgot about her confinement. His boasting, in which she took quiet delight, reminded her of her brothers. When they reached their turf dwelling, which he himself called a house, she was in the most cheerful of moods. They lit lamps and kindled the stove, cooked fish and rutabagas, and he told her about his plans to buy a boat—no little two-oared thing, but a four-ton boat—"to start with," he said, holding up his index finger to emphasize this, and then an even bigger boat when he had the money for it, and finally a good herring boat.

"Won't you need a good captain, then?" she asked, to add something to the conversation. "I'm the captain," he answered, surprised at such a silly question. "I have a degree from the Maritime College." Her mouth opened wide. "Oh, I didn't know that." And it struck her that she actually knew nothing about the father of her child. "You didn't know because you never ask anything," he said, looking sternly at her. "You have little interest in others." "What nonsense," she said, a little annoyed. "Of course I'm interested in others." "Their faces and bodies," he said. And she knew that there was a grain of truth in what he said. Just a tiny one.

In an attempt to make up for her disinterest, she tried, once they were in bed, asking him about his childhood and upbringing, but he wasn't keen at all on talking about himself, answering only in one-syllable words and preferring to kiss her, so she gave up, but asked if he knew when Högna was thinking of making clothing for her. "She'll bring her sewing machine here after the New Year," he replied. "It wouldn't surprise me if she brought the whole gaggle along, too."

"What gaggle?" she asked, sitting up in bed.

"Oh, her five daughters: Guðjóna, Sigurjóna, Magnúsína, Erlendína, and Eiríka," he yawned.

"Where is the blue jug?" she asked, standing in the workshop door. He was at a loss. He had no idea what blue jug she was talking about, had never seen a blue jug in this house, only the white one in which Kára always brought the milk. "My first morning here, I saw a blue jug," she insisted. But he just gave her a bemused smile, as if she weren't completely awake, so she said no more and went back into the house. She searched high and low for the blue jug, tore open all the cupboard doors, peeked under the beds, went out again and over to the storehouse, where she turned everything upside down, and ended up in the cowshed with the cow, which mooed with joy when it saw her, but found the blue jug nowhere. She stood for a long time at the kitchen window and stroked the white jug, which she was convinced had been blue. Then she sat down and didn't know what to do with herself.

Outside, an icy north wind blew, and now and then a few snow-flakes flitted through the air. Christmas was just around the corner, and she had nothing to do. I'll lose my mind if I stay here much longer, she thought. She tottered to the door, tore it open, and looked out to sea, where the tender was coming alongside the coastal steamer, and thought how easy it would be for her to leave for Reykjavík, if only she didn't get so seasick. Sigmar came out of the workshop, and when he saw her at the door, he asked if she would like to go to the village with him, but she declined, saying that she had nothing to wear and was feeling a bit indisposed, besides. On the other hand, since he was going to the village anyway, he could buy them a new pot. As soon as he left, she lay down and pulled the duvet up over her head. It was getting dark both outside the house and inside her soul, and the house was growing cold, for she hadn't had the energy to replenish the coal stove. In a drowsy haze, she heard him return. It was pitch-dark inside and she heard him light the lamps and pull something heavy into the sitting room, and then he came into the bedroom with a lamp in hand and said: "I've brought something for you, Karitas."

"Is it a pot?" she asked.

"No, it looks as if it's from your mother."

She got up out of bed.

Her easel, her paints in their wooden box, the brushes in their holder, her palette, canvas, a bottle of turpentine, all carefully packed, the spaces between them stuffed with hand- and machine-knitted woolen garments, and, wrapped in brown paper, a half-length, wide wool jacket made for a woman with a protruding belly. She brushed the jacket against her cheek and said, with a lump in her throat: "I miss Mama so much." And she had to sit down to steady herself. Her long johns with their wide elastic waistband brought tears to her eyes; her legs had been so cold for so long. Sigmar waited sullenly as she fingered the garments and squeezed them, unable to understand why she needed to examine every single one over and over. He wanted to set up the easel and see real paintings on it. They went to the workshop to nail some frames together. He would see to that part of the enterprise, in order to be of some use to her: "You'll get them in different sizes, and when I'm not around, you can nail the canvas onto them yourself, just as you need." She had already decided the sizes of all the frames, and as he was sawing and hammering, she chattered freely, telling him stories about artists in Copenhagen. "The girls and I talked a lot about their pictures, and once or twice, I got to go with them to exhibitions, but some of them didn't like the modernists, and were outraged at some of the pictures, saying that they were just abstract rubbish, but for me, a new world opened up. I remember when I saw Vilhelm Lundstrøm's works, which were kinds of collages, pieces of fabric and the like, all cut into pieces, shaped, and painted as well—I was captivated. And then there were Olaf Rude's compositions; he was so inspired by Picasso—everyone could see it. I don't know if he saw Picasso's paintings in Paris or Copenhagen, but it doesn't matter. I suppose I was most fond of Harald Giersing's paintings. He was a master of the pared-down palette: black was predominant and used to great effect; many were still lifes of everyday objects, all in those deep, dense blacks and whites. Yes, they certainly weren't painting mountains and faces, like some are always doing, but those fellows definitely knew how to paint. It's a shame that I never got to make their acquaintance. They all stuck together, you see, went to Paris, Rome. I was once on the verge of going to Rome; goodness, how I longed to go, but I had no money, and besides, I felt as if I were expected to return home. Oh, I regret so much that I didn't just go."

"And I am so glad that you didn't!" he said.

He moved the sitting-room table over to the wall to give her plenty of floor space, set up the easel right next to the window, so that she would have plenty of light, and then she stood there motionless, staring at the white canvas. He stretched out on the divan, which was too short for him, placed a pillow under his head and waited patiently for artistic inspiration to arrive. He had to wait a long time before she lifted her pencil and began to draw indistinct lines here and there on the canvas, and finally, she opened her box of paints and fiddled with each tube, acting as if he weren't present, squeezed paint out of three of the tubes, mixed colors on the palette, thinned them out with turpentine, and finally, daubed blue paint onto the middle of the canvas, stood unmoving, brush aloft, looked at the color, then thrust her nose toward the easel and inhaled the aroma. She applied the paint to the surface, feeling as if she were alone in the world, forgetting that he was behind her until she heard him sigh as people do when they're overcome with drowsiness. She had been painting for a long time and her lower back had begun to ache, when he suddenly exclaimed loudly, as if he hadn't actually fallen asleep: "It's a blue jug!"

"It's the blue jug I saw my first morning here," she said.

"It was white."

"No, it was blue."

"You won't paint mountains, and no faces, so what is it you're after?"

"I'm after chaos."

"I don't see any chaos in a blue jug."

"The chaos will come; it's inside of me. It will come when I've gotten to paint freely, for a long time, and to be myself. One of my schoolmates who went to Rome told me about the futurists in Italy. I was no less fond of them than the modernists, or rather, their agenda, I should say. I never saw their works, but they seek inspiration in speed and modernity. Their subject is technology: all the machines, cars, airplanes; they try to capture the beauty of speed, not the beauty of silence, like the old masters. Isn't it exciting? Imagine, renewing culture through painting—but then, of course, one must also have perfect mastery of technique itself, you see, the brush, the paints. I need to paint and paint. Then she left, that schoolmate of mine. One day she just went to Berlin, just disappeared from my life, when I still had so much to say to her about chaos. Everyone disappears from my life, Sigmar; they just disappear."

"It's because you're after chaos. If you painted mountains and faces, nothing and no one would leave you."

This idea of his made her stop and think for a moment.

"I'm hungry," he said, getting up.

"You're always hungry," she said.

"But what about you, my little one? Aren't you hungry at all?" he asked, coming and standing behind her, putting both his arms around her belly and stroking her breasts and loins. Unbelievable that he has this in mind when he's famished, she thought, baffled at the man's inexhaustible amorousness, but he got what he wanted, perhaps because she was feeling happy again and had nothing against a little cuddling. So they tumbled around in bed, two famished souls, until they were panting for breath. As they lay side by side, playfully bickering over who had the most beautiful legs, she said slightly reproachfully that he would soon have to stop doing this, and he knew what she meant; it was becoming uncomfortable for her because of her stomach. "You'll have peace and quiet enough when I leave for the fishing season after the turn of the year," he said, and the first thing that occurred to her was that she would then have peace to paint. All day and night, if she wanted to.

But that night, she sat up abruptly in bed and shouted into the darkness: "Fishing season! So who is going to clear away the snow from our door and fetch the water?" He didn't so much as mumble one word, and she lay back down again. But she had only been lying there for a few minutes before she sat up again, her eyes open wide: "Sigmar, it's moving inside of me!" That roused him. They both pressed their hands to the little bulge, which was newly woken and lively, like a third person in their bed, and whispered to each other while waiting for the next kick. "Sigmar," she said, "you mustn't disappear early in the morning without saying goodbye."

Karitas

Buckets in Snow 1924

Oil on canvas

Deep snow and utter stillness, as if the sea has fallen asleep.

Ravens croaking beyond the house.

I in men's trousers in the farmyard. Waterless.

Deep tracks in the snow reveal that the animals were fed earlier that morning. With a little dexterity, the tracks can be followed up to the well.

I dread having to lug the water, but make my way over the snowdrifts with the buckets rattling in my hands.

At the lava rocks I stumble, fall into a dip, swear, though I know that pregnant women mustn't, and hoist myself back to my feet. When I reach the well and have trampled snow beneath my feet, I shake the snow out of my trouser legs.

Smoke rises from Kára's chimney. Her door is closed, the cats are nowhere to be seen.

I lower the well bucket, hoist it up, which strains my arm muscles, pour the water from it into one of my buckets, lower the well bucket again.

The water splashes all over as I pour; it's horrendously cold. I grasp the buckets' handles, straighten my back, they're heavy as lead, I lower my head and count the steps to my house in my mind.

Slowly and carefully, I go back the way I came. After a few steps, I need to rest. I do the same a few times and now feel so sure-footed that I start walking faster.

I'm a few steps from the house when I stumble and fall flat. The snowdrift gives way a little beneath me; I'm not hurt, but watch the buckets roll down the slope toward the seashore. Finally they stop, gape at each other in lonely silence, dark brown in the white snow, with the blue-gray, sleeping sea behind them.

I lie there unmoving in the snow, arms outstretched, looking at the buckets. It feels good to rest in this position; I don't want to get up. I lick the snow and think.

Then I hear the snow crunching behind me, Kára's voice: "Get up, you poor thing, and go into the house. I'll bring the water to you."

The white jug of lukewarm milk was there every morning, framed by the window with the elf city as a backdrop, but Karitas never managed to wake up early enough to thank Kára for her trouble. She didn't stir in the slightest when Kára came in; that woman must do the milking in the dead of night. It struck Karitas that, without Kára, she would probably wither away, as she got the milk and the water, which often lasted for several days when there were no large washings to be done. Karitas had just finished mixing the dark brown color to paint the buckets, deciding to make them darker than they really were in order to create greater contrast, when she realized that it would be most convenient to put the clotheslines down where the buckets had come to rest. A large washing was needed, and as a woman, she could hardly ask Kára to do it for her, even though she had washed Sigmar's clothes when he was single. She would be considered a show-off or a wretch, if not both. It might have been different had she been a lady in a distinguished home, or the astute wife of a parish administrator in Skagafjörður who had her maids scrub away on washboards. But Karitas was neither, and it was time to wash the duvet covers. She would probably have to boil them in the old pot on the coal stove, if she could lift that blasted thing. And where was she supposed to hang them to dry? It was out of the question to bring white, clean laundry to that stinking storehouse, where oilskins had been kept for years; she didn't want that stench getting in the fabric. Best would be to find some string and hang the clothes up between the buildings. Somehow, she had to figure this out, which she certainly ought to be able to do, experienced washerwoman that she was. She looked at the hands that had washed all those heavy loads of laundry in Akureyri back in the day, and then at the brush resting in those same hands, and it dawned on her that it was clotheslines, and not art, that occupied her mind. The old masters would never have let such a thing happen.

She sat there like someone condemned to death, wondering if she had lost her mind. Was she focused on art, after all—or were there artists who thought of clotheslines? Could one be a true artist if one's mind and heart weren't always on art? She sat there pondering these questions until her back felt so stiff that she had to get up. "This just won't do," she said bitterly. "I'm getting nothing done." She laid the palette on the table so that she could keep her left hand pressed to her lower back as she painted, and was struggling with the coloring of the snow when a new thought struck her: Of course! I'll have him turn the storehouse into a laundry room.

The sun reddened the windows, as it had done for a full seven days, and Karitas let it caress her face, grayish pale from the December darkness. It wasn't until the sun had begun to shine again that she noticed how much she had missed it, yet she hadn't celebrated its return with a "sun coffee," despite that custom being imprinted on her soul since childhood, and she felt slightly ashamed of her laziness. Of course, she'd been craving crepes but just couldn't bring herself to make the dough—apart from how sad it would be to have sun coffee alone. So she just kept working as if nothing had changed. "If I'm going to hold an exhibition, I've got to have material to choose from"—but she avoided thinking about when that exhibition might be, and in fact avoided thinking about what might become of her—"in any case, right now I have peace and quiet to paint, and I had better take advantage of it." Which was what she did. The sun had given her energy despite her hardly having set foot outside her door; it was the light in the sitting room that made the difference, so quiet and warm. It made it easier to concentrate; she didn't feel lonely, despite being alone, and she had also begun to chat with the little one inside her. It felt more natural with each passing day, and the peaceful atmosphere did her good—it was nice to hear the surf, the ravens, and the sheep in their shed bleating with wanderlust.

When she heard a gruff female voice in the distance, she could scarcely believe her ears. Feeling as if the voice were a harbinger of disturbance and unrest, she instinctively screwed the caps back on the tubes of paint, as if she feared that someone would tinker with them. Then she looked out the west window.

A woman on a gray horse, along with five others on foot, had stopped at Kára's well, and together they were looking around for a trodden path, regarding her house like troops surveilling land to be occupied. A cart was attached to the horse, and the woman on the horse was giving orders while the others stood silently. Karitas peered at them. She was unable to distinguish their faces but saw them raise shovels, making ready to clear away the snow from the well to her house so that the cart could get through. She couldn't make out their faces until they were a short distance from her door, shaking their light red locks in the winter sun. Karitas quickly removed the painting from the easel, placed it in a corner alongside the painting of the blue jug, turned them both to the wall and moved the easel, but didn't manage to gather up the tubes of paint. What should I serve them? she thought in horror as she tidied up.

Högna and her five daughters crashed down on Karitas like a huge wave, dragging her with them into a swirling river and washing her back ashore, dazed and exhausted. They tore boxes and bundles from off the cart, and when Karitas stepped hesitantly into the farmyard with her hand over her mouth, Högna said: "Well, dear, I have come to make clothing for you," speaking as if she had come alone. She blathered incessantly while the daughters carried in the luggage. Hers was a hand-powered sewing machine, not one with a foot pedal, as she could see, but plans had been made to order a pedal-driven one from the capital after the fishing season, which Karitas mustn't trumpet all over the village, because then others would just buy their own, "and goodness gracious, Sigmar lives nicely. Where did he get hold of this pretty cupboard and fine dinnerware? You didn't bring it from Reykjavík, did you?" Without waiting for an answer, she pointed suspiciously at the paints and brushes covering the table: "This will have to go," she said, as if it were rotten meat or worse, and Karitas hurriedly cleared the table to make room for the sewing machine. Högna wanted the table from the kitchen, too; less than that wouldn't do for her to be able to cut and sew, and when her daughters had moved the table into the correct position, the whole house sprang into motion like an old clock that has been cleaned and ticks away the hours like new. Karitas stood in the middle of the room and watched the feverish activity, unable to do a thing about it. They were like flies, now here and now there, behind her or in front of her; sometimes she turned in circles, trying to follow what they were doing. One sat down straightaway at the sewing machine and began to hem diapers, another took out knitting needles and cast on a baby's sweater, the third soaked laundry, the fourth began to scrub the floor and walls, the fifth rummaged in her cupboards and then started making crepes.

She needn't have worried about what to serve them with coffee.

And all of this they did without being told. The one in charge stood there thoughtfully, holding fabric for a dress, muttering and saying "mm-hmm" and "ah-ha" to herself, until finally, she asked: "Would you like your morning dress to be brown or blue, or would you perhaps prefer it to be green?" But she didn't wait for an answer, and instead, put her hands on Karitas's belly, poked at it, and pressed it: "Yes, it's a boy, it's best that you have blue." Then she pulled out a tape measure, measured Karitas back and front, reeled off her measurements without writing them down, and said: "Well, you can sit down for a bit," and Karitas sat down with an exasperated look, like a visitor in her own home.

The daughters acted as if she weren't present; if they happened to meet her gaze, they turned up their noses and looked peevishly in the other direction. If, now and then, they hadn't answered their mother when she called out to them without so much as a glance in their direction—"Erlendína, coffee! Magnúsína, scissors!"—Karitas would have thought they were foreign on both their father's and mother's side and didn't understand Icelandic. So incredibly alike they were, with their light red hair, white eyebrows, and aquamarine eyes, that Karitas had the hardest time telling them apart. She stared at them, and when Högna saw this, she gave Karitas something of a mischievous look, as if she enjoyed witnessing her confusion. Her heavy eyelids over sprightly eyes lent her that look, but she said nothing, and when she said nothing, no one else did, either, so Karitas tried conversing with her. She couldn't really think of anything to say, though, so she asked, just to break the silence, if she knew Kára at the next farm over. "Everyone knows Kára," said Högna. "She's a bit unsociable," said Karitas. "She has nothing to say to others and never comes out of that cat cottage of hers," replied Högna. Hoping for a fateful story, Karitas asked if something had happened to her at some point, but Högna said, "That's precisely the problem; not a single thing has ever happened to her. She has never had anyone and never lost anyone." Karitas, however, pressed on: "But she must be fond of Sigmar; otherwise she wouldn't feed his sheep and milk his cow." "She isn't fond of him at all," Högna spat. "It was his mother she was fond of." "Oh, well now," said Karitas. "And you must also have been a friend of his mother's?" "We were all her friends. She fished, helped with births, directed theater performances, and walked alone over the heaths in snowstorms in the dead of winter, when the men didn't dare. She was a great woman, and was mourned by us all."

"Winter here is very snowy."

"The summers are immensely beautiful."

"Was his father so robust, too?"

"He was a kind man and well liked by all, but when he drank, he could disappear for months, as happened one year when he said that he was going to Seyðisfjörður, but apparently ended up in Scotland. He had a kind of wanderlust in him, the dear man. He would sit for long stretches down by the Kiðubjörg cliffs and stare out at the sea, as if there were something to see on it. In the last years of his life, he was a miserable wretch, having suffered an internal ailment for years. But he never complained. No, we here in Borgarfjörður never complain, as we've always had enough to eat."

From the kitchen came endless refreshments: the crepes were placed on the table, and Karitas had hardly gotten a few of them down before dinner was served. By then, the hemmed diapers had been laid in a pile; a baby-sized cardigan had been knitted, and two dresses cut and stitched together. "And now, undress," said Högna, and when Karitas was standing there in her slip, all of the daughters, as one, stopped working and lined up around her, cornering her as hunters do their prey, and after Högna had slipped one of the stitched-together dresses over her head and they knelt to check the length and pin up the hem, she suddenly felt as if they were ladies-in-waiting and she a noblewoman. She shut her eyes and enjoyed standing there idly and letting others fuss over her, relishing the fantasy of her royal role. And then it was over. She washed back ashore. The visitors packed up their things just as quickly as they had unpacked them, put on their coats and bundled themselves warmly, but left behind the day's yield and the sewing machine. "I'll be back tomorrow to finish the dresses," Högna said, kissing Karitas fleetingly on the forehead before disappearing into the moonlit night with her horse and the ladies-in-waiting.

Karitas made sketches of the sewing machine. She had been contemplating its form all day, wondering how best to shape and exaggerate it without losing its quiet character, the unobtrusiveness of its soft, curved lines, the rebelliousness of the handle on the handwheel, which spun her life round and round. She moved the easel back into its place in the middle of the room, took out her tools, nailed canvas onto the third and largest frame, and sketched the outlines of the machine, filling the entire picture plane. Then she sat idly as she thought about the machine's black color. The light had faded; she refilled all the lamps and lined them up around her, as if enclosing herself within a wall of flame, and went on the attack with the color black, which, in itself, was no color. She had to rest a few times over the course of the night, not because she was sleepy, but because of the ache that reached from her belly to her back. No sooner had she lain down and begun massaging her belly on both sides than the kicking began. Was this child going to be a night owl? she wondered, because it never moved more than in the evenings and nights, just when she would rather not have to talk to it. She felt as if her bump had expanded at an alarming rate in recent days—the new clothes were being made in the nick of time. Then she remembered the cardigan and diapers that lay folded in the cupboard, and she went and got the cardigan, which was artfully knitted, ocher yellow. "It's for you," she told the night owl.

She painted for as long as she could remain standing, but sometime toward morning, when she wanted to rest for a moment, she fell fast asleep with the turpentine cloth in her hands. When she opened her eyes, the first thing she saw was a white milk jug on the kitchen table. All but one of the lamps had been extinguished. She gulped down the milk, relit all the lamps, and painted until day began to dawn. Then she carried the painting to the window, scrutinized the color in the daylight, lay down for a while to think, and fell asleep again.

A loud banging startled her from sleep.

The seamstress had returned, but this time she was alone. She had taken off her coat and was staring at the easel as if she couldn't believe her own eyes. "Is that supposed to be my sewing machine?" she asked, not even looking at Karitas to make sure that she was awake and able to answer. Karitas dragged herself to her feet and began gathering her things, but Högna continued reproachfully: "But this is just a black splotch, my dear. Can't you paint better than that—trained artist and all?" Karitas had heard similar comments before and knew that it was pointless to start explaining different types of artistic expression to Högna, let alone trends and movements, so she held back, but still, the woman's words stung, and she grew annoyed with herself because of it. Doubts about whether she was on the right track harangued her, and the purpose of it all became unclear. If people didn't like her pictures, it made no sense to keep going, she thought as Högna started up the sewing machine and blathered about the colorful mountains she should paint instead. She had heard that that was what real artists painted—it would never occur to them to paint insignificant things, and least of all sewing machines. Not that her machine wasn't lovely and well worth painting, but it would have to be done properly, with the machine depicted as it truly was—masterfully built. She turned the handwheel deftly in order to emphasize her sewing expertise, while Karitas went out to the farmyard to compose herself. They spoke not a word to each other over the next hour, as if both were a bit put out, one because of the remarks about her work, the other because of the work itself. Karitas had made coffee for Högna and served her bread and pâté, too, because seamstresses need to be fed regularly, her mother had said when Jenný made dresses for her back in the day, and the light was beginning to fade when she finally sat down across from her with her sketchbook.

She knew from experience that women didn't appreciate artistic liberties when it came to their own faces, so she refrained from sketching Högna's portrait in the way that she herself would have preferred, and instead, put herself in the shoes of the old masters when they painted distinguished noblewomen, refining her subject's features, beautifying them, more than anything, lifting her eyes, exaggerating the contours of her lips, filling out her cheeks, making her younger by around twenty years. Högna must have been pretty in her younger years, she thought, and she shaded the portrait and took great care with it. The Högna of twenty years older went on sewing energetically, having come quite far with the second dress, but it was obvious from her movements that she knew she was being portrayed on paper and felt a bit insecure about the situation, as if she feared that her comment about the black splotch could have unpleasant consequences.

Without a word, Karitas handed her the portrait.

Högna took the picture impassively, prepared for the worst, but uttered a half-suppressed cry of joy when she saw herself. As if she herself were masterfully built. She groped at her face, hemmed and chuckled to herself. She rolled up the picture, tied a piece of thread around it, and stuck it in her bag. She said not a word about the picture in and of itself, but was chatty while helping Karitas put on the finished dresses, wanting, of course, praise and compliments for her handiwork, which she got, because seamstresses must be praised especially, her mother had said, and as they admired the workmanship, Högna had a great deal to say about art, reiterating that Karitas should turn to painting mountains, she would have no difficulty doing so, and asked whether she had seen the altarpiece in the church that their local artist had painted—the mountains on it were so beautiful. And speaking of the church, why hadn't Karitas come to mass with Sigmar at Christmas, nor to the play that was put on between Christmas and New Year? "I had a part in that play," she said disappointedly, and it took Karitas a long time to convince her that it was neither a lack of faith nor interest that had been the reason for her absence, but quite simply, a lack of clothing. Högna understood this, having often been in a similar situation. "And often having had no time to sew anything for myself," she said. But as they were loading the sewing machine onto the cart, Högna couldn't refrain from telling Karitas about the play, the audience's warm response to it, and the dance afterward.

"Oh, you don't say, was there a dance afterward?" said Karitas. "And did Sigmar dance?"

"Of course Sigmar danced, he dances better than anyone else in all of Borgarfjörður, if not in the whole country. You should already know that."

But she didn't know that. There was the rub.

Karitas had thought that she would be so happy when all this hustle and bustle was over and she could return to her work in peace and quiet, but as she stood watching the seamstress ride off with her sewing machine, she was seized with a feeling of emptiness, and it was a long time before she could bring herself to go back inside. She wanted to be among other people, listen to them, watch them eat, see them dance. Lonely and distracted, she went to bed, thinking to herself that it was probably best to head off to dreamland; tomorrow would be a new day, and then she would be herself again. But sleep was reluctant; she lay awake until the early hours of the morning, fighting back bitter thoughts.

Worst of all for her was that he had danced.

She felt that he had no business dancing when she herself couldn't. Because it was largely his fault that she was in this state. And he would probably do some dancing this fishing season; she was quite certain that the girls in the Westman Islands knew how to dance. As she lay there alone and abandoned, not yet twenty-four years of age, Karitas whimpered into the darkness and was kicked from within, as if someone were agreeing with her. She wouldn't even get hot chocolate on her birthday, which she always got from her mother, and this thought made her miss her mother so badly that she could no longer hold back her tears. The kicking in her belly now began in earnest, distracting her from her tears, and after she'd composed herself a little, she wondered whether she shouldn't just pack her things and go home to her mother. That would serve him right. She could see it so clearly in her mind: Sigmar coming home to discover that the bird had flown. She liked this idea so much that she stopped her whimpering, that is, until she thought of the sea voyage to Reykjavík, not to mention the shame that she would bring upon her mother by returning home unmarried and pregnant, after all that her mother had taken upon herself to raise her children. She began crying again, until she had had enough. "I can't allow myself to behave like this. I'm an adult," she said to the little night owl, but at the same time, she knew that she wasn't yet an adult, because if she were, she wouldn't behave like that.

The ravens made a racket on her roof. They couldn't find food in the hard frost and kept her awake with their hoarse croaking. She felt like shutting them up by tossing them a few pieces of meat, but couldn't bring herself to do so; she just stared at the cupboard where the meat was kept. In the moonlight, she could see all the way into the kitchen, but her old fear of the dark retained its hold on her. She thought she heard noises, footsteps, and one night, she felt as if someone whispered something in her ear. In the morning, she was certain that it had just been a wooshing in her ears, one of those annoying side effects of pregnancy, but then it happened again, leaving her feeling a bit frightened of falling asleep. Maybe it was best to let the ravens croak as long as possible.

But they began making even more of a racket than before, until finally, she could no longer bear their noise, got hurriedly out of bed, but stopped first to pee in her chamber pot—she felt like she always had to pee—put on a sweater, and stuck her feet in a pair of wool socks.

When she entered the kitchen, she could feel the warmth from the coal stove, put her hands on it for a second, and then pulled out the plate of meat, intending to cut some of it into smaller pieces for those dratted ravens, for which she felt a bit sorry even if they did keep her from sleeping, but then she looked out the window. The moon was reflected in the snow's frozen crust, as if it were an ice-covered pond, and before her towered the black elf city. She thought she saw something moving by the rock face, but assumed it must be horses grazing and continued to cut up the meat, not even needing to light a lamp to do so, but it suddenly struck her that horses could not be grazing in the hard-frozen snow, and she looked out again.

Five women came walking out of the rock face.

They walked side by side, wearing long gray dresses with large black collars, and on their heads peculiar white coverings, with upward-curving front and back edges.

She stood there gobsmacked, staring at them. Who could be out and about so late, dressed that way, and where were they going? They walked briskly. At first, it looked as if they were going down to the shore, but then she realized they were headed toward her. She threw down her knife in horror, rushed aimlessly back and forth, not knowing whether she should leave or stay. She felt that she needed to hide, but nowhere seemed safe, and at last, she tore open the front door, ran to the cowshed and into the cow's stall, and sat trembling on the milking stool. The cow raised her head, looked at her with big sleepy eyes, seeming to recall that it was still a long time until milking, uncertain whether she should clamber to her feet or not. Karitas stroked and patted her hurriedly, shushed her, and it was as if the cow understood that she should keep quiet.

They waited in silence and looked each other in the eyes.

Time passed; she heard only the rhythmic rolling of the waves below the shore ridge. The ravens made not a sound. She didn't dare go back into the house but remained leaning against the stall's wall, trying to keep as close as possible to the cow. They dozed together until morning. She was startled from sleep by a nudge. Kára helped her to her feet without asking what she was doing out in the cowshed so early in the morning. She simply wanted her milking stool. "I was seeing things and became so frightened," Karitas said through chattering teeth. Kára didn't reply at first, but as Karitas shambled out, she said: "I'll loan you two cats."

"Cats? What for?"

"They keep them at bay."

She waddled down to the Co-op and bought coffee, which she herself didn't drink because it made her pulse race and gave her heartburn, but she wanted to have it in her house like a normal person, along with raisins, which she simply couldn't do without. She could eat raisins with a mixture of cream and milk at every meal. In fact, it was all the same to her whether she ate nothing else, and as she wandered home again, she thought about the looks that the women outside the Co-op had given her; they weren't the same fleeting glances as before the New Year, but rather, longer or even shy gazes, as if she were an important person. She was still wondering about this when someone called to her from a one-story wooden house.

It was a young woman with a crowd of children around her. Some of them stood in the doorway, others were out on the steps, and the young woman said, "Good morning, aren't you Sigmar's Karitas?" and Karitas said, "Yes, of course," but found it strange hearing the words "Sigmar's Karitas." And the woman said: "I'm his cousin, my name is Karlína, and I'm married to Þorfinnur, who left for the fishing with your Sigmar," and Karitas had never heard anyone say that before, "your Sigmar," but she liked hearing that he had gone fishing with a family man, meaning that he might not be larking about so much, and Karlína continued: "And I'm going to lend you my cradle. I'm not expecting at the moment; don't you need a cradle?" Karitas hadn't thought about it and felt slightly ashamed. She had imagined having the child in bed with her, but, of course, all normal people had a cradle, so she said, since this woman was so closely related to Sigmar, "Yes, thank you, I'll gladly accept your cradle." The young woman came all the way up to her, with her full bosom and a child on her arm, plump cheeks, warm, genial eyes, her hair as auburn as Sigmar's, looked searchingly at Karitas's stomach and asked, "Do you think that you can hold it in until he comes home shortly after Closing Day?"

"I really hope so," stammered Karitas, relieved that someone had brought this up, as she'd been worried about it herself. Karlína said, smiling broadly: "You can expect it to take a few days; it took me four days to deliver my first." They looked straight at each other. Karitas felt that she had hardly ever seen such a cheerful face, and imagined that it could be quite complicated to draw, to capture its joy on paper. As if Karlína had read her mind, she leaned in closer and whispered: "Listen, do you think you could draw me when I bring the cradle?" Karitas couldn't refuse, seeing as how the woman was going to lend her a cradle—and then Karlína added: "If you suddenly start having contractions while you're all alone, hang a white sheet in the window. I'll have someone keep an eye on your house."

As if a siege were impending.

The surf brought solace when Karitas's shortness of breath became almost too much to bear; it was as if the pressure on her sternum lightened when she looked at the waves, and she did breathing exercises in the morning while emptying the chamber pot, the salty spray hitting her face as she drew in as much of the raw, cold air as she could before going back in to the cats. At night, they lay on her feet or nestled in the hollows that formed on the bedspread depending on how she was lying, and stared grimly. During the day, they settled on the divan in the sitting room, one at each end, lying there like a pair of Egyptian lions with their chins on their forepaws and their yellow eyes closed. At those times, they seemed a little less dismissive, and she chatted with them, asking their opinions about her choices of colors, telling them how tiring it was to be pregnant—"which you both probably know already. I'm sure I don't need to enlighten you about that side of life, but don't you think this will end up being just a black splotch?"

Högna had started bringing her fish. She came on horseback twice a week, saying that she didn't feel like trudging down to her house. She never dismounted, just gave Karitas's belly a good looking-over from on high and asked if everything was all right. Karitas said yes, apart from everything going full steam inside of her, and one day when she said she felt as if her stomach had dropped and detached from her sternum, which made it easier to breathe, Högna said with a frown that it was nearly time. And after Högna handed down this verdict, more and more people began showing up in the vicinity of the house. Kára was always prowling about; Karitas saw her here and there with a cat on her shoulder, at the sheep shed, up on the hill, and down by the sea. Little boys began frequenting the shore, adolescent girls sat on the rocks, all positioned so that they could keep an eye on her house. She felt as if she were being kept under constant surveillance.

One night when she had trouble sleeping, which happened less frequently once the cats began standing watch over her soul, Karitas dragged herself out of bed. The spring night had driven away the blackest darkness, and she went out to breathe in the surf, as she put it to the cats. She had only been standing for a moment down at the shore ridge when she felt as if a dart had been shot from the lower part of her stomach up her back. "It's coming," she said on the verge of tears, before going back inside the house, doubled over and holding her belly in her hands. She sat down on the edge of the bed and rocked forward and back. The cats grew restless, glanced to the right and left, jumped off the bed, and lay down on the divan in the living room. She tried frantically to recall stories of childbirth, how the contractions came prior to delivery, but couldn't remember any apart from the one that her mother had told as they circled the country those years ago, and that recollection only filled her with anxiety. Her mother had started having contractions, and then they just shot out, the sisters; one landed in the potato patch, and the other on the shore. However, she recalled that Halldóra, the first child, had come out on the bed, which was a bit of a relief—but then she began thinking of her sister Halldóra, who had of course been a midwife out here in the east, and she missed her so much and her mother, too; it would have been so good to have them both by her side, and she started to cry. The next contraction came much later, after she'd been bawling and lamenting her misfortune for a long time, and she still had no idea what to do. She dared not move for fear that the child would come. Toward morning, however, she pulled herself together, despite being so tired she could barely keep her eyes open, tore the sheet off her bed, and hung it from her window. "At least I tried," she said before crawling into bed and falling fast asleep. She woke with the sun in her eyes and a strange woman leaning over her. She heard footsteps and women's voices, and the woman who had pulled the duvet off her and had both hands on her stomach said firmly: "This will take some time, my dear."

The white sheet had mustered an army of women. They waltzed freely about her home: Kára, Högna, and Karlína, two women she didn't recognize, and then the one who had woken her, the midwife herself. Why they were all there, apart from the midwife, she had no idea, but as the day went by, she came to understand that they were in the habit of gathering when a woman was delivering, considering it their sacred duty to provide whatever assistance was needed. And despite the fact that they gave her porridge to eat, washed her high and low, changed her bedding, and kept track of all the labor pains that came and went, Karitas felt a bit as if she were an uninvited guest at their merry gathering. They chatted and laughed in the sitting room, drank enormous amounts of coffee, told endless comical stories about themselves and others. Now and then, they called to her, told her to grit her teeth, that's what they were there for, and then laughed loudly. Sometimes they came to her, stroked her gently, told her to try to sleep between contractions and not to worry, they would take care of everything; and she wanted to believe them, even if she knew better. Karlína whispered: "Try to hold it in a little longer. Sigmar is on his way," and she tried her best, without having any idea what one could do to delay the process. Over the course of the evening, they went home one by one, saying that they needed to go feed their families—apart from Högna and Kára, who stayed put, as if they had been ordered by a higher power to watch over the expectant mother, while the midwife yawned and went to lie down in the sitting room. Calm fell over the house; Karitas remained in bed, safe under the supervision of the two women despite her constant discomfort. She was deeply nervous, and sweaty on her back and between her thighs. Still, she tried to sleep, but after midnight, woke with a start, no longer able to hear the surf. The utter silence outside and in was ominous, and she waddled into the sitting room, where the three women were sleeping either lying down or sitting up, and called out: "Have the breakers stopped?" As one, the women jumped up and bumped into each other, confused and still in another world; just as they moved to get her into bed again, she felt a stinging pain and moaned, and therewith, the little night owl began its painful journey into the world's light.

The contractions were unusually severe; with sweat beading her forehead, the midwife said again and again: "This child is too big, this child is too big, what have you been eating the last few months?" "Raisins and cream, day in and day out," Kára answered dryly. Karitas screamed at every throe, and whimpered in between: "Let me die, just let me die," and Högna, bathed in sweat and trembling, shushed her. "Stop your shouting, woman, you'll wake the whole neighborhood," but Karitas could not have cared less even if she woke the dead. She was being torn apart from the inside and below, and she screamed until her voice failed. But finally, he slipped out; a crinkled little thing. Three days after Closing Day—right on schedule. The midwife, practiced and confident, got the baby to cry, as her assistants sat down on the stools, shaking and exhausted.

The boy was washed and examined.

"He's the spitting image of Sigmar," said Högna and Kára. They gazed raptly at him. "God is so good; He makes them look like their fathers at birth, and then they become like us," the midwife said. Karitas stared at her son as he was laid in her arms, newly cleansed. She tried as best she could to detect a resemblance to her mother, her sisters, brothers, even her father who was long gone, but didn't see the slightest sign of any relationship between the child and his family. "Still, your name will be Jón," she muttered. Then the women took this Jón-to-be, laid him in the cradle, and let the mother sleep.

In her slumber, she seemed to sense his arrival. She was aware of his movements, his smell, and before she opened her eyes, she knew that he would be standing at her bedside. And so he was. He was winded, as if he had been running; he was tanned, almost weather-beaten, but beautiful as ever. And just as always, she longed to draw him as soon as she saw him, but didn't say so. Sigmar bent down and said softly: "My little one?"

And she said: "We need poles for the clotheslines."

Karitas

Laundry at Sunrise 1924

Oil on canvas

The sun comes up from the sea.

The water's surface is mahogany red.

The sky is dark violet.

Both colors grow lighter, so slowly that we don't discern it, but we can feel our minds becoming clearer with each minute, until it leaves us, is sucked into the beam of light that formed on the tranquil sea, shoots into that flaming golden fireball.

Happiness fills our minds.

We sit at the cliffs, hold hands, watch the sunrise. Sigmar's hand is warm and big, in his arms rests Jón, bundled in a woolen blanket.

The morning is mild and wonderful.

Then the sun rises, as majestic as a fairy-tale princess who wakens from a spell.

The fjord and the mountains become jewels.

We are as if hypnotized, hardly daring to breathe as this sublimely beautiful work of creation takes place.

Finally, I turn my head, look toward the countryside, see the elf city glow, our house rose gold at the mouth of the river and my laundry on the clotheslines, yellow and cheerful.

It flutters in the morning breeze, light and playful, its shapes so amusing, seen from the cliffs.

Sigmar had put up four clothesline poles in a square, which I'd never seen done before, but I hung the laundry on all the lines, and now it reminds me of cheery children doing a ring dance. I give a little chirp of delight; Sigmar thinks it's because of the sun, and says: "Karitas, now you must paint some pictures of the sunrise, the sea, and the mountains." "Yes," I answer, "and then I'll send Mama a few of them in gratitude for the clothing and the duvet covers she sent Jón." He likes this idea very much, but I look at the duvet covers and sweaters belonging to Jón, Sigmar, and myself leading each other in their ring dance on the clotheslines, and know very well what it is I will paint.

We've been sitting on the cliff for a long time when it occurs to me that I've forgotten yet again to take the laundry down before bed.

It wasn't little Jón who bothered her—he slept all day and night—but the women who were constantly on the move from house to house. The higher the sun rose in the sky, the busier they became, which meant endless comings and goings and chatter. They stopped to see Karitas, some with whole groups of children in tow, such as Karlína, or with neighbor women at their heels, such as Högna, and they all wanted to know how little Jón was doing, whether he needed anything. She was extremely grateful to them for their concern, but sighed to herself because the constant stream of visitors meant endless coffee brewing and bread baking. Luckily, Kára was always just around the corner when the disturbance was at its worst; she would show up without warning in the kitchen and be kneading dough with a pained expression long before Karitas had even given a thought to doing so. "I don't understand why they're so keen on visiting me now. They didn't come this winter when I was alone," Karitas complained to Sigmar, because she never found any time to paint, and his only explanation was that they probably would have liked to have come, but hadn't felt comfortable doing so without a real reason or having something to talk about, and little Jón provided them with both. Sigmar himself had business with many people, or rather, many did with him, it being the busiest time of the year: rowing out to fish every day, cleaning the fish and salting it, haymaking in between, and the men were both hungry and thirsty and turned up in the kitchens every chance they got. Karitas's kitchen was no exception, and no one would have imagined her to be dabbling with her brushes at this time of year.

One morning when Sigmar was out fishing and she was finally painting, having gotten a good hold on her subject after several days of mental wrangling, Högna and one of the other women from the village appeared in her doorway, smiling buoyantly. Taking a little break from their chores, they had come to bring her some first-rate rhubarb jam they had made and were gobsmacked to see what she was up to. They asked in astonishment what she was doing, and Karitas replied that she was working. "Oh, indeed," they said evasively, as if they had caught her in the act of some impropriety, which, for her sake, they would keep quiet about, and then they took off their coats and made themselves at home. Later, after she had served them coffee and listened to them talk about their lives and some women up in the valley whom she didn't know and in whom she had no interest whatsoever, Högna's friend, who, like Högna, had avoided looking at the easel, now turned to Karitas and said: "Yes, things are so busy at the moment that I couldn't even imagine trying to sit down to embroider or the like, what with all the chores—it will just have to wait until winter, my dear." When they finally left after a nearly three-hour visit, Karitas felt entirely drained of strength. She sat down and stared at the baby in the cradle.

Little Jón slept. Sometimes she wondered whether it was normal that the child could sleep for so long, and often tested his reflexes to make sure that he was still alive, tickling his cheek and mouth, which he would then open wide, thinking that he was going to get a sip of milk, but when nothing came out of the finger, his lower lip began to quiver. But he didn't cry, little Jón. "He's a real man, just like his father," Sigmar said proudly, but Karitas could never look for long at the baby's little lip quivering. She breastfed him. "A remarkable child," muttered Kára, who, following the birth, was frequently there outside of milking time, having taken upon herself so many of the household chores, slipping silently in and out like a housefly but always stopping for a moment or two to peek into the cradle, slipping her hands under the baby's duvet and rubbing his little feet. "Women of her age appreciate children who are as silent as cats," Sigmar said, as if he had years of experience with elderly women. But it was much the same with him as with Kára; he returned from fishing and stormed in without so much as a "hello" for Karitas, went straight to the cradle, stared, stroked the baby's little head, sighed and said: "This child looks exactly like me." Did you expect otherwise? Karitas wanted to say, and it occurred to her that it might not be so easy to be a man and never be able to be one hundred percent sure when a woman was telling the truth about her baby's paternity.

In a letter that her mother had sent along with the baby gifts, she recommended that Karitas marry Sigmar. "I don't know what merits the father of your child possesses, but he must be thrifty, seeing as how he is saving up for a boat, and as long as he has no penchant for drinking or dissipation, you should marry him." But she wasn't at all certain that she would or could. The man had never proposed to her formally; it couldn't be considered courtship when a man said, while yawning into the wind: "Would you like to get married?" As if she were some old maid who needed to tie the knot posthaste. If he wanted to marry her, he could propose to her in the conventional way. But she wasn't entirely sure she would say yes. If she did, she would become a sailor's wife, which wasn't a fate she coveted. His whole life revolved around the sea and that boat he was planning to own. "After the next fishing season, I'll have enough money for it," he'd declared, and then been surprised when she didn't react happily to that news—though he'd forgotten that she'd asked him numerous times to buy a new pot, which was much more of a pressing need. And that was how their lives would be: as soon as he had bought that four-ton boat, he would probably save up for a fifty-ton boat, "because I'm not going to keep fishing from other men's boats all my life," and she would still have no new pot. That was what their conversations in bed were about—the boats he intended to buy. "A larger house and lots of children," he sometimes added as he lay there, splayed out over the bed, but he never mentioned her work or how she should find the time to paint in a large house full of children. Yet he was the only one who admired her pictures, whether they were naturalistic images of the sunrise and the child in the cradle, like the one intended for her mother, or avant-garde, abstract pieces that he didn't understand at all. "You are the greatest painter in this country," he occasionally said, enthralled, even breathless, and she ate up his flattery, even though she sometimes had the suspicion that he didn't know nearly as much about painting as he'd initially let on. After such praise, she became extremely coy and docile when he became amorous, and even showed interest in his intended boat purchase and planned house extension, but when he came tramping in with a line of men behind him, those with whom he went to sea, did the haymaking, or planned to have help him with the house extension, and demanded coffee and bread for all of them at once, despite her standing there with her brush and palette in hand, she felt furious. Still, she never dared to show her displeasure openly, for fear of getting a bad reputation or something even worse, whatever that might be. At such moments, she had no desire to spend the rest of her life with him. And when people began to suggest that she could let Kára take care of the boy and come out to salt and spread the saltfish to dry, that it would do her good to move a little and be in the company of other young women, she was terrified. Did they expect her to sacrifice her hands to the salt yet again, and didn't she have enough to think about, what with her child and home, along with her painting? She was also supposed to go and salt fish? To show Sigmar how serious the situation was, she got up out of bed in the middle of the night and started painting. "What are you doing, Karitas?" he shouted sleepily into the sitting room. "I'm working," she snapped. "Since I don't get any peace to do so during the day." "Oh, my little one," he sighed. "You can paint in the winter, when I leave for the fishing."

When he was at his most boisterous, she looked forward to his departure in the winter, despite it being many months away. But then the thought also crossed her mind that since she was looking forward to being rid of him, she could hardly care for him very much. As she was doing her chores, Karitas racked her brain over her vague longings, and sometimes, when she was sitting on the bed feeding Jón, she lost herself in daydreams, toying with the idea of traveling to Reykjavík and setting up an atelier. Her mother would surely welcome her grandchild with open arms, and while her mother looked after Jón, she herself would be able to paint. If people didn't want her real work, she would doubtless be able to support herself doing portraits, and even if those kinds of paintings bored her, she would simply put up with it. Perhaps she could save enough money for a trip to Rome. See all the works of art that her colleagues in Copenhagen had told her about. She saw them in her mind's eye, and saw all the palaces and ancient monuments, the cypress and olive trees, the fruits ripening in the orchards, and the people who, according to what she had been told, were so beautiful, so jovial and fond of singing. Apparently, this was due to the sun's shining there day in and day out; they couldn't help but sing in so much sunshine. She envisioned herself enjoying the good life, dressed in summer clothes and smiling, and she thought so long and hard about Rome that she forgot about little Jón, who made the best of the situation, breastfed twice and slumbered blissfully in between. Sigmar never appeared in her daydreams, never once even walked the streets of Rome with her. She took this as a sign that she would have to walk those paths alone. It would probably be best if she left for Reykjavík late in the winter, while he was still away fishing; it would stir up the least trouble. And then she could inform him in a letter that she no longer loved him. But that he could visit Jón whenever it suited him. Or her. So certain she was of how she felt about Sigmar at those moments that she was dumbfounded when the opposite came to light.

At that time, the sun was shining in the middle of the night, which it apparently never did in Rome, and everyone gathered to sing and dance. As usual, though, the gathering began with speeches and debates, and ended with dancing and carousing until morning. Fun and dancing were Sigmar's cup of tea, not least after debates, which he enjoyed listening to, despite having no interest in participating himself—"It's mostly just useless blather about nothing"—but Karitas was unenthusiastic about attending these gatherings, and least of all with her breasts bursting with milk. So, when Sigmar left, she stayed at home under the evening sun, quite happy with the arrangement; she had set up her easel and spent quite some time making sketches—the clotheslines were still bothering her—when two boys of around twenty appeared in her doorway with a somewhat bewildered Kára between them. The cat had jumped down from her shoulder, apparently unhappy with the idea of being dragged off to a strange home, and the boys said somewhat breathlessly that Sigmar insisted she should come to the community hall right away, and that Kára should look after the boy in the meantime. Karitas was livid: "What's the meaning of this insolence?" In the face of Karitas's reaction, Kára came back to her senses and exclaimed, "Yes, what bluster is this?" The boys were told to clear off back to the village and tell Sigmar Hilmarsson to find some other women besides them to boss around. As the boys moved slowly and embarrassedly out the door, they said that Sigmar had told them to say that if Karitas refused to come with them, he would come there himself, grab her, and carry her back to the village. The two women scoffed.

Kára returned to her cottage, and Karitas resumed painting, despite her agitation. From experience, she knew how determined the man could be; he was used to getting what he wanted. And then he did indeed appear, striding across the farmyard with Kára in tow. Without a word, he dragged the woman to the cradle and let go of her, turned grimacing like a troll to Karitas, grabbed her by the shoulders and backs of her knees, lifted her, and hurried out of the house with her bent double in his arms. She was still holding her pencil. She seethed with rage all the way up to the village; her hair was unbrushed and she was wearing an everyday skirt. She looked at him from the side and thought about how she was going to kill him when this was all over. He tightened his grip as if he knew what she was thinking, but at the same time, stared straight ahead with screwed-up eyes, dashing with her over terrain both easy and tough. A curlew whistled at them, a snipe screeched, dogs leaped to their feet with tongues dangling and trotted friskily after them, and then the dance music resounded from the community hall. A group of partygoers stood outside and took sips from their flasks, and Sigmar tightened his grip even more, ran the last few meters, burst through the group and into the building, stopped in the middle of the room, and put her down on the floor. Karitas jumped to her feet and slapped his face. He ignored her rebuke, grabbed her with both hands by the waistband of her skirt, and whirled her into the dance. She was forced to hold on to his shoulders so as not to stumble.

They danced and sweated, the sun set and rose again, the night was young, and when the accordion player finally gave up, the partygoers went out under the newly woken morning sun; lovers walked hand in hand to the rose-gold cliffs, where they sat down and told each other their dreams. Karitas and Sigmar followed, holding hands shyly as if they were just getting to know each other, saying nothing because they were content and neither wanted to be the first to speak for fear that it might disturb their harmony. As they danced, he had repeatedly whispered in her ear how beautiful she was, how much he desired her and loved her; he knew what he was doing, did Sigmar, and little by little her anger had evaporated. She no longer thought about how she was going to kill him. They sat down under the morning sun like the other couples; she lay down in the grass and felt so free with the endless sky above her. He tickled her face and the soles of her feet with a blade of grass, and then he picked violets, lady's bedstraw, and northern bedstraw and made of them a bouquet, which he handed to her with a deep bow. When the village roosters began to crow, they got up to go. Her bosom was soaking wet by then, and when they reached the farmyard, they could hear Jón's screams. They were both a bit sheepish and surprised, having never heard Jón scream so loud, and Kára was in a rage, having had to hold him in her arms and walk back and forth all night. "I simply don't understand this fiddle-faddle," she exclaimed furiously, referring to the frivolity of the baby's parents, and slammed the door violently as she left. Little Jón had to drink from both breasts, still heaving with sobs and, in between sucking, let loose with angry howls over the neglect to which he'd been subjected. When he was finally full, the other man in the house wanted to do his own breast fondling, which he was eagerly allowed to do, and Karitas was astonished at her own cursed passions.

Then, she could hardly imagine life without Sigmar.

But when the commotion began again in the autumn—he needed to build an extension to the house, go round up the sheep, slaughter the lambs—all of which bustle she was forced to take part in with him, Karitas wished desperately and earnestly that he would depart as soon as possible for the winter fishing, and preferably from her life. And in the midst of all the goings-on, he was in constant contact with men in the capital who were building him a boat, trotting several times a week to the telephone office to keep after them, as he told her when he came home—"Those southerners like to take their bloody time with things, I can tell you"—and knuckled down twice as hard on his own projects after every phone call. One day, he brought home a letter from the post office that did nothing to improve her mood. It was from Bjarghildur, wife of the parish administrator and model housewife. True to form, she began her letter by apologizing for her tardiness in writing; due to all the work that needed doing on such a large farm, she hadn't had a moment's peace to sit down and write until now, but her sister mustn't think that she had forgotten little Jón; she would soon receive a trunk full of clothing that should last him until he was two years old, if not longer. All of the women on the farm had sat down to sew and knit garments for him as soon as they heard news of his birth, although the haymaking had of course complicated things, but the stepsisters had seldom put down their knitting needles, hardworking and God-loving as those two were—"They know all about your struggles, dear sister, and wish to do everything that they possibly can for you, and although it was of course I who provided all the materials, the work is mainly theirs"—and the trunk would come sometime after the slaughter. As the eldest sister and more staid one—this about being more staid, she apparently said more in jest than seriousness—she simply had to admonish her younger sister to perform her housekeeping duties in an exemplary manner, especially during the slaughter, for no matter whether a woman eked out an existence or ran an estate, she must comport herself impeccably; it was her duty to God and her country.

Upon reading this letter, Karitas quivered with anger, though scarcely knowing why. She was mainly angry at herself for letting Bjarghildur upset her. Again without really knowing why, she abruptly asked Sigmar if there was any chance of his cleaning out that stinking storehouse of his and installing a wash copper there. Not knowing what the letter had said, he didn't realize the seriousness of the matter and asked her to be patient; as things stood, everything he earned was going into the boat, and besides, he really had no time to start fiddling with installing a wash copper while he was putting a roof on the house extension. That was all it took. She woke little Jón from his cozy nap and, still in her apron, hurried over to Karlína's. She left the blood-pudding filling lying in a tub in the middle of the floor, the stomachs half-filled and unsewn on all the tables, and told him to slosh in it himself. Two hours later, he came to find them. He stood in front of Karlína's kitchen window without saying a word, and when Karlína opened the window and asked him if it was her he had come to visit, answered reluctantly that she might as well tell Karitas that she could come home; he would get to work installing a damned wash copper that week.

They didn't say another word to each other for the rest of the day, but after going to bed that evening, he blew on her hair to catch her attention and asked what had gotten into her there at the blood-pudding tub. "Nothing got into me," she shot back. "I just want a wash copper like the other women in the village." He didn't find this sufficient explanation, so she added, in order to torment him a little: "I'm not particularly pleased that rumor of how we barely manage to scrape by here has reached as far north as Skagafjörður." He drew a deep breath, let his head drop onto the pillow, and said no more.

Although Sigmar wasn't a man of many words—in general, she often wished that he were a little more talkative—his silence over the next few days was striking. He installed the wash copper silently, put the fresh meat into the barrels and salted it silently, and put the finishing touches on the roof of the extension silently. She called him in for meals and coffee, and he ate and drank in silence. She considered trying to appease him in some way, but every time she saw his icy gaze, she decided against it. "If he wants to say nothing, it's up to him," she told little Jón. "At least then we get some peace and quiet at night." But one morning before daylight, when she wasn't yet fully awake, he stood, fully dressed, leaning over her, and said curtly, as if it didn't matter whether she heard or not: "I'm going up to Hérað to sell fish, and afterward, I'll be going ptarmigan hunting." Not a word more. She was so irritated that she couldn't go back to sleep. "And this he allows himself," she said to little Jón, and repeated the same thing numerous times that day. "And I don't even eat ptarmigan," she said bitterly before getting into bed.

The night after he left to go ptarmigan hunting, she dreamed of a man. It seemed to her as if he was walking toward the house, slowly, as if he were timid by nature. He was a tall man with dark hair, and he stopped outside the sitting-room window and looked at her as she stood there at her easel. She felt as if he were going to say something, but then she woke up. She lay there for a while thinking about him, unable to recall his face, but she vaguely remembered his dark-blue eyes looking at her. She found his timidity charming, and for this reason, she thought about the man and the dream as she painted and took care of Jón. When she snuggled under her duvet again that evening, she hoped that she would see him again. But there was no sign of him that night or those that followed—and the same went for Sigmar. She tried to take advantage of the peace and quiet and paint. Little Jón, that tranquil child, didn't disturb her at all, except when he was hungry, but she was plagued by an inner turmoil. She was upset with Sigmar, feeling as if he had left only to make her uneasy, to get back at her. And worst of all was that he had succeeded; she had such a hard time concentrating on her painting with people wading around in her thoughts. After several unsuccessful attempts with the white laundry on the clotheslines, she went to bed in a resentful mood, with no expectation whatsoever of dramatic dreams. But then he returned, the dream man.

As timid as before, yet this time, he had been able to bring himself to come inside. Now he stood there in the middle of the kitchen and looked into her bedroom, where she was undressing for bed. As she slowly pulled her dress up over her head, he stared at her ardently; she looked down quickly and saw that she had forgotten to put on her underwear that morning, and he drew nearer. She felt her body begin burning with desire, and he came right up to her and stroked her breasts, which began to drip with milk, and then he laid her down on the bed and joined her there, now stark naked. They made love and she let it happen, did nothing, nothing at all until she heard her baby make a noise, at which point she jumped up and shouted, "Stop, stop!" and she fought against him; she felt as if she were awake, was finally able to open her eyes, look into the darkness, see the outlines of the cupboards and doors, and then she knew that she had been dreaming. But her body was on fire and she was wet, both above and below. Sweaty and breathless, she snatched up little Jón from his cradle and held him to her breast, her heart filled with shame. When he had drunk his fill, she went into the kitchen, lit all the lamps, wiped her breasts, her armpits, and her lower parts clean, got dressed, and brought the lamps into the sitting room. She forced herself not to think about the dream man, focused on her colors as she mixed them, ran her eyes over the canvas, made one brushstroke, then another; it was as if her hand were being guided, no hesitation, no thoughts. She painted resolutely, until the darkness outside had given way to the light.

She heard him come in and froze. Stood as if nailed to the floor, brush aloft. Felt his gaze on the back of her neck, her heart pounding as if she had been caught in the act of adultery. She didn't dare turn around. "My little one," he said, "shall we not be friends? I was so upset because of you that I couldn't shoot a single ptarmigan."

"That's perfectly fine," she said with a lump in her throat. "I don't eat ptarmigan."

When the ptarmigan hunters went south for the fishing season after the turn of the year, the ptarmigans that had escaped them in the autumn crept down into the village. They sought out the birch scrub sticking out of the snow, and the women, who were always so happy to see them, kept the children inside as the ptarmigan wandered around the houses. Kára locked her cats inside, because even though they had little interest in this species of bird, they could easily scare them away.

When Karitas came out one still, cold winter morning, she heard the ptarmigans clucking, saw them slip through and around the scrub, scrape and dig under the snow to find food, looking small and plump despite the scarcity of the same, and as she watched, she felt a touch of nausea. "I ate too much blood pudding last night," she said, taking hold of her bloated stomach, but then she had a bad premonition. Yet she was reluctant to believe this foreboding and did everything she could to avoid unpleasant thoughts, throwing herself into her chores both outside and inside until noon, by which time her nausea was gone. But when she sat down with little Jón after bathing him, the nausea returned, this time overwhelmingly. She felt such a deep restlessness that, after breastfeeding Jón, she dressed him and bundled him up. "And now we shall pop over to Karlína's, my man, to have coffee and crepes, the best in the world." She put on a good face, but she was shaking inwardly.

Karlína was always so cheerful, no matter what. A mere twenty-five-year-old with six children, she could sing while kindling the wash copper and recite playful verses as she shook the contents of diapers into the privy pot. "Do you never get tired, what with all these children?" asked Karitas, and Karlína answered immediately: "No, dearest, there are only six of them. After all, I could have had nine by now, since I started when I was sixteen, and apart from the diaper washing, there's not really that much work where they're concerned." She toiled away all day, washing, cooking, baking, cleaning, knitting, milking, and feeding the animals in Þorfinnur's absence. Yet she said the children were no trouble at all, and she took time to chat with women who stopped in, and made crepes for them, besides.

Karitas looked the group of children over. "Tell me, Karlína, did you ever get pregnant while breastfeeding?" She wanted confirmation of something that she had once heard, trying to make the question sound natural, as if it meant nothing, really, and received a burst of laughter in response: "Yes, I suppose I did, dear. Once when Þorfinnur was at home all year long, I actually had two children the same year, one in January and the other in December. There is only one safe period, dear, and that's from the New Year until the end of the fishing season in May. We're protected for the duration of the winter fishing season." And then she laughed at her own humor and seemed as if she would never stop, and Karitas squeezed out a few noises to play along. "Wouldn't you like a crepe?" Karlína asked, slightly offended, when she saw that Karitas hadn't touched the delicacies, which she had of course served with the coffee. "Aren't you aware that these are the best crepes in the entire village?" "Yes, of course," said Karitas, reaching out a trembling hand for one of the rolled-up crepes. "In fact, I was just wondering how you make them taste so good." "It's because I always use the milk that's left in my breasts after I'm done breastfeeding," Karlína said, with a knowing tilt of her head. "Breast milk is so much better than cow's milk." Karitas turned pale: "I've had such a sour stomach all day. If you don't mind, I'll take my crepe home with me and eat it when I get my appetite back."

Sitting in the dark on the edge of the bed at home, she pondered her next steps. She recalled all the methods that she had heard that women used to rid themselves of an unwelcome pregnancy, but found them all quite disagreeable except for one, perhaps: shaking. She saw Kára go into the sheep shed, followed her in, and, claiming to have pressing business in the village, asked her to look after Jón for a short time. Horses were standing in a field at a farm near the elf city. Wearing long woolen underwear beneath her dress and with a piece of string in her pocket, she approached the one she liked best, letting the winter darkness hide her, tied the string around its lower lip, led the horse to the nearest rock, and mounted it. She rode up the valley, letting the horse choose its own course but urging it on, driving her heels into its sides, and she leaned her head down to its mane and hissed: "Witch ride, witch ride!" as if she were flying on her broomstick, which she thought she was, to a certain extent, and she bounced and shook and shook and bounced, just as she wanted. After returning the sweaty horse to where she'd found it, she hobbled home, where she had to stop and lean against the doorpost. She stared with bloodshot eyes at Kára, who looked her up and down without saying a word, then walked past and out the door with a resentful frown.

Karitas waited half the night for something to happen.

When all hope was gone of her witch ride having produced its desired effect, she thought things over again, but could come up with no other solution than to induce violent vomiting, heave up everything inside her, her guts, smoke it out. She found Sigmar's special-occasion cigars in a box in a drawer, took two of them and a box of matches, snuck behind the house under cover of darkness, squatted, and smoked as hard as she could into the night. This method proved to be extremely effective: she broke out in a cold sweat, became miserably nauseated and threw up, feeling as if she had never in her life experienced such torments. She vomited over and over until she felt as though her body was entirely drained of fluid. She lurched back inside, shivering and shaking from the cold, crawled into bed, and waited for milking time. She neither heard nor saw Kára when she came in with the milk jug, so quiet was that woman, and would have missed her if she hadn't sensed that someone was in the kitchen. And she called out to her in a weak voice: "Kára, is that you? I think I've come down with something. I feel horrendous." As soon as little Jón was lying in Kára's arms, Karitas fell asleep. She slept until the afternoon, but then woke refreshed and rested, feeling right as rain. Kára stood over her, and when she saw that Karitas had opened her eyes, she asked dryly, "What balderdash has gotten into you?"

Karitas surrendered to Mother Nature. But sadness assailed her. And nausea. She sat staring into space: there was no way she could paint with two children on her arm. She didn't even try to paint while Jón slept. She felt like it wasn't worth it. She would have to give up on art, anyway. The days passed, it snowed outside, and little Jón crawled around on the floor. The pants that Bjarghildur had sent him were now too short and tight—she could see this but lacked the drive to do anything about it, despite telling herself that this simply wouldn't do. But Kára had her eye on them, and one day when the weather was unusually still, the north wind being busy in other parts of the country, the seamstress showed up with her retinue. Karitas welcomed them impassively, sat with Jón on her lap through all their hurly-burly, undressed and dressed him as they checked and adjusted the sizes of the garments, and did as she was told. The red-haired sisters, silent as usual, cleaned the house from top to bottom. She didn't interfere, asking only once why they were scrubbing all the walls, only to be told that they were so sooty that their like was not to be seen in the entire district. "Why on earth do you turn up the lamps so high, woman?" asked Högna. "To have more light," Karitas answered truthfully, and Högna said, flabbergasted, "Light? What do you need light for?"

There was no longer any light in her soul, but at the start of March, when the days began to grow longer again and it was bright almost all day, a boy came running down from the telephone office and said that she had to come right away; there was a call for her. She took little Jón with her, even though holding him strained her arms, so heavy had he become. But she drew strength from him, as well; it was good to have someone to hold on to when receiving bad news. Because people didn't put calls through to the telephone office unless something was wrong, someone was dead, sick, or injured. And when she arrived, she was breathless and panting, not only due to her burden, but also to her heart, which raced out of control. She handed Jón over to the operator, took the phone, and whispered: "Yes, this is Karitas," and waited for the awful news. It was her mother on the other end of the line, and she said, "Karitas, how are you, how is the weather over there?" "Just fine," stammered Karitas hoarsely. "There's a bit of a cold wind, but it's reasonably clear." "I had better not talk for too long, it's so expensive," said her mother. "But it's about your pictures."

"My pictures?" repeated Karitas shrilly, straightening her back.

"Yes, I thought you should know that your brother Ólafur has arranged for them to be exhibited here in Reykjavík this Easter, along with paintings by other young artists, two men, I think, who went to art school like you. Are you there, Karitas?"

"Yes."

"There will be around ten pictures per painter, if I remember correctly. Hello, are you there?"

"Yes."

"Since, of course, it won't be possible to exhibit all of your paintings, we've just chosen the ten ourselves, and your brother Páll took it upon himself to make frames for them. He's so deft, the boy. Karitas, are you there?"

"Yes."

"He's been apprenticing to a carpenter along with his studies, and is allowed to make the frames in his workshop in the evenings. Karitas?"

"Yes. Oh, he's been working there?"

"Yes, he has a natural talent for it, but otherwise, he's been attending the Teachers' College, as you know. Oh, and Ólafur's studies at the University are going well; I suppose he'll end up a lawyer in three or four years, and your little brother is planning on starting at the Commercial College this autumn. Hello?"

"Hello."

"Well, that's all I have to tell you. But how are you all doing there in the east?"

"What?"

"What's the news from there? Is little Jón doing well?"

"He's gotten pretty heavy."

"He hasn't started walking yet, has he?"

"No, but he's crawling."

"Tell me, are there any changes in the offing? I dreamed that there were. Hello, Karitas, are you there?"

"Yes, apparently so. Something like that."

"I thought so. But how has the weather been?"

"Not bad. It got down to twenty below in early February."

"It was eighteen below," said someone on the line, feeling compelled to correct her.

"Well, little Karitas, that's how life goes, I suppose. Perhaps you could write me a few lines?"

"I'll try. What pictures did you choose?"

"I don't remember now, Karitas, but they were incredibly beautiful, in my opinion. Let me know in good time if you're going to get married, so that I can send you a little something. Karitas."

"Yes."

"Well, I'll just say goodbye now. Your brothers all say hello. Ólafur will write to you and tell you what people think of your pictures. Goodbye, Karitas, and God be with you."

She hurried home, talking nonstop to little Jón the entire way and confiding in him that she would soon become famous—"which is not to say that I have ever longed to be famous, dear Jón, but good Lord, I think that soon I'll be famous, Jón," and she squealed with excitement like a little girl. As soon as she got home, she speedily set up her easel, threw an unfinished painting on it, and painted as if her life depended on it—"because, little Jón, I must have enough paintings for the next exhibition"—and he understood that well and crawled happily all over the floor. She was exultant; she felt as if she had made a connection with the cosmos itself, and floated there through the firmament in blissful intoxication, painting and muttering to herself, and lost herself in her work until she suddenly heard Kára's sharp voice: "Are you out of your mind, woman? The boy was out in the yard!" She let this lapse be a lesson to her and waited to continue painting until Jón was put to bed.

She lay down with him in the afternoon, and her nap gave her enough energy to paint well into the night.

Karitas had been working nonstop for twelve nights when she again saw the strangely dressed women coming out of the elf city. It was four o'clock in the morning. She was putting away her tubes of paint when it seemed to her as if the ravens were croaking unusually loudly. She had an eerie feeling, remembering what had happened the last time they made such a racket, and sure enough, the same thing happened now. She looked out the window and saw them coming, walking side by side at a brisk pace in their peculiar headgear. She was about to rush out to the cowshed like last time, but changed her mind, not wanting to wake little Jón, and instead, locked herself in the bedroom and pushed the terribly heavy dresser in front of the door. But first, she snatched the kitchen knife from its drawer. Then she sat on the edge of the bed in front of little Jón, who didn't move, and waited. She heard them enter the house with a great tumult; the wood creaked as when a sharp gust of wind blew through. She heard them open and close doors and cupboards, move furniture, stomp on the floor and knock on the walls, and she clutched the knife so tightly that her knuckles whitened. Then suddenly, everything went quiet. But she didn't dare open the door, nor put the knife down. When, however, it grew light outside and little Jón woke up wanting his breakfast, she felt compelled to open the bedroom door. She looked around carefully but saw not a soul, nor any trace of the visit. "They cleaned up after themselves, those cursed things," she muttered, before dressing Jón. She strode with him over the snowdrifts to Kára, and, without any explanation, asked her curtly to loan her the cats again.

Once the cats were back in her house, she stopped noticing anything unusual and was able to work unhindered. But she began feeling incredibly sleepy, despite her midday naps. One day, when the sun shone so brightly on the snow that people's eyes were dazzled when they walked out the door, she decided to put on nice clothes and go up to the village with little Jón so that he could meet other children and she herself could visit Karlína. But Karlína spared her the inconvenience by coming to her. She walked with heavier steps than usual, plodding along as if carrying a heavy burden, with her youngest child in her arms and two others trotting beside her. After she and the children had come inside, she had to sit down for a good while to gather her breath. Then she said: "Do you know what your Sigmar has done?" Karitas didn't. "No, of course you don't know," said Karlína, "so now I shall tell you. He and some fellows from Siglufjörður have bought a twenty-ton fishing boat." Karitas saw nothing tumultuous in this news, which, however, was told to her with such gravity and pain, so she said only: "Oh, I didn't know that. But wasn't that his plan all along?" "No, that was never his plan, Karitas Jónsdóttir," said Karlína. "His plan was to buy a four-ton boat along with my Þorfinnur. But Þorfinnur just phoned me and said that Sigmar signed off on a twenty-ton boat without so much as talking to him first. And now my Þorfinnur can't get a boat because he can't afford to buy one on his own; he needs a co-owner, and there is no one in the village prepared to join him in purchasing a boat right now. And they had been planning to fish together. How could Sigmar do this?" she asked, but Karitas had no answer; the man had said that he couldn't even afford a wash copper, let alone a twenty-ton boat. Karlína burst into tears again and again as she spoke about the boat purchase, and Karitas took it very badly—it was simply awful seeing such a cheerful person so sad. But she could do little more than pat her on the shoulder and curse Sigmar. "This will cost him dearly, that Sigmar," sobbed Karlína, that genial woman. Upon parting, she said she would try to phone Þorfinnur the next day and cheer him up. "He's devastated," she wept. "I'll also tell him how upset you are; maybe he'll tell that to Sigmar." "Yes," said Karitas eagerly. "And ask him to remind Sigmar, if he sees him, to buy paints for me."

Karitas

Cradle 1925

Charcoal drawing

Out the window, I see the white boats.

Come rocking up the fjord with their fish.

Under the window is a cradle, painted white.

A small white boat that has sailed into my life.

My little child in the cradle. Sleeps all day in the sunshine in the sitting room. So deeply that I have to flick my fingertip against the sole of his foot to wake him.

Tranquility surrounds us here inside.

Outside, work is in full swing. Never before has so much cod been caught.

The women wash the fish and spread it out, the men salt and stack it, wherever you look lie fish—on gravel banks, on the drying lots, on rooftops, the village is riddled with fish. At the same time, the haymaking is being done; there are men with sickles, women with rakes, the fields all around are dotted with haystacks, like giant tussocks.

It is the busiest time of the year.

Then the little child sails into the world.

Sigmar had to go straight from fishing for cod to fishing for herring. I am home alone with the boys.

I've run out of paint.

I use the coal with which I fire up the wash copper.

The charcoal drawings grew in number. To keep her hands from turning black, Karitas partially wrapped the piece of charcoal in a cloth, applied it to the surface, and spread it with her fingertips. She felt as if she were getting a grip on the technique when the letter from her brother Ólafur arrived. It was extremely enthusiastic. He told her that her pictures had received good reviews. "They said, dear sister, that you have a highly agreeable talent for painting, that the interplay of light and color in the landscapes is very effective, that there is a deep serenity and quietude in the pictures. They said that one might think that a man had painted them. You even sold two of them. It was a goldsmith who bought them, and he said that you would be famous someday! We're enormously proud of you." Enclosed with the letter was payment for the pictures. Karitas looked for a long time at the banknotes. For the very first time, she had made money as an artist, but felt no joy in her heart. They had submitted the pictures that she had painted for her mother, of the sunrise, the sea, and the mountains. Not the abstract images from her Academy days, the experiments with form that were supposed to have marked her future as an artist. They had probably been worried that these would be considered amateur or slapdash, not the works of a true artist. Agreeable talent for painting? How was she supposed to interpret that? Worst of all was that she couldn't talk to Sigmar about the reviews. And it was nearly impossible to talk to Kára about anything. The woman was in a foul mood these days, having not only had to get her relatives to help her with the peat cutting and sheep shearing, but also having had to cut the grass, gather, bind, and store it herself. She didn't say a word to Karitas. As if it were Karitas's fault that her husband hadn't shown up. Worse, Karlína was very abrupt with her, and the women in the village hardly looked at or spoke to her. They were upset with Sigmar due to his absence and his boat purchase with the men from Siglufjörður, and Karitas was made to suffer for it. "It should have been I, rather than they, who was offended by his actions," she said to little Jón.

She was sweeping the floor when she saw him coming. The coastal steamer lay at anchor out on the fjord; she had seen it sail in and the tender depart from it, carrying passengers and goods, but she hadn't expected him. She had thought he would come sailing in on that twenty-ton vessel everyone was so upset about. But then he simply came walking up, carrying his duffel bag. To her, he looked even sturdier—and she recalled having heard once that men continued to grow until they were nearly thirty. When he was still several yards away from the house, Karitas stopped sweeping, went and stood in the front doorway with one hand on her hip and the other on the broom, and stared straight ahead, truculent and narrow-eyed. He stopped, put down his duffel bag, and grinned. She spoke first: "You haven't been home in eight months." He nodded sheepishly in agreement. She continued: "You haven't seen your elder son for months and haven't phoned home once to ask how the younger one is doing." "I didn't know anyone who had a phone," he then said, having stopped grinning, "and I didn't have time to stand in line at the telephone office; we just landed the fish and sailed back out." She refused to hear excuses: "Þorfinnur phoned Karlína numerous times during the fishing season." This, of course, was a lie. He had phoned only once, but Sigmar didn't know that, and he hung his head. She went on in the same vein: "And then you betrayed Þorfinnur, your best friend and childhood companion, didn't buy a boat with him as you had promised, but with some men from Siglufjörður." He straightened up, said nothing, but looked at her sharply. She tightened the screws: "You're the only man in the community who hasn't made hay for your animals." Then he stared hard at her, slung his bag over his shoulder, and strode determinedly toward her. Threw the bag down at her feet; they both breathed rapidly, she didn't move, he said, "Move." She didn't move an inch. "You will not bully me, Sigmar Hilmarsson," she said gravely. "No, that I won't do," he said, and he took her by the waist with both hands, lifted her in the air, held her for several moments above his head as if to check whether she had gained or lost weight in his absence, put her down behind him, and walked in.

He sat for a long time with the baby, ran his eyes up and down him as he slept, looked at little Jón, who was taking a midday nap, and then again at the infant. "He is so beautiful—he looks a lot more like you than me. But he doesn't seem as robust as Jón was." "Of course he's robust," she said emphatically. After sitting there looking at the boy for a long time, he asked politely if she had anything for him to eat. "You can have saltfish," she said scornfully. "Yes, please," he said, "but do you have some seal blubber to go with it?" "No, unfortunately," she replied with feigned sincerity. "I used the blubber to kindle the wash copper, it burns so well, and besides, I've had to be sparing with the charcoal, because I use it for drawing, since I ran out of paint a long time ago. But now I'll cook you some saltfish in this one battered old pot, the only one I have."

They both said nothing as she worked. Neither of them would yield to the other, and would probably have kept quiet for days had it not been for little Jón. To Karitas's annoyance, Jón smiled when he woke up and saw his father, and then reached out to him, probably because he was so happy to see a man, finally. All that was missing was for him to say "Baba"—and Sigmar laughed and lifted him with both hands over his head and couldn't stop commenting on the handsomeness of his children. Then Karitas gave in and started talking, having also yearned for so long to be able to chat with someone about the children, and about her lack of paint—and naturally, she told him about the exhibition and the reviews, which she wasn't sure were good or bad, but they must have been good, because he was so happy and proud of her, and his enthusiasm melted her heart yet again. Once her defenses were broken down, he needed no more than to stroke her hair and kiss her on the neck to get what he had been dreaming of for months, as he told her.

Later, in bed, with both boys between them, they threw themselves into their daydreams. He told her, just to get it over and done with, that he had indeed forgotten to buy her any proper pots, which he regretted, but he had tried to find her paints—the store just hadn't had any in stock; they had to be ordered, and he simply hadn't known what kind she wanted, and concerning the boat and Þorfinnur, he'd realized that he and Þorfinnur didn't share the same ambitions. "He just wanted a small boat to use for fishing from here in the summers; it's impossible to fish from here in the winters since there's no actual harbor. But my dreams are about other, grander things. I want to have my own crew for both the winter fishing down south and the herring fishing up north, captain my own boat, because I intend to become a rich man, Karitas. When I was eleven years old, I went with my mother to Akureyri. She bought a pastry for me at the bakery. I had never before tasted such a delicacy, and I said to her: 'You know what, Mama, when I grow up, I'm going to be so rich that I can buy myself pastry every single day.' And she said, 'Yes, then you will certainly be rich, Sigmar.' Once I've caught enough fish and paid off my share of the loan on this boat, I'll buy a new one and name it after you, Karitas. And then I'll be my own boss and fish from Siglufjörður or Akureyri, and we'll move there. Where would you rather live?" She had to think this over a little: "I think I would rather live in Akureyri. They're so spacious and bright, the houses there." "Then we'll buy a house in Akureyri," he said. "One or two stories? It probably doesn't matter much, I just need a small space where I can work, the attic would probably be enough for me." "The attic? No, it would be too dark to paint in." "But we'll have electricity, yes?" "Yes, that's true, there's plenty of electricity in Akureyri." "And running water?" "Of course. And you can have a telephone, as well, like the merchants."

They both fell silent and listened to the surf and the cries of the seabirds as they tried to imagine a life with electricity, water, and a telephone, and then he said: "All the same, I'm not going to sell the house here. This is the most beautiful place in the whole country, and we've got to be able to come here in the summers. This house will be our summer estate."

Then he remembered something, got up from the bed, rummaged in his duffel bag, pulled out a small box, and held it in the palm of his hand. "I may not have bought you any pots or paints, my little one, but I did buy you a ring at a jeweler's in Reykjavík." He opened the box, took out the ring, and put it on her finger. "The stone is light blue, just like your eyes," he said. "The jeweler said that it's called Mary's Tear. And now, I would like to ask you if you will marry me tomorrow." She stared wide-eyed at him and the ring in turn. He ran his finger down the middle of her face, as if to divide it in two: "You have until then to think about it."

He wouldn't hear of anything other than a church wedding, so first thing the next morning, after Karitas had said yes to him, he went up to the village to speak to the priest, as well as to let Högna and her husband know that he would like them to act as witnesses. He was back before noon, after having stopped at Kára's to tell her to dress up because she would be holding the boys during their baptism. All of these people heeded him without objection, despite it being just an ordinary Wednesday. He came riding back with two extra horses and told Karitas to hurry and put on her Sunday best, while he himself dressed the boys, got the whole family on horseback, picked up Kára on the way to the village, and arrived at the church with his whole regiment shortly after noon. Högna and Kára, who took their duties very seriously, had put on their national costumes, and Högna, who normally never let anyone boss her around, said not a word, knowing that this was an important moment in the history of the parish, if not in Icelandic church history, with her, a woman, acting as a witness. Besides the bride and groom, there were seven people present at the wedding, the organist included. He was wearing his new rubber boots, having just returned from sea when he was hurried to the church. The ceremony was unpretentious but intimate, all of them trying to sing as loud as they could and with all their heart, to make up for the absence of the choir. Karitas was distracted, being more interested in the painter's altarpiece than the priest's words, feeling as if he repeated too often that the two of them should be as one. She had imagined them having separate souls, if that was all right with the priest, and she also felt it unnecessary for him to say that what God had joined together, no man could separate; there was surely little danger of her getting herself mixed up with any more men, whatever Sigmar did. Naturally, though, the priest had to read something from the Bible; she understood that; and then he blessed them and she was a married woman. She, who twenty-four hours ago had been sweeping the floor of her house, unmarried and unsuspecting of the overwhelming power of love. Well, she thought to herself, since that's how things went, at least I got the most beautiful man in Iceland. Then the baptism began. Kára's national costume was too big for her; she had shrunk somewhat in recent years. She trembled nervously as she held Jón, but spoke up loud and clear when it came time to tell the priest what the child was to be named. On the other hand, when she took the infant in her arms, her face paled, for in all the hustle and bustle, she had forgotten to ask the parents what the boy's name was to be. Even worse, the parents had also forgotten to discuss the matter, so Karitas whispered to Sigmar: "I suppose you would like him to be named Hilmar, after your father?" And he whispered back, as the others held their breath: "Not at all. Just pick a good name," and the first male name that came to her mind was Sumarliði. So the couple stood there with their sons, Jón and Sumarliði, and looked at each other perplexedly, because neither of them had thought about what they would do with the guests after the ceremony.

The witnesses and godmother, tidied up and dressed in their finest, had to have something for their troubles, so Sigmar finally said, looking over the group, "Won't you all ride home with us for crepes?"

The women handled the preparation and cooking, and the reception turned out to be lovely indeed. The weather was exceptionally fine, so the table was set up south of the house and covered with a white tablecloth. The fine tableware was taken out, steaming-hot coffee and crepes filled with whipped cream were brought to the table, and Sigmar fetched shot glasses and cigars for the men, including the priest and the organist in his rubber boots. The men talked about the weather and the fishing in the east and north, taking care not to mention the boat purchase so as not to offend the groom on this festive day, and the women fussed over the newly baptized boys. The gathering reminded Karitas of the high-society garden party in Akureyri that she had seen when she was a teenager, and she told herself that when she and Sigmar moved to the north, into their fine house with electricity and water, she would invite guests as frequently as possible for afternoon coffee in her garden. After a few shots of liquor, Sigmar felt it a grand idea to go for a ride with his bride up the valley, and it fell to the festively dressed Kára to look after the boys. Smiling, the two newlyweds rode through the countryside, occasionally stopping to exchange kisses and gaze into each other's eyes, then rode down the fjord and back to get a better look at the country's most beautiful mountains and form a picture in their minds of their summer estate in all its glory.

Kára liked children as long as they behaved like cats, that is, slept most of the day and otherwise kept their mouths shut. Although Sumarliði met these conditions, which was no longer the case for his big brother, who had begun to cry while under her care, she wasn't as taken with the infant as she had been with Jón. "He's sweet, the little fellow," she said, "but terribly weak. Why not try giving him cod-liver oil?" Karitas reacted crustily every time someone brought up Sumarliði's weakness, but in her heart, she sensed that there was something wrong with the boy. He didn't latch on to her breast as greedily as Jón had; she had to pinch him or flick him lightly with her finger to wake him and get him to suckle, and in the rare moments when his eyes were open, they were distant and staring, two light-blue but lifeless pearls. Maybe he's blind, she thought, or deaf, and she snapped her fingers in front of his nose to see if he would react; she clapped her hands, coughed, sneezed, did all sorts of tricks, but he slept like an angel. At night, she often started from sleep and checked whether he was breathing. One night when she woke, she saw Sigmar standing in the middle of the room with the baby in his arms, holding the child's lips to his ear. "We must have a doctor look at the boy," she heard him mumble. "He isn't normal." It was exactly as she had feared.

As soon as Sigmar had left to go round up the sheep—"This is the last time that I go herding sheep"—Karlína came to the house and whispered a secret in her ear, which everyone knew but no one talked about. She was in a lively mood, though not as cheerful as she had been before the boat purchase. "I just came to give you a wedding present," she said, producing a fine lace tablecloth and handing it to Karitas with an apology, and they chatted like the closest of sisters about the children, the wedding, and the baptism. Then their conversation turned to Högna. Karitas said that Högna's daughters had obviously never liked her, but she didn't know why, and Karlína told her with a slightly scornful laugh, which was out of character for her, that it was only because they'd had their own sights set on marrying Sigmar. But he, of course, hadn't wanted any of them, knowing, as did everyone else, that they were only half-human. Their other parent was an elf man from the elf city—"as if you can't see that for yourself, my dear. They're not like anyone else."

A chill ran down Karitas's spine. She hadn't forgotten the strange night when he came to her, the dream man. "Might this be an elf child?" whistled the wind as the daylight faded, and by night, she slept with

242

the child at her breast, while by day, she kept him bundled in a cloth that she tied around herself, for fear that someone would take the boy if she so much as took her eyes off him. When the doctor came to the village on his rounds, they asked him to look at the child. He had them remove Sumarliði's clothes and examined him carefully, peered into his eyes, listened for a long time to his heart and lungs, but couldn't find anything, he said, except that the boy's heartbeats were somewhat weak. "We'll wait a bit and see. You should breastfeed him at three-hour intervals around the clock until he has reached normal weight. I'll stop by the next time I'm in the village." He didn't seem to take into account the mother's own need for sleep, and neither did he give her any good advice on how to go about waking the child, so she continued as before, pinching Sumarliði's little thighs and continually flicking him with her finger. She longed to hear him cry, and when she went to bed exhausted in the evening, she often let herself dream that the boy would scream so loud, the mountains would resound.

In the middle of the slaughter, Karitas traversed the house like a sleepwalker, sewed the stomachs up without filling them first, dropped everything, retched over the blood puddings. Sigmar asked Kára to come and help, which she did, despite being plagued by a stomach ailment and unhappy with his decision to slaughter all of the sheep, while he himself undertook to look after little Jón and cook for them. Karitas had almost no appetite; her diet consisted mainly of skyr and raisins, and the weight dropped off until she resembled an undeveloped girl of confirmation age. She tried to sleep at night between breastfeedings in order to resemble a human during the day, but was like an edgy sheep, jolting wide awake at the slightest sound. One night, she was startled from sleep by the croaking of the ravens, and she shook Sigmar in terror. "Can you hear that?" Sigmar woke. "Can you hear the ravens? The women are coming to get him." He shushed her gently and managed to calm her down, but she remained awake, holding the child tightly. In the morning, after Sigmar and little Jón were up and she sat on the edge of the bed with Sumarliði, poised to give the sole of his foot a flick, he opened his eyes. Looked at her. With a radiant, clear gaze. She thought she was dreaming. But there was no mistaking it; he looked at her, regarded her, and it seemed to her as if a smile played on his little lips. "My little angel," she said, weeping with joy. She called loudly to Sigmar, but when he finally heard her, the little one had fallen asleep again.

That day, Karitas slept. They had to pinch and shake her, both Sigmar and Kára, to wake her so that she could breastfeed the baby. Sumarliði didn't look in her eyes as he had done that morning, but she was still overjoyed; that one little look had given her hope. The night was cold. She woke, pulled the baby closer to her, longed to sleep a little longer before breastfeeding him, she so desperately needed sleep, but suddenly she was wide awake. Something wasn't right; the baby was so strangely quiet. He didn't move. His little hands were motionless. She screamed at Sigmar, they jumped out of bed, lit the lamps, shook the child, turned him this way and that, lifted him by his feet, but Sumarliði was lifeless. Was gone from them.

Sigmar ran up to the village and returned with the midwife. She pronounced the child dead. "Congenital heart defect," she said, as if she had known this since he was born. "There was nothing you could have done; it was inevitable."

Karitas sat all day with the dead child in her arms.

They were on their way home from the funeral when a girl came running up with a letter that had been waiting for them at the telephone office. From Bjarghildur. Toward evening, after Karitas sat for a long time, head hanging, she finally opened the letter. It was bursting with triumphant joy. Bjarghildur had been elected chairman of the Women's Club. She described in detail the events leading up to this, the election itself—"which took place in the living room here at Þrastabakki the day before yesterday"—and the dance party that she had held that evening. She'd been expecting this for quite some time—"I'd overheard them saying that they were thinking of electing me, so I made arrangements. I had already cleared out the main rooms in the concrete house before the meeting was held, had hired an accordion player, and prepared the refreshments well in advance. The Creator Himself must have ordained the chairmanship for me, because the weather was on my side, and all sorts of unexpected events took place. In exceptionally fine autumn weather, we Women's Club members walked up the slope after the meeting, had our coffee there, recited poems and sang patriotic songs, as must be done on such occasions, and when we walked down the slope again later in the afternoon, the most surprising, interesting thing happened. The accordionist, Lárus, had brought a violinist from Hungary with him—I shall tell you later how it happened that he came to this country, and when this dark-eyed violinist saw us women coming walking down the slope in the autumn sun, with me leading the way, he stuck his violin under his chin and began playing a cheerful melody. I was told later that he had been playing the Hungarian Dance no. 1, by Brahms, who is a German composer you may not know, but in any case, we all come gliding and smiling down to the farmhouse with the Hungarian Dance in our ears, and I was told afterward by people standing in the farmyard that it was magnificent to see all those young, bright-headed Icelandic women come trotting down the slope, light-footed as hinds, to the music of the violin. But to make a long story short, Hámundur and I hosted a dance for fifty-seven people, which, to the great delight of our guests, went on until morning. Well, this was a bit of a digression, dear sister; an enjoyable weekend is behind us, and duty calls. Otherwise, everything is fine here, and everyone is healthy. The haymaking went well this summer, as did the autumn work, especially since I kept both of the maids that you got for me, and for which I thank you once again. I would be happy to hear how the farming is going for you and Sigmar out east; have you gotten yourselves any more animals, or do you still have twenty sheep? Is there a Women's Club in the area?"

"She danced down the slope while I sat with my dead boy in my arms," Karitas said.

A storm hit, bringing cold from the north, and waves as tall as a man crashed over the shore's boulders and slabs, shaking off the rubble before pulling back to prepare for the next assault. At their most energetic, they slammed against the west side of the house and drained off on the east, having gone the whole way round. A circle dance. Karitas woke and listened to them, recalling their wild dance in the bay at home out west, when their fury had frightened her—but now she wanted to dance with them. She looked at her husband and son, sleeping deeply next to her, slipped out of bed, barefoot in her nightgown, and groped her way to the front door. She heard the north wind raging outside, and when she opened the door, it stormed madly in, punched and beat her. She wasn't going to try to get past it and out, which she never would have been able to do, anyway. Sigmar woke, rushed to the door, pushed her back behind him, attacked the wind violently, and managed to slam the door in its face. "What the hell are you thinking, woman?" he exclaimed, pulling her into the bedroom, but softened when he saw how miserable she was. "Where were you going, Karitas?" he asked, taking her in his arms. "I just wanted to clear my head," she said. "It's full of foul muck." He helped her back into bed, had her lie down beside Jón. "Hold him, my little one, and then I'll hold you." She repeated that she needed to clear her head, but he said: "Now I'll lay my hand on your forehead and stroke it lightly until the foulness disappears." He did so, and she immediately felt her head clearing. "Won't he be freezing in his grave, in such cold weather?" she asked. "No, not at all," he said. "The ground is warm and soft, and besides, he's no longer there, my little one, as you know. He has long since gone up to God. I'm sure he's with your sister Halldóra; I could well imagine that." She thought for a moment in silence. "Yes, you're absolutely right," she said. "Of course he's with Halldóra."

There were seventeen cats. Most were tabby cats, although there were a few blacks, whites, and grays among them, and Kára knew the needs and dispositions of each and every one, even though they all had the same name: "Kitty." "I've never put down a cat, but one or two have disappeared," she said. Karitas didn't want to know where they had gone. She went to Kára when she was called. Karlína didn't want to set foot in Sigmar Hilmarsson's house, so instead, she went to Kára and had her go fetch Karitas when she wanted to speak to her. She was worried about Karitas because she "lost her child and has no relatives nearby, only that horrid man, and has shrunk down to nothing." She hugged Karitas and stroked her hair, brought her treats like freshly baked hot-cakes and raisins, knowing that Karitas loved raisins. When Karitas came to Kára's cottage, Karlína had her sit down, grabbed the cats by the scruff of the neck and moved them out of the way, and then tried to get her friend to eat something, "because you're the best friend I've ever had, Karitas." Karitas let her do as she pleased, sat obediently, and pretended to listen. She herself had nothing to say, just counted the cats over and over in her mind. Kára paid no attention to the commotion in her cottage, but lay in bed during such visits and allowed the cats to strut over her. Then Karlína would bid farewell and say that she would come again soon, at which point Kára would finally open her mouth and say: "There are seventeen of them, Karitas, and I would like to ask you to feed them if I should go away."

One day, when the weather was so mild that it made people suspicious, Karlína narrowed one eye, looked at Karitas for several long moments, and asked, "Do you think you might be pregnant again, Karitas?" The cats lay down on Kára's stomach, drooped their eyelids, and waited for her answer. "How do you come up with such twaddle?" whispered Karitas, putting her hands over her belly. "I just haven't had any appetite for a long time, which is why I haven't had my period," she said, but as soon as she'd let slip the truth, she knew the game was up. The women inhaled audibly through their noses and shut their eyes for a second. "I need to go," muttered Karitas, lifting little Jón off the floor. "I need to get dinner ready," she added, even though it had only been a short time since lunch. With misery in her heart and little Jón in her arms—despite being hardly able to lift him anymore—she hobbled home, looked around for Sigmar, and found him out in the dusky workshop, where he stood looking over his rifle. She let Jón sink to the floor and said breathlessly, with a lump in her throat: "You've done it again." She could tell by his body language that he knew exactly what she meant, despite acting as if he'd had nothing to do with it, instead raising his rifle and blowing down its barrel. And when he made no reply, offered nothing in his own defense, she pushed Jón toward him, saying, "Here, take him, isn't that what you want, to produce as many children as possible?"

Then she ran down to the beach.

She slipped on the slick seaweed, held her arms crossed beneath her bosom as if doing so helped her to keep her balance, hopped over the sleek shore rocks with her shoulders hunched up to her ears until she came down to the water's edge, where she sat down on the sand, legs outstretched. Small waves inched their way toward her, withdrew, returned just a little more pluckily, repeated this game over and over as she stared alternately at them and her shoes. They were terribly old and worn. She recalled her first leather shoes, the scent of the leather; she couldn't bring herself to wear them the first few days so as not to lose the new-shoe smell. They had made fun of her, Bjarghildur and Halldóra, and she also remembered the shoes she had bought herself in Copenhagen. Their toes had been a tiny bit narrower, and when she and the girls at the Academy sat together making sketches of plaster figures, she had tried to stretch one leg as far out from under the hem of her skirt as possible so that the others could see her new shoes in all their glory. She actually hadn't been able to concentrate on her work because of those shoes; it certainly didn't help that she hated sketching those stone-dead plaster figures—and, now that she thought of it, that was the first and only time the teacher had reprimanded her. The shoes had had deep-red edging at the heel. How pretty they were, those shoes; she'd worn them only when she was at school, so that they would last. The other female students had owned many pairs of shoes and hadn't had to support themselves by washing dishes well into the night. And they hadn't even been as talented as her. Where were they now, all those girls?

"I will never paint again," she told the waves.

They withdrew dejectedly, as if it were their fault. She watched as they disappeared into the sea, which was constantly changing, just as she was; now it had turned gray. The fog that crept into the fjord used the gray color. She heard footsteps in the gravel, and, knowing that Sigmar had come to fetch her, did not look over her shoulder, but just said, when she knew that he could hear her: "I can't have any more children, Sigmar, just to lose them."

He sat down behind her, with his legs on either side, and wrapped his arms around her.

"She always rowed out to sea early in the morning," he said, as if he were in the middle of telling her a story, "and most often, I was asleep. Once I woke up early so that I could go with her, but was too late; I had to watch as she rowed out toward the morning sun. I sat here at the shore, determined to wait for her. After waiting a long time, and perhaps dozing a little, I suddenly saw a girl come up from the sea, a lovely girl, beautiful and dainty, with flaming golden hair. She glided toward me on a wave, but the sun was so strong that I was forced to squint for a moment, and she disappeared. When Mama finally returned from her fishing, I told her about the girl, and she said: 'It's love, Sigmar—but you'll have to conquer it, like the sea.' And then I saw you in the morning sun at the salting lot in Siglufjörður, and immediately recognized the girl who had come up from the sea."

"Where's Jón?" interrupted Karitas, who had little interest in a poetic story about a woman from the sea. "He's taking his midday nap," he said, clearly disappointed at her lukewarm response. "You must never leave children alone," she said gruffly, tearing herself from his embrace and trying to scramble to her feet. "Would you like me to carry you home?" he asked, after they had both gotten up. "No, I have to hurry, the blackest fog is coming in," she said. "Let me carry you out of the fog," he pleaded. "No," she repeated, but he didn't listen. He tried to grab her in his arms, which only made her angry, and she struck him with her open hand and kicked him in the calf. "I shall tell you this, now, Sigmar: even if you're a little bit bigger than me, don't you dare try to overpower me! I said that I would go by myself—now try to understand that!" And he, who was more than a little bit bigger than she, was helpless in the face of her ferocity. "Forgive me," he said in bewilderment as he let go of her. She dashed up the rocky shore, scrambling and slipping over the boulders with him following at her heels, apologizing, trying a gentler approach: "Karitas, when is the baby due?" She didn't answer immediately, but then barked, without looking back: "In May, as usual!" despite having given birth only once before in May. "Before or after Closing Day?" he called out after her. "You and your damned Closing Day," she hissed from higher up the shore, now turning toward him. "And, of course, I'm supposed to be here alone and sick, up to my ears in snow, yet another dratted winter?" Seeing her standing still, he took the opportunity and hurried to her. "But, Karitas, how would you feel about traveling south with Jón and staying with your mother while I'm away for the winter fishing?" He clearly thought this an excellent idea, because he nodded eagerly, as if expecting her to agree to it immediately. But there, he was wrong. She could barely breathe from indignation: "How could it ever cross your mind, Sigmar Hilmarsson, that I, a married woman with one child and expecting another, would go crawling home to my mother like some miserable wretch? Do you have any idea how hard she had to work to bring up me and my siblings? She circled the entire country with us just so she could give us an education, and in case you never knew it, my dear man, I'll just tell you now that Halldóra attended the

Midwifery College, Bjarghildur the Women's College, Páll the Teachers' College. Pétur is in the Commercial College, Ólafur at the University of Iceland, and I, as you may faintly remember, I graduated from the Royal Academy of Fine Arts in Copenhagen! And yet you expect me to go crawling home to Mama like some stray dog in order to have a roof over my head and something to eat, because you, the proud man from Borgarfjörður, need to sail from harbor to harbor instead of finding yourself honorable work on land like other family men!" She was going to go on, being only halfway through her speech and having worked up steam after her instructive introduction, but he suddenly clamped his big hand around the neckline of her jersey, lifted her up so that her toes barely touched the shore rocks, bent his head down close enough to her face that she saw herself reflected in his burning eyes, and snarled: "And I, little Karitas Jónsdóttir, have a degree from the Maritime College and am planning to make fishing my life's work, putting my life at risk along Iceland's shores to generate income for the national economy, so that we can stand upright like men, crawl out of these damned turf huts and wooden sheds, live lives fit for human beings, have lawyers and artists, feed landlubbers and whiny women who don't have the slightest respect for us seafarers—and just you remember that this is the first and last time I offer to carry you out of the fog!" He released his grip on her so abruptly that she fell onto her bottom in the seaweed.

She watched him make his way up and along the shore ridge toward their house, then lost sight of him in the fog. She herself crawled up onto the ridge, her bottom smarting, and burning with rage, saw the vague outline of the house, and started running. She wasn't going to let him have the last word—and then she practically ran into him in the farmyard. He was holding his rifle. Hardly able to stand upright, she threw her arms over her bosom in horror and whispered, "Are you going to shoot me, Sigmar?" He didn't answer, pushed her aside, and disappeared into the black fog. With her hands outstretched, she staggered toward the house, slammed the door shut behind her, and bolted it.

The fog took the house in its arms, darkened the fjord, suffocated all sounds, the birds fell silent and stuck their heads under their wings. Little Jón woke up as she was lighting the lamps, confused, at first, by the darkness in the middle of the day, and then became restless and began to whimper, wanting only to be in his mother's arms. But she hummed and whistled to show that she cared not a whit about the fates of men who wandered around in the fog. She did, however, stay away from the windows, as if she expected to be shot if she stood in front of them, for she knew that he was mad, stark raving mad with his gun somewhere out there in the fog; she imagined him dashing around those immense mountains with his head lowered, shooting at anything that moved, reindeer as well as trolls. "I don't know your father," she said to little Jón. "I swear I don't know him, although I've always known that he had this violence in him. I just beg of you, for goodness' sake: don't end up like him," she said, before putting a new diaper on the child—but then, not knowing what else to do with herself, she tore off all his clothes and began washing him from head to toe. As she did, she sang every verse she could, and Jón stared at her in astonishment with his pacifier in his mouth, having never heard his mother sing so loudly before. And as it grew dark and the fog became even denser, she sang as energetically as she could. She couldn't care less about Sigmar! Then she heated water and washed the children's clothes, taking a long time doing so. Yet when night itself descended over the village, she could no longer pretend. Now she imagined him high up in the mountains, lost in the fog; at any moment, he could fall off a cliff or into a deep crevice. She saw how awful she had been to him. Sobbing, she went to the front door and drew back the bolt; perhaps he would find his way home after all—one never knew with Sigmar. Then, unable to resist, she opened the door straight onto that blasted fog, stepped out, and called out softly: "Sigmar." She repeated this several times, sitting down in between on the edge of Jón's bed. He had gone back to sleep—he could sleep through anything, that boy—and then, carrying a lamp, she went out again and called, softly and tenderly: "Sigmar." Ahead of her, the silhouettes of the outbuildings appeared like a black cliff face, and she felt an urge to pet the cow, that doing so might make her feel safer. She held the lamp high. The cow lay chewing her cud, perfectly calmly, unafraid of the world's fogs; Karitas approached her and saw a shape in the corner of the stall. She held out the lamp toward that corner, illuminating it. There lay Sigmar Hilmarsson, sleeping like a baby.

They said little as they walked together back into the house. He was stiff from lying in the stall and limped a little, but wrapped his arm tightly around her shoulders as she held firmly to his waist. When they came to the kitchen, he ran his hands over her hair and body and kissed her, and she kissed him back, but tried to get him to slacken his caresses because she wanted to talk to him first; the other thing might come afterward. But he wanted that first, and then maybe to talk; and to keep the peace, she let him have his way.

On winter evenings, they encouraged each other. "We've got to fight," Karitas told him anxiously when he became taciturn. "There's nothing else for it," she said in the words and spirit of her mother. But when she herself thought about little Sumarliði and was so overwhelmed by sadness that she had to crawl into bed, it was he who gave a fiery speech about their future, and before she knew it, she was listening attentively to him, it being rare for Sigmar to speak for any extended amount of time. When his silence grew too tedious for her, Karitas would ask if he was sad, but he just said that he saw no point whatsoever in blathering endlessly about everything and nothing. As if she herself really enjoyed being around talkative people. But he sat with her, stroked her arm, divided her face in two with his finger, and tried to inspire some zest for life in her again by telling her about his future plans for them and their children, either in Akureyri or Siglufjörður. Around Easter, they would have to make a decision about where they would settle—and he calculated for her how much he would make during the winter fishing season, not to mention during the herring season, as great as the catches had been this year, so that, as she could see, his profits would not only go toward paying off the boat, but also into the purchase of their house and other things pertaining to the family. She didn't want to interrupt him to ask what those other things might be, although she did let the thought of pots cross her mind. But when he saw her pensiveness, he hurriedly said: "And I'll order paints for you as soon as I'm in the south; just tell me what you want." Then she drew a deep breath and said, "I can't paint with one child on my arm and another hanging on to the hem of my skirt; you yourself know that." "My little one," he then said, "once we've settled in, we'll hire a girl to look after the children and another to do the housework, so that you can paint in peace all day long. I don't think you realize how rich I'll be, dear Karitas." They avoided discussing the winter months ahead and their separation. But of course, she, like other sailors' wives, had to get used to running the home, and in fact the entire village, while the men were away. The women had no problem doing so, either; they viewed it as a kind of cooperative project, supported each other, entertained each other, made sure that everyone had enough to eat. Many of them didn't find it such a bad time at all; it was even possible to embroider a little. It was nothing to worry about—quite the opposite. Karitas wasn't going to worry, either.

But then one morning, the milk jug wasn't in its place.

Maybe she overslept, was the first thought that crossed Karitas's mind, despite knowing for certain that women like Kára never overslept. "I wonder if she has the flu, and a fever?" she said to little Jón as she dressed him, having no one else to talk to. Sigmar had rowed out to sea at dawn with another man. Little Jón answered her questions with meaningless babble, but made it clear that he wanted his milk right away, so she bundled up both herself and her child and lumbered with him over to Kára's cottage, anxious about the latter's health. The frost nipped their cheeks, the day was still dark and quiet, but she could see that the sea was calm.

Kára lay next to the well, motionless. She was facedown, one hand resting on the handle of the water bucket, which had overturned. The spilled water had begun to freeze. The cats strutted around the well, arching their backs in the cold. Karitas put Jón down slowly, knelt, and turned Kára gently onto her back. Her eyes were open and staring, as if she had seen something astonishing. The cats came closer, sniffed, stuck their noses in her gray hair, and little Jón laid his hand on the woman's cold cheek, clapped and blabbered, trying to be sweet to his Kára. "She was looking at the stars," said Karitas to Jón, in a tone of surprise. She stroked Kára's icy forehead and cheeks, straightened her jersey a little. Slightly pensive, she said to Jón, as if in confirmation: "Yes, she was looking at the stars and was dazzled." Then she added, "But now, dear Jón, we've got to bring her inside before she freezes out here. Here we go, upsy daisy, now we'll pull her in." Grabbing Kára under her arms, she pulled her into the cottage, with the cats and little Jón getting in her way as she tried to heave the woman onto the bed. "And now Kára is going to take a little nap, Jón. We'll pull the duvet over her and let her be."

The cats took their places, staying off the bed.

With Jón on her hip, Karitas slowly and carefully traversed the slippery patches up to Karlína's house in the village, and, numb with cold, knocked on the door. "You wouldn't happen to have a drop of milk for little Jón, would you?" she said apologetically when the housewife came to the door with half-dressed children at her heels. When she and the baby had been pulled into the warmth and both had been tended to with warm milk straight from the cow, Karlína asked if Karitas's cow wasn't giving milk. Karitas said that she thought that it was, but that Kára hadn't milked it that morning; that was the problem. "And why didn't Kára milk it today?" Karlína asked suspiciously, eyeballing Karitas, that poor woman who couldn't milk a single cow in the absence of the milkmaid. "Is she ill?" Karitas knitted her brow and tilted her head: "Yes, darn it. I would definitely say that she's come down with something." Karlína wanted to go back to Kára's with her. She called for Þorfinnur, who was out in the workshop, and instructed him to put together another bed "because the family's growing so quickly." Then she asked him to look after the children while she popped out. They put little Jón on a sledge—"He's well beyond carrying, after all, as heavy as he is"—and then they hurried down to Kára's cottage, chatting, as usual, about their lives and livelihoods. Once at Kára's, they parted ways. Karitas said that she had to get little Jón home, wet as his diaper was after drinking all that milk.

She didn't know what went on at Kára's cottage for the remainder of the day, as no one told her anything, and it wasn't until late in the afternoon that she saw them approaching, Sigmar and the priest. "What might the cleric want?" she asked Jón.

They conveyed the news to her extraordinarily gently, tiptoeing around it for a long time before informing her that Karlína had found Kára dead. "We think she had a heart attack," they said, "but of course, the doctor will determine that when he finds time to come." "It's a pity about the body," the priest muttered to Sigmar. "I don't want it lying there in the church until the funeral, what with all the Christmas fuss, and it isn't appropriate to leave it in the care of the cats, even if they do an excellent job when it comes to mice." Sigmar said that it was out of the question for him to store the body, there being no room for it in his house, but he would construct a coffin for her, the blessed woman, and a handsome one at that. "Such dratted bad luck that she should up and kick the bucket now, right before the holiday," the priest continued, still distressed. "I'll have to lay her to rest on the Feast of St. Þorlákur. I simply don't understand the woman, doing this. She should have known better, as sensible as she was."

Karitas had been on the go when they arrived. She didn't have time to sit down with them in the sitting room, but came rushing in now and then with hot coffee, and said little. They spared her the practical considerations that follow every person's death, it having been not so long ago that she herself had to deal with such things, and after the priest left, she went on diligently with her chores. She had nothing to say to Sigmar, but did look up now and again, as if listening for comings or goings. Finally she said: "Tell me, isn't it long past time for the evening milking, and no one has gone to the cowshed?"

Sigmar said he was afraid that they'd have to sell the cow; Karitas could hardly start doing the milking and mucking out the dung trough after the New Year. "I expect that you already have enough on your plate." "Where is the blue jug?" she then asked. "The white jug, you mean," he said. "No, the blue jug," she said petulantly. He looked at her for a long time, before saying, "What an awful day this was, my little one; I'm going to pop down to the cowshed, and then we'll just go to bed."

"Where are they taking Kára?" she asked Sigmar as they lifted the coffin onto a cart after the funeral. "Up to the churchyard," Sigmar answered in a low voice, looking around to see if anyone had heard his wife's peculiar question. "Why am I not surprised," she snapped, without elaborating. The cortege slowly approached the churchyard. Most of the village's adult residents had gathered; children under confirmation age had been put in charge of all the little ones at home. The snow fell thickly, and the attendees shivered. "What drudgery to have had to dig her grave in this hard-frozen ground," they muttered, although it wasn't a complaint, per se. They crowded around the grave. Karitas turned into the wind as the coffin was lowered and blew her nose as she made the sign of the cross over the grave, but otherwise didn't show much emotion, people felt, despite her having been closest to Kára, at least in the last couple of years. They also found her a bit on the impassive side when she walked over to her child's grave after the milkmaid's burial, "but maybe that's just how they are, those people from the north or west or God knows where." Nor did she attend the funeral reception, which the women of the village had, in the midst of the Christmas bustle, prepared out of great generosity in the primary school, saying that she had to hurry home to feed the cats. "I almost forgot about it," she whispered worriedly to Sigmar, "but Kára asked me to feed them if she should go away." Somber and taciturn, Sigmar brought little Jón with him to the reception.

The cats meowed in complaint from within the darkness as she opened the cottage door, but reacted quickly to the smell of fish that came with her, rushing to the door and blocking her way. Some of them latched their claws onto the canvas bag that she had filled with fish tails and heads, and hung on as she slowly made her way to the table. "There now, you poor things, let me light the lamp and kindle the stove," she said, setting the bag down on the floor. They pounced, all seventeen cats, pawing and scratching, and she let them go at it as she poured water into a pot and lit the stove. Then she shooed the cats away with the broom—otherwise, she wouldn't have been able to get near the bag—gathered up the pieces of fish and put them in the pot, and then waited for the water to start boiling. "Well now," she said, looking over the group, all of which had sat down and were licking their mouths. "So you've been behaving yourselves while your mother was away?" They meowed in chorus. "So nice to hear," she said, and blew her nose. "And you've been tidy, too," she added, looking around approvingly. She took the plates out of the cupboard, four in all, placed them on the table, and went back to waiting for the water to boil. The diners rubbed themselves against her legs, one after the other, meowing politely, and she got goose bumps of delight when they brushed against her calves. The water began boiling; she took the fish out of the bubbling water, divided it among the four plates, and lined them up on the floor at appropriate intervals. "Bon appétit," she said festively. They tiptoed around the plates while the fish was still steaming, but little by little, began to partake of the food. She sat down on the bed and watched them contentedly. Then she dozed off, and that was how Sigmar found her—lying in Kára's bed with all seventeen cats on top of and around her. All sound asleep.

The day the men had been planning to head south, and several days before the sun began to redden the windowpanes again, Sigmar went out into the storehouse and returned with his rifle in hand. They had made love for hours; it was their last night together before the fishing season. They had gotten so little sleep that Karitas assumed he was groggy when she saw him with the gun. She called out cheerfully: "Sigmar, dear, you're not going ptarmigan hunting now." He stood in the farmyard and said softly when he saw her come out: "Go back inside." She retreated in fear when she saw his stern gaze. What had gotten into him, what was he going to shoot? She slunk to the sitting-room window, hid behind the curtains, and watched him walk to Kára's cottage.

A shot rang out. Then another. And a third. The reports echoed around the fjord in the tranquil morning. The seabirds fell silent. The salvo turned into one long rumble. Little Jón began bawling. She sat down with him and rocked back and forth. Much later, when all had gone quiet and the birds were once again soaring over the house, she heard voices. She could make out those of Sigmar and the parish administrator; the third she didn't recognize. They drew slowly nearer to the house, talking loudly, stopping now and then to unburden their minds, and ended up outside her sitting-room window. "I'm never doing any damned job like that again," she heard Sigmar say. "They jumped all over the walls, hung from the ceiling at the height of it. Some I had to shoot thrice, those bastard cats have nine lives, they would have scratched my eyes out if I hadn't shot them from outside and had the windowpane to protect me." The parish administrator said in a whiny tone: "We couldn't ask anyone else, Sigmar; we had to have a master shooter do it. After all, there was no point in letting them live. Who would have taken care of them? I don't understand the old woman, hoarding cats like that. Especially with things being so difficult. Best would be to get rid of that shack, as I said—set it alight. Then we wouldn't need to gather the carcasses into some goddamned sack."

"Do you have coffee for us, Karitas?" Sigmar called from the doorway. They came inside. She got up and walked into the kitchen icily, not greeting or looking at the men. They tried lightening the mood by chatting with little Jón as the coffee was being served. Sigmar came to her in the kitchen and looked her cautiously in the eyes. She turned her back to him, and he said: "There was nothing of value in Kára's cottage. I, the administrator, and Kára's nephew here were just there, and the only thing she had that was in fairly good condition was her cutlery. Her nephew thinks that you should have it, and I also took this notebook that she'd been scribbling poems in; her nephew thought you might enjoy it. Here you are." She tore the notebook from his hands but acted as if she didn't see the bag of cutlery. Unable to deal with her silence, Sigmar returned to his guests.

They watched her from the sitting-room window as she walked up to the village, bareheaded and gloveless, notebook in hand. She didn't stop at Karlína's, as anyone might have expected. She didn't even look up at her windows, but, with her gaze fixed rigidly ahead, took a direct course for the churchyard. Once there, she kicked the snow away from the lychgate so that she could open it. The snow lay over Kára's grave like a woolen blanket. She made the sign of the cross, but words would not come; made the sign of the cross three times in the hope that the gesture would help loosen her tongue. Finally, she gave up, wiped her eyes, and sighed: "I'll just read your poems to you. You may never have heard them read out loud." She stood in front of the grave, and in the still, clear air, she solemnly read the poems, which were written in a delicate hand. She shuffled her feet a few times to keep the blood circulating in her legs, and looked up from the book at the cross over the grave to check whether the listener was paying proper attention. There were many poems and reading them took a long time, so she asked their author for forgiveness, and said that she simply had to sit down on the stone wall for a moment to rest her legs. She stopped reading and glanced toward the spit, where there was a lot going on: wares and luggage were being brought to the tender that awaited the coastal steamer. She sat quietly for several minutes, smiled apologetically at the cross on the grave, then got up again and positioned herself to read once more.

"How could you think of rushing out like that when you know that I'm leaving? Weren't you going to say goodbye?" someone called from the lychgate. She continued her reading.

"Are you going to say goodbye to me?" he repeated.

"Don't disturb us," she said tersely.

"Come here," he ordered.

"Inside the lychgate, I am safe from evil spirits," she said, and continued to read as if these words had been in the poem.

"If you don't come here, I'll come in there to get you."

She slammed the book shut, went to the lychgate, and stood there looking him sternly in the eye. "You're not getting me unless I will it."

He grabbed her and pulled her outside the gate. She slapped at his hand. "Have you washed the smell of cats off your hands?"

They stood facing each other silently, and neither of them looked away. His trunk and duffel bag lay in the new-fallen snow; the ship waited out on the fjord. Finally, he said: "You'll understand later. I've sold the sheep that were left, and the cow as well. I've made arrangements with old Stefán for him to bring you milk every day. Högna will help you with the water from time to time. You need to go fetch Jón from her now. I'll try to stop here between the cod and herring fishing, and then we'll be moving north in the autumn."

He took his trunk, slung the duffel bag over his shoulder, and stood there for a moment. Then he leaned in close enough that she could look straight into his sea-green eyes, straightened up again, and walked away. She didn't move. He was only a few strides away when he stopped abruptly, put down his luggage, hurried back, grabbed her in his arms, and kissed her face and neck. She closed her eyes. Then, without looking at her, he let go and walked away once more. Said without looking over his shoulder: "I'll get you whenever I please."

As long as it was light, there were always people out and about near her house, riding down the fjord or up the valley or catching horses. When Karitas looked out the window, she saw both women and men, and sometimes youngsters, out strolling around, which made her feel as if she were never alone. But as soon as darkness fell, she became restless; she felt on edge and didn't know why. After putting little Jón to bed, she lit all the lamps and made sure she had enough to do, washing the clothing and herself until well into the evening; she felt safer when she was busy. Finally, she could no longer stay on her feet, and sat down on the edge of the bed and listened to the croaking of the ravens. If, in her opinion, it sounded ordinary, she turned down the lamps and lay down, but if it was loud and importunate, she peered through the window at the elf city. Even if she rarely saw anything in the black of night.

One evening, when the croaking reached new heights, she saw the women coming. They were five, as usual, and moving fast. "Cursed things," she muttered through clenched teeth, and she went to get the kitchen knife, locked herself in the bedroom with Jón, pulled the dresser in front of the door, extinguished the lamp, and waited. She heard them enter the house and go into the sitting room, then suddenly withdraw and go out again, as if someone had frightened them away. She heard them outside, the rustling of their skirts as they walked along the wall; she peeked out the window and watched as they walked away in the moonlight, dressed in their strange attire. She pushed the dresser away from the door and was about to go and put the kitchen knife back in its place when she heard a soft noise in the sitting room and froze.

"You're not going to stab me with that thing, are you?" said a cheerful voice from within the room. A soft female voice that Karitas knew well. A voice that she had longed to hear for many years.

"Is that you, Halldóra?" Karitas asked in a tremulous voice.

"It certainly is. Now, put away that knife and light the lamp."

She obeyed silently, trembling as she lit the lamp, and then held it high to illuminate the sitting room. There she stood, Halldóra, smiling in a blue dress with her hair tied in a beautiful knot at the nape of her neck.

"Have you been here long?" asked Karitas. "No, I just arrived," said Halldóra. "I came right before the five women." "Yes, those cursed things," said Karitas. "Are you going to stay long?" "A few days, perhaps," said Halldóra. "Isn't Sumarliði with you? Who's looking after him while you're here?" "Don't worry about him," said Halldóra with a yawn. "He's in good hands."

As Karitas made up a bed for Halldóra on the divan in the sitting room, she told her about her interactions with the five women, and Halldóra said that she was quite certain they were elves, and not exactly sympathetic—that, she had seen right away. After Halldóra lay down to sleep, being tired after her long journey, she advised Karitas to ignore them and keep a lamp lit every night. "Even a glimmer will do." And then she said: "But for goodness' sake, Karitas, don't let anyone know that I'm here, because otherwise, the women will start sending for me at all hours, and I'm in no condition to be tramping around the countryside in waist-deep snow and pitch darkness." "But won't you stay here with me until after the birth?" Karitas asked breathlessly. "I'll try to, of course, but I can't be away from Sumarliði for too long," said the midwife, closing her eyes.

It made all the difference to Karitas to have Halldóra to talk to while she was doing her daily chores. The tedious ones went quicker, it seemed. They talked about everything under the sun. Halldóra, who loved art, was eager to hear about Karitas's studies and life in Copenhagen, and Karitas told her how much she had enjoyed going out into the hustle and bustle of the city in the mornings, automobiles, carriages, and carts clattering along the cobbled streets, and how, in the summers, people bought their wares at outdoor markets and stalls. "It was so fun to look over all the goods in the sun, but I seldom bought anything. I had to watch my money and use it for paints and canvas, but now I have more. Sigmar always leaves some behind when he goes away, but I can't buy any paints or canvas now, because the Co-op only sells goods that people can eat or use for practical purposes." Then Halldóra said: "Why don't you just use what's at hand? You don't need paints or canvas to create works of art. You can use everything around you: rocks, pieces of wood, cloth, tools, containers. And, Karitas, where is Kára's cutlery? Can't you use that, too?"

Karitas

Cutlery in Heaven 1926

Assemblage with varnish on wood

In heaven, the cutlery is white.

In the storehouse, I find a good wooden board, carry it into the house, and lay it on the sitting-room table.

Pull Kára's cutlery from its bag.

Seventeen pieces in total; lacking only one knife to make a full set for six. I arrange them on the board's surface. Rearrange them many times but am never satisfied with the result. I need more cutlery.

I go to the Co-op, but they're sold out, as is the case with most desirable wares. Instead, I buy white lacquer since it's in stock, and the clerk chortles: "Planning on painting the pantry?"

I ask Karlína to collect cutlery for me, bent old forks, knives, and spoons that people can part with, and she says, "How have you been able to manage all this time without cutlery?"

She collects a good bagful for me.

I'm ecstatic.

I spend several nights arranging the cutlery. Then the gluing begins, messy work; the glue is strong, it gives me a headache. I glue close to eighty pieces onto the board, mainly forks, which people had the most of, or maybe they used spoons and knives more often and were reluctant to hand them over. Then I paint over the whole surface.

It's all white.

White cirrus.

In heaven, people eat with white cutlery.

Karlína was first to see the cutlery assemblage—besides Halldóra, of course, who said that it was very avant-garde, as such works are called abroad—and she seemed flabbergasted; she gasped and coughed, despite not having had a drink of anything since coming into the house. "Is that cutlery I'm seeing?" she finally managed to splutter, and Karitas said that it was indeed, happy with the attention her art was receiving. Still, she began to have her doubts when Karlína plunked down onto a chair, hid her face in her hands, rocked back and forth, and repeated over and over: "Jesus Christ." After invoking him a few times, she jumped up, dashed through the house, scrutinized the kitchen and bedroom with a look of desperation, as if searching for evidence, rushed outside, then came in again. Karitas asked, "Are you looking for my sister? She needed to pop over to the Co-op." And Karlína sat back down. She still hadn't taken off her overcoat, but her dress could be glimpsed underneath; it was practically bursting at the seams. Without looking up, Karlína said, "Oh, so your sister was here, too?" Karitas realized that she had put her foot in it, and said hurriedly: "No, I was just joking. Bjarghildur can't get away, what with the responsibility of that big household on her shoulders." Then Karlína wanted to hear all about Bjarghildur: where she lived, to whom she was married, and what telephone office was nearest her. Upon receiving this information, she stood up and said goodbye.

"And she just groaned when she saw my cutlery picture," Karitas complained to Halldóra later. "That's the sort of reaction you can expect, dear Karitas," said Halldóra, while still encouraging her to continue in the same vein.

The next day, after they had washed their faces and were giving little Jón his morning cleaning, they saw Högna come riding up, escorted by her five daughters. "There they are, those cursed things," said Karitas, and Halldóra asked whether she ought to go and hide.

Högna glanced around, and the daughters walked carefully through the house as if expecting little devils to leap out from the corners. Högna looked askance at Karitas and narrowed her eyes: "Weren't you painting a picture, Karitas?" Had the woman's daughters not been there, Karitas would have gladly shown her the cutlery work, but since Högna wasn't alone, Karitas said that she hadn't painted anything recently. Högna behaved very strangely, saying that she had come to take Karitas's measurements since she would probably need a wider skirt before long, but she did little more than measure Karitas with her eyes. The daughters set about cleaning and tidying, emptying the chamber pot, filling a jug with water, fetching more water, heating water, pouring water into a bucket. Little Jón kept getting in their way, wanting to splash in the water. One of them picked him up, but Karitas grabbed him from her. "Why can't they ever hold Jón?" Högna asked in an offended tone. "He's afraid of elves," said Karitas, scowling.

They left soon afterward. Halldóra emerged from her hiding place. She said she'd been worried they would scrub her into the light during their cleaning frenzy. Halldóra made fun of the sisters, and Karitas laughed with abandon. It had been a long time since she had laughed so heartily, and little Jón looked at her in surprise. But Karitas had to hand it to Högna's daughters, despite their elvish nature: they always fetched water for her when they came with their mother. In the evening, Karitas and Halldóra poured heated water into the large tub and took baths, each in turn. Halldóra washed her hair with fragrant soap, and Karitas told her stories about Copenhagen. There were many things she could tell Halldóra, but not Sigmar. The sorts of little things that girls talk about with each other. "But you know, Halldóra," she said, "I've never told this to anyone, but I was so terribly lonely abroad. I never had a good friend at school, even though most of my classmates were very sweet and took me with them to exhibitions, but many of them were from sophisticated, privileged families, some of them even related to the king, I think, and I swear they looked down on me just because I was an Icelander and was always washing dishes when I wasn't in school. I never told Mama this in my letters. I didn't want her to think that I was ungrateful. I've never actually had a girlfriend except for Pía, maybe, but she disappeared so abruptly from my life." Halldóra was full of empathy; she understood about the girlfriends and felt sad on her sister's behalf, but Karitas hurriedly changed the subject. She couldn't bear to see Halldóra melancholy, and entertained her with stories about all the elegant people she had seen at the Glyptoteket and the fishwives at the harbor. The sisters sat and chatted late into the night.

The darkness left them in peace.

Högna and Karlína, however, had gotten into the habit of looking in at any time of the day, prompting Halldóra to say: "They never leave you alone, do they?" "Oh, what can I do about that?" sighed Karitas in despair.

"Ask if you can paint them. Naked."

So she asked Karlína if she would model for her. And Karlína perked up; her eyes gleamed and her cheeks flushed, but then Karitas added: "I know it doesn't seem very comfortable for a model to have to take off her clothes in the middle of winter so far north. There's no 'Roman heat' here as there was for Bernini, but it has always been easy to keep this house warm, and the floors aren't cold." Karlína looked at her silently for several moments, trying to figure out what it was the artist wanted, and then asked suspiciously, "You want me to take my socks off?" Karitas explained with gestures what garments besides her socks Karlína had to remove so that her body could come into its own—and of course, they all had to go—and then she hurried over, propped a pillow on the divan, and showed her how she should lie. Karlína turned blood red. Finally she whispered, stressing every syllable: "You mean you want me lying here bare-bottomed for your picture?" Karitas replied that that was exactly how it had to be. "And you'll be a fine model, Karlína, with your soft flesh."

Karlína stormed out of the house with her gaggle of children in a line behind her. She didn't show herself again for several days, and the two sisters sighed with relief. But just before the weekend, when Karitas needed to go down to the Co-op for raisins and a few little things for Halldóra, she ran into Högna—who wasn't particularly affable toward her. She coughed and cleared her throat, looked at Karitas's stomach, hemmed and hawed before pulling herself together and saying, "You can't be rude to such a good girl as Karlína. I heard that you wanted to paint her in the nude. You who are a wife and mother. How could you suggest such a thing?" "How pretty it would have been had Botticelli painted Venus bundled in clothing," Karitas replied dryly, not yielding an inch. Högna tossed her head, and with a touch of contempt, snapped: "It's all the same to me what lewd lives the women in Copenhagen choose to lead, but here in Borgarfjörður, such things are not tolerated, that much is certain."

Karitas had managed to infuriate and offend both women, Karlína and Högna, which hadn't been her intention—well, perhaps to a small degree. She had simply wanted to free herself from their incessant visits. Just for a while. She had no particular desire, in any case, to paint the female figure. But in the aftermath of this uproar, she began to think that she, a graduate of the Royal Academy of Fine Arts, in fact had every right to paint naked women without heaven and earth being shaken to their core, and she said so to Halldóra. Who agreed with her fully.

They were left in peace for a few days, and Karitas went on a rampage in the storehouse and the workshop, collecting nails and screws, rusty little tools, and rags. She cut one of her sweaters into small pieces, because the knit structure made an excellent addition to the patterns that she envisioned. She sacrificed two saucers from her fine tableware, and glued all that she had gathered onto wood. She wanted to go up to the village to buy brown paint, but had such pain in her abdomen that she didn't think she could cope with the trip. In any case, there was a fierce wind and crashing surf, and it was hard to carry Jón when he refused to walk. "My belly didn't give me so much trouble the other two times," she complained to Halldóra. "It's as if my stomach stretches out and becomes hard for a few minutes." And Halldóra said that it was probably a girl, that they behave differently, need so much space to begin with.

The surf grew even wilder over the next few days, and one evening the waves reached higher than ever, towered over the shore ridge, crashed down on the house. The sea surrounded it, hit it from the north, ran along it and then down at the south wall. Karitas sat in bed with little Jón, waiting for the seawater to seep under the door and into the room, but nothing happened. There was just a slight bit of moisture at the front door. "This is a good house," she told Jón and Halldóra. "It's watertight and stays warm."

As the storm raged, she dreamed of an elf woman. This woman didn't look like the five sisters at all; she was dark haired and slender, and she said: "It will be a hard winter for you, but I will help you because you took care of my hill out west." That was all there was to the dream, and when Karitas woke, she immediately told Halldóra about it. They both remembered the elf hill back home. Their mother had forbidden them to play on it, and asked them to make sure that other children didn't do so, either. "The hidden people don't like us playing on their houses any more than we would," she had said. "I remember looking after the hill as if it were the apple of my eye," Karitas told Halldóra, "but I would never have imagined that the elf woman would reward me for doing so! Just think, she's found me here in the east! And how is she going to repay the favor?"

The answer to that question became clear that same day, when she felt stabbing pains in her abdomen. That sort of pain, she knew well. "How can this be?" she asked Halldóra. "I'm barely into my eighth month!" "It's too early, and not as it should be," said Halldóra. "Hang the white sheet." She hung the white sheet in the hope that folk would be out and about once the storm calmed down, and then she lay down, as Halldóra advised. Little Jón was unusually fretful. He didn't want to play with his toys, but just clung to her and cried. Karitas was hugely relieved when Karlína came running. "I just wanted to see if everything was all right with you after the storm," she said breathlessly, holding on to her heart, "and then I saw the white sheet fluttering out the kitchen window, but, my dearest dear, you're not due to give birth until May!" Karitas thought so, too, and they couldn't understand why she was having these contractions, yet contractions they were, and something had to be done. The doctor happened to be in the village, which was fortunate, because the midwife was in Akureyri for an operation. The doctor had had to amputate a leg and hadn't been able to leave yet due to the storm, so Högna and Karlína put him on a horse and rode with him out to Karitas's house. He remained silent while examining Karitas and didn't offer the women any information, only asking, after looking her over thoroughly: "Are you here alone?" Karitas nearly pointed out Halldóra to him, but Karlína quickly interjected, "Yes, she's alone, but Högna and I are keeping an eye on her." The doctor said that he would wait in the village until the afternoon to see how things developed, and asked the women not to go far. Which they didn't do, and instead, began washing clothes and cleaning the house. "You do an awful lot of cleaning every time you're here," Karitas sighed, but they didn't answer her; they just shook their heads and looked at her worriedly. "It's going to take us a long time to tidy up the sitting room, what with all that junk from the workshop in it," they muttered. "It's sheer luck that the child hasn't injured himself on any of it. And there are no clean bedclothes!" "We've had no dry weather at all," whined Karitas from her bed, but they didn't listen, just discussed how best to take care of everything, get it all into acceptable shape before the birth, if it should happen now. They took turns going home, made arrangements regarding their own households, fetched clean bedclothes, their knitting, bread, and plenty of coffee—one never knew how this might go—and brought toys for Jón to keep him happy. He didn't need clean clothes. "He's the only thing in this house that's clean," they said so loudly that the childbearing woman could hear it.

The contractions seemed to subside that evening, and the women calmed down a bit, got Jón ready for bed, dandled him, and sang lullabies. Night fell. The women made themselves comfortable in the sitting room and dozed off. Toward morning, however, when they had started to hope that the worst was over, the contractions returned in full, excruciating force. Karitas moaned, felt as if she needed to use the chamber pot, and then her water broke. Högna rode quickly up to the village. As fast as she could, Karlína put a pot of water on the stove. Karitas groaned in agony and called out to Halldóra. She was nowhere to be seen. "Where has Halldóra gone?" shouted Karitas, but Karlína asked her for the love of God to hold the child in until the doctor came. "She had to go home to Sumarliði," groaned Karitas disappointedly, despite feeling better knowing that she was with the child. Finally the doctor and Högna arrived, weather-beaten and wet; the storm had returned with high winds and sudden lashings of snow, and at the same time, Karitas crowned. She was having twins.

They arrived ten minutes apart. "The boy weighs a thousand grams, the girl seven hundred and fifty," the doctor said in a natural tone, as if they were fully developed babies, but his hands trembled as he handled them. Högna and Karlína couldn't hold back; the tears streamed unremittingly down their cheeks as they looked sorrowfully from the children to the mother, who seemed to be the only one able to maintain her composure. "Pity that I have no bed for them," she said thoughtfully, wiping the sweat from her forehead. She raised herself onto her elbow, looked attentively at the children, who were the length of a book, blind, and had nearly transparent skin, and then said sharply to the women: "Aren't you going to bathe them?"

The children were wrapped in flannel diapers and laid on a linen cloth on the dresser. "The poor little things," said the doctor, stroking them. He looked at them pensively for a few moments, then took off his wedding ring and slid it over the little girl's leg to her thigh. There it remained for a moment. Then he took back his ring, sat down with Karitas, held her hands, and said: "Karitas, it isn't certain that the babies will survive, you must prepare for that, but if they do, they will live to be ninety." He gave her good advice, asked her to swaddle the children well, keep them warm, and breastfeed them at two- to three-hour intervals around the clock. "When am I supposed to sleep?" she asked, but received no answer, as this wasn't about her. Then the doctor left, but said that he would come and see her later. Silence fell over the house. The women were as if in a trance, standing bewildered next to the dresser and staring at the babies, who were still breathing but hadn't been bathed. Their mother took charge. She ordered the others to bathe the infants, swaddle them in cotton, prepare a bed for them in one of the dresser drawers, put a three-quarter-liter bottle of hot water in a wool sock between them, and place the dresser drawer on a chair next to the coal stove.

Then she fell asleep, exhausted in soul and body. The women stood watch. Högna sat down next to the drawer and stared at the babies, as if by doing so, she could prevent them from slipping away from her into the great beyond. Karlína dressed little Jón, who had woken refreshed and energetic, without the slightest awareness of the night's events. He was captivated by the little children in the drawer, thought they were dolls he could play with, and got a bit upset when he was handed other toys. In the afternoon, they woke Karitas and told her gently that the little girl was probably gone—the life seemed to have gone out of her. Karitas took this calmly, with barely a reaction. She tried to milk herself, squeezing out a few drops with great effort. "This isn't enough, but we've got to try to get some nourishment in them," she said, as if she hadn't even heard what they said about the girl. They poured cow's milk into a small medicine bottle, and Karitas used its dropper to drip the milk into the boy's mouth. He accepted and swallowed it. The little girl showed no signs of life. "We'll just let her rest a little," the mother said. She returned to her bed, took Jón with her, and told him stories about animals, making the corresponding sounds. The women whispered together in the kitchen, unable to decide whether to prepare the little girl's body for burial or not. They could hardly let them lie there together, one alive and the other dead, but they thought the mother should be allowed to decide. They boiled water for coffee and prepared food, having to do everything carefully, being sure not to bump into the dresser drawer, moving like frightened mice. In the evening, after Karlína had put little Jón to bed, she had to go home to tend to her own children, but couldn't refrain from taking a look at the little ones one last time before she left. Tucking the cotton in better around the little girl, she let out a cry. "She's moving her little toe; she's moving her little toe!" Karitas and Högna ran over; there was no mistake: it was moving, that little toe the size of the head of a nail. They cried, laughed, and kissed each other. "I knew she would live," said Karitas. "The elf woman promised to help me." The others didn't ask anything about this woman, considering it only natural that such folk should take matters into their own hands at critical moments.

The world outside became an unknown dimension, but the one inside was marked out by floors, wood-paneled walls, and a ceiling—a safe, warm enclosure for the children and herself. She kindled the stove night and day, sometimes having to shed clothing in all the heat, and stood watching over the children in her undershirt as the north wind pounded the windows and a furious westerly tore at the roof. It was a harsh winter, as the elf woman had predicted, but it didn't matter to Karitas; she rubbed the babies with oil, changed their cotton, fed them milk with the dropper. Often, their small mouths twisted as the liquid trickled into their throats. If Högna or Karlína couldn't come to help her, the men who hadn't left to fish took it upon themselves to do so, struggling through the storm to deliver milk and coal and peat, and in return, were allowed to see the little children. People could stare at them endlessly. In between the snowstorms, the village women came, having knitted and sewn clothing for the little dears and wanting to see if the garments fit, which they didn't, of course, but first and foremost, they came to see the tiny things for themselves. "Just one person at a time, and hold your hands over your noses and mouths," ordered Högna and Karlína, who had formed a shield around the mother and children, and the visitors were happy to stand outside and wait, even though the wind whistled up their skirts. They crossed themselves and said, "Jesus Lord," when they saw the little ones, marveling that they should be alive, and praised the Creator for His mercy. When the doctor came to visit, however, he preferred to leave the Lord out of it, although he did struggle to restrain his astonishment when he saw that the children were not only living, but thriving. He said: "They have strong hearts."

This spread throughout the village. Their hearts were so strong. People exchanged affirmative nods. Borgarfirthian hearts. They doubted that the children would have made it had the father been from the south.

In the meantime, Sigmar had received the news by phone. And had sent a message back that he would call home the next time he came ashore. The weather had improved slightly by the time Karitas was summoned to the telephone office. "My little one," he said on the phone, "a number of things have happened, I've heard." "No more than usual," she answered. "So small?" he asked. "So small what?" she replied brusquely. For a moment or two, he said nothing, but then asked: "How small, big, were they?" "Weren't you told?" she snapped. "Yes, yes yes," he said awkwardly. "What did you do with them, where did you put them, did we have a cradle?" "No, we've never had a cradle, Sigmar. I just put them in a dresser drawer." There was a long silence. Finally, he drew a deep breath, and, adopting a more authoritative tone, said:

"We'll try to move north in the autumn, but I don't know if I'll make it home between fishing seasons in the spring. I must do all that I can to earn enough for the house; we're fishing so much that we always head right back out as soon as we've landed our catches, yes, not much sleeping is done aboard ship here in the south." "Nor in the east," she said. Before saying goodbye, he added, "Wouldn't it be best to give them an emergency baptism?" "No," she said, "they will be baptized like all other children, and not in any other way."

Her mother's suggestion for the same didn't change her position, either. Steinunn sent the children hymnbooks, accompanied by a letter. "My dearest Karitas: While sincerely congratulating you and Sigmar on your little son and little daughter, I hope with all my heart that the Almighty will watch over the blessed little angels. Your friend, Karlína, told me on the phone that they were so tiny that they could fit in the hand of a large man. I have slept little since receiving the news, and deeply regret not being able to be there to support you. But I know, my beloved daughter, that God Almighty will never turn away from you, and He must have some purpose in letting the children come into the world so early. In spite of that, you must not delay too long in having them baptized, and I am sending these hymnbooks that you can write their names in once they've been given them. You have such pretty handwriting. We here in the south are fine. Your brothers are in good health, but I myself have recently been plagued by arthritis, and often have difficulty walking first thing in the morning. Otherwise, the weather has been relatively nice."

In the north, the weather had been bearable, too, although at the time the letter was written, there had been lashing rain and sleet, but the housewife at Þrastabakki was as energetic as usual, despite having been struck speechless at the news that Karlína had phoned to tell her. "Dearest Karitas, children are truly a gift from God, but why such burdens are placed on the shoulders of an artist goes beyond my comprehension."

"Burdens? Are you burdens?" Karitas asked the children, looking so tiny as they lay there nestled around the hot-water bottle. She sat down beside the dresser drawer and tried not to be upset. Jón climbed into her lap, and she told him that his aunt Bjarghildur was going to come visit after the main haymaking. He didn't understand, and she added, "But in the meantime, Papa will come home. Perhaps." "Baba," the boy said happily, holding out his arms. "But I haven't seen Halldóra," she continued. "So it is with midwives; they're called out in the middle of the night, and then, of course, she needed to get home to little Sumarliði. But I'll probably name your little sister Halldóra. How would you like that, Jón? And then, wouldn't it stand to reason that your brother should be called Sumarliði? Then at least their names will be interknit, even if the two of them weren't destined to be together. It's so sad when lovers can't be together."

Although the days had begun to grow longer, darkness lay heavy over the house at night, but she no longer feared it since the lamps were lit, and she tended to her babies as if it were broad daylight. Every two hours, they were given drops of milk, and a new hot-water bottle was placed between them. She kindled the stove until she was sweating, and the house creaked and cracked from the temperature difference outside and in. Between feedings, she threw herself onto the bed, but never managed to finish a dream, always starting from sleep as if someone shoved her. Then it was time for the next feeding. Once, when Högna came to visit, the woman looked inquisitively at her and asked when she had last slept a whole night through. This, Karitas could not recall. "You need to sleep," Högna said. "You've begun spouting gibberish." Then she took the night shift, sitting by the dresser drawer and knitting all night long. Karitas slept for an entire fourteen hours and felt refreshed and vigorous when she woke.

Spring cleaning was in full swing when the men returned shortly after Closing Day. Some of the women, however, had only finished half of the indoor cleaning, having also had to look after the sheep and assist neighbors who had recently given birth or who were struggling due to illness, Karitas being one of them, although, in a figurative sense, things were a bit brighter in her house. The twins' weights had doubled, and they had left the dresser drawer. Now they looked more like children than dolls, dressed in flannel clothing and lying head to foot next to each other in Karlína's cradle, wrapped in tiny woolen blankets beneath a down-filled duvet. Otherwise, there wasn't much light. All the walls were black with soot from the relentless heating during the winter, and that sort of grime, the women had a hard time tolerating, whether in their own homes or elsewhere. An entire army showed up one morning, making it so cramped inside that people could hardly move. "Incredible that the children should have endured such bad air," the women said, moving the infants from room to room as needed and giving themselves plenty of time to babble to them in a language that has never been written down. Everything was scrubbed, aired, and washed. At the same time, there was baking and a great deal of laughing, and there they stood in their aprons and rolled-up sleeves when an adolescent boy came running up and, panting, announced that the men's ship had arrived.

They tossed aside their scrub brushes and rushed up to the village, leaving Karitas turning this way and that in the soap-cleansed house, unable to decide whether she should wash herself first and then the children, or vice versa. She decided to start with herself, and, wanting to make sure she smelled good in the right places, scrubbed her armpits thoroughly. Despite their cold parting at the churchyard, she still had some slight butterflies; she knew this man—that he would grab for her sooner or later. But she washed both herself and the children high and low, made coffee, and laid out saltfish and seal blubber without any new developments. She began listening for his footsteps, wandering out into the farmyard and back in again.

After the spring clouds over the fjord had displayed all of their hues and themes, she finally saw someone approaching. But it wasn't the one whom she wanted to see, it was Karlína, alone and dejected. She neither waved nor called out when she saw Karitas in the farmyard, but looked down at the ground and drew nearer in silence. When at last she looked into Karitas's face, it was as if she saw the devil himself; her lips twisted into a scowl. "I have a bag here for you," she spat, "a shipment from the south. It's tubes of paints; that would be my guess, anyway," and she slapped the bag into Karitas's arms. Most natural would have been to inquire about the sender, but the anger clearly boiling in the woman led to a different question: "Karlína, have you and Þorfinnur been quarreling?" "Quarreling, quarreling?" shrieked Karlína. "How could we be quarreling when the man isn't even here?" Something had happened, there was no doubt about it, so Karitas tried to persuade the other woman to come into the house with her so that she could calm down enough for a chat, but this only agitated Karlína even more: "No, I'll be damned if I enter his house!" The time had come. "And where is Sigmar?" asked Karitas, barely breathing. "Out at sea, out at sea. He went straight north for the herring fishing and took my Þorfinnur with him!" There was the crux of the matter. At first, the thought struck Karitas that the man had found himself another woman. But this she kept to herself; Karlína was upset enough already. "So they went straight to the herring," she said bitterly. "And what are they going to do up north for a whole month? The herring doesn't usually show up until late June." Karlína shouted: "It doesn't matter when the bloody herring comes; what matters is that my husband stooped so low as to join the crew of the devil that you're married to!" Karitas looked out to sea, which, for certain people, held far greater attraction than her little children in their cradle. Then she pressed the bag to her chest and, without another word, turned to go back into the house, but Karlína grabbed her shoulder and said hoarsely: "Karitas, how can Sigmar have gotten him to stoop so low?" Karitas looked her straight in the eye: "Sigmar has a diabolical charm."

Karitas

Coal Stove 1926

Oil on canvas

A summer night in the east.

Timeless serenity.

Every little sound goes into motion, flies between mountains, soars over fjords, crawls up the valley.

The serenades of lovers, the whispers exchanged before and after embraces.

I sit beside my sleeping nestlings, hold my breath so that I can better hear the lovers out on the rose-gold cliffs.

Sit with my hands in my lap, staring into the kitchen, at it, black, rugged.

I'd wrestled with the subject before but gave up; it was as strong as a settler woman, impossible to defeat. But perhaps I hadn't approached it in the right way, perhaps I hadn't respected it enough. The one who had saved my children, held the fire, aroused it until the house trembled with the warmth.

Its sounds had been my serenade.

The coal stove.

I slip out to the storehouse, choose a larger-sized frame, position it on the easel, move extremely slowly so as not to wake the children, mix the colors, paint the stove directly on the canvas. It fills the entire picture plane, black yet blazing. There is movement inside it, which one doesn't see, but senses.

There is also movement inside me. A little ember waiting to burst into life. It isn't the big events that change the world, but rather everyday things and unspoken words.

I paint until morning, finish the picture. I'd painted it in my mind before I started.

"How are the poor little dears doing?" asked the old man every morning when he brought the milk, and Karitas replied each time: "They're getting along really well." And he returned home convinced in his heart that the children's well-being was thanks to the fresh, warm milk from his cow. He had thought it best that he himself bring the milk after the little ones were born, because the adolescent boys tended to dawdle, he told Karitas, and she had grown very fond of the old man, he being the only person apart from the children whom she saw daily. Karlína came sometimes and took little Jón home with her so that he could play with other children and avoid becoming unsocial, and she put so much emphasis on the word "unsocial" that Karitas began apologizing for their isolation. It was true, she and the children were quite far away and far too much alone, but she simply didn't know what to do about it. At such times, Karlína would say: "Why don't you take the children south to your mother, or north to your sister? What are you waiting for?" But if Karitas complained unprompted about her solitude, Karlína did an about-face and bristled. "Do you ever hear me complaining, Karitas? Even with six children? Aren't all fishermen's wives in this country alone with their children and households?"

The words "fishermen's wives" got on her nerves. She was an artist. It was as if people were trying at all costs to forget that. But even though the old man didn't remember that she was an artist, she didn't hold it against him. "They're so restless," she groaned one morning when he came with the milk. "Damn," he said sympathetically. "I haven't slept for many nights; they take turns being awake!" she practically whined another morning as he handed her the milk jug. "Bloody awful situation," he said.

Despite the brevity of his comments, he apparently let the right party know about the awful situation, because one day, Högna came tearing down on her favorite saddlehorse and had barely dismounted before launching into her business. "If you don't sleep, Karitas, you'll lose your mind. I kept vigil over my children every night, and one day I was so muddleheaded from lack of sleep that I almost stuck one of the children into the copper instead of the clothes. You look awful. You've got to have people around you, under these circumstances." Karitas agreed wholeheartedly; the thought of boiling one of the children was terrifying. But where she was to find people to have around her, she had no idea, because all the women in the village were fishermen's wives, and they had enough on their plates taking care of themselves and their families. Högna was well aware of this and shook her head resignedly. She was no less downcast when she looked at the children, who, however, were sleeping soundly just then, dead tired after their sleepless nights, and said: "They're growing and fattening up, no problem there. But why are they such a bother at night?" Karitas replied that the boys could easily sleep, but that they were never given any peace to do so by the girl, who howled all night, that rascally rag doll. She said she thought the child's stomach might be troubling her. She had to walk around with her every night. "I'm going home now to make dinner, but I'll come back and look after the children so that you can sleep tonight," Högna said. She stuck to her word. By midnight, she had everything under control in Karitas's home. She told Karitas to lie down with the boys in her own bed, while she herself brought the girl to the sitting room and said authoritatively before closing the door: "Sleep, Karitas."

Which she really tried to do. Squeezed her eyes shut, curled up in a ball, stretched out again, tossed and turned, tried to think of something beautiful, the motif for her next picture, which could, most often, make her fall asleep, but every single nerve in her body was tense and unruly. When Högna was about to leave the next morning, they were both dejected after their sleepless night, pale, lacking appetites, and unable to express themselves in a comprehensible language. "This simply won't do," Högna finally managed to say. "Something must be done, though I don't know how we can fix this." Karitas, who felt ashamed about not having been able to sleep after all the trouble the woman had taken, said: "My sister was planning to come after the main haymaking and stay here until the men returned from the herring; perhaps Bjarghildur can put this to rights."

Apparently, folk there did not soon forget the day the woman in the riding habit disembarked from the coastal steamer. It wasn't just the clothes that made her unforgettable, but the way she comported herself, issuing orders right and left with a gloved hand—orders that were obeyed without a word, though that wasn't mentioned in the retellings—and that she smelled so nice. Folk weren't used to people smelling good in the middle of haymaking. But they were quick to discern the circumstances; the men, realizing that this woman was a dame, if not a veritable gentlewoman, did their best to please her, making sure that her footlocker and trunk took precedence in the unloading, supporting her firmly, perhaps more of them than necessary, both when she stepped into the boat and then when she stepped out of it onto the quay, where they pushed everything else aside and loaded her luggage quickly onto a cart. She didn't have to wait long for a horse; the swiftest among the men ran to fetch the best in the village, while the rest went and got a wooden box, which they invited her to sit down on and then spoke politely with her about the weather while she waited. The other passengers just had to wait, as did their luggage. When everything was ready and she was asked where she wanted to go—although it wasn't customary for ship passengers to be taken to their destination—she replied that she had come to visit her sister, the local artist. "It must have something to do with Sigmar," someone said, and when the dame raised her eyebrows, the man added, rather proudly: "Sigmar is our Catch King."

They rode off at a leisurely and dignified pace. As the procession passed by, people stopped working and wiped their sweaty foreheads, but the gentlewoman looked neither right nor left, and not so much as a drop of sweat could be seen on her, despite her being all bundled up in her riding habit. When the regiment reached the lava rocks, Karitas first thought that a funeral procession had taken a wrong turn, but then she recognized the riding habit and went out into the farmyard. Bjarghildur stepped gracefully from her horse, but when she saw her sister standing by the vestibule, she froze for a moment. With a puzzled expression, she approached slowly, looked her up and down, and said indignantly: "You look as if you've crawled out of your grave!" Then she glared at her entourage, as if it had something to do with the woman's appearance, and said curtly, "Thank you, you may go now." When discussing this later, the men agreed that the woman's farewell could have been a bit more warmhearted. They did, however, carry her footlocker in for her.

Momentarily forgetting their different social positions, the sisters kissed each other and looked into each other's eyes as they had under the duvet in Akureyri, but then the elder sister remembered who she was, glanced around, and said: "So this is where you've been muddling through—the artist herself." Karitas wasn't exactly in the mood to think about her circumstances, and had little to say to this proclamation. She just stroked little Jón, who, when the woman appeared, had stuck his head under his mother's skirt, despite normally being unafraid of strangers. But the children in the cradle were above reproach. Bjarghildur was elated when she saw the two little things, lifted the duvet, stroked them, bent down to them, sniffed at them, and muttered, "Oh, how adorable they are, with their plump cheeks, the darlings!" "I've just begun giving them a little porridge," said Karitas wearily. With nothing to say to that, Bjarghildur went on: "And Mama said that they were so little; I need to phone her down south and tell her they've grown! But all this dawdling won't do! We'll unpack the footlocker before preparing dinner and tidying up. I've brought clothes for you and the children, which we made at home at Þrastabakki, and there are tablecloths and various delicacies, boiled meat and raisins, since you like them so much. And where am I to sleep?"

Despite the commotion that blew in with the housewife from the north, Karitas found her life even brighter now; she felt much less on edge, having another person to share the responsibilities with her, looking after the children, and deciding what to cook and when to go to bed. Bjarghildur didn't want to sleep in the sitting room, saying that the bed in the bedroom was much softer, and if Karitas didn't want to move, then they would just have to sleep together, which, of course, they had done before. They changed the children's diapers and cleaned their bottoms, taking turns telling each other about their lives in low voices. They fed the children before bed, and then Bjarghildur leaned over the cradle and said brusquely: "And now you must sleep." Then the sisters crawled under the duvet and whispered to each other. There was so much to tell about Bjarghildur's household, and the poor baby girl, who hadn't slept at night in three months, obeyed her aunt's order and didn't make a sound.

Children sleep best when they hear women whispering.

After Bjarghildur fell silent, Karitas had difficulty sleeping, constantly anticipating the little whinny that was the precursor to crying, but around midnight, she, too, finally slipped off. The next morning, she woke feeling so refreshed that she was finally able to get a spoonful or two of porridge down without retching. On the other hand, she had a hard time keeping pace with all the activity going on now both indoors and out, while at the same time listening to her sister's theories about bad marriages and the recklessness of fishermen who shirked their duty to participate in the building up of a healthy Icelandic society and instead binged on brennivín and women around the slimy herring-salting lots. Before going to bed and after getting up, Bjarghildur read the Bible aloud because she was a Christian, and in the morning sun, she set up a table by the south wall, covered it with a tablecloth, and batted away the bluebottles with her Bible. She opened all the doors and windows—"All the bad air that comes with seafaring needs letting out"—and hung everything that could possibly be hung on clotheslines to let it air out. Mealtimes were regular, but she was dumbstruck at Sigmar's slothfulness, not to have brought running water into the house, and pitied the women who had to cook their meals in those dented excuses for pots. She set fixed times for washing both the children and the laundry, "because in good homes in my district, Karitas Jónsdóttir, the housework is done according to timetables from morning to midnight, though it might be done differently in fishermen's homes and by housewives who never attended a women's college."

Although sleep after midnight is taken for granted in good households in the countryside, that was unfortunately not the case in this fisherman's house. Before long, the little girl was back in form, howling all night, and the sisters took turns walking with her around the room. Neither of them could get any sleep. The child's crying, the most heart-rending sound in the world, contained an accusation that made them believe they were to blame, even if they were not. "The child needs to breathe the clear, healthy air of the countryside," said Bjarghildur. "The eternal swell and salty air in these fishing villages make children terribly ill; their lungs fill with rubbish. Just imagine what comes from the sea—all sorts of foreign bacteria!"

However, when Högna and Karlína finally decided to go and greet the gentlewoman from the north, the fishing village became one of the most beautiful places in the country, perhaps even more beautiful than Skagafjörður itself. "The hinterland here is wonderful," said Bjarghildur, throwing out her arms. "Surrounded by the most beautiful mountains that I have ever seen in my life; the colors so magnificent that they leave me awestruck, and inspired by the might of the Creator." Tears welled in her eyes as she praised the village, and the women, who squirmed at all the superlatives, were touched and had to wipe tears from the corners of their eyes, as well. Each outdid the other heaping praise on the place, and when Bjarghildur mentioned casually how much she longed to explore the area on horseback, and take a look inside both the schoolhouse and the church so that she could tell those at home about life in Borgarfjörður, both women eagerly said that they would hurry home and prepare dinner, and return afterward to look after the children so that Karitas could ride with her out under the evening sun and show her the village.

"We'll ride in a circle," said Bjarghildur as she mounted her horse in her riding habit. "Let's go clockwise, starting with the countryside and ending in the village." "A grassy valley," she said, after they had ridden for a while. "It reminds me of the valley by the bay back home in the west, although that one was smaller," she continued, speaking a bit like a poet composing verse in his mind. "Do you remember, Sister, how secure and happy our lives were when our father was alive? Days of sheer sunshine. But we were given a good upbringing by our mother, Karitas. She taught us beautiful rules of life, probity and diligence, respect for people and animals, honesty in words and deeds, and last but not least, she told us that we must always keep our promises." The sisters gave their horses their heads, the fresh air trickled slowly through their minds, and they had reached the western side of the village when Karitas said: "There's the churchyard. I'm going to stop in." "Do you think that's a good idea, Sister, as indisposed as you are?" asked Bjarghildur, but she, too, dismounted and entered through the lychgate. "The poor little thing," she said as they stood over Sumarliði's grave. "He couldn't tolerate the salty air." Karitas's temper flared. "The two of us were brought up in salty air, and we're still here. Salty air has never killed anyone. On the contrary, in foreign countries it's thought to be beneficial for health. He was sick from birth; some children aren't destined to live." Bjarghildur sighed: "All that those foreigners know is how to kill each other. But who is lying there?" she asked when Karitas stopped at Kára's grave. "A woman. Just a woman," said Karitas, making the sign of the cross over the grave three times. But the fresh air had vanished from her mind; she rode distractedly behind her sister into the village. They rode to the schoolhouse, but Bjarghildur contented herself with viewing it from the outside: "A very fine house; here is where the children are educated. It reminds me of our mother. Education was one of her top priorities, and in the end, she achieved her exalted goal, to provide all of her children with an education—even if some of them haven't succeeded in using it as well as others. But the duty rests on us, dear sister, to provide our own children with an education, and I have delivered many a lecture on the value of education for a thriving Icelandic national life, both at Women's Club meetings and at the political meetings of the householders in my parish. While it isn't customary at those meetings for a woman to discuss matters of national interest, the men asked me to speak on education, and my talks were always well received. But shouldn't we go and have a look at the church now? It will be useful for me to see how the choir is accommodated in this parish."

After entering, Bjarghildur shut the door behind them, stood there for a few moments, and took a deep breath: "There's nothing like the smell of a house of worship. Let's go take a closer look at the altar cloth. Oh, the women here do seem to know a thing or two about embroidering!" She fingered the cloth in great astonishment, examining the stitching thoroughly, and whispered, "They must have attended women's college." Karitas pointed at the altarpiece: "Their painter created this." Bjarghildur glanced at the image and frowned. "Yes, yes, anyone can splash colors onto a surface, but only those who know what they're doing can embroider an altar cloth." Viewing the cloth's elaborate embroidery seemed to have tested her spiritual strength, because when she finally tore herself free from the altar, she sounded slightly testy as she asked where the choir stood during mass. Karitas didn't know. She couldn't remember having seen any choir, had only been to the church that one time, when the boys were baptized, and then, only the organist had been there, she said. She didn't mention either the wedding or the two funerals. On the other hand, she added, after rubbing her forehead, "The little ones are to be named Halldóra and Sumarliði."

For a moment, there was silence in the church. Bjarghildur looked askance at her sister, undid the top button of her riding jacket so she could breathe easier, sat down on the front pew, and said tenderly: "Sit down here with me, dear sister. Let us pray together for their souls." Bjarghildur crossed herself and folded her hands in prayer; Karitas looked at the organ, regarded its lines and corners, gave the painting of Christ a sidelong glance, heard the endless murmur beside her; her sister's prayer was long and wide-ranging, touching on many different individuals. Finally, it ended with an amen and the sign of the cross. Bjarghildur took a deep breath, looked at the altar cloth, then into her sister's eyes, and said, "Here in the house of God, I ask you, dear sister, whether you will now fulfill your promise?" Karitas couldn't remember having ever promised her anything, and asked: "What promise, Bjarghildur?"

"If I have two, I'll give you one."

Karitas looked at her sister. "Two what, Bjarghildur? Do you mean paintings?" "You know very well what I mean," her sister said breathlessly, and then it dawned on Karitas what she was talking about. She was aghast. "Have you lost your mind, woman?"

"I'm offering you my help," Bjarghildur said hurriedly, doing an about-face, before adding in a resentful tone, unused to being accused of losing her mind, "I'm only talking about fosterage for a short time." She got up, went and stood next to the organ, and laid one hand on its edge. She looked elegant in her riding habit. In the tone of a parish priest, she addressed her sister: "Our life will only be a reflection of the life of our Savior, but in our privation and powerlessness, we must always remain focused on the grandeur of His light, try to dwell in His luster by supporting each other in love and faith. I am offering you a helping hand, Karitas, offering to foster your little girl for a time so that she may gain health and tranquility in the pristine air of the country-side. I am offering you relief, as weary and weak as you have become, so that you can care for your children, reinvigorated and refreshed." Bjarghildur went on and on, just like a priest. Karitas heard some of it, and some of it not. Toward the end, the pious words dwindled in number, and practical words of everyday life gained the upper hand.

The little girl stood only to benefit from being in the clean coun-tryside air. Then, she might be able to sleep, and if she should suffer anything besides colic, she could be taken regularly to be seen by the doctor in Sauðárkrókur. "You must first and foremost think about the child and her well-being. You cannot always be thinking only of your-self, Karitas. But it is also clear that you, as much as the girl, need to recover your health; you risk becoming bedridden if this continues. I wonder if your intestines have gotten twisted or you have a worm in your stomach. I can easily imagine that. You look like a ghost. And it is simply awful seeing your children, skinny and pale, with bags under their eyes from lack of sleep and the malnutrition that goes hand in hand with it. If your closest ones do not intervene, higher powers will sooner or later. Is that what you want, perhaps? Are you perhaps waiting for the whole family to drop dead in that fishing hut out there? Who is to help you, if not your sister? You cannot trust a husband who disap-pears for months at a time, leaving you wondering if he will ever appear again. I'm just asking you straight, dear sister: how can you be sure that he has not found another woman?"

This, she heard. Karitas looked up, with dark circles under her eyes.

"Sigmar? No, Sigmar will not find another woman. One is enough for him." She laughed. "No, Sigmar doesn't love other women." She laughed louder. "I alone know what Sigmar loves." Then she tossed her head and laughed her loudest.

"Are you out of your mind, woman? How dare you laugh in here; have you gone stark raving mad?" Bjarghildur glanced around sheepishly and grabbed her sister by the shoulder.

She pulled her sister, laughing, down the church aisle and out into the August evening.

The evening was still bright.

Then dusk enveloped the house.

Bjarghildur and the other two women sat at the table in the sitting room, while Karitas lay in her bedroom, trying to decide whether she should turn over so that she could see into the sitting room and follow their conversation, or whether she should follow her sister's advice and take a nap while the children were calm. She decided to do both: turn over in bed so that she could see them, and nod off to their chatter if it suited her. The bedroom was half-dark; it was slightly brighter in the sitting room, where there were two windows, but the color of the women's sweaters had faded somewhat, taken on a grayish-brown hue. They spoke softly so as not to wake the children, but she caught a word or two now and then: "monastery stitches," "cross-stitches." She had never been interested in embroidery, and her ears numbed. With her eyes half-closed, she looked at the outlines of the three women, the shadows on their cheeks, the six fists that met on the tabletop. Feeling drowsy, she shut her eyes. She liked knowing that they were there, their chatter accompanying her into a dream. Then she seemed to hear her sister's voice: "She must get away from this place if her health is to improve." And Högna's deep voice: "Someone must take care of her; she is far too much alone." She realized that they were talking about her, and tried to lift her head from the pillow and tell them that she would be fine, she would regain her strength before winter, but then she heard Karlína say: "But she wants to be alone. She thinks differently than we do. She is an artist; that is her cross." And Bjarghildur's sharp voice: "No. The children are her cross."

There was silence, and the word "cross" began to buzz in her ears. She tried to whisper, to make them aware that she was awake, but her head felt so heavy that she couldn't utter a word. She just heard their voices as an incessant buzz that gradually ebbed away: "Someone has to take care of her. Can't you take her with you to the north?" "I'll take the girl; there's nothing more that I can do." "Someone has to take care of her. A good woman who can get some flesh onto her bones." "I have a kindhearted aunt who would take good care of her and invigorate her with her herbal teas. Let's send her there before she dwindles to nothing. Let's send her off before Sigmar arrives." "Where does she live, your kindhearted aunt?" "In the Öræfi district."

The ship sailed north with the infant. Not a peep was heard from the little girl as she was being prepared for the journey, wrapped in flannel and wool; it was as if she knew what was going on. That she was leaving her mama because she had been so naughty. And her mama sat there numbly at the bedside as this was going on. Not a sound was heard from her, either; it was as if she knew that her little girl was leaving her because she had been such a bad mother. They handed her her daughter so that she could say goodbye. "No need to be so crestfallen, Karitas. It is only a matter of a few months, while you both recover your health," and she closed her eyes and stroked the little girl's face all over with her lips, inhaled her wonderful scent. Then they took the girl from her. When Bjarghildur came to say goodbye, she turned away. The ship sailed north, and the house fell dead silent. The boys were quiet as mice, and she herself crawled into bed and turned toward the wall.

Another ship was heading south. Which was what Högna and Karlína were waiting for. They had tracked down a woman who would accompany Karitas to Hornafjörður. They packed clothing for her into the trunk that had come from the north. "Would you like to take your woolen skirt with you, Karitas? And the green skirt, if you should go to church? Won't you need all of your shoes? Look, we're putting your box of paints in the trunk; then you can paint pictures. It's so divinely beautiful in Öræfi."

She didn't answer them.

The night before the ship arrived, she retched repeatedly. She was wearing her nightgown but had to go stand outside in the cool evening air, feeling time and again as if the vomit were coming. But her stomach was as good as empty, so all attempts to vomit were in vain. The women didn't like the look of things. "She will have to be in shape to travel tomorrow. I'll sleep here on the divan tonight," Högna said. She forced Karitas to eat some gruel and laid cold compresses on her forehead, all the while telling her stories of Karlína's aunt in Öræfi, who was renowned for her kindness and could cure all ailments with her presence and her herbal teas.

The August twilight fell over the house, and Karitas dozed, lay half-asleep, listening to its creaking, which could always be heard when cold and warm air clashed. Högna had fallen asleep on the divan and was snoring.

Karitas was on the verge of falling asleep when a croaking outside combined with the snores.

"The ravens have come," she mumbled through clenched teeth, rising up in bed. Their croaking grew more importunate; an unbroken, hoarse song sounding from the roof, culminating in a devilish squawking. "You cursed vermin," she hissed softly. "You mustn't think you can scare me"—and she jumped out of bed and rushed out into the farmyard, clad only in her nightgown. She clambered onto the wooden barrel next to the gable, climbed up onto the vestibule, heaved herself from there up onto the roof, sat astride the roof ridge, and pushed herself along it.

Then she saw the ravens. They were at the edge, two pitch-black birds, looking at her, not moving. They were the size of the largest cats.

She was startled; it felt as if all her strength drained from her momentarily, but then her blood began boiling with unrestrained anger. Beside herself with rage, she pushed herself quickly and jerkily toward them, shrieked and swung her fists at them, spread her arms wide and howled and laughed after she'd driven them off the roof.

Seen from a distance, she looked like a cross on the roof of the house.

III

Karitas

Guest Room 1939

Collage

White lace curtains, blue sky.

The farmhouse faces the sea, behind it rise the mountain and the glacier, the highest peak in the country.

A sleeping giant that can lay waste to the land with fire and ash if it stirs.

Behind the lace, people act as if they're safe, but an awareness of the power above resides in every nerve.

In the guest room is a cheerful window. Two beds with woven covers, a bookshelf, a cupboard holding the fine tableware, a small table for the washbasin, a French wicker chair retrieved from the wreck of a fishing boat that ran aground many years ago, and in the middle of the floor, a round table with four chairs.

All with an air of feminine virtue and good taste.

Only men, however, stay in the guest room.

Which explains the contrasts in the image: a strip of white lace, a snippet of floral-patterned wallpaper, a patch of woven material in bright colors, contrasted with dark, gruff colors and a piece of coarse sackcloth, painted over.

The housewife's youngest son stays in the guest room.

He is sophisticated, has traveled both to Reykjavík and the Westman Islands.

But when guests come from the south, he has to give up the room.

The river guides brought visitors in the spring.

Then Karitas began to feel restless. She lingered near the housewife, followed her like a dog out into the farmyard and back inside, hung around her in the old kitchen, tripped behind her up the stairs to the family room and back down, ambled after her into the passageway leading out to the cowshed, waited in the doorway while she did her chores, and stood over her as she changed the water in which the women rinsed their sanitary belts. And Auður allowed Karitas to shadow her, acted as if nothing were more natural than to have the woman at her heels, did everything unhurriedly, but after tossing the blood-tinged water out the door and letting fresh water stream into the enameled pail, she hummed: "Is there something on your mind, bright heart?"

Karitas stuck her hands under the bib of her overalls, said that there was nothing on her mind, she'd just been wondering if there was any news of who might be coming to the parish this spring, that is, apart from all the children, if she'd heard whether anyone else would be coming, that is, adults, and while waiting for the answer, she stood there shuffling her feet as if needing to pee. "Karitas, no one is coming to get you," Auður said, as she said every spring. "You can relax. Why should that man come and get you now after all these years? Didn't he settle down overseas long ago?" Yes, that's what she thought. "But it occurred to me that he might want to come get the boys." "The boys?" exclaimed Auður in surprise. "He didn't show up for little Jón's confirmation last year." "No, but maybe he just couldn't make it," said Karitas, beginning once more to defend Sigmar, although she didn't know why. Auður looked at her, stroked her arm, and said: "Let's go to the kitchen, have a cup of coffee, and hear a few verses."

"A lifelong line of sore dismay, drawn from a single point of sin, no tears can ever wash away, nor weeping cleanse the woe therein," said Auður as they sipped their steaming coffee. And Karitas wondered whether the "single point of sin" part was directed at her; she couldn't be sure. But then Auður said: "It doesn't matter who it was that sinned, maybe it was just me, as I'm twenty years older than you and have had more time to sin—but in any case, what's past is past, and there is no need to wallow in it. But I am convinced that your husband still loves you, for otherwise, he would have sought a divorce long ago. Yes, you were ill when you came here, but my word, how you have improved over the years, and it was a blessing that you and the boys came to me. I can't do without you, and I don't understand how I got by before you came." So said the housewife who had eight mouths to feed besides herself, and would have gotten by quite well, at least in terms of having company. "But, bright heart," she continued, "perhaps it is time for you to make some decisions. If you still want your husband, you will go to him across the rivers, but if you prefer to remain here, as I wish and hope you will, then the day will inevitably come when, for the sake of the boys, you two will have to put your affairs in order." "I was planning to do so next summer, when Sumarliði is confirmed," Karitas said, despite being unsure of whether or how she would do so, it did feel good to say.

In any case, that was still a long way off. But in spite of the house-wife's spring speeches, which were held every year over coffee, she was never able to relax until she had seen whom the river guides had brought. If she saw a group of men come riding, whether from the east or west, she fetched both her boys, washed their faces, combed their hair, changed out of her long trousers and into her skirt, had the boys sit with her up in the family room, and ordered them to behave and read aloud to themselves as she sat at the window and kept her eye on the riders. This she did every spring. She couldn't help it. But the men only ever brought the summer children, trembling with eager anticipation, prepared for their days and nights in the countryside, and her sons, jabbering joyfully, accompanied them to the surrounding farms.

Then the rivers on both sides of the parish flooded the sands, and only the birds of the air could cross over.

The stream flowed down a ravine where the wind couldn't reach it, and there in the still air, the women rinsed the laundry and pounded the dirt from their socks. "Not in the stream!" Karitas shouted to her sons, but they waded straight in because it was so boisterous and clear, even though it was cold as the glacier it ran from. "Let's see whose legs can last the longest," they shouted, and got away with their shenanigans because their mother was distracted, staring constantly into the water. She had wedged the wicker basket of laundry between two stones so that she could think in peace while the water flirted with the duvet covers. After staring long enough, however, at the stream running to the sea, she said: "Now then, boys, wring these." And they came at once; each grabbed one end of a duvet cover and twisted vigorously, but ran into trouble with the twisting, as they knew they would, since one of them was left-handed. So, the operation didn't end with a wrung duvet cover, but with fits of laughter and roughhousing, and then Karitas lost patience as she knelt there on all fours by the river, jumped abruptly to her feet, tore the wet duvet cover from them, gave them a poke and told them to go back inside; she wasn't in the mood for nonsense. They weren't expecting such irritability, the brothers; in general, she allowed them to splash and play whenever they helped her with the laundry, so now, they were startled—and she added gruffly: "And tell Hallgerður to come out and help me." Shamefaced and sopping wet, they returned to the farmhouse, and after a moment, the housewife's daughter, who had been sitting in the potato patch in front of the house, lost in her own thoughts like many others on this cold spring day, joined Karitas at the stream. She was serious as always as she tried to solve the mystery of the world, with her hair unrestrained and wild, being named Hallgerður and knowing, despite having read none of the old sagas, that the name obliged her to have long, thick hair. She had been reminded of this numerous times by her brothers. Washed with soft soap and rinsed with stale urine, her hair shone in the spring sun, and Karitas looked longingly at her locks as the two of them wrung out the snow-white duvet cover; she nearly forgot about her sad thoughts and unruly sons, but just then, the beautiful-haired girl asked a question. Hallgerður never talked about life and existence; she only asked questions, and because, for genetic reasons that were seldom spoken of, her memory reached only a short distance back, she often asked the same question over and over, and which she now asked once more, furrowing her brow as if to lend her words more weight: "Where is your husband?"

"South of the sea in a beautiful town," Karitas replied as always, knowing that the answer would satisfy the girl as usual, but perhaps because her thoughts were still floating around in the past, this time she added, addressing the duvet cover: "From under my duvet, he went to sea, sailed in the south and north, shoveled up the silver of the sea. Everyone called him the Catch King because he always knew where the fish were to be found, and then, after a long and rewarding herring summer, he finally came home to his fjord in the east, to find his wife and all his children gone. Now, let's put the duvet cover in the tub with the others, Hallgerður. He was furious and ran riot in the village, then went back to sea, sailed north once more, where he and some others owned a fine vessel, but one night in a violent storm, he lost his ship. Grab the sheet by the corner here, Hallgerður, and twist it hard. And they sank into the deep, cold sea, a huge wave took them down, and they all drowned but him. Now, put these pale sheets here in the tub, and then we'll turn to the socks. And when, at dawn, a boat reached the accident site, he was hanging on to a life buoy, alone in the middle of the sea, and they pulled him aboard. He lay in the infirmary for many days, having lost his comrades and his ship to that cruel, greedy creature that kills everything, devours everything, and they said that he couldn't sleep due to sheer rage. Line up the socks on that rock once you've soaped them. And then a Norwegian came to him and invited him to sail with him to Norway, and the doctor advised him to go, because his anger was pushing him toward madness. Now, hand me the mallet there, and we'll pound the dirt out of our socks with it, and apparently, he only intended to stay in Norway over the winter and then cross over to Öræfi with the river guides in the spring to fetch his wife and children. We must pound the socks hard with the mallet, Hallgerður, to get the dirt out. But then he and the Norwegian sailors began shipping curbstones from Norway to Italy, and one fine day, he decided to remain in Rome. Pound harder, Hallgerður, harder, or the dirt won't come out, and since then nothing has been heard from him, but people who know him think he has gotten himself a new ship and crew. Now, we'll put the socks in the basket and rinse them in the stream, but he never saw his youngest children, and I, dear Hallgerður, I still haven't been to Rome."

After dinner, the men lingered in the guest room while the women washed themselves. Not because they had been banished from the kitchen—no one had said any such thing—they just felt as if their presence wasn't desired, even if they couldn't have explained how they got that feeling. But the women's murmurs in place of replies, their conspicuous indifference, a slight furrowing of their brows, all suggested that they had more important things to do than attend to them. So the men ambled out of the kitchen, and the last one had hardly disappeared before the women pulled out the washbasin and placed it on the small table under the kitchen window. It wasn't as if any major washing was done in the kitchen; the women either tidied things or sat at the big table, fulled socks or sewed on buttons, while one sat by the window with the washbasin in front of her, ran the washcloth over her face and chest, under her arms, and perhaps between her legs, but it went so quickly and quietly that before those who were doing the mending or heating water for the next woman knew it, it was their turn. Auður went first; she had to hurry so that she could put together the refreshments for the evening coffee later, and she was followed by her sister, Hrefna, and then her younger daughter, Hallgerður—her elder daughter, Guðrún, had moved away from home—and finally Karitas, for she was the last to have joined the household. No one ever suggested changing the order, even though Karitas was older than the daughter. On the other hand, old Bergþóra, who was largely bedridden, was washed every morning after the milking, in the family room upstairs. Her daughters, Auður and Hrefna, took turns doing so, and the old woman always smelled lovely. In the guest room, on the other hand, the sophisticated son, Skarphéðinn, read aloud from the sagas to Karitas's boys. Supposedly, it was in order to instill manliness in them, but in fact it was done for the benefit of Hallur, who was collecting dust at his sister Auður's due to the region's lack of marriageable women. Skarphéðinn would read a hefty chunk, then stop abruptly and look at Hallur, who would clear his throat for a fitting amount of time before recounting from memory what came next, often verbatim if he could, without taking his eyes off the floor. "Bloody hell, he's good!" shouted Höskuldur every time—he being the elder brother who lived on the closest farm and often came over in the evening—while Karitas's sons were struck speechless, overwhelmed by Hallur's knowledge. Which was more comfortable for those present, as the boys were in the phase of male development when the voice breaks during exclamations. But as the clock struck ten, the men made their way back into the kitchen, glancing around and hemming and hawing, and it was as if nothing had changed or happened during their absence; the women sat there calmly sewing buttons, and the housewife had everything ready for the evening coffee. The radio was turned on, and everyone sat and listened to the ten o'clock news while quietly munching their cake. Usually, by the time the announcer was finished, people had started yawning and preparing to call it a night, but in recent weeks, Hallur and the sons had shown a matchless interest in battles and armaments, saying that everything was going to hell in Europe and making no secret of their satisfaction; the world news was an excellent diversion from the endless talk of the economic crisis in Reykjavík and other parts of the country. They could easily have discussed submarine warfare until well into the night, and were in no doubt that such battles were about to be repeated. "But we're about to go to bed," said Auður, clearing the table to remind them that their own warfare consisted of tending horses and sheep. Then she nodded to Karitas, who, at that signal, ordered her sons to bed while she herself went to the old kitchen to fetch her painting equipment.

After the household went to bed, the kitchen table was hers, and she wiped it carefully with a rag before placing the empty frame on top. Then she took some cardboard, old newspapers, dented pieces of sheet metal, and canvas sacks out of an old wooden box and laid them out to the left of the frame as she mumbled to herself and prepared the glue. She handled the materials as if they were pearls from the Orient, and began tearing them apart very slowly, ripping, cutting. Often, she had glued nothing by the time she stopped working well past midnight; had only torn and arranged, rearranged and thought out loud. Sometimes she created the image in her mind as she did her daily chores, allowing her to glue and paint over some of it the same evening. Once, shortly after she had started doing collages and was working hard on one, Auður came down to pour herself a cup of herbal tea, and when she saw the frame filled with various bits and pieces, she couldn't help but say, disappointed to see the trained artist simply tearing up cardboard and other rubbish: "What is this, bright heart?" And Karitas, who didn't want to lie to this good woman who made sure she got the kitchen table to herself after the ten o'clock news, replied that it was a composition. She didn't explain it any further to the housewife—having never really given the foreign term much thought, herself—and Auður coughed as her tea went down the wrong pipe. But the housewife never commented on Karitas's pursuit, even if she didn't think much of it. Instead, she only said before returning to the family room: "Don't let your art keep you up too long. You need sleep to regain your strength."

Her solicitude and unequivocal recognition of Karitas's artistry strengthened Karitas's determination never to leave Öræfi. Nowhere was the light better than here. It came from the sky, the sea, the glacier. She felt as if she were bathed in light all year round, and when the light was in her eyes and in her soul, no shadows could pursue her. She was convinced that she had never been so free, and often told herself the same when she felt the old heaviness in her chest. "Here is where I'll be buried," she said as she pressed her hands to the grass to feel the power of the glacier. But when Skarphéðinn came bustling into the kitchen in his long underwear after everyone else had gone to bed, having had to pee after a long round of saga reading and wanting a glass of water, and bellowed: "Damn, to be wasting electricity lighting up crap like that," it occurred to her that she might not be buried at the foot of the glacier, after all. Ever since her arrival, he had nurtured certain feelings toward her, vague and unevenly intense, depending on the weather and the growth of the grass, and after she began drawing and painting again, after she had started sleeping again at night like everyone else and felt much better in her stomach after drinking Auður's herbal teas, he often came to the kitchen after the others had gone to bed. Not necessarily wearing only long underwear, but often with his hair slicked back. Skarphéðinn was a handsome man, like all of these glacier folk, tall and lively, seven years younger than she, but the mere thought of a close relationship with a member of the opposite sex was enough to make her break out in a cold sweat. It irritated her that just when she'd considered herself free from the yoke of men's insatiable amorous desires, which resulted only in hungry mouths to feed and sleepless nights, just when she'd felt safe between the sandy wastes and great rivers, she should be subject to attack from within. He came and stood behind her, breathed on her hair, touched a lock of it as if by chance, brushed up against her, and, overwrought after these passionate overtures, she lost patience. "It isn't fair that he should be hassling me," she told the housewife, making sure to speak in a choked voice so as not to lose the woman's boundless compassion, and Auður's son was upbraided. Because of this, he was occasionally a bit aggressive toward Karitas—especially in the spring when nature began calling—behaving either like an infatuated teenager or a cranky brother. In order not to increase his suffering, she did her best not to tempt him with her femininity, but cut her hair short and wore long trousers.

It saddened Auður to hear of her son's amorous longings, although she did take him to task for them. "I'll have to send him south for the winter fishing again," she said slowly as she dropped salted lamb heads into a pot. "He's always so calm after such trips, and maybe he'll find himself a wife there, too. All of the young women in this area are relatives of his; you never know what can come out of that sort of mishmash," she said, pouring sago into a casserole dish. "My dear departed Grímur and I were cousins, which has left a bit of a mark on my Hallgerður, although the boys are unscathed," she said, putting potatoes on to boil. Her son's longing for female companionship strained her patience for a few days, but then she pulled herself together, borrowed a novel from the nearest farm, and before long, had regained her former vitality and self-confidence. She even tried to push books on Karitas, always doing so in a special way, saying that if she felt like reading and could stay awake, she should try this or that title—particularly ones that suggested fateful or romantic tales, neither of which Karitas had any desire to read. If she did, she would have to go out and press her hands into the grass and feel the power of the glacier. Instead, she chose to stay up late creating art, rather than reading books that fatigued her. Worst of all, she felt, was being able to work on her pictures only in the winter. The light was so heavenly at the peak of haymaking.

The summer children came shortly before lambing, pale and puny after their long, rainy winter indoors in the capital, but beaming with joyful expectation, and the entire parish welcomed them with freshly baked cakes. There was a buzz of anticipation in the air; the animals sensed what was going on and outdid each other with their bleating, barking, and whinnying. It was so fun when the summer children showed up; it meant that spring had finally arrived. They were distributed among the farms that formed a little community there below the glacier, going to the central farms, the eastern farms, and the southern farm, but no children came to their farm, which was one of the two western ones, because Karitas's sons were already there. This, however, did not prevent large-scale baking in that household, because the children went from farm to farm the first day to say hello to everyone, and of course had to be treated to something. Other shipments from the south came along with the children, goods and whatnot from relatives and friends, books, newspapers, tablecloths, and the mail—it came, too. After Karitas got over the realization that none of the newcomers had any particular business with her and was able to put on trousers again instead of her skirt, her tension about the postman's visits took over. Despite not wanting to be without the letters he brought her in the spring and waiting impatiently for them for several weeks, she dreaded the emotions that overwhelmed her upon reading them. For many years she had received two letters each spring, one from Bjarghildur, the other from Karlína. One contained news of her daughter, the other of her husband—or rather, the message that there was no news of him. Both letters drained her of energy, although the letter from Karlína was, of course, easier to read. Just like the lava, time slowly became overgrown by moss. But her heart always beat harder when she read the letters from Bjarghildur; she had to press her hand to her chest as she read them, so much did it hurt. The first years had been the worst, when her daughter was so small and such a great light. She had a photograph of her as a five-year-old— so incredibly beautiful, with bright locks, a high forehead, and round cheeks that she longed so much to kiss. She had sewn the photo into a small cover, double-lined; the inside lining was waterproof, allowing her to carry the photo around her neck, keep it under her clothing, at her chest, without her own sweat and tears ruining it. She never took it off apart from when she washed herself at the washbasin under the window. Auður knew what the little sheath contained. She always asked about the news of Karitas's little daughter when she saw that she had finished reading the letter behind a hill. "She's so sweet and kind and talkative," Karitas said. Later: "Hámundur simply adores her; he has given her the finest, most expensive saddlehorse in Skagafjörður." When she reached school age: "They have rented out Þrastabakki and moved to Sauðárkrókur so she can go to school there." And after they'd been living in Sauðárkrókur for several years: "She always has the highest marks in school. Apparently, her teachers say that she's the most talented, hardworking student they have ever had." "How wonderful it is to receive such news of your daughter," Auður exclaimed, clasping her hands in admiration, but Karitas rubbed her lower lip and said, as she stared stiffly at the hayfield: "I wonder if she'll always hate me for having given her up." Auður cupped her hand under Karitas's chin and asked how on earth such nonsense could occur to her. The child couldn't possibly have things any better; she was attending school and being lovingly cared for. "Just imagine if all the foster children in Iceland started hating their mothers—half the country would be aflame with hatred!" "Maybe they do," Karitas said, feeling the cold streaming down from the glacier. Auður screwed up one eye as she tried to find a suitable answer to this new theory about the country and its people, without, however, finding one she could stand on. Instead, she said: "We probably have too many children, we Icelanders. It's incorrigible, the dratted call of nature."

Most often, the letters from the east were about nature, in both a literal and figurative sense. After an eight-year break from having children, for reasons Karlína avoided explaining, she made a concentrated effort and brought two more children into the world—"I don't know why, dear Karitas, but one has to occupy oneself with something"—but she rarely mentioned Sigmar, not after he sailed to Italy and basically disappeared, although she did mention regularly that Högna was looking after their house and cleaned it in the spring and before Christmas. Although the news from Borgarfjörður was far from earth-shattering, Karitas's hands usually trembled when she opened the letter from Karlína.

But this year, there was only one letter. "Only one?" she asked the postman. "I'm supposed to get two letters." The postman was sorry, but unfortunately, that was how it was. "Are you sure the other one didn't just fall in one of the rivers when you crossed it?" asked Karitas, grimacing and grabbing his arm. Auður had to step in: "Karitas, maybe Bjarghildur has come down with something and been unable to write to you." But Karitas wouldn't listen to reason. She had waited all winter for news of her daughter, even if it was only about her marks in school, whether she'd gotten the highest one in mathematics, whether she was growing at a natural pace. It was ominous, not receiving a letter from Skagafjörður. "I'll call my mother in Akureyri, she ought to know something," she said bitterly to the postman. She gave him a little shove as if he were standing in her way, stormed past the others in the farmyard without looking to the right or left, and headed for the central farms.

The sisters in the nearest of the central farms had set the table in the guest room, as they always did in early April in preparation for the arrival of the first spring visitors. They laid the fine china on an embroidered white tablecloth with a crocheted lace border and turned the cups upside down on the saucers to keep them from getting dusty inside while waiting. Sometimes the set table waited untouched all summer, when neither a parliamentarian nor priest showed up, but because of the unpredictability of the political situation in the south—one never knew whether snap elections would be called, in which case MPs would come galloping up to secure votes—experience had taught the sisters to have everything prepared ahead of time. Their own neighbors, however, had never been invited into the guest room; such pageantry just didn't happen, although everyone was allowed access to their telephone, and for that reason, the sisters remained well informed of the private affairs of their neighbors. "You want to call now?" asked one of the sisters in astonishment. "But your mother's birthday isn't until October!" "I'm well aware of that," muttered Karitas; it was difficult to break traditions. For several years, she had called her mother on her birthday, and her mother had in turn called her on her birthday in February. It was her mother who had originally initiated this excellent custom, finding it better to phone people than to write them letters after the arthritis began bothering her. She had moved back to Akureyri after accomplishing her mission in Reykjavík: to provide her sons an education. "I feel much better among all the greenery up north," she declared—and had settled into the upper floor of an excellent house at the base of the slope, not far from Jenný, whose phone she was allowed to use. They sat and waited by the phone, the sisters and Karitas. It was "call time," meaning that the telephone offices were all manned, but it took a while as one office transferred the call to the next all the way north. In addition, they had to guess how long it would take for Jenný to go to Steinunn and tell her about the call, and then how long it would take for them both to go back to Jenný's house, adding a little time to account for their slow pace due to Steinunn's arthritis. Then one sister looked at the other, who was focused on the clock, and when the call finally went through, they said, like a well-trained choir: "Now pick up the phone," and nodded gravely. They waited ceremoniously behind Karitas for a moment as she picked up the phone and screeched, "Hello!" and then politely withdrew into the kitchen, closing the door behind them.

"Has something happened?"

"Nothing at all, Mama. How is your arthritis?"

"It's always bad after the winter, the cold creeps into my joints. Are the boys doing well?"

"Indeed they are, they're getting along just fine. Jón is growing so fast that we can barely manage to make him new trousers before the old ones are too small. Sumarliði isn't as tall as Jón, but is slightly bulkier."

"And what about yourself? How are you feeling?"

"I'm fine, but is there any news of little Halldóra? I haven't received a letter from Bjarghildur."

"Oh, you haven't? Yes, little Halldóra is doing very well. Goodness, what a splendid girl she is. She studies so hard but isn't so skilled with her hands, according to Bjarghildur. She has tried to teach her embroidery and knitting, but it isn't going well at all. The apple rarely falls far from the tree, as they say. But she's a skilled rider, the dear, and is quite tall and mature for her age."

"Well, I just wanted to know if everything was all right. I don't understand why Bjarghildur hasn't written to me as she usually does."

"Oh, that Bjarghildur. Yes, she's been a bit ill, yes yes, but I was wondering whether you would send Jón north in the autumn so that he can start preparing for high school. Your brother Páll is teaching here now."

"Send him north? Little Jón? My little Jón? Well, I hadn't thought of that at all. I'll consider it, yes, I'll give it some thought."

"It would probably be best if you sent both boys here to me in the north."

"She won't be sending them north during haymaking!" interrupted an indignant voice on the line.

"Well, dear, so it goes. I also just wanted to tell you that the drawings you did before you traveled abroad are all down south with your brother Ólafur, and I had Högna out in Borgarfjörður send him all the paintings that you did there in the east, so all of your pictures are now in Reykjavík."

"They are? My word. Well now. But what's that you said—is Bjarghildur ill?"

"Yes, she has the same stomach thing that you had when you stayed with her, the summer that you worked in the herring."

"Do you mean just after I returned from abroad? That—you mean she has what I came down with in Siglufjörður?"

"Yes, that's what I mean."

"But that's impossible!"

"Everything is possible in this life."

"And when, when do you think she'll be herself again?"

"She'll probably have it until September, the way it looks now."

"Well, so that's how it is. Goodness me. I think we'll have to say goodbye now, Mama."

"All right, dear girl. Take good care of the boys, and God be with you."

When the phone call was over, she dashed to the sisters in the kitchen and looked from one to the other without being able to utter a word. They began fingering their aprons perplexedly, and then she said, as if it were their fault: "My sister Bjarghildur is pregnant!" The sisters looked at each other as they tried to decide how best to react to this news, before saying, "What a nice surprise." "Nice?" Karitas exclaimed. "Now, finally—when she's forty-one years old!" "Yes, yes, that's quite all right," they said in unison, having collected themselves again, and they patted her soothingly on the shoulder. "We were at it until well over fifty. Everything will be fine with your sister," they added, seeing that she was far more emotional than usual after a phone call with her mother. And she hurried back over the hayfields with the same lump in her throat that she always got after hearing her mother's voice, besides being highly upset at the news. When she was halfway home, she remembered the unread letter from Karlína in her trouser pocket, and thought, when it rains, it pours. And it certainly did. In just a few words, Karlína informed her that she was now a widow. Þorfinnur had died of exposure in a blizzard in the mountains while searching for a few sheep that hadn't returned during the roundup. It had happened eight months ago, and Karlína ended her short letter by saying that they were now in the same boat, alone with their children. Karitas had to sit down right in the hayfield: How many people had the sea and sheep killed in Iceland? Then it occurred to her that she might have to write back to Karlína. Which she had never done before. Nor had she ever answered her sister's letters. Only sent her little daughter drawings of her brothers and of the horses on the farms. "I'm as vindictive as my sister Halldóra," she said to herself, surprised at this discovery.

In the increasingly bright nights, insomnia plagued her.

Karitas

Ship Arrival 1939

Collage

The ship arrives once a year.

Loaded with goods from Vík and the capital.

Everyone who is able to goes down, down to the channel with horse-drawn wagons and carts, and the unloading commences. The men row the tenders out to the ship, fill them with foodstuffs, dry goods, tools, and at the shore, they have erected a winch, which they use to haul timber and iron ashore, building materials that the boats are unable to carry.

I stand at a distance and watch the bustle. I ought to be back in the farmhouse with the women who have stayed behind; they have other things to look after, but the ship draws me to it.

I look at the ship, see both imprisonment and freedom.

Have an awareness of the world that only the ships can reach.

A world beyond the sea.

The shore is awhirl with activity.

People, dogs, horses, carts, wagons, chests, crates, timber, iron, the winch, the ship itself.

I use small pieces of fabric, strips and scraps to depict the chaos. Warm colors for the shore, cold for the glaring light all around.

The goods are transported in numerous trips to the building at the base of the cliffs, a building in which a small cooperative store is run at one end, and a slaughterhouse at the other.

The next day, when people have gathered their breath after the unloading, they come to pick up their orders. The rest is stored in the building: coffee, sugar, grain, delicacies and drinks for Christmas.

Dress fabric for the farmers' unmarried daughters.

The women stuck their heads out their front doors at regular intervals and looked out to sea, straightening their backs as they did—their work indoors bent and stiffened them—and when they saw no one returning home, they went back inside; the food was ready. During one of their detours out into the fresh air, they saw Jón come hobbling along. In the hustle and bustle down at the channel, someone had inadvertently stabbed his leg with an iron bar, and they rushed him, bleeding, into the kitchen, removed his bloody trousers, and cleaned the open, ugly wound with alcohol. It hurt and burned, but he didn't flinch, just clenched his teeth, and they praised him for his bravery. Then they took a gray-willow leaf and applied it to the wound to stop the bleeding. "He has long legs, our Jón," said Auður as she held the leaf to the wound, and Karitas looked at her son as well, as he sat there on a stool, long-legged in his underpants, and knew they were both thinking the same thing: When Jón is full-grown, will he be one of the tallest men in Iceland? He had only just turned fifteen and already towered over the women. Everything he ate, however, went into his height; his ribs could be counted—and his kneecaps, see how they protruded, just like all of his bones, in fact. He barely had any flesh on him. "But he's tough, our Jón," said Auður when she had stopped the bleeding—and it was no exaggeration; not a single boy in the parish was as diligent, as hardworking; he never complained, was always cheery, took everything serenely. Unlike his parents, felt Karitas. "He got his tenacity from a certain person," she said, because she never mentioned the boys' father by name in their hearing, "but he inherited his gentle disposition from my father, his namesake—of that I am quite certain." She didn't think for a moment that he could have inherited any character traits from her, nor did she know what traits those ought to have been. They put another leaf on the wound, this time with the opposite side against it to prevent infection, and bandaged it. "Come upstairs with me," said Karitas. "We'll find another pair of trousers for you." All of the residents had their own footlocker beside their bed, but when she opened his to pull out a pair of clean trousers, Jón said: "I'll do it, Mama," and she understood that he didn't want her rummaging through his things. Which, from a material perspective, didn't consist of much as far as she knew, but at that very moment, she discovered that her boy was becoming his own person. She said nothing as he dressed, and the family room was silent; her ears barely caught the clinking of Bergþóra's knitting needles as the old woman sat on her bed and said not a word; she would, in the end, take all words with her to her grave—as she preached to everyone else. After dressing, he said he was going back down to the shore, but Karitas said: "Sit down here for a second, Jón." And the old woman knitted faster.

"Jón, do you want to go to school?"

He looked at her with his clear eyes, in surprise, as if it had slipped her mind that he had been going to school in one of the neighboring parishes between the rivers for most of the winter. "Comprehensive school and then high school," she added. "Your grandma up north will let you stay with her." He stared straight ahead, wide-eyed. He didn't even know how his grandma looked or what she was like, but Karitas said: "Your grandma is a good woman, Jón. She is pious and wise, but if you want to live with her, you must work." His breathing quickened. "I would rather just work here." "I understand that," she said sympathetically, glancing at his chin to see if he had started growing any facial hair. "But soon you'll have to start thinking about what you want to do when you become an adult." "I've thought about that for a long time," he said, looking her determinedly in the eye. "I want to be a farmer here in Öræfi." "Oh, you don't say," she said after a moment's silence, feeling a certain sense of relief, yet not wanting to back off just yet: "But you enjoy reading so much, Jón. Don't you want to be a learned man who can spend all his time reading?" "I just want to be here," he answered impatiently. The unloading was in full swing down at the shore; this prolonged blather was completely uncalled for at the moment. He heaved himself up and hobbled hurriedly down the stairs.

Karitas sat there thinking, and was just about to get up when old Bergþóra said: "Yes, let the boy decide for himself. They have it incredibly good, the farmers here in Öræfi. They've always had enough to eat: sheep, birds, seals, and trout, and they can join in the fishing in the winter." When she heard those last words, Karitas turned around abruptly and stared for a moment at the old woman, then stomped down the stairs with such a ruckus that she was lucky she didn't break her leg, rushed out into the farmyard and chased after Jón, who had hurried down the hayfield, and roared: "Jón, you're going to school in the north this autumn! Do you hear that?"

"You're not sending Sumarliði north, too, bright heart?" Auður asked gingerly, cautious of Karitas's current peevishness. "No, he needs to learn moderation first," Karitas replied shortly, as if the boy's upbringing had gone completely awry due to lack of restraint, and she made no secret of her opinion that others besides herself bore the responsibility for that, even if she didn't say so directly. "Jón will go first, and Sumarliði the year after," said Karitas, and the housewife's gait revealed her relief at hearing that she would get to have Sumarliði with her a little longer. He was the favorite of all the women there, the child they had gotten to cuddle and pamper from the beginning. It had been completely different with Jón, who had allowed no one, except perhaps his mother, to touch him, and if they simply had to kiss his cheek, he would rub the spot afterward as if it had gotten dirty. They had quickly given up on him. If, on the other hand, Sumarliði wasn't given his kisses and hugs voluntarily, he worked hard for the attention, clambering onto the women's laps even before he could walk, clutching their legs after he'd begun to stand upright, and then their bellies after he grew taller, warmed his hands in their armpits, laid his cheek against their backs as they sat working, crawled into bed with them if his toes were cold, and they showered him with kisses, all the kisses that would otherwise have been wasted due to the ongoing shortage of husbands. With him, they had an outlet for their longing for love—which helped keep them balanced emotionally. And he had them eating out of his hand. There were few things that Sumarliði wasn't allowed to do—almost none. And so incredibly beautiful he was, too, they thought, tilting their smiling heads left and right as they drank in his beautiful eyes, his long eyelashes, his kissable mouth, and sighing as they pressed long kisses into the crook of his neck. When their coddling got out of hand and left the housework waiting, they excused themselves by saying: "Premature babies need so much affection. Just think, he weighed barely a kilogram, the little fellow." And then they stuck an extra bite of food or a sweet treat in his mouth, as if to make up for his weight at birth. He belonged to all of them, and each raised him in her own way—being careful, however, never to upset him so that he wouldn't turn his back on them. That was the lack of restraint of which Karitas spoke, the carelessness that resulted from him always getting whatever he wanted. Still, there was only one person to whom he ran howling if he hurt himself; only one person who got to comfort him, or chastise him if necessary. But even that woman he could wrap around his finger, and now she could see its consequences. She could send the elder son to her mother; he was level-headed, well-behaved, but she could just imagine her mother's indignation at the younger son's impertinence.

Karitas began relentlessly drilling good manners into her sons, finding fault with everything. "Eat politely, Jón. Your grandma isn't accustomed to people slurping down their porridge. Sumarliði, you mustn't make faces at Jón at the table; and I won't have you endlessly fighting with the boys on the eastern farms." The others ate their porridge and blood pudding in silence, being unused to such chiding during meals, but they didn't interfere in the remonstrations because the radio news was on—it was not the time for big speeches. However, they clearly couldn't understand what had gotten into the woman. She sat staring, brow furrowed, into her milk glass, feeling as if she had been woken from a long, sound sleep by a kick in the shin. Such an awakening was very unsettling. And as she stared stiffly at the white milk, her thoughts turned to the glacier above the farm, which could waken without warning—but wasn't such a thing always preceded by tremors in the earth's crust, some subterranean movements invisible to all? What was she thinking, living here beneath the glacier with her boys—where could they flee if it woke? The glacier to the north, desolate sands and roaring, uncrossable rivers to the east and west, the deadly cold sea to the south. An erupting volcano underneath the glacier, fire lava ash, no way out, and she there with her children. Buried alive under ash with her children in her arms, like the inhabitants of Pompeii. They had talked a lot about Pompeii back when she'd been asked to go visit Rome. She had always longed to see Pompeii. Now, she never would.

"How many people died when the glacier last erupted?" she asked dryly, out of the blue.

The others stopped eating for a second. The sons looked hopefully at the men, relieved that their mother had quit her reprimands and turned to geological topics, but the men didn't answer, not letting old, recent, or impending volcanic eruptions disturb the radio news. It was only after the radio was turned off and the housewife said cheerfully to the whole group, probably having been thinking of it as she ate her cured blood pudding from last autumn, "Won't we be needing some fresh meat soon?" that the mother's child-rearing methods got to be too much for the others. She announced curtly: "The boys aren't going out to the gravel plains to club skua chicks anymore, nor are they going down to the estuary to drive seals together for you men." Scowling, the men to whom she was referring got to their feet without so much as looking at the childrearer and said to each other: "Does she think that folk in Öræfi live off the air?" Which they did, in a certain sense, but the men didn't see the connection. Her sons stood up along with the men and looked at their mother reproachfully, making no secret of how much disappointment she'd caused them, but she just sat there looking at the empty porridge bowls. The longer she looked at them, the stronger grew her longing to smash them. Then it suddenly struck her that she might in fact be able to smash a few plates, pile up the shards on a picture surface, glue them on, paint them over. She considered this idea while the women stacked the plates for washing. Hrefna said, "The boys must learn to get by on their own, provide food for their households like other men, and how are they to learn such things if they aren't allowed to go hunting with the men?" Karitas said, "They're going to school, so they won't need to hunt or fish." "That's still a long way off, a whole summer," snorted the other woman. But it wasn't far off; time was racing by, soon she would lose her boys to life, and she regretted not having better appreciated their time together when they were little, when they wrapped their arms around her neck, hung on to her skirt, snuggled with her in bed. Those days would never come again. Then, she had thought only about peace and quiet and sleep, about when she would be free again. And now, once they were gone, all her days would be like the Icelandic spring: cold and bleak.

She gave a start when someone touched her shoulder; it was Hrefna, who whispered: "Come with me into the pantry; there's something I want to show you." And when they were standing in the pantry, to which no one had access but Auður and Hrefna, the latter said: "And now we'll each have one piece." She glanced around despite their being alone in the pantry, and then opened a box and took a large bar of chocolate from it. "From the ship," she added in a whisper, and she broke off a piece, stuck it in Karitas's mouth, broke off another, and stuck it in her own. They sucked silently on the chocolate, looked at each other's mouths, rolled the pieces over their tongues and teeth, rested them against their palates, closed their eyes, opened them wide again, exchanged inquisitive glances, assented with their eyes to continued pleasure, stuck another piece in their mouths and then more, until a hundred grams had gone the only right way, comforting the younger woman and satisfying the older one's need for sweets. "Oh God, we mustn't eat all of it!" said Hrefna, covering her mouth. But they had already finished the whole bar.

Even though chocolate, according to Hrefna, helped with a good night's sleep, and few people could snore with as much gusto as she—should she happen to snore, that is—Karitas lay awake that night. Most often, she fell asleep before midnight, like everyone else, but usually woke with a start around three, or even before. At first, she tried not to let her insomnia bother her, but listened to the whirring sound of the snipe as it dove from high in the sky and the buzzing of the bumblebee as it threw itself at the windowpane. But the longer that she couldn't sleep, the darker the thoughts that began to beset her in the bright spring nights. She propped herself on her elbow and looked around the family room at all the sleeping heads: Hallgerður and Hrefna, who lay in the beds next to hers, Bergþóra and Hallur in the beds opposite, the empty beds of the children who had moved away from home, the master bedroom at the end, where the housewife now slept alone, and then she turned and looked at the bed under the window, where her boys still slept head to foot even though there were enough empty beds for each of them to have his own. She heard the boys' tranquil breathing amid the various noises of the others and asked herself, "Why am I the only one awake?" She tried to find an explanation for it, dug deep into her thoughts, tried to stay focused, think logically, but lost hold and her thoughts flew in all directions—and just at that moment, it happened. Just when she felt almost as if she were slipping into sleep, that her muscles had relaxed, it was as if a claw gripped her heart. It fought for its life; she had to sit up, sweating, to catch her breath, before finally being able to lean her head back into her pillow, overwhelmed by a menacing feeling. Am I possessed? she thought, stuffing the edge of the duvet into her mouth in terror and regretting that there wasn't a single cat to be found in all of the Öræfi district.

"No, there have never been any cats in this area. We don't need them, because there are no mice, either," Auður said proudly, stroking her chin as she rummaged through her memories. "Although my grandmother apparently saw some cats in Hornafjörður. She said they startled her when they began rubbing against her legs. But we've never seen mice here. We've only heard the summer children's descriptions of them— most of them not very nice, either," she added with a shudder. She wanted to change the subject, but Karitas snapped: "Cats are good creatures, and as far as I'm concerned, they can fill the farmhouse— maybe then I could sleep better!" And she took out her frustration on the floor, scrubbing it vigorously with sand until the boards whitened. Auður said nothing, but patted Karitas gently on the back as she knelt there. "Stand up, bright heart, just for a moment so that I can look in your eyes." Karitas did, but when they stood facing each other, Auður did not say anything right away, and instead, brushed Karitas's hair from her face, straightened her blouse a bit, fiddled with her buttons, and said: "As I recall, my niece Karlína told me that some cats had kept you from sleeping out east. But we'll not fuss about that now. On the other hand, I know that you've had a lot of trouble sleeping recently, which worries me. Insomnia is your worst curse, bright heart, and we have to get it under control somehow. Let me think about it until dinner."

Out in the farmyard under the evening sun, the men made predictions about the weather while relieving themselves. Auður came and stood next to them, turned her head from east to west, and said: "Yes, the air out here is refreshing; it isn't healthy for anyone to hang around indoors in such weather. Wouldn't it be best, Skarphéðinn, if Karitas went with you and the lads to hunt skuas tomorrow? She missed out on it completely when she was a child. It would do her a great deal of good to move about a bit in the fresh air outdoors." That was all; the housewife had said her piece, and her will was law, whether one liked it or not. Karitas tried to object, but when she saw her sons' obvious excitement at having their mother come with them on a skua hunt, she settled for staring coldly at the housewife. "I have never in my life killed a single living thing, not so much as a fly." Auður whispered in her ear: "Run off now and tire yourself out as best you can; it doesn't matter if you kill anything or not."

Armed with a stick, she rode out onto the gravel plain with the men. Skarphéðinn said not a word, which she took to mean that he didn't like having a woman along. But when the attack was launched and he swung his stick like a soldier wielding his sword in battle, striking to the right and left with wild abandon, she realized that her presence actually whetted his lust for murder. The frenzied skuas dove at her head one after another, causing her to do little, in fact, but swing her stick over her head while running over the gravel, instead of clubbing the chicks as she ought to have done. Her sons ran after the chicks, knocking them out with quick blows as if they'd done little else all their lives, and if the chicks' parents made the mistake of diving at them, they were struck, too. Karitas was appalled by the ruthlessness and felt miserable. Her heart was beating in her throat by the time Skarphéðinn said that that was enough. The men pulled slipknots tightly around the necks of the chicks and a few of the adult skuas that had tried to defend their offspring, and her sons said encouragingly: "You'll do better next time, Mama." She didn't answer them. She refused to help transport the catch back home and rode quickly ahead of them. When she reached the farmhouse, she announced dryly to the housewife that she would rather scrub the floors with sand all day and night than rob birds of their young, but Auður said, with a gleam in her eye: "It appears to me that you have gotten some sun, and have a red glow to your cheeks—which is a good sign."

If Auður had imagined that the bluster and fresh air of the hunt would help Karitas sleep, she was wrong. The boys slept like stunned skua chicks, as did everyone else in the family room, but the screams of the skuas echoed in Karitas's head half the night, and in the morning, when the housewife looked into her swollen eyes and saw the sadness there, she said, "Well, then, that didn't work." But it was as if Auður had become obsessed with the idea that only hard work and fresh air could put insomniacs to sleep. Since the haymaking hadn't yet begun, Auður had no other option than to send Karitas out to the estuary to hunt seals with the men and children. "No, I'm not going," said Karitas bluntly. "Oh yes you are, bright heart. Your sleep is more important to me than a few dead seal pups or skua chicks."

Once again, Karitas had to ride out with the men and children. Höskuldur, the other brother, joined them and brought some of the summer children along, and when they reached the estuary, they dismounted, while she remained sitting on her horse. "I'll wait here," she said tersely to her sons, while the rest went down to the beach ridge, looking this way and that. One of them pointed westward: a large group of seals. Encouraged, the men raised their heavy staves, their predatory instincts tensing their shoulders. The boys ran over to their mother and more or less pulled her off her horse—"Please, Mama, come with us"—as if they were ashamed of her sitting there idly while the others slaved away to provide food for the farm. She let herself be persuaded, though with dread in her heart.

The seals had been sleeping under the sun, soaking up the bluish-white silence. The female seals glanced with their big curious eyes toward the glacier, feeling safe with their pups in this stunningly beautiful place, and slumbered on. Then the men nodded, signaling to the children to wade into the estuary, herd the animals together, and drive them onto the beach, where they would receive the coup de grâce. One hard blow to the nostrils—and then they could fly into infinite tranquility, up to the glacier, too, if they wanted, lie on the white expanses so near to the sun. In a flash, the estuary turned into a bloody battlefield. The water turned red, clothes, hair, hands, and arms; the blood splashed over them. Karitas had let her boys lead her into the water and she was going to join in, clapping her hands along with the others as they did when herding sheep into the sorting corral, but when the blood of the dumb animals began to flow, it was as if her own blood froze in her veins. She stood there petrified in the estuary, with outstretched arms, staring at the bloody water and looking into the eyes of the seals. "Move toward the beach, Mama!" shouted Jón, pushing her forward, and she stumbled over the pups, crawled to the beach with half-suppressed groans, wet and bloody. And there stood Skarphéðinn, waiting for her. He grabbed her arm, yanked her harshly toward him, trembling with suppressed fury, held her in an iron grip, bent his face to hers, stood stock-still for a moment as he stared wide-eyed at her lips, and then hissed: "Try to be of some use, woman. Since you can't herd them like the children, here's a club. Now hit them in the nostrils; show what you're capable of!" He thrust the club roughly into her hands, gripped her wrist firmly: "You swing it like this!" She tore herself loose, swung the club, and hit him in the nose. Blood gushed over his face. She tossed aside the club, set off running up the beach ridge, scraped along on all fours, got to her feet, ran to the horses as if the devil were at her heels.

She galloped home, threw herself off the horse, and rushed into the farmhouse. The smell of fried skua chicks filled her nostrils and she covered her nose and mouth with one hand, ran up to the family room, grabbed some clothes from her footlocker, tore off the ones she was wearing, and left them lying on the floor as she put on clean underwear, her hands trembling. Bergþóra looked up: "Do I smell blood?" Without answering, Karitas wrapped her smelly, wet clothes together, grabbed a clean jersey, trousers, and towel, hurried out of the house and down to the stream in her underwear. She filled her hands with the ice-cold water, splashed it over her arms and legs, rubbed them, splashed more water over, dipped her head into the stream, gasped for breath because of the cold, rinsed her hair, wrung it, was drying it when she saw Auður's legs beside her. "I think I killed your Skarphéðinn," she said in a trembling voice. Auður bent down to her, handed her the jersey. "How so?" "I hit him in the nose; I think he may have bled out." Auður handed her the trousers. "I expect it would take more than one whack on the nose to do away with Skarphéðinn Grímsson." She looked to the south, shading her eyes with her hand. "And I would be right. Here he comes on his horse." It was the horse that brought Skarphéðinn home. He himself couldn't see very well with his bloody sweater covering his nose and mouth and his head tilted backward. The man had been badly injured, and the women came rushing out of the house with shouts and cries. They helped him down from his horse, led him into the guest room, nursed him, pulled off his boots and clothing, removed the sweater from his face, and wailed loudly. Karitas fled to the cowshed.

Skarphéðinn received the best care imaginable. The women cleaned his face with alcohol, rubbed ointments into it, examined his nose thoroughly; they weren't quite sure if it was broken or if the cartilage had shifted, but he was in a lot of pain, he said, and they were disconsolate at not being able to do anything about it. They had camphor drops, Hoffman's drops, and heart strengtheners, but no painkillers apart from a combined gastric pain and flatulence reliever, and after conferring for a little while, they decided to give it to him rather than nothing at all. And then they fed him fried skua chicks.

The seals had been dragged home. Hallur saw to skinning and salting them, scraping the skins and hanging them to dry on the door of the storehouse, and the next day, fresh seal meat was eaten, along with salted seal blubber from the year before. Karitas had no appetite for the fresh meat, neither skua nor seal. Both disgusted her, which bothered no one, since few gave much thought to her appetite in the days that followed. Her boys prevaricated when she addressed them and stuck close to the hero lying in the guest room, blind in both eyes. No such black eye—red and purple, both eyes hidden behind the swollen flesh— had been seen in this parish since around the turn of the century. "He looks like a monster," the boys whispered to each other. Karitas tried to keep a low profile, emptying the family's chamber pots after her restless, sleepless nights, mucking out the cowshed for the recuperating son, and standing over the washtub all day with bloodshot eyes.

When the men went out to the Ingólfshöfði headland to catch puffins and guillemots, Auður called to Karitas as she stood at the stream, pounding dirt from the household's socks, and told her that a cup of coffee was waiting for her in the kitchen. Karitas knew that she was about to be subject to a powerful reprimand and said with fullest sincerity: "I never meant to hit him." Auður raised her eyebrows: "Hit him? No, I'm quite certain that that wasn't what you had in mind, but I've given the matter a lot of thought and feel that being outdoors isn't enough, in and of itself, to help you sleep. The body bends to the will of the soul, I believe, so it is best that I ask you directly, bright heart, if anything in particular is disturbing your soul?" "I wonder if I'm just possessed," Karitas said resignedly. Auður sputtered and asked in a low voice if she had been seeing the dead. "No, I haven't seen anyone," replied Karitas, although she wasn't quite sure that was indeed the case. She added that people's snoring probably kept the dead away—though she didn't want to say that most of the snoring came from the master bedroom—but on the other hand, even when no one was snoring, she still couldn't sleep. Deep in thought, the two women sipped their coffee, until Auður asked, as if out of the blue, whether Karitas could do her the favor of popping over to Þorgerður at the far-central farm with the *Guide for Housewives*. A little past noon, when the men were napping; it would be quiet then. Auður asked Karitas to thank Þorgerður for the loan and tell her that she had used the veal fricandeau recipe, "and then ask her if she has the Northerner's spiritual poems for me to read." The housewives in the parish weren't in the habit of wandering from farm to farm, having to do so much else with their time; they saw each other only at mass and other sorts of gatherings, or when they came together to weave. They never called on each other unless they had pressing matters, had to use the phone, pass on messages, hand off the shared baking oven, or occasionally borrow or return books. Despite their limited interactions, however, they knew everything about each other.

Þorgerður, who was older than Auður, a serious, soft-spoken woman, took the book, shifted it from hand to hand for a few moments, and said: "Did she use any of its recipes?" "Yes, the recipe for veal fricandeau," said Karitas, "and she would like to borrow the Northerner's spiritual poems from you." "Oh, did she say that?" said Þorgerður, looking out over the hayfields. "Well, so it shall be." She whispered: "Sit down here on this stool out in the sunshine while I go get the book for her, but we had better be quiet, because the men are napping." Then she returned, but with another stool in place of the book, and sat down beside Karitas, praised the fine weather, and said, as if nothing were more natural, "Yes, my dear Auður is quite spiritually minded. I don't suppose that you are, too? Do you read the Bible often?" Karitas said that she herself read it very little, but on the other hand, it had been read a lot at home when she was a child. Þorgerður asked if she believed in God and Jesus Christ, and Karitas said that she thought so, although she hadn't had much time to think about it, what with all of her chores. "How strong is your faith?" Þorgerður asked her directly. Stunned at being asked such a question so soon after lunch, Karitas replied: "Well, just so-so." Then she added, a little hoarsely, that she didn't go to church unless she had to; it was such a bother. Þorgerður whispered: "No one has been hovering around you, have they?" "Who should that be?" Karitas asked in surprise. Þorgerður shushed her and looked around: "You haven't seen any of the deceased recently?" "No," replied Karitas quickly, with the woman's face close to her own. "Well, in that case, everything is as it should be, but if such a thing should happen, my best advice is that you sleep with the Bible on your pillow and pray constantly. Think about God and Jesus Christ; let Him envelop you and pour over you, inundate you, become a reflection of your own life." Karitas felt as if the woman were suffocating her, and she moved her stool up against the wall, plucked a few buttercups growing out between its stones, and tickled her nose with them, fanned herself with them, and said rather sharply: "They've never been a great help to me, the Father and Son in Heaven. They took both my son and my sister from me. And then sent Bjarghildur away with my daughter. They probably wanted to punish me for going abroad, when I should have stayed with my mother and siblings. Bjarghildur said that the devil would follow my every footstep, because he settles in the souls of those who betray their nearest and dearest." Þorgerður grabbed her hand, tilted her head, and whispered: "In times of despair, all sorts of gods are born who are more like devils than humans, but you mustn't let guilt gnaw at you. Turn to the Lord, tell Him that you repent and ask Him to be allowed to enter the light." Karitas raised her voice again. "Who says that I feel guilty? I think that Bjarghildur should be the one plagued by guilt, having taken my girl from me, and then becoming pregnant herself—even though she's forty!" Þorgerður winced and shushed her again, but Karitas was really angry now: "Fortunately, I'll never have children again—and love has never been more favorable to me than anything else in life!" She got up angrily and would have stormed off, had not Þorgerður grabbed her jersey. She patted her soothingly, hemmed and hawed a little, and said, "Now, now," without adding any further wisdom, and then said that she would pop in and get the book for Auður. After a few moments, she returned somewhat distractedly with the *Guide for Housewives* under her arm and a pencil in her hand, which she hurriedly stuck in her apron pocket when she saw Karitas, and whispered that she hadn't actually found the book with the spiritual poems—she'd probably lent it out— but she asked Karitas to bring the *Guide for Housewives* back to Auður. "Tell her to try the rissole recipe, which I find splendid. And please give her my greeting, yes, and tell her that as far as I recall, Hildigunnur has some love poems by some northerner or other. Maybe she would like to read them, since I can't find the pious poems."

In her sleeplessness that night, Karitas tried to make up her mind whether she believed in God. She wasn't entirely sure but envied the people who were willing to let Christ inundate them. They were so secure in their existences. They didn't lie awake at night. At first, she forced herself to lie still, but then tossed and turned, and finally sat up to relieve her aching back. She sat and stared stiffly at her boys and the sleeping people, alternately leaned back and sat up again, dozed off for a bit, started to the buzzing of the bumblebees. Some mornings, she woke feeling like a decrepit old woman who refused to get up so as not to prolong her wait for death.

Auður watched worriedly as she ate her mixture of skyr and oatmeal, and said "Sleep doesn't covet you, bright heart; that much is certain."

It was incredible how avidly she read, Auður, even in the middle of the summer. One beautiful evening when the men and boys headed down to the shore to lay nets in the channel and catch trout, she said to Karitas, as if it had just occurred to her: "Listen, perhaps you could go over to Hildigunnur at the inner-eastern farm and pick up that excellent book that Þorgerður was talking about. I think her family has gone on some sort of outing, so she is home alone and would have nothing against a little company. You could bring her the *Guide for Housewives* at the same time; at the last mass, she mentioned that she wanted to make princess cookies. Tell her there's a recipe for them in the book."

Once again, Karitas had to saunter over the fields, and as she approached the eastern farm, she heard singing, or rather the kind of singsong made by someone who thinks he's all alone, and when she showed up at the farmhouse's doorstep, the housewife was startled. She gasped as if she'd been caught in the act of something and crumpled the garment that she was holding. On the flagstones and grass lay dresses and skirts, and on the wall hung an Icelandic national costume, smiling respectfully at the evening sun. "I was just airing out, yes, airing out my clothes," she said breathlessly, turning this way and that as if trying to decide whether to continue what she was doing or gather everything up, things being as they were. "You mustn't let me disturb you," said Karitas. "I'm just here to pick up the Northerner's love poems for Auður and let you have the *Guide for Housewives* in its place. There's a recipe in it that you mentioned to her." Hildigunnur, recomposing herself, took the book and looked at it for a moment or two. "Oh, did she say that? So Auður said that, well. Do you remember what recipe it was?" Karitas remembered it well, as princesses and stories of love and eternal happiness were inextricably linked in her mind, and when the housewife was given that information, her life seemed to return to normal. She went inside with the book, saying that she was going to bring refreshments for them both, and Karitas sat down on a stool among the dresses and felt as if she were in the company of good women. Stepping lightly, Hildigunnur came back out with glasses of milk and Christmas cake on a plate, and said, as if she couldn't quite remember what this was all about: "Yes, so Auður wants to borrow the love poems, does she? I'll need to find the book. Yes, it's not a bad thing to read about love, Karitas; it is complicated, after all, and not easy for ordinary mortals to deal with when at its most rambunctious. I expect you know all about that, being a married woman. Have you heard anything from your husband?" "No," Karitas replied, showing greater interest in the cake than in her missing husband. Hildigunnur inched forward: "How strange of that man not to show himself, when his wife is so good and beautiful, because that is what you are, Karitas, an utter delight to the eye." Karitas saw no reason to object to these last words. She ate her cake noisily and opened up a little more: "Well, he's probably met an Italian woman and forgotten that he is married." Hildigunnur's voice quivered a little, her question being so personal: "But you haven't forgotten him; your heart is still bound to his embrace?" "I don't know about that," said Karitas, continuing to munch her cake. Hildigunnur's expression lightened: "Well, my dear, so you might consider remarrying?" "I haven't really thought about it," said Karitas through her nose. Hildigunnur straightened up and jerked her head, because things had taken a new turn. "Have some more cake, more cake, and now, let me tell you, Karitas: in my opinion, it isn't good for any woman to go through life alone. Women who do so just wither away over time. They grow thinner with each passing year, having no man to provide for the household, and have to depend on others for their daily bread. Women belong in a man's arms; alone, they can never be happy for long." Karitas replied, "What utter nonsense. As far as I can tell, Auður is both happy and thriving in spite of her widowhood, and as far as I can see, you feel quite fine here alone on this farm—where you've strewn all your clothes around you like seeds in a vegetable bed."

The last remark could well have been left unsaid, Karitas realized afterward. Actually, she found it quite a clever whim, and could see it as an excellent picture. But the outspread garments suddenly became embarrassing for both of them. Hildigunnur was clearly itching to gather up the clothes; she fiddled with her skirt but maintained her composure, obviously wanting to preserve her dignity. All she said was: "Oh, wouldn't you know it—here comes a breeze. It's probably best that I go in and look for the book for you." She returned holding the great *Guide for Housewives*, and said that she just remembered that she'd loaned someone the Northerner's love poems: "But let Auður have her book back; I won't be getting the baking oven anytime soon, and I've heard there's something wrong with it, anyway. But on the other hand,

I found a good recipe here for an Alexandra pudding, if Auður should be interested." She handed Karitas the book and asked her to convey her greeting to Auður. She had meant to leave it at that but couldn't help herself, probably feeling it best to have the last word as things stood, squirmed a little and said in a shrill voice: "It hasn't occurred to you that your husband might be dead?"

Auður was out in the cowshed, sitting on the skull of a large animal as she did the milking and conversing with her daughter Hallgerður when Karitas came storming in with a fierce expression and handed her the book. "Here's this blasted recipe book for you again!" she exclaimed, without even attempting to hide her discontent. She went on: "And I'm not going to keep traipsing all over the place and letting old biddies lecture me! They're out of their minds. Your friend on the eastern farm is flat-out claiming that my husband is dead!" The mother and daughter tilted their heads and looked at her intently. The assertion about the man's death, however, didn't seem to shake Auður as much as Karitas's disparaging remarks about the neighbor women. She got up, cleared her throat a few times, held the book to her chest as she walked pensively through the cowshed and back again, patting the cows on the loins, one after the other, and saying: "Many people, because they don't know better, think cows are stupid. If they're outside when it's raining, they come home by themselves, stand there sopping wet at the cowshed door, and look reproachfully at you. Some of them are wise, others are simpleminded. Héla here, for example, is big and strong, housewifely and kindhearted. Rifa here in the next stall, on the other hand, is the crankiest of them all, but is growing gentler with each passing day; see here when I pat her—she pretends it bothers her, shaking her head like that, but then lifts her tail and lets the cat out of the bag. Yes, and this is Sunna, always bursting with curiosity, but terribly full of herself. And here is Rauðbrá, the most beautiful of them all. Absolutely perfect, so beautifully built." Auður stroked the cow. "With such beautiful eyes." And the cow looked admiringly at her mistress, who continued: "And she's constantly washing herself; there's never a spot of dirt to be seen on her, and her coat always smells so nice." And Auður buried her face in Rauðbrá's coat and took a big sniff, and the cow sniffed just as lovingly at her. Then Auður sighed and moved to the next stall: "And here is my Hyrna, who is going to calve this autumn and therefore gives no milk yet; she's so gentle but can never stand still in her stall. And then there's little Dúlla here, the smallest and cheekiest, and Frekja who always stole the milk from the other calves when she was little, and here's Lína, who's the wisest, and here, here is Madame Fenja herself, the greatest milcher."

Auður went and stood in the middle of the cowshed, still holding the cookbook as unassumingly as a priest would a hymnal, tilted her head, and stared wistfully. Her sermon was finished. The message had hit home. Karitas took one more look at the madams in the cowshed, bowed to the ladies, and backed out.

"To be able to think clearly, you need a lot of light," the housewife said one Saturday night as she stared stiffly out the kitchen window. No one bothered to answer her, as they were busy eating, besides being accustomed to her remarks about life and existence, which often had nothing to do with whatever had come before. As they expected, she didn't add anything else. So the radio news wasn't interrupted any further, and the others simply forgot what she'd said, as usual. Karitas, however, recalled her words the next evening. After the ten o'clock news, when the women were done washing themselves and the men had finished their saga reading, and everyone had started yawning and muttering, "Well then," at every other sentence, Auður said that she was going to go up to the mountainside the next morning to pick herbs, and that Karitas should come along. They would return in the afternoon. To this, the others said, "Well then," except for Hrefna, who said that she would like to join them; Auður said she couldn't, but that she would like to borrow Hrefna's overshoes and wool jacket for Karitas to wear;

it was often so nippy up there in the early morning. Karitas wasn't even asked. She gasped, "I don't want to go to the mountainside. I don't like mountains, I get sore legs from such hikes. Do you have to go now, don't you always go in the spring, can't you take Hallgerður with you?" But Auður said, "Do you think it's asking too much to have you help me gather herbs just this once?" And with that, the matter was settled. Warm clothes were gathered. "But it's summer!" screeched Karitas. She didn't get an answer. The housewife began to pack a sack of provisions for them and was still doing so when Karitas went to bed. Shortly before her customary insomniac hours, she was woken. She looked up into the face of Auður in horror, and whispered: "But it's the middle of the night!" She didn't get an answer this time, either.

At three o'clock in the morning, they headed eastward over the hay-fields with sacks on their backs and walking sticks in their hands, setting course for the slope above the uppermost farm, and the land soon began to incline upward. It was the time of night when the birds are silent. The two women were silent as well as they put the slope behind them. Karitas didn't understand why they had had to leave so early. She had thought they might leave around six, when the sun had pushed away the gray haze. They came to a flat area, and she finally asked, "Why did we leave so early?" "To be ahead of the sun," Auður replied, and then another steep slope began. Auður climbed determinedly and sure-footedly, while Karitas dragged herself along behind, slipping at every other step. She began to sweat, had sore calves, pain in her groin, and couldn't catch her breath; she stopped, gripped her chest. Auður had disappeared in a greenish-blue fog. Then the thought crossed Karitas's mind that Auður might be one of those unforgiving women, after all, that she was taking revenge on her for the way she had treated Auður's son and was going to let her get lost in the mountains. She looked over her shoulder, saw the precipice below, felt dizzy and nauseated, and thought, I can go neither up nor down; I'll die here. Then she heard a shout: "Clamber on up, and we'll take a rest." When she reached Auður, she was drooling from fatigue; she simply had to lie down on the slope, but Auður sat there erect, looking around genially despite the visibility being zero, and said: "Such nice weather we're having!" She reached into her sack, pulled out a bottle. "Here you go, have a sip of water, and then you'll feel better." Karitas doubted it. The night was still in her body; she asked in a weak voice when they would start picking herbs. "Soon," Auður replied, pulling Karitas to her feet. She crawled on after her mistress for what felt like an eternity. Seeing nothing but the rocky slope, she stumbled, fell, and whined: "Auður, go on without me; I'm going back down." Then Auður sat down beside her, a little breathless herself, and opened her sack. "We'll have some flatbread before going a little farther, very slowly, and then the worst of it will be over." "These herbs of yours certainly do grow high up," bleated Karitas.

They had been climbing for ages. Karitas had grown sullen and irritated at herself when Auður finally said: "The worst stretch is behind us now." Karitas sighed with relief, but then she caught sight of the glacier ahead of them in all its splendor, and was taken aback. "Auður, haven't we gone too high? There isn't a single blade of grass around here." She received no answer and was gripped by the suspicion that the woman wasn't in her right mind. She probably had no idea where they were and knew it, but didn't want to tell Karitas that. Karitas followed her as she pondered what to do, before grabbing Auður's shoulder and asking gently, so as not to frighten her: "Auður, have you ever come here before?" "Yes," said Auður, "around fifteen times." And she handed her one of the walking sticks and went on resolutely. They had reached the mass of hard-packed snow. Karitas followed with icy anxiety in her heart, until Auður stopped and said, "Now we've reached the Sléttubjörg ridge. From here, we'll head east to Kambabrúnir and look out over the mountains from there."

The newly woken morning sun tickled the mountain peaks below them, and a haze lay over the lowlands. Karitas had never before seen mountains from above, and she gasped. "So this is how they look from above?" she said in astonishment, and Auður nodded, her expression blissful: "Yes, aren't they wonderful, my mountains?" It slowly dawned on Karitas that she was standing on the highest peaks in her country, that she had made it to this place all by herself, without help, as brave as could be—and, unable to control herself, she threw her arms around Auður in her joy. "Imagine, me, up here!" They laughed. Then became solemn in the face of such beauty. "I guess we're about twelve hundred meters high," said Auður. "It's good to look back over your life from up here. Go through it in your mind, pick out the best and store it, take the worst and throw it out. Can you remember it all in a single moment?" Karitas looked at the mountaintops, both smooth and sharp; each of them symbolized a chapter in her life. She felt as if she could remember them all, except perhaps one—there was one chapter she couldn't remember. "I remember everything except for the days before I came here to Öræfi," she said. "Nor do I remember sailing to Hornafjörður or the journey over the rivers. Those were bad days."

"The most bitter experience is of the most benefit later," said the woman from Öræfi in an unusually deep voice. She looked over her shoulder at the white expanse and said that they should go on. "Go on?" said Karitas skeptically. "When are we going to pick herbs?" "On the way back down," Auður replied. "But this is terribly dangerous!" cried Karitas. "People have fallen into crevasses up here and died!" Auður looked sharply at her: "Life is full of crevasses. That is why every single step is significant. People have fallen into crevasses but pulled themselves out through courage and perseverance. Have you never fallen into a crevasse? Aren't you in one right now?" Walking onward, she muttered, "The crevasses are still closed. We'll head north to that point there and have our lunch."

Karitas drove her walking stick into the snow and stared gloomily at the woman ahead of her. Auður had had no business depriving her of her joy at the beauty all around and making her recall those bad days, and she tried as hard as she could to come up with hurtful words to pay her back. She still hadn't come up with any when they sat down on pieces of leather that Auður pulled from her sack, but the crevasses of her life had deepened quickly in her head. They munched on salted lamb heads, boiled potatoes, and rye bread spread with a thick layer of butter, but Karitas was still angry. Auður then said, "What an extraordinary woman your mother is. She loses her husband at sea and picks up and leaves with her six children in order to provide them with an education. Circumnavigates the country with them in the dark hold of a ship but makes it to her destination, washes fish, knits woolen clothing, and manages to get all of her children into school. She never lost sight of her goal, that woman. They have always been known for their toughness, those people in the Westfjords. Though they've always dabbled in black magic, of course." "She was never involved with anything of that sort," Karitas said hurriedly. "She believed only in God and herself." "Oh, did she?" said Auður. Karitas replied: "Yes, and she also believed that new days were dawning for women, a new age, she said, a new age for women." "Oh, did she say that?" said Auður. Then she looked straight into Karitas's eyes. "Well now, bright heart, should we head up onto the glacier?"

Karitas couldn't believe her ears. "Do you mean," she said, pointing at herself, "that we two, we women—that we should go up onto the glacier?" Auður raised her eyebrows and smiled: "Women have gone up onto the glacier before—you know that as well as I. Some went on the excursion up here with the boys the year before last, remember? When you didn't want to go?" "Yes, but it's just the two of us now!" said Karitas. "Should that make the trip worse—it being just the two of us?" asked Auður. "I know my way around these parts, come here regularly, it strengthens the lungs," she added. She packed up the remainder of their lunch and stood up. "Wouldn't it be fun to hike over to the knob there, which you've only ever seen from the shore, and tell your sons about your accomplishment afterward? They would be so proud of their mother." Karitas was torn; she couldn't answer, and Auður took advantage of her momentary hesitation. She reached into Karitas's sack, pulled out crampons, said that they should tie them on, pulled a rope from her own sack, tied it around her waist, and, making sure there was a good amount of space between them, knotted the other end around Karitas and said: "Yes, that will do it. Let's go."

A haze lay over the snow-white glacier. Karitas struggled with images and memories from her life; it was as if they demanded to come alive in this dead stillness. Some were clear, colorful, others vague, gray; they vanished in a fog, reappeared, vanished; the silence made her uneasy. She stopped. "What now?" said Auður. "I feel like the silence is devouring me," whispered Karitas, grabbing her head in her hands. Auður pulled her along. After a few moments, she stopped again. "Are you sure we're on the right track? Couldn't we get lost in the fog? It's all white here, dead; there are no landmarks." Auður called out over her shoulder: "I'm on the right track, but are you? If you ever had the feeling of being on the right track, try to find it again now."

Karitas had stopped trying to understand this woman, and even worse, she had stopped trying to understand herself. "I've lost my mind; this isn't real. I'm in a dream. I'm a ghost." "Be careful! There's a crack here right in our path," she heard Auður say. "We've got to cross a little snow bridge." Karitas clung to Auður, looked neither right nor left, could think neither about her life nor her death, just stared at the back of the woman's neck until they had crossed over. She no longer had the strength to reprove the older woman for dragging her along on this deadly expedition. She thought, maybe I'm sleeping or just dead without knowing it, and in her mind's eye, she saw Halldóra and Kára and her little son who had looked into her eyes only once, and all of a sudden, she felt good to be up there in the snow-white silence and fog, to be able to think of them in peace and quiet, feel their presence, how they walked with her, upward, endlessly upward, as she kept her eyes on the ground. She found her breathing and heartbeats so loud in the heavy silence and wanted to say so, but she didn't dare speak, feeling as if it would disturb the Almighty Himself. She started in alarm when Auður said: "How do you like our knob now?" Karitas looked up distractedly at the white rock face. "It's a crag," she declared. "Well said!" exclaimed Auður. "Now we'll have a bite to eat."

While eating the ice-cold meal, it struck Karitas that they had reached the final destination of their white journey. The sun had ambushed the fog, making it clear who was in charge so close to the sky, which enveloped them in cloudless blue. She felt quite fine and had no qualms about descending, she knew the way. Then Auður said: "Look to the northwest—there you see the country's highest peak. Isn't it lovely in the sun? Don't you want to go there?" "No, Auður," laughed Karitas, assuming that the woman was joking. "It's not one of my goals." "What are your goals, then?" asked Auður. "We only have a short way to go to the summit after this long, hard ascent. Wouldn't you regret it all your life, to have let timidity prevent you from reaching it? I'll leave the decision to you, bright heart. Now it's you who will decide our course. Are we going to the summit, or are we going down?"

Deep inside, she'd had a suspicion that their journey wasn't complete, even if she had been hoping that it was. She couldn't see that it served any purpose to go higher; the landscape up there was probably no different from here, but on the other hand, timidity was not what one wanted to be known for in the Öræfi district. "We can go on a bit, since you really want to," she muttered, shifting the responsibility for their recklessness to Auður. "It's your decision," said Auður. "So let's go."

They walked across the smooth surface of the glacier with the sun smiling on their right cheeks, and she thought that it would be best to see this through to the end. She would never go up into the mountains again, in any case—that she could promise the one who had created them. Still, she was surprised at how vigorous she suddenly felt—she must have had a hidden energy reserve—and her mind became so strangely serene, as if all thoughts had fled. It was a huge relief. The heavy silence gave way; everything became so light and free. It's as if I'm walking in heaven, she thought. She found herself longing to talk, she just didn't know about what; it had been so long since she had let her tongue wag, but then she suddenly recalled Pía, who had wanted to see the trolls in the mountains, and, breaking the silence, she said it would have been more like Pía to tramp across this glacier than her, and now that she had mentioned Pía, she thought that she really ought to say more about her character and circumstances, and she told Auður about their herring years and their stay at Þrastabakki, when Pía decided that she wanted to help with the winemaking and got them both drunk in the churchyard. She burst into such raucous laughter that she doubled over and had to stop and clutch her stomach. Auður stopped as well, what with the rope tying them together, and she let her laugh to her heart's content, and just when Karitas had recomposed herself and they had walked a short distance, she thought of how Bjarghildur had reacted when Pía took off on her favorite horse, and she went on and on, describing the expression on her sister's face as she stood there with the pillows in her arms when Sigmar slammed the door in her face, and if she knew her sister well, as haughty and complacent as she was, Bjarghildur would surely take revenge someday and slam the door in his.

"Wasn't that exactly what she did?" asked Auður dryly. Karitas stopped abruptly. It was as if she had suddenly sobered up. "So now we're at the foot of the peak," said Auður. "We'll follow it to the northeast and take a rest." They plunked themselves down on the snow and said nothing. Karitas felt a tightness in her chest and heard a buzzing in her ears, as if her head were filling with muck. Her entire body ached, and an enormous weariness overwhelmed her. Patting her lightly on the thigh, Auður said, "We won't eat anything here; it's customary to have a bite of something at the summit." "The summit?" exclaimed Karitas in astonishment. "Are you going all the way up this slope?" she asked exasperatedly. And she didn't wait for an answer, for at that moment, it was as if everything burst inside her. The dikes gave way before the onslaught of the heavy surf, and the rocky debris was scattered throughout her body; she had to release the raging forces, those mad breakers. Tears ran down her cheeks like a cheerful stream freed from its coating of ice; her nose was stuffed, and, having no handkerchief, she was forced to blow the snot out her right and left nostrils by pressing one closed and then the other, and wiping her fingers on her trousers in between. "I don't understand this at all," she sobbed, looking around. "Why should I feel this way in this utterly lifeless place?" Auður said: "It's because of the fire here beneath you." She didn't move, but looked up at the sky, tilted her head as if listening for birdsong in the distance. Then she reached into her sack and pulled out a dish towel: "Here, blow your nose into this, bright heart." "I've lost everyone," Karitas cried into the cloth, "my children, my sister, my Kára, my husband—they're all gone, all gone." Auður stroked her back firmly, determinedly. "From the moment we're born, we're headed for death, and neither you nor I can do anything about that. But we can weep for what we lose; that we are free to do. It is for us to decide." "Auður, it's so awful to lose a child. There is nothing worse in the world. You lose yourself at the same time. And now God is punishing me, I know it," wept Karitas. "Why should He punish you any more than me?" said Auður. "Oh, there is so much that you don't know. Karlína didn't know it, either, so she couldn't tell you, even though she told you all about me. No one knows." Now she wept even louder than before. Auður stroked her back: "We all have secrets. I have a little one, too, but I keep it to myself, because that's how it should be. It wouldn't be pretty if everyone poured out their secrets over all the world. You have lost yourself, that's true. But don't try to find yourself again. It never works. Instead, find another Karitas, a new one. But it's still your decision whether we go all the way to the summit or not." Karitas looked sluggishly up the slope. "Are there more peaks here?" "This is the highest one," Auður said cheerfully, getting to her feet. "Oh, I don't care what we do!" wept Karitas, hiding her face in her hands. "Well then, that must mean we're going to the top," said Auður. "There now, on your feet! You can whimper your way up."

And so she did. She let Auður lead her, crying, to the summit of the highest peak in the country. She had trouble shoving her walking stick into the hard-frozen snow and her nose ran even more, forcing her to stop and blow it into the dish towel as Auður waited. The housewife gazed out over the land, said that it made a great difference wearing good shoes with crampons, and shook her head as if remembering the footwear of centuries past. She yanked on the rope when she wanted them to continue, and sometimes, when Karitas suffered another crying fit and hung heavily on to it, she had to get down on all fours to brace herself. They were nearing the top and were both quite breathless when Auður stopped without prompting, looked over her shoulder, and said, "Despite your losses, you still have one thing that is all your own, and that is your art. I think that you're a great artist, and that you will become famous one day." "You think so?" asked Karitas. Her crying came to an abrupt end. "Yes," said Auður. "Something inside me tells me so. The pictures of yours that I have seen are quite strange, but they have a kind of inexplicable magic to them. Perhaps the best art is that which one doesn't understand." They walked a little farther, until Auður stopped again to catch her breath. She said, "Karlína told me that you are an outstanding portrait artist. But you have never drawn me." "Oh, what was I thinking?" exclaimed Karitas, feeling quite heartened now. "You could have just asked me, my dear woman."

And then they had reached the top, and Karitas asked incredulously, just to be sure, if they were at the summit. Auður said that they were indeed; closer to the sky they could not come in this country— that much she knew. And they fell silent, acted almost bashful, as if they had been catapulted onto the white marble floor of the palace of the sun without knowing the courtly etiquette. They stood back-to-back, moved their heads slowly from left to right, turned in a circle. The fog had receded, revealing the whole country. White peaks and blue, perfect harmony and beauty. The silence sucked in their souls, their consciousnesses opened, everything became so light. Auður drew a deep breath and said: "Isn't it worth coming up here, even if only to experience this feeling?" "Such was the world before we shaped it," Karitas said. And they had to embrace each other for fear that one or the other of them would float off into space if she wasn't held down. It was only for a moment, and then the feeling passed.

Karitas took a whiff of the air. She sniffed around like a dog searching for tracks, and looked puzzled. "I smell the sea."

"The sea? Up here? Well, I'll be!"

"I can smell seaweed and ships' decks."

"It must bode something. Perhaps you have a voyage ahead of you. Unless someone is sailing to you."

They took out their food, feeling as if they deserved a hearty meal. They munched it all with gusto; gulped down trout, salted lamb, potatoes, followed by dried figs, raisins, chocolate. In Karitas's opinion, there could be nothing better, and with her mouth full of raisins, she declared, with a touch of arrogance: "Sigmar may have been to Rome, but he has never climbed Iceland's highest peak." Auður finished chewing and swallowed her mouthful before saying, "I have long had the feeling that you wish to travel abroad. Perhaps you should go, so that you reach your destination before your life is over." Karitas felt relieved. "Auður, that was exactly what I wanted to say to you. I think it's best that I leave Öræfi soon." Auður nodded calmly. Karitas continued: "The only problem is that I used up all of my money long ago." "I'll give you money," Auður said. "No, I can't possibly accept it," hemmed Karitas. "You have worked for me for thirteen years; I owe you," said Auður. "But, Auður, you fed us, my boys and me, for which I am incredibly grateful." "No need to be grateful," Auður said emphatically. "I'll pay you. I'll just sell a few horses."

As Auður had wished, they had gotten there ahead of the sun, but now it caught up, romping with the white heaps of snow, which tossed its rays between them. The light became so bright and dazzling that the women had to shade their eyes. "It's best that we get out of here now," Auður said, and, after bidding the peak a cordial goodbye, they pulled out their pieces of leather and slid on them down the slope whenever they could.

The sun had seized power from the glacier and thawed the snow with its aggressive heat, and was now doing all it could to light a fire in the faces of the women who had snuck into its realm as it slept. The going was heavy and tough; they trudged through slush and got their feet wet, their faces burned, they had headaches behind their eyes, but even so, they felt immensely proud of themselves. Auður was light-hearted, as if she had just finished a good day's work. Her tongue loosened and she spoke loudly, recounting her youth and countless trips up the mountains—"I've always been a great mountain woman"—and intertwined her own stories with many others of valiant men and their adventures. Karitas listened with one ear as she tried to order her life and future in her mind. Time passed much faster on the way down; they had come to Sléttubjörg ridge when Auður suddenly said, as if remembering just in time: "Listen, bright heart, we had better not say anything about our glacier trip right away. They get so terribly worked up, the men, if they hear about such things. They always want to be the ones in charge of such expeditions. They don't trust the women. But Hrefna and I sometimes sneak up here, pretending that we're going to pick herbs. It's so good for the health. We'll let them think we were lolling on the slope, among the herbs, if you don't mind. And then in the autumn, I'll tell your boys about your trip to the summit. I promise. And so that our sunburns don't give us away, I've brought along a bit of flour that we can powder our faces with before we reach the hayfields of home."

Dead tired, with the glacier air in their lungs, but positively glowing within, their eyes sparkling and off-color, they walked back into the farmhouse around four o'clock. Auður gulped down a cup of coffee, then said that she was going to lie down for a while before getting dinner ready. Karitas sat against the wall of the house with her boys and sipped hot coffee, longing to tell them about her trip to the summit but holding back, as agreed. She did, however, say that the mountains had been rather harsh and steep. They felt that she had accomplished a great feat by hiking all the way up the slope—"And you saw the glacier, Mama, didn't you?"—and acted as if she had been gone a very long time. They cuddled up to her. And she told them, as they sat there all huddled together, that all three of them would be leaving Öræfi for good in the autumn. The brothers would both be going to school in Akureyri. First, they would go south to her brother Ólafur in Reykjavík, and then north. "Will we go by car?" Sumarliði asked excitedly. She said that she thought so. She would then either go north with them or come later. The main thing was for her to get a good job and good housing so that they could always be together. Whether it would be in the south or north, she didn't know yet. "Do you think that our papa will return someday?" Jón dared to ask, pulling his legs up underneath him. Karitas said that she didn't think so. Then she yawned and, trying to lead the conversation in a different direction, said, "I think I'll go upstairs and lie down, like Auður." But Jón wouldn't let her go: "Mama, Skarphéðinn says that you were ill and confused when you came with us here to Öræfi." There was anxiety in both the boys' faces as they waited for an answer. She stroked her sunburned face; her lips stung. Without looking at them, she said, "That Skarphéðinn is mad at me right now, which is why he's spouting rubbish. But it's true that I was very ill when we got here. I couldn't keep anything down and hadn't slept for many weeks, many months. Lack of sleep makes you ill." She got up, moved to go, stopped, stood in front of them, and said thoughtfully: "Still, I felt as if I were sleeping the whole time. I was sleeping but knew while I slept that I hadn't fallen asleep."

For the summer festival, the men had set up a dance platform near the cliffs and pitched tents in which the women could sell refreshments. The women's preparations had been going on for more than a week. They had baked until late at night, made all sorts of treats including whey cheese and English puddings, and some of them had sewn themselves new garments in the quiet of midnight. Karitas dressed her sons in nice shirts and herself in a skirt, and shortly after noon, the guests began streaming in from near and far with bulging saddlebags, arriving early so that they could roam from farm to farm and say hello to their neighbors before the festivities got underway. Both accordion players had arrived, filling the farmyard with gaiety as the sisters Guðrún and Hallgerður danced in fun for those gathered as a warm-up for the evening, and the kitchen was so crowded with folk that Auður had to elbow her way through them with the coffeepot. Then everyone began making their way down to the cliffs, the children excited and noisy, the young people giggling and whispering, and the outdoor games began. The children ran relay races, played red rover and duck, duck, goose, and wrestled, and when the adults had had their fill of coffee, they were ready for the main contest, a tug-of-war between the men and women.

Karitas, who, as in previous years, had been tasked with bringing provisions from the farm to the cliffs, sat down next to the tent with a cup of coffee at a quiet moment and watched the rope being pulled left and right to shouts and cascades of laughter, and she watched the birds as well, crying out over the gathering, and the horses on the mowed hayfields. The hay from the manured fields had all been brought in; only the hay from the meadows was left, and when that had been brought in, she would pack her things and leave with the river guides. She focused on the tug-of-war. The men seemed to have the upper hand, and the women shouted for reinforcements: "Come here, Karitas!" She hesitated, but then decided to help them this one time and pulled herself to her feet. She grabbed the rope at the front of the line of women and looked directly into the eyes of her sons facing her. The certainty of victory in their eyes fired her up; did these kids think they could defeat their mother? She pulled with doubled strength, putting everything she had into it and screaming to the troops behind her. And they pulled and bared their teeth, growled and roared like wild animals in a bloody battle, so hideous to see that the lads were thrown momentarily off guard, and the women took advantage of it, tugged hard one last time, and won. Afterward, they had to lie flat on the grass, eyes closed. But even though their bodies were momentarily overcome, their souls had never been more lively—thanks to their victory. The winning team's joy was so great that it took their vanquished opponents all they had to swing their partners when the dance began on the platform. The evening sun was warm and cheery, the dancing went on and on, and the women sweated and gulped down milk and whey until their faces swelled, while the men took swigs from flasks pulled secretively from their saddlebags. There was no drunkenness, however; everyone was peaceful, apart from a few who didn't know how to dance and tried to cover up their ignorance by indulging in some unusual wrestling moves. No one paid them any attention. Both men and women sang along to the tunes that had lyrics, and Karitas danced with Hrefna, as usual. No one in the parish danced as well as Hrefna, but in the circle dances, Karitas often ended up with one of the men, which she didn't mind so long as they weren't using snuff—and suddenly, Skarphéðinn was standing before her. With shining eyes, due to his having taken quite a few swigs, but unassuming, and almost shy. The rascal still has feelings for me, she thought, and if the circumstances had been different, he would have gotten a cold reception, but the evening was so beautiful and she herself was so happy inside, though she hardly knew why, that she allowed him to grip her tightly around her waist. But it is with men as with puppies, becoming more persistent if you don't keep them at bay through aloofness and indifference. He awaited his opportunity, grabbed her again during the dance, this time taking her away from a renowned horseman, and tightened his grip on her waist. He danced well, Skarphéðinn; she had to give him that. He was powerful and unrestrained—and she definitely noticed various feelings kindle within her. She decided to put a stop to this before it got out of hand, but danced that particular dance to the end, enjoying letting a strong man hold her.

The accordion players had to wet their whistles and rest their fingers for a few moments. She thanked the man for the dance, but once the music stopped, they had nothing to say to each other. People were still in high spirits, even though it was well past midnight. Her sons were doing complicated gymnastic exercises with the other children and weren't in any mood to go to bed—and customarily, such gatherings went on until it was time to drive the cows in for their morning milking. The summer night was long and bright—it simply had to be danced away. The birds' cries had died down, but instead, their melancholy notes could be heard from the cliffs, and the same wistfulness had slipped into the hearts of the young, unmarried folk. Some stole away in pairs as the musicians rested, others sat enjoying themselves; none showed any signs of fatigue—apart from Karitas, who yawned. Skarphéðinn stared at her. He was sitting between two girls, both of whom had come with the sole purpose of making him their husband, and they had no intention of letting him rejoin the dance with a woman who had been married for years; this they made clear to her with sharp glances. Karitas took the looks in stride, especially since she wasn't the least bit interested. But glacier folk seldom let go of their prey. When the dance started up again, she pretended to need to go get something at home, and disappeared around the cliffs and up over the hayfields. He followed at her heels, calling out after her: "Listen, is it true that you're moving to the south?" "No," she replied, "I'm not leaving until the autumn." "That's what I meant," he said, stopping her. He took both her hands and squeezed them so hard that she thought he would crush every single bone in them, before finally saying, "I can come south, too, if you wish." She understood that this was something like a declaration of love. The horses in the field stood stock-still, staring at them and following along with the progress of this matter. Which was actually rather complicated. But there was no reason to be peevish toward men who danced well, so Karitas said, "It could be fun to meet you in Reykjavík." Skarphéðinn was clearly relieved to hear these words. His face brightened, and he squeezed her hands again: "May I perhaps kiss you on the cheek to confirm this?" She had no objection to his doing so but found his behavior quite comical. He, on the other hand, was completely serious. Determinedly, he pulled her close, bent her head back, and kissed her long and passionately on the mouth. "Unbelievable," she sighed when the kiss was finally over. Then she stormed off, leaving him standing there, shuffling his feet awkwardly, as if he weren't quite sure whether he had done the right thing. At the farmhouse door, Karitas glanced behind her. Saw him disappear in the direction of the cliffs.

Upstairs, Bergþóra was sleeping the sleep of the righteous; she hadn't kissed anyone. Karitas took off her clothes and pulled the duvet up over her head. She was convinced that the man was desperate; that he simply couldn't restrain himself, and that she was lucky to be more frightened than hurt. But she had hardly been sleeping for more than a few hours when she woke, bathed in sweat and deeply ashamed. She had dreamed that a man had come to her. In her dream, she had remembered him and asked herself what he was doing here at the foot of Vatnajökull Glacier. Shouldn't he be in the east? She had remembered his eyes, having seen them before—she couldn't remember where, but she remembered the man himself—and she had never forgotten her dream out east. Now it had repeated itself here, near the glacier, up in a family room among blameless people. Karitas was deeply upset, there was a buzzing in her ears, she was damp with sweat from top to bottom and felt as if her blood were boiling. She groped at her body in a panic to check if her underwear was where it should be, and was relieved to discover that it was, but lifted her head and looked around, ashamed. Had anyone seen her writhing beneath her duvet? Opposite her, the old woman lay sleeping; the others' beds were still empty. She heard the cows mooing outside in the early morning.

Karitas

Horses Transporting Hay 1939

Collage

Mirages flicker over the warm sands below the meadows.

I look toward the burning sun, shade my eyes with my hand, see the line of horses transporting hay slowly upward. My boy is riding the lead horse, with another in tow, pulling a cart, and then comes another, and so on down the line. Five horses, four carts, four bales of hay in each cart.

The caravan resembles a snake slowly winding its way up the fields toward the barn.

Across the picture surface.

Above is the sun-white sky.

Below is the dark-green grass.

I use burlap for the hay, cardboard for the carts, canvas for the horses. The wood chip is the boy.

In the farmyard stands the housewife, with a treat for the boy. Rhubarb in sugar syrup with whipped cream.

She is pampering my boy. He delivers her the hay.

When he comes home from the meadows in the evenings, she has warmed his bed.

Put two bottles of boiling water in wool socks, laid one at the foot of the bed, the other against his pillow.

Horse-drawn carts were the only vehicles on wheels that the boys had ever seen, but despite that, Sumarliði thought he knew everything about automobiles. While everyone napped in the tents down on the meadows after lunch, Karitas sat at the foot of a haystack with her boys and told them about the life that awaited them on the other side of the desolate sands, the bustle of the farms, the traffic in the city, and they asked endless questions, Jón about buildings, Sumarliði about automobiles. He knew that a bus drove from the sands south to Reykjavík, and couldn't wait to get in it and hear the sound of its engine with his own ears. "It's all about the ignition, Mama," he said solemnly, as if explaining the salvation of mankind. They discussed this while the others dozed inside the tents, having little other opportunity to chat, what with haymaking being at its peak. They worked all day, from dawn until close to midnight, as long as the dry weather lasted, and Karitas was either in the meadows raking or in the farmhouse, where the women cooked and baked until the sweat dripped off them. Only Bergþóra, old and blind, led a comfortable life. Everyone else's rest times were determined by the glaciers; the men could tell by the smell if a glacial flood was underway. At such times, a strong odor of sulfur hung over the meadows, and if it was Hólajökull Glacier that shifted, they could expect dry weather, and would shout: "Spread it out!" But if Stigajökull Glacier shifted, they could expect rain, and would shout even louder: "Rake it up!" These weather forecasts never failed.

When it rained, it was less busy, and the women sewed dresses and aprons.

Auður had mentioned to Karitas that she would probably have to sew herself a new dress and perhaps two skirts since she was going south to Reykjavík. She would be leaving soon; hadn't she given any thought to this? And she was right, Karitas had been preoccupied with getting things ready for her sons, the future schoolboys, and had gotten Hildigunnur, who was the best at making trousers, to help her. It was important to her that her mother receive them well-dressed and impeccable, knowing that if they arrived wearing worn-out old clothes, there would be talk of her ineptitude. But the same went for Auður; in her opinion, she was sending Karitas out into the merciless world beyond Öræfi, and the responsibility for her attire would be laid on the women of this parish. "You must be properly dressed when walking the streets of the capital," she said, trying to sound carefree, but she couldn't hide how dispirited she felt. The dresses and skirts would probably have been thrown together without much fuss had not Guðrún, the eldest daughter who lived on an enterprising farm in the neighborhood, come to visit her mother. The housewife's eldest daughter and her youngest son had sophistication in common, as Guðrún, too, had been to Reykjavík, but as far as experience went, she won, having worked at both a cookie factory and a hospital for two years before she married.

"What, may I ask, is this supposed to be?" Guðrún asked, looking indignantly at the pieces of cloth on the kitchen table. They answered truthfully: "A calico dress for Karitas." "And what pattern have you used?" "Oh, the same as the dress we made for Hallgerður the other year; the two of them are the same size." "That dress has long since gone out of fashion," Guðrún said coldly. Hallgerður burst into tears. "I knew it all along, Mama, I told you." Auður, with scissors poised at the ready, turned pale. Hrefna felt she ought to intervene, now that Hallgerður had been brought to tears. "Well, since you've come bursting in here with all of your knowledge about fashion in the capital, how about sharing some of it with us?" "The skirt isn't wide enough," Guðrún said dismissively. "You should have cut it at an angle." Auður looked dejected. "But then you waste so much of the fabric that there will be nothing left for the aprons." "Not if you do it this way," Guðrún said, and now everyone in the room began to gesticulate wildly, with the exception of the one who, in the fullness of time, would be wearing the dress. She was standing over a washbasin at the window, rinsing out sweaters. When the debate, whose volume had increased considerably, shifted to sleeve lengths, old Bergþóra appeared with her knitting, to everyone's surprise. How she had managed to come downstairs alone and unsupported was a mystery, and she had barely made herself comfortable in the nook by the stove when Hrefna remarked grumpily, "Hold on a minute, how long has it been since the young lady," as she always called her niece, despite her being married and therefore entitled to a different honorific, "was pottering around the capital? Five years, hasn't it? And does she perhaps think that fashion hasn't changed since then?" The women's hands dropped. Guðrún glanced at Karitas, who was staring into the washbasin. When no comments came from that direction, Guðrún shot back: "Well, it should be easy enough to find out if I'm right. I'll just phone my friend in Reykjavík; she's always fashionable." Then she mounted her horse and sped over the hayfields to the sisters at the central farm.

The women hadn't waited long with the coffee when she reappeared with four women in tow: the sisters who owned the phone, along with Þorgerður and Hildigunnur, who'd happened to be there making a phone call in connection with a youth-association activity for which they were responsible. They had thought it best to accompany Guðrún back to the farm, all of them having listened to the telephone conversation with the big-city dame and having the sewing skills that fashion in the capital demanded. They encircled the table, nine in all, mothers and daughters, sisters, aunts and nieces, letting their light shine as usual on such occasions, loudly voicing their opinions and interrupting each other. From what Karitas could make out, Guðrún had been right about the skirt's width, but hadn't taken into account the rapid developments in the design of lapels, collars, and sleeves. The lapel should be buttoned, the neckline rounded off with a white collar, the sleeves slightly gathered, and there should be shoulder pads, too.

"And the skirts are getting shorter," Guðrún said. "Again!" shouted the women, before clapping their hands over their mouths, sighing, and praising God for not having lengthened them. Because if they had, the old dresses could not have been reused. Many of their musings also had to do with the future uses of the dress, whether it would be worn daily or taken out solely on special occasions. This was important to know with respect to the collar, but Auður said, clipping with her scissors in the empty air in order to silence the assembly, that it didn't matter which it was, she had to be well-dressed on a daily basis, did her bright heart, because in just a few days, she would be living in the home of her brother, the trial lawyer, who was married to a woman from a fine family of civil servants, and Auður wanted that woman to know how well the women of Öræfi dressed in their everyday life. They glanced at Karitas, who was wringing out the sweaters as best she could, and, doubling their efforts, the women threw themselves upon the fabric like surgeons upon a lifeless patient.

With the entire distaff side of the family gathered in the kitchen, the discussions became so fervent that no one noticed the man who had ventured in twice, covered in blood. It was Skarphéðinn, who had run into an iron bar in the storehouse and lacerated one eyebrow, and, being such a sanguine man, the blood poured from him. His face was bloody, his shirt and trousers were stained with blood, leaving barely a dry thread in them, as if he had just slaughtered a vicious bull. He had simply wanted to ask if the women could spare him a bandage, and perhaps find him some clean clothes, but, startled upon seeing how many of them there were and how loud they were, he had immediately withdrawn, but had been forced to try again when the bleeding rendered him nearly blind. Only Karitas saw him the second time he came in. She didn't even try to point him out to the women, but signaled to him to sit down on the stool by the window, fetched hot water and clean cloths, cleaned his face and his wound, applied a willow leaf, gauze, and a bandage, went and got clean clothes, and led him through the old kitchen and into the cowshed so that he could change—and all of this happened without any of the women at the table so much as looking up. She was pouring out the water from the washbasin when the picture sprang to her mind. She stood stock-still for a few seconds, envisioning the form, the contours, the dress on the operating table, cut, clipped, sewn roughly together. She put down the washbasin, hurried to the old kitchen, rummaged in her box, took out the largest of the drawing pads and a pencil, slipped back into the kitchen, sat down under the window, and plunged headlong into sketching.

One of the women inadvertently looked up. Stopped talking. Stared in astonishment at Karitas. Another noticed her surprise and silence and turned to look, as well, and was no less dumbfounded. Finally, they all fell silent, some turning halfway around so they could look at her as she sat there under the window. And she drew them, glancing up and down, her pencil flying over the paper, and it was as if they suddenly remembered that this was the woman who was supposed to get the dress, and that this woman was an artist—educated abroad, in fact. They stood there as if nailed to the floor, not daring to move, aware that they were being drawn. They straightened their backs, brushed hair from their cheeks, put on solemn faces; it was clear to them that at that very moment, their faces, bodies, and clothing could very well be immortalized before the world. The woman with the pencil had taken control; she was moving to the capital and would take this picture of them with her. "Do I smell blood?" asked old Bergþóra.

The laundry boiled in the black pot over the sheep-dung-fired stove in the old kitchen, and Karitas stirred it with the stick. Rarely had she boiled her sanitary belts as happily as she did now. Anxiety had beset her since the dream man appeared to her for the second time, although she was well aware that conception could not take place without the presence of a man of flesh and blood. Experience had taught her to take nothing for granted. So she boiled her belts with a contented smile on her lips, fished them out of the pot, and laid them next to the wet linen pads. Lumbered with the pot down to the stream, self-contented and serene; from now on, nothing could hinder her journey south. She rinsed the pads and her belts in the cold stream, talked to herself about the weather, this peculiar stillness day after day—perhaps it was a precursor to a storm or something even worse? Would it start snowing before they brought in the hay from the meadows? Wouldn't that be typical?

"We can hear it all the way down in the meadows, Mama, when you talk to yourself," said Jón behind her, and she could tell he found it embarrassing. "Well, since you're here, you can give me a hand wringing out the laundry," she said, shaking off his remark. "Now stand still while Jón twists," she told the left-handed Sumarliði. She was in a lighthearted mood and indulged herself in preaching to them, which she had done so often lately, instructing them in proper manners, and at the same time, teaching them about life in Akureyri. For the third time, she told them where the school was located, how many shops there were, what wind directions were the worst when it came to the weather, and what kind of clothes they should wear—"I assume that they wear galoshes in the north, just as we do here, I mean on a daily basis, but when you go to school in Akureyri, you have to wear leather shoes, so we need to invest in pairs for the both of you when we get to Reykjavík." And then she couldn't help but go over the names and main characteristics of their relatives, in case they had forgotten. "You'll be spending two nights with my brother Ólafur before continuing north, and as you know, Ólafur is an important man with a fine title. He is a trial lawyer, as I have told you, and then there is my brother Páll, the teacher, who will hopefully give you lessons in Akureyri at some point, and my little brother Pétur, who is a distinguished merchant in Reykjavík, I don't remember if I told you that—I do believe that his shop is on Laugavegur Street, no less; yes, they all have fine titles, the boys, your uncles, and your aunts, too; see, Halldóra was a midwife, and Bjarghildur is a housewife, with a diploma from the Women's College, yes indeed." She stopped and took the duvet cover from them, which Jón had wrung gently as he and his brother listened. "Yes," she continued, "such fine titles they all have. I'm the only one who is untitled."

"But you're an artist, Mother," Jón remarked earnestly. "You can't get a job as an artist, so it isn't a title," she replied, suddenly grouchy. "But at least you're a Mrs.," said Sumarliði, "and that's a title!" "Yes, my dear gentlemen," she sighed, "I'm still a Mrs., and that's the title that most of us women have, I suppose."

When Karitas stepped outside that morning, she found the sound of the wind quite strange, like a piteous howling in the distance. She looked at the southern sky over the sea; the clouds had lined themselves up from east to west and resembled a long mountain range with sharp peaks. They remained still, as if awaiting orders from above. She stared and listened, holding the tub full of wet men's trousers, then made her way to the clothesline with difficulty, inching along the wall of the house without taking her eyes off the clouds. She pulled the trousers from the tub, fastened them onto the line, sensed that something was in the offing, and glanced up at the sky. The clouds were now at full sail, like warships charging toward each other, and the wind's howling drew nearer. She threw everything down and ran inside. Auður asked if the weather wasn't good and dry. Karitas said that there was nothing wrong with the weather, except that the wind was behaving so strangely. Auður found this noteworthy; her cows had also behaved strangely as she was milking them. They both went out to the farmyard to look at the clouds, which had ceased their bluster and now sailed slowly along. "But do you hear the wind?" asked Karitas, and Auður listened intently. She said that she couldn't hear anything, but that nature often behaved strangely at the turning of the seasons—then, she often heard a cracking and rumbling from up on the glacier, as if an entire household within it were being moved. Were those the sounds that she had heard? "No, it was more like the howling of a dog being beaten," Karitas said.

They went about their work that morning lost in thought, and didn't notice that Hallgerður had disappeared until Skarphéðinn came out of the workshop with a saddle he wanted his sister to try out. The men immediately began searching for her, riding here and there throughout the parish—the last time she'd disappeared, she had been found in a haystack—and finally, they found her down at the estuary, wearing few clothes. She was furious with them, insisting that she had just been trying to free the trout from a curse. She was brought home and put to bed like a small child, despite being over twenty years old. "Where is your husband?" she asked Karitas sharply as the latter dressed her in clean socks. And Karitas was forced to croon the verse "south of the sea in a fair valley" to calm her down, even though she would have preferred to slap the girl for her caper. Auður seemed quite unaffected by her daughter's misadventure, and served lunch with characteristic serenity and balance, but said that she was going to take a nap following lunch, like the men. But Hrefna grew anxious and whispered to Karitas as they did the dishes: "What do you think it will be like in the winter, with only Auður and me to take care of Hallgerður, with you all gone and Skarphéðinn, too? The only man here will be Hallur, and he's getting old. Can you imagine Auður and me rushing out into a blizzard to look for the poor chit?" After washing up, Hrefna headed anxiously to the pantry and gobbled up all the chocolate she had set aside for Christmas. "I need this now; my hips are bothering me so much," she said with her mouth full.

Karitas was standing out in the farmyard listening to the wind, which still behaved belligerently in the distance, and watching the clouds dance over the sea, when Skarphéðinn touched her shoulder. "Will you come with me to the guest room for a moment?" As it wasn't like Skarphéðinn to ask her to speak with him privately, this made her a bit uneasy, but she followed him in. "Listen," he said, and it was clear that he had practiced the speech that followed. "It is just over a week until you leave, whereas I am unable to go anywhere until after the roundup and the slaughter, and therefore can't keep you company on your trip south, so it crossed my mind that you might like to have something to read along the way. I would like to give you a book." Karitas looked at the shelves containing the home's treasures, a complete collection of the Icelandic sagas, and, after careful consideration, said that he was a noble and generous man, but that she had never had any particular interest in the old sagas, and that she therefore felt it wrong to take any of them from him. It was best that the valiant man himself kept them. "Would you perhaps like something more recent?" he asked eagerly, and she didn't know how to answer, but he opened his footlocker, which was crammed with printed matter, rummaged around, and pulled out three books. He held them in his hands for a few moments as if for show, and then chose one: "Here you have an excellent story that can make you forget time and place, *The Aviator of Tsingtao*, which is about a German naval officer and aviator, or 'pilot' as they are called nowadays, from Berlin, who, at the start of the war, is stationed in China, whence he travels to America, and then makes his way to Gibraltar and from there to England, where he is put in a prison camp from which he later escapes, manages to get to Holland and finally back to Germany, where he is able to continue serving his homeland, because the war isn't over at all, and it really is a damned cracking, fantastic book. It's probably best that I write your name inside so that there can be no doubt as to its owner." She thanked him and left, and he shut the door to the guest room so that he could lie down for a bit. She sat down on a stool in the farmyard, peeked at the dedication, and couldn't help but smile. "Best wishes to Karitas, with thanks for a warm summer night, Skarphéðinn Grímsson." She found it an earnest dedication, and since no one was there to disturb her, her boys being busy with something, she began to read, and did so eagerly, completely forgetting to keep an eye on the clouds. At a noise from the farmhouse, she looked up and discovered that the clouds hadn't been able to withstand the onslaught of the wind.

The boys had herded the cows back into the cowshed, where they suddenly began to moo, each louder than the next, eyes wide. The eerie sounds were as if made by a choir from the underworld, and the boys shushed them, yelled at them, and ordered them to stop, but they mooed even louder. The cowshed trembled, horses in the pastures galloped away, dogs tore off to the hayfields—never had such a bellowing been heard on the farm. Everyone ran in mortal anguish to the cowshed. "What the hell is going on here!" shouted Skarphéðinn, and his exclamation seemed to hit the nail on the head: it was as if the devil himself were running amok in the stalls. Everyone dashed in bewilderment from cow to cow, patted them, tried to calm them down, but nothing did the trick until Auður grabbed hold of the head of the lead cow, Fenja, with both hands and pressed her head against her chest, holding the cow as tightly as she could. Fenja stopped mooing, and the others fell silent as one. The household members wiped the sweat from their foreheads. Auður said, "It's an omen." She began milking Fenja, whose mood had suddenly changed. Now she behaved in the most dignified manner and acted as if she had had nothing to do with this at all.

When the household sat down to dinner, they were all rather quiet. They gave each other sidelong glances in the hope that someone could offer a plausible explanation for the cows' behavior, or perhaps knew stories of cows mooing madly when a natural disaster was imminent or the end of the world was at hand, but even old Bergþóra was baffled. "Whatever caused it, it's an omen," Hallur proclaimed, and he turned on the radio. When the first news of the evening was announced, they all stopped eating and stared wide-eyed at each other.

Out in the big world, war had broken out. The Germans had attacked Poland. The announcer was audibly upset.

"Well, there we have it," said the old woman. The housewife, who always ate standing up, sat down on the stool next to the stove. After the announcer had finished delivering this news, the men quickly began jabbering, having long suspected that submarine warfare was imminent. They recapitulated everything they knew about the war that had raged on the Continent more than twenty years ago, and made predictions for the coming one, which they thought would soon be over, naval and land forces being much more effective and powerful now—not to mention the improved equipment of the well-drilled soldiers. "What do these soldiers look like?" old Bergþóra hazarded to ask, having never in all her life seen such a phenomenon, although she suspected that it was a type of person. She was given detailed explanations and descriptions, and the discussion at the table was enthusiastic and high-spirited; it wasn't every day that such news was delivered—but the housewife still sat silently by the stove. "Well, Mama," said Skarphéðinn, "now we know why the cows mooed like that." "No, Skarphéðinn Grímsson," she answered. "We still have no idea."

At sunset that evening, the area's residents went into motion. In a southwesterly breeze, the men hurried from farm to farm, wanting to make sure that everyone had heard the radio news and taking the opportunity to check on their neighbors' knowledge of the antecedents to the war and its leading players, besides making predictions on its course and outcome. This went on until the ten o'clock news; people came and went, stood or sat down for a brief moment in the kitchen and speculated particularly on how the Icelandic government would respond. Karitas grew tired of the perpetual racket in the kitchen, besides feeling that her sons were too young for such war talk, and said slightly petulantly, to make it clear to everyone that it was now bedtime, that the Icelandic government had no influence on world affairs—that much she knew after her years in Denmark. And at that, all the visitors went home. She went out to the clothesline with an empty basket to bring in the laundry before bedtime.

Silence lay over the hayfields, the evening air was cool, the moon was new. The trouser legs flapped lightly against each other in the breeze, now completely dry following the onslaught of wind, and she stood there unmoving, enjoying the silence after all the jabbering in the house. She tilted her head as if having spotted a new dimension in the laundry, moved closer to the clotheslines, walked all the way around them, looked at the trouser legs from all angles. Came up to them again, tied them together so that it looked as if they were dancing a circle dance in the twilight.

Hoofbeats sounded from the east, at first indistinctly. She felt no need to check to see who might have come so late in the evening; it was probably more men wanting to gossip about war. The hoofbeats grew louder in the evening silence, yet mainly in her head, she felt; she could hear a whole herd of horses, envisioned horsemen racing toward the northern farm and a young girl standing in their way. At last she looked east and saw that there were two riders, riding fast with the moon at their necks. A sharp gust of wind stirred the trousers on the clotheslines into momentary action, and the legs of one pair hit her in the face. She tried to tame them, reached for one of the clothespins on the line, no longer heard the hoofbeats but got goose bumps all over her body. The riders had halted their horses on the other side of the stream. She held on to the trouser legs, didn't move. The riders waited. One dismounted. Moved slowly toward the gully. His outline revealed that he was dressed in riding clothes of a foreign style, with high, narrow riding boots. For a second, he held his hands in front of his face, and she saw smoke rise from him; he had lit a cigar. He smoked for a few moments with one hand in his pocket, regarding her and the farm. She peered back, still holding on to the trouser legs. Then he threw his cigar into the gully, inched his way down into it, disappeared from her sight, reappeared on the bank on her side. Came walking toward her, tall, slender, headed for the clotheslines.

His movements seemed familiar to her.

She clutched the trouser legs tightly, felt as if her legs were giving way. When he reached her, he leaned with one hand against the clothes pole, stuck the other in his pocket, and said: "My little one?"

She pulled the trousers off the line, stuffed the clothespins into her pocket, folded the trousers, and laid them in the basket. Did the same with all of them, taking her time, acting as if she were alone. She looked up at the sky as if checking whether she could see any stars, took out a handkerchief and blew her nose, buttoned a button, and said without looking at him: "I thought you were going to come and get us thirteen years ago."

His traveling companion on the other side of the stream had grown impatient. She saw him deal with the horses and go down into the gully, heard the swishing of the grass as he came walking toward them. The two men stood side by side, politely waiting for Karitas to attend to them. She laid the last pair of trousers on top of the others in the basket, straightened up, and finally looked at them. His face was darker, sharper, but his eyes looked the same. Curse him, she thought. He's as handsome as ever. And he looked intently back at her. The other man, a head shorter yet of average height, bowed earnestly and said in an inquiring tone: "Signora Ilmarsson?" Then he kissed her hand. She thought she was dreaming. She bent down to lift the laundry basket, but the foreigner reacted quickly, grabbing it in order to spare her the inconvenience. She, however, yanked it out of his hands and stormed into the farmhouse. She pushed open the kitchen door, and the lively chatter stopped immediately. Those in the kitchen could see from her expression that war abroad was insignificant compared to the major news that she would be announcing to them. When she hesitated to speak, not having had time to decide how best to announce the arrival of these men, the housewife stuck out her chin and looked over the household members slowly, as if to remind them of the infallibility of her cows. "What is it that you wish to tell us, bright heart?"

Karitas looked at her boys. "Your father is outside and would like to see you."

News of an eruption in the glacier would hardly have had a greater effect. The boys stiffened, and the others looked at each other in stunned amazement. It was Auður who said, "Well, it's a good thing we have fresh-baked crullers."

The boys went out. Karitas, watching them from the doorway, saw them stare helplessly at their toes, hunch their shoulders up to their ears, stand close together, and stare at the man she had said was their father. He was tall, dressed in a three-piece suit of dark tweed and high leather boots. Like a nobleman on an evening inspection of his lands. He made no attempt to touch his sons, merely scrutinized them with a sharp expression, as if they were poachers. They pressed even closer together. Karitas grew angry. She was a hair's breadth from pulling the boys in again, when their father took one big step forward and grabbed them both in his arms. Holding them close, he rested his cheek against first one and then the other's head, inhaling the scent of their hair. They didn't move. Karitas went inside, having to elbow her way past the others, who had gathered at the door behind her. They craned their necks, looked over each other's heads, stared in astonishment at the well-dressed strangers.

The discussion at the kitchen table was now as stiff as it had been lively earlier in the evening. The sun in the lands to the south hadn't made Sigmar any more talkative; the foreigner didn't speak the language, and Skarphéðinn, normally the best among them at engaging strangers in conversation, sat there glum-faced and silent. Hallgerður and Hrefna, overcome with shyness in the presence of such well-dressed, distinguished men, glanced up from time to time as if to assure themselves that Sigmar was of flesh and blood, and Auður was in a similar state, trying to concentrate on serving the refreshments but clumsily dropping everything. The boys acted as if they were in a trance, and Karitas stood at the door to the old kitchen, arms crossed, staring at the window. Only Hallur, who had never mastered the art of conversation, tried to chat with the guests, resorting exclusively to the interrogation method. He asked them the news—this, he knew how to do—where they came from, where they were going. "We've come from Hornafjörður," Sigmar answered, looking at Karitas as he spoke, "and we're going to Akureyri." The answer allowed Hallur to ask how the weather had been in Hornafjörður. If Auður hadn't pulled herself together once the coffee and crullers were on the table, the entire conversation would have revolved around the weather in the southeastern corner of the country. The coffee also seemed to help loosen the tongues of those who normally didn't say much. Auður asked who Sigmar's companion was, and everyone held their breath. Sigmar apologized, saying that he had momentarily forgotten his manners; of course he had intended to introduce his friend, Andrea Fortunato, from Rome. The Roman bowed his head slightly when he heard his name and looked warmly into the eyes of the others, but they all looked away. Karitas couldn't help but glance at the man when she heard where he was from, and immediately took note of his fine-featured yet manly face, his black hair, and his gentle demeanor, but then her gaze met the sea-green eyes of the man from Borgarfjörður and she turned her attention back to the window. The man from Borgarfjörður, however, had noticed the flash in her eyes, and added, "Karitas always wanted to go to Rome, but never made it, so I have brought Rome to her."

As this remark did nothing to lighten the mood in the room, Auður politely asked if the weather wasn't always nice in Rome. And looked tenderly at the man who had come from there. Sigmar turned to the Roman and said something to him in a foreign language—apparently telling him what the housewife had asked. The Roman sat up straighter in his seat and began to speak in his strangely melodic language. He raised his arms and described his country and his people in detail, before going into the climate down south, talking with his hands and wiping imaginary sweat off his forehead and then suddenly changing his expression and hitting himself with his arms, as if to warm himself up. The household members dangled their crullers as they listened devoutly, considering it impolite to bite into them until the foreigner had finished speaking. No one said a word until Auður looked at Sigmar and asked what the man had been saying, it sounded so beautiful. "He said that it can get hot in the summer, cold in the winter," Sigmar replied. Since the Roman was asked nothing further about the summer heat, the conversation stalled again. Finally, Skarphéðinn sniffed several times and asked the strangers, without looking at them, if they had heard that war had broken out. Sigmar sipped slowly at his coffee, and then looked at Auður, as if it had been she who asked: "We had long heard talk of impending world war." The others clearly thought that his use of the term "world war" for the German invasion of Poland was a bit of an exaggeration. Still, they couldn't help but shudder. Auður hastened to say, "I expect that the gentlemen will be spending the night?" And the Icelandic visitor replied: "Yes, we would appreciate that."

The boys had been sitting silently the entire time, stuffing crullers into their mouths in between staring at their father and Karitas, who had stood like a sentry at the door to the old kitchen and acted as if she had nothing to do with those present. The housewife, who had never had any difficulty directing houseguests to their beds when the day was at an end, now seemed a little insecure, and said first: "Skarphéðinn, you'll sleep up in the family room in your brother Höskuldur's old bed," but then hesitated for a moment before saying to Sigmar: "You'll sleep in the guest room." Then she looked questioningly at Karitas. And then alternately at her and her husband. The only married couple under her roof. Sigmar looked at Karitas, who was still staring at the window. She saw their duvet in Borgarfjörður—white warm fragrant—reflected in the windowpane, their divan, her easel, heard the surf, looked at the napes of her boys' necks. She yawned. "I'm going up to bed now."

The door to the guest room was opened wide.

The women opened the window, let in the cool evening air, made up the beds, dusted off the tables, shook out the lace curtains, tidied the books. Asked the guests to come in. They went and got their saddlebags. With a smirk on his face, Skarphéðinn had gathered his bedding and brought it up to the family room. One by one, the others went to bed, acting as if nothing were out of the ordinary and no one had come to visit. Karitas lay open-eyed in bed, numb in body and soul like one who has been pulled up from a deep crevasse. The silence in the room was oppressive; many had difficulty falling asleep after the evening's dramatic events, but in the end, the varied tones and rhythms of breathing hinted that sleep had triumphed. At first, Karitas dozed rather than slept, or so it seemed to her, rising now and then onto her elbow to check whether her boys were definitely in their bed. Toward morning, she fell into a deep sleep. She dreamed that Sigmar came to her and ran his finger down her face as if to divide it in two. When she woke, she saw that the others had already gotten up. She lay still and tried to determine what time it was by listening to the sounds from below. She heard Hrefna's affected laughter down in the kitchen, the cheerful tones of Auður and Hallgerður, men's voices. Clearly, everyone was in high spirits this morning and had a lot to talk about. She reached under the bed for the chamber pot, pulled it up and under the duvet, and sat over it a long time. Her mood was surly as she considered her next moves.

Her absence from the kitchen had eased some of the others' reticence in the presence of the distinguished gentlemen. She could hear it as she walked down the stairs. They seemed to have had quite a jolly time over their porridge. A certain person had even entertained them with tales of his stay in the sun-blessed country of his Roman companion, or so she gleaned from the housewife's statement that it was good to hear he had felt so well in the sun down south. Then Karitas stepped in through the kitchen door, and everyone stopped talking. The Roman sprang to his feet and bowed his head slightly, while the Icelanders remained fixed to their seats. When it became clear that she would neither wish them a good morning nor nod to them, Sigmar got up, looked over the group as if it were the crew of his ship, thanked the housewife for the good porridge and the excellent blood pudding, and looked at his sons. "Well, my lads, we had better get going." As he passed Karitas, he said to her: "The boys will be riding with me to Skaftafell. You can start packing in the meantime. And then early tomorrow morning, we will leave for Hornafjörður." He was extremely polite, and went to the door as if everything were settled. Yet he couldn't refrain from turning for a second to see the expression on her face, and she, who knew his methods and recalled his behavior back in Skagafjörður, was suddenly able to think clearly. Pretending as if she had heard nothing of what he said, she looked at Auður and asked with a touch of puzzlement, "Where did Skarphéðinn go? Weren't we all planning on going to Salthöfði today?" The others, put in a tight spot, hemmed and said, "Well then," as they got up and jostled each other to be first out the door. Sigmar looked coldly at his wife, and then signaled his sons to follow him out. The Roman sat there looking nervously at the two women. Without looking at Karitas, Auður smiled at him and said: "That wasn't a wise thing to say, bright heart." The foreigner took her words as encouragement to have more to eat, and that was what he did. But Karitas, being in no mood for admonitions, hastened out to the farmyard, where she stood and watched her boys and their father saddle the horses. "Where do you think you're going?" she asked her sons. They stopped what they were doing and looked at each other. "We're going to ride to Skaftafell with our papa," said Jón, trying to sound determined. "Have I given you permission to do so?" she asked. Being completely unprepared for any opposition on her part, the boys were lost for words; they just stared at the slender, trouser-clad woman who had, in a single morning, become unrecognizable. But it was Sumarliði who defused the situation. Knowing the way to women's hearts, he went to his mother, put his arms around her, and begged her with a smile: "Dearest Mama, please let us go. We'll be back tonight." And she stroked his head: "Go then, but watch out for the foxes."

They rode west and were barely gone from sight when she regretted having allowed them to go. Now, Sigmar Hilmarsson would have all day to interrogate his sons about their mother's circumstances ever since their paths had diverged, and if she knew her boys, they would report everything thoroughly and conscientiously. She, in turn, would be no wiser concerning his life in the land of sunshine for the past thirteen years. Auður read her mind and said that it had been right of her to allow them to leave. They would have to get to know their father sooner or later and had every right to do so, and he needed to know what they had been up to here in Öræfi. "Is that so?" retorted Karitas bitterly. "But ought we not to know what he was doing all those years overseas?" Regarding this, Auður apparently had some pertinent information, but before she was able to comment, Karitas hurried inside, threw dirty socks into a tub, boiled sanitary belts in a pot, laid washcloths on the washboard and flew at them as if she wanted to scrub the life out of them. The other members of the household went about their usual work all morning, despite such noteworthy events having taken place both there on the farm and out in the world. After all the drama, they had to gather their thoughts before delving further into any of it and immersed themselves in their chores, there being so much to do now that preparations for the autumn work were in full swing. So violently did Karitas pound the socks with the mallet down at the stream that brown water splashed everywhere. She neither saw nor heard Auður until the housewife touched her hand: "I have never seen you in such a state. Now put those socks aside for a moment so that we can talk." And she plunged straight into the intended conversation, which was in fact a monologue, when it came down to it, saying, as she pointed toward her farm, "The dark-eyed man in the guest room is a learned scientist who is writing a book on the ancient Romans and their rule in Spain, or so said Sigmar this morning before you came down. He got to know the Roman and his family several years ago, and helped them run a shipping company in a town called Naples, and now you know, bright heart, where he has been all these years, and he sailed here aboard his own boat, which is waiting now in Hornafjörður. The other thing that I would like to say to you is this: you two are still married, and for your sons' sake, you need to sit down together and talk about the future. And I would also like you to put your house in order as far as my Skarphéðinn is concerned. He suffered quite a jolt when your husband suddenly showed up, and has been a bit beside himself ever since. This morning he refused to eat anything, just stormed out to the workshop without a word. Do you hear that hammering? I think he's getting a bit out of control—but goodness me, how handsome your husband is! It makes the heart throb, seeing such a man."

When Karitas made no reply, thinking only of the ship that was waiting in Hornafjörður and feeling both anxious and nauseated because of it, Auður added as she turned away: "That's all I had to say, but how fun it would have been for my Skarphéðinn if the foreigner had been able to speak Icelandic. The two of them could have discussed their countries' ancient heroes until the cows came home."

"So he came by ship," said Karitas. "How many tons is it?"

Everyone noticed how the couple said little to one another, despite having now slept under the same roof after thirteen years of separation—but the real dratted shame, for the women, was that the foreigner couldn't speak Icelandic. At lunchtime, they found themselves in a terrible quandary where he was concerned. They had taken pains with the cooking, boiled salted lamb, dug up rutabagas, made gravy, baked flatbread, and prepared rye-bread soup, but when it came time to summon the man to his meal, they were overwhelmed by shyness and balked, one after another, at going to knock on the door of the guest room, where he had kept himself all morning without making the slightest sound. "He could be sleeping and not have any appetite at all," Hrefna said, despite having taken extra great pains with the rye-bread soup just for him. "He can't talk like I do," said Hallgerður, who was all hunched up—though in general, she gave little thought to whether people talked or not. "I'm afraid of disturbing him in his research," said Auður as she stood there motionless, staring at the salted lamb—though realizing that the task would probably fall to her. But then Karitas came in, wet to her knees, and they looked commandingly at her: "You can knock on his door. You've been overseas."

She gave the door a quick knock with the knuckle of her middle finger, and then opened it resolutely. The Roman sat hunched over the table, staring at the things that he had arranged there, apparently with great precision. Books on the far left, a flower vase and a few glasses in the middle, an alarm clock on the right. Is he going to draw these things? was her first thought. When he saw her, he rose and bowed his head, which he seemed to do every time he met a woman, but when his eyes met her cold gaze, he sat right back down again. She stood before him with her arms crossed over her chest, staring at this foreigner who knew more about her husband and the father of her children than she herself, and said: "I don't know how it is with you down south, where you probably dance all night and sleep through the day, but here in the Öræfi district, it is customary to eat lunch at the proper time. But because the women here have never seen a foreigner before and don't know whether such people need to eat salted meat like us Icelanders or whether they draw their nourishment from the sun, they have asked me to ask the gentleman if he would be willing to join them in the kitchen so that they might get a better look at him."

She pointed with her outstretched arm toward the door, which he took to mean that she was asking him to come to the table, after describing what was to be served and how it had been prepared. When he stepped into the kitchen, the women glanced this way and that, having plenty to attend to as he could very well see, although they did make it clear to him with hand gestures that he should take a seat. They arranged the bowls and plates around him so that he didn't need to reach for anything, poured milk into his glass, and hustled hemming and hawing in and out of the kitchen. Out of the corners of their eyes, they watched how he used his fork and knife, how he laid them in a cross, upside down, on his plate before raising his milk glass to his lips. It was clear that he found it perfectly natural to be surrounded by a group of women whose one and only task was to serve him his meal. He obviously liked the salted lamb, because he looked warmly at the housewife and said, *"Buono buono,"* which she easily understood, because she nodded, though without looking at him. The hammer blows from the workshop, however, reminded the women of their duties to the other men, and they were about to summon them when Hallur entered. He grunted when he caught sight of the foreigner, but quickly switched on the radio and sat down, saying that it was pointless trying to deal with Skarphéðinn in his current foul mood. He hadn't answered at all when asked if he was going to come in to eat. Auður shot Karitas a glance, went out to her son, and returned with red blotches on her neck, which usually appeared when she was upset about something, but she didn't say a word.

The news of the world poured from the radio over the lunch table. It seemed that the Germans' declaration of war the day before had escaped the rest of the world's notice—and even the Germans' own, because, said the narrator in a strained voice, the residents of Berlin were sitting in sidewalk cafés, enjoying the fine weather. The same was supposedly true of the French and the British, according to the latest news from Britain, which caused Hallur considerable disappointment. He had expected sharper reactions from the British. Hrefna noticed her brother's dejection and said: "They may just be waiting until after the weekend."

It was drizzling outside, and world affairs were put on hold for the time being. The foreigner bowed his head slightly and disappeared into the guest room. The hammering in the workshop stopped. The son, who had declined both breakfast and lunch, appeared in the farmyard, leading a horse by the reins. Auður reacted quickly, putting salted lamb and flatbread in a bag and running out to him. She dashed back into the house and said that he was going out to Salthöfði to put the tables in the slaughterhouse in order. "You go with him," she directed Hallur, and he got up, as obedient as always, but to her sister and daughter she said: "Once you've done the dishes, go up to the rocks and pick berries. Fill a few tins; we need more juice for the winter." Looking at Karitas wearily, she said, "Bright heart, don't you think it's time for you to start packing?" Then, before anyone could argue, she went out the door and disappeared into the storehouse.

After being left alone, Karitas didn't know what to do with herself. Since there were guests in the house, she couldn't start scrubbing the floors as she usually did on Saturdays. There would be no big washes to do until after the weekend, and if the thought had previously occurred to her to use this time to pack her belongings, the journey south being so imminent, she certainly couldn't do so now. People might think that she was obeying Sigmar Hilmarsson's orders. She wanted to go upstairs and take a nap along with old Bergþóra, but she knew that as soon as she laid her head on the pillow, thoughts and images from past times would crowd her head, and she needed to keep her head on straight and her spirit balanced. She didn't want to see any images, neither in color nor black-and-white, and in any case, she had painted them all over a long time ago. In the frame there was only white canvas, as at the start. No one knew what was beneath it; she herself couldn't even remember. Or could she? She suddenly thought of her collages in the box in the old kitchen. She had to do something about them before she left; keep the best and take them with her, throw the rest away. She went and got the pictures and spread them out on the kitchen table, but there wasn't enough space; she had to use the floor, as well. They covered the table and the floor, her best pictures from Öræfi, and as she regarded them, she tried to remember everything she had painted in her life. But then her whole life began to flash before her eyes, forcing her to rub her forehead and temples with her fingertips to ward off the needles pricking at her head. She wasn't on her guard and didn't hear it when the door opened behind her, only noticed an unfamiliar smell and turned around. The stranger stood in the doorway, staring at her pictures. A moment passed, and then she raised both hands and brought them down hard on his chest, pushed him backward over the doorstep, and slammed the door furiously in his face.

In the absence of her sons, Karitas herself had gone to fetch the cows—when the thought struck her that the boys and their father might not return. An excursion to Skaftafell—he was probably well beyond the rivers. Sigmar was the man who left, the man who didn't return. For a second, she thought she might lose her temper. She urged the cows on, poked at their loins, begged them in God's name to try just this once to hurry, but then left them standing at the foot of the hayfield and ran into the workshop. She had the saddle in her arms and was on her way out to the western field to catch a horse when Auður came out and asked her to wait a second. "Where might you be going, bright heart?" Karitas said it as it was: she was going after her husband, who had abducted her sons. Auður replied that she doubted whether her pursuit would yield the intended result, since the man had a full day's lead, besides the fact that it was a bad idea to go rushing away now, "as it will soon be dinner, and I can't see why he would have headed west, that man, when his ship is waiting out east." "You don't know this man," said Karitas, "but I do. Why do you think he has come here, if not to take the boys, and who besides he himself said that he came from the east? Couldn't his ship just as well be in the south?" "But I thought he asked you to pack all of your things, both yours and the boys'," said Auður, who could no longer follow Karitas's speculations. "He came to get all three of you, and I am sure that they will all be back before darkness falls. But tell me one thing: Does no flame still burn between you?" "There isn't so much as a spark," Karitas replied coldly. For the next two hours, she stood out in the farmyard and stared west, refusing to eat or drink anything, and was so peevish that everyone left her alone except for Auður, who came out at regular intervals and said: "They'll be here soon."

"What did I say!" she then exclaimed, when three men on horseback appeared silhouetted against the dark-blue western sky. One large and broad-shouldered, the other two half-grown. There was no mistaking it; the father and sons were returning. As they rode up the hayfield, Karitas could see in the way the boys carried themselves that their trip had made them feel more vigorous, masculine. They held their heads high, puffed out their chests, wore previously unseen expressions of haughtiness. Continuing to act as if their father were a barely noticeable breeze, she commanded: "Into the old kitchen with you. It's Saturday night, in case you have forgotten, and your hair still needs washing."

Karitas

Wooden Tub on a Stool 1939

Pencil drawing

Evening in the old kitchen.

The icy silence of the glacier lies upon the roof.

The drizzle wets the little window beneath the rafters.

The creamer, the butter churn, and the coffee grinder rest in shadow on the bench against the wood-paneled wall. Opposite them is an old, silent chest.

The water boils in the black pot on the sheep-dung-fired stove.

The steam ascends to the rafters.

From the ceiling hangs a light bulb that illuminates a wooden tub, which stands on a stool in the middle of the sand-scrubbed wooden floor.

I wash my boys' hair.

Have them crouch over the tub, apply soft soap to their hair, rub it in, and work up a lather. Pour lukewarm water from a large jug over their heads and rinse their hair thoroughly.

Their father, who has come to take us from the countryside, stands by and watches the hair washing.

The four of us stand around the tub.

Say nothing in the glacial silence.

Karitas's assertion that there wasn't a single spark between her and her husband wasn't credible, in the opinion of the other women. Hrefna claimed that she had seen sparks flying around the tub that the couple stood over, opposite each other. Yet they hadn't exchanged a single word, and while Hrefna had interpreted the sparks as love, Auður was of a different opinion, being more experienced in such matters. She clearly didn't like the look of things. There was something menacing in the air, reminiscent of the feeling that people from other farms in the parish got in the outlying sheep sheds haunted by ghosts, a feeling almost of physical discomfort. Her younger children had had the sense to find themselves another place to sleep for the time being. Skarphéðinn had sent Hallur home with the message that he would spend the night with his brother, Höskuldur. The two of them had to write an article for the journal of the youth association, and when Hallgerður heard this, she pretended to have pressing business with her cousin at the central farm, and would even have to spend the night, so important it was. The foreigner still hadn't left his quarters except when summoned for meals, so the only ones who remained to gather in the kitchen were the elders, who had a bad feeling in their guts. "I will have peace in my house before bedtime," Auður said. She went into the old kitchen, where there was an icy silence, and said to Sigmar, who was staring at his wife with a piercing gaze: "I have changed your bedclothes, if you would please." She signaled to him to leave the room and didn't move until he had gone to his own. A day and night had passed since the guests arrived, and Karitas still acted as if Sigmar were little more than a breath of air.

The mother and her sons finished their Saturday washing. Karitas rubbed dry the boys' heads until they winced, but at the same time, they found their tongues again; words gushed from them after the frigid draft over the tub had dissipated. "Oh, you should have seen the faces of the boys on all the farms when we rode past with Papa," Sumarliði said, and she felt compelled to listen to all of their detailed descriptions. It had been a long time since they had been so exuberant, her boys, and now they practically talked over each other as they told of their neighbors' reactions as they came riding by in the company of that elegant, splendidly dressed man. The neighbor boys had been so dumbfounded that they could barely pull themselves together to greet them. "And then you should have seen their expressions when we told them that he's our father, the captain of a ship waiting out in Hornafjörður!" While recounting their experience, the boys punched each other lightly. She had no difficulty imagining people's reactions—or the women's expressions—when they saw Sigmar. But it was the next comment that kept her from sleeping that night: "And then, Mama, the boys said they'd always thought we were just sons of a poor maid—that they'd had no idea that we had a father somewhere, let alone one so well-off!" It was Sumarliði who said this. Jón was somewhat more thoughtful as he bade them goodnight and spread the duvet over himself and his brother, as he usually did. He said: "Mama, Papa is going to sail north on his ship, taking the eastern route, and we would really like to go with him."

Now, the married couple would simply have to talk to each other, but it couldn't be done without outside assistance—Auður had to step in. The next morning, she didn't set places for them at the table, but instead, saddled her best horses, packed a bag of provisions, and asked them please to go for a ride and talk together; she preferred to have peace in her house, if they didn't mind, and they understood that this was an order, not a request, and mounted their horses without objection. They rode slowly down the slope and out onto the path. Their sons had climbed onto the roof so that they could follow their progress as far as possible—these parents of theirs whom they had never before seen together. Jón had seen them, of course, but he was so small when they'd lived together in Borgarfjörður that there was no way he could remember the house's sighs when their passionate caresses reached their climax.

But there they rode, toward the hills to the east, and the expression on Karitas's face was so harsh that the sun, which shone from a cloudless sky, gave up trying to soften it.

They had ridden for quite some time and Sigmar had begun talking about the weather, looking in all directions and saying, as if to himself, "I wonder if the wind will turn soon," when she abruptly snapped: "What do you want here, Sigmar? Why did you come?" Clearly having no further interest in polite chat, he went straight to the point, saying that in his opinion, she had no right to be contemptuous and arrogant toward him; it hadn't been he, after all, who had run away with the children, but she. It was like setting fire to an oil barrel; she tore into him so furiously that it frightened even her, but she had held it all in for so long that it flew out of her like a shower of arrows—it was a miracle that he didn't fall off his horse under such an attack. And she reminded him of all the months, weeks, days, hours, and minutes that she had had to spend alone with her children, ill and crying while he was making money and dawdling down south, and she burst into tears as she recounted the most painful moments. Then she wiped her eyes and nose with the back of her hand and said: "But there is one thing you need to know, Sigmar Hilmarsson, and that is that I don't give a pin for where or with whom you were traipsing around for thirteen years. Your life no longer concerns me."

She kicked her horse into an amble.

He followed closely, looking rather meek after hearing her story of suffering, and it was only after they had reached the sheep sheds by the eastern hills that she stopped the horse, turned to him, and spat: "Would you prefer to eat here or somewhere else?" He said that it was all the same to him where they ate, and they dismounted. This sunny Sunday, he was wearing his foreign riding suit and high leather boots, and she, as usual, was wearing overalls, wool socks, and galoshes. That the distance between them as they sat down in the grass was so great could also perhaps be explained by their vastly different clothing—as if they weren't cut from the same cloth at all, and therefore couldn't sit next to each other. Despite this difference, they were both quite warm. He took off his jacket, and she her galoshes and wool socks. He sat up on a large rock and looked south, toward the sea, while she used a tall tussock as a backrest and looked north, toward the mountain. They sat there opposite each other and munched flatbread. She stared at the green vertical stripes on the mountain, which she had seen so often before, and was always amazed at the Creator's sense of form, at his skill in combining colors. She let her eyes wander toward the rock pillars at the western end of the mountain and regarded the strange black formations. Giant profiles in the rock, fantastic creatures with gaping mouths, a man and woman. The white glacier in the background. The man and woman looked to the west, one standing behind and slightly higher than the other, but it had never been decided which of them loomed over the other; it was always as if they changed places from one moment to the next. She focused on the contrasts in the colors up there; he stared at her bare feet. To still the waves that had previously crashed over him, he made an attempt now to lead the conversation down other paths, saying that it must be difficult for people to live in such a remote area. What prompted him to start talking about the way of life of people in this district, she didn't know, but replied that people here hadn't known the meaning of the word "difficult" before getting the radio. "But you're quite far behind the modern world here in the countryside," he asserted, although he should have known that this remark could easily make her blood boil again. Which in fact, it did to a certain degree, because she said sharply, "As far as equipment and techniques go, we may be a bit backward, but when it comes to know-how and ability, we're far ahead of those who turn up here uninvited."

There he had it. He said nothing more, but the fire in her was already stoked. Unable to let it rest, she said haughtily: "Despite the fact that my sons have developed into such fine boys, thanks in part to the fine treatment they have received here in the countryside, I have decided that they must have an education, and am sending them north to my mother so that they can go to school, and I am going to bring them there myself. On our way to the north, we will be stopping in at my brother's, the lawyer in Reykjavík, so that he can arrange our divorce, which of course will be easier to effect now that the deserter has finally come forth."

Sitting there across from this man, as arrogant as he was, was so intolerable to Karitas that she felt practically compelled to torment him a bit. But instead of provoking his anger and making their conversation even more heated, she inadvertently caused him to change tactics. He stood up, and she saw immediately where this was heading. "Sit back down!" she ordered, but of course, being Sigmar, he didn't obey, and instead sat down beside her. It was her slender, sockless feet that drew him to her; he stroked her instep as if in a trance, ran his fingers toward her toes, and she hardly dared to breathe, for if she did, she would catch the scent of his skin, and once that happened, those thirteen years could become as one day. He took her hand and asked, "Where is the ring that I gave you in the east? Wasn't it called Mary's Tear, the stone?" With solemn affectation, she said: "The Mary's Tear is in the arms of a tin soldier that the boy in the north gave me when I was young and free, and now they're both lying at the bottom of my chest."

He turned away, looked up at the mountain, and then said, "Are you still after chaos?"

She went on the defensive, knowing that he was referring to their conversation about art that had taken place in the sitting room at home in Borgarfjörður and was trying now to gain the upper hand. Even so, she didn't try to stop him, because she really wanted to see how he intended to do so this time. He fiddled with the legs of her overalls, moved his hand up under them, and stroked her calves. Incredible how warm his hands always are, she thought, feeling the chaos intensifying in her head. Then she remembered that the next move was hers. She played her pawns: "I couldn't attend to chaos with children in my arms, you see. Children can't tolerate chaos, they need order and security, which is what they have gotten here in the countryside. Chaos had to give way." He said, "My friend says that he has seen some of your pictures. He says that you spread them out all around you." Her temper flared. "Leave my legs alone. I was just picking out some collages that I created after the ten o'clock news in the evenings. I wanted to get rid of them before heading south." He was taken aback; this she could see. He took his hands off her legs but moved his face closer to hers. She looked at his lips and wished that the two of them were birds flying through the beautiful blue expanse. How can this be? she thought, on the verge of tears. I hate him. He said: "Every one of your pictures is unique. Art runs in your veins; not blood, as in the rest of us. You must never get rid of any of your pictures."

Now he's saying the magic words, she thought. She hastened to turn the tables, asking scornfully, "Well, have you become as rich as you intended, Sigmar Hilmarsson? Can you buy yourself a pastry every single day?"

He waved away a crane fly.

"My little one, I have come to offer you a house. Two stories or three stories, whichever you wish, running water in the sinks and bathtubs, lighting in every nook, electricity and a telephone, a salon for your guests on the ground floor, a bedroom for us and the boys on the floor above, and a studio for you at the top."

He awaited her answer. She looked at his face, smelled his scent without inhaling deeply, knew that he could throw himself upon his prey at any moment, such a skilled hunter Sigmar was. She had seen a falcon dive at a ptarmigan—and take it. "You haven't shaved," she said. She should have said something more sensible, because now that irresistible smile of his spread over his lips. He drew nearer, came closer and closer until she saw herself reflected in his eyes, but when their lips were just about to meet after the long separation, he moved his mouth to her ear and whispered: "And you haven't brushed your hair, my little one." The sky arched over them and the moment for which everyone longs. He spread his wings over her. But then a small gust of wind came from the east, stirring a lock of his hair and blowing on her bare feet. She wriggled away.

"I can't bear the cross of living in your house. And stop this 'little one' talk of yours. I'm no smaller than you."

She staggered as she stood up, then grabbed the bag, and was mounting her horse when he pulled her back down to the ground. Holding her tightly with both hands, he said: "Why is that a cross?" She reached under her shirt, grabbed the case holding the photograph of the little angel, tore it off, and clapped it into his palm. She let him look at the photo of his daughter for a moment, long enough for her to see her feelings reflected in his: guilt, grief. Then she took the picture from him, and said: "You can't have it. It's the only one that I have. But she looks like you, don't you think?" She stuck the photo back under her shirt and swung herself onto her horse. "Well, we've talked, as Auður asked, and now we can go home for dinner. I'm not certain, but I think we're having smoked horse meat and rhubarb compote."

She kept him behind her all the way home. She thought she heard him snort and growl, but wasn't sure; it might just have been a noise in her head or the wind changing direction, but as they rode up to the farmyard, she brought herself to look back and saw that those strange sounds had probably come from him, because she had never before seen Sigmar scowling so fiercely. It was unfortunate that Skarphéðinn chose just that moment to provoke the ship captain. "He could have just left it alone," Auður said later. "Yes, it damn well served him right," said Hrefna, cursing for the first time in her life, as far as anyone could remember. But they were all gathered there in the farmyard under the noonday sun, apart from Hallur and the foreigner: Auður, Hrefna, Hallgerður, Skarphéðinn, and both the boys, taking a look at a stallion that Höskuldur had brought to show them. And the couple had only just ridden into the farmyard when Skarphéðinn turned away from the stallion, grimaced, and called to Karitas: "Before I forget, I wanted to tell you that I put another book I would like to give you in your chest, and inscribed it as I did the first: 'with thanks for a warm summer night.'"

The fuse was lit. Those few words were enough.

But just at that moment, when the others were trying to make up their minds about how best to prepare for battle, Hallur came running out of the house, waving both arms and panting happily: "War has begun! They just announced it on the noon news! The British prime minister made a statement this morning, saying, 'This country is at war with Germany!'" When no one responded, he lowered his arms and fell silent. The others were still standing there, stunned by Skarphéðinn's announcement, and therefore paid no heed to the one that the British prime minister had made to the world. War had broken out; there was no doubt about that.

Skarphéðinn was surely able to see from Sigmar's stinging gaze and threatening demeanor that it would be best to get away as quickly as possible, because he abruptly leaped into action, swinging himself up onto the stallion and racing down the path at a full gallop. With Sigmar on his tail. The others stood motionless by the potato patch, watching the action without a word; the foreigner walked out in his stock-inged feet, holding a book. They all stared at the heroes dashing toward the cliffs. Höskuldur gritted his teeth and said: "Damn it." He pulled Karitas down from her saddle, jumped onto her horse, and rode off after them as if the devil himself were at his heels. Then the others found their tongues again; the boys flew into a rage and wanted to run off and fetch horses, save their father from Skarphéðinn's terrible clutches, but then they saw the riders turn in a wide arc and head back toward the farm at full speed, with Skarphéðinn in front. Those watching moved instinctively back to the farmhouse wall; Karitas grabbed the boys by the shoulders and pushed them behind her. The galloping heroes drew nearer, came up the path to the farmhouse, and everyone thought that the two men might end this feud with a proper fight in the farmyard. But that was not the case. On the roof of the old turf-and-stone farm-house, the workshop farthest to the west, lay two scythes and a few rakes, and without reining in the stallion, Skarphéðinn reached out for one of the scythes and continued riding west, brandishing the weapon above his head. The man from Borgarfjörður, the famous hunter and expert shooter, followed his example, grabbing the other scythe and continuing his pursuit of his adversary. And finally, those in the farmyard saw Höskuldur attempt to do the same as the other two, except that he had to settle for grabbing a rake, the scythes being taken. The foreigner clapped his hands enthusiastically, and a torrent of words poured from him. But the women were far from thrilled. They saw the men speed back toward the cliffs, watched until they disappeared from view. "They'll all be killed," Hallgerður said. The boys cried out and tore themselves free from their mother, but Auður finally snapped back to her senses. "Take the boys into the house," she ordered, and, as the mother didn't seem to be all there, Hrefna carried out her sister's order. She hooked her hands under the boys' arms and pulled them in against their will. Then came back out again, scarlet-faced and with a gleam in her eyes. "Go down there and try to stop this madness," Auður then ordered Hallur, who had stood there with his hands in his pockets, befuddled and with his mind still on Chamberlain's statement. "And take the Roman with you," she said in a sharp tone. "You're going to need help stopping Skarphéðinn." She didn't know Sigmar's character, which was perhaps just as well, as matters stood, but Karitas knew it quite well and feared the worst. She wandered over to the potato patch and sat down on one of the dirt beds. But the two men rode off, determined and lofty, as men often are when they set off to fight for their country. The Roman had managed to put on his leather boots.

The other women stood there with their arms crossed over their chests, not quite knowing what to do with themselves. They shaded their eyes with their hands a few times to see if they could spot the men, but were dazzled by the sun's glare. Karitas fiddled with a potato leaf. "We can start digging these up." "Yes, the plan was to start doing so after the weekend," Auður replied. She was still looking south, restlessly. Finally, she said heavily: "To think; making us wait on lunch like this."

Old Bergþóra up in the family room, however, had to have her lunchtime porridge, no matter what, so that she could take a nap after the meal, so Hrefna headed in to take care of her. She came out again quickly and asked if she should bring a bit of horse meat for them to nibble on while they waited for the men to come home. Being hungry, the women didn't object to this idea, but first wanted to know what Hrefna had done with the boys. "I locked them in the pantry," Hrefna said contentedly. "They have plenty to eat and drink in there and can tell each other stories while the men beat the foolishness out of each other!" The others stared at her in amazement. Not because of her harsh treatment of the boys, which was the best solution to keep them out of the fray, but because no man had ever been allowed into the pantry on this farm, as far as they could recall, and for this reason, this was something of a sensation. Since there was no need to worry about the boys as far as food was concerned, they sat down in the potato patch and munched on horse meat, and Hrefna went back into the house over and over to fill up the serving dish—they were terribly hungry, after all—and finally, they rounded off their meal with rhubarb compote and cream. After they had licked the insides of their bowls, the conversation turned back to the potatoes and whether they should check if they were ready to be harvested, since they were just sitting there waiting, anyway. They reminded each other that the potatoes last year had been too big; the medium-sized ones were better, like the ones the year before, but of course the small ones were the best, there were no two ways about it, and it was best to sort them out and use them for special occasions in the autumn months. They went and got a shovel, dug up a plant, looked closely at each potato, and agreed that now was the time to harvest them, and not a day later. So they went and got another shovel and a wooden box; two dug up the plants, the others gathered up the potatoes, and they talked about the autumn work, estimated how many lambs they should slaughter and considered reducing the number of barrels of salted lamb, since the boys would be leaving. Karitas ate so little that her presence or absence made no difference in this matter, but then she said, as she lightly shook dirt off a few potatoes: "He has offered me a three-story house in Akureyri, where we all would live, with a telephone, electricity, and a bathtub, a studio on the top floor and a salon for guests on the bottom one. He wants us to sail north with him via the eastern route."

This announcement was so overwhelming that they all had to sit down on the potato beds. "Sweet Jesus," said Hrefna. "The moment I saw your husband, I simply knew that you would become a fine madam." Silently, they envisioned Karitas in that position. Hallgerður said: "If you sail north with him up the east coast, you won't be able to show the folk in Reykjavík the dress we made for you." They were speechless, having never dreamed of hearing such an astute comment from Hallgerður. They scratched their foreheads. "The boys want to sail north with their father, and shouldn't one stay with one's children?" said Karitas. "I'm not letting them go with him by themselves." Hrefna replied: "Wouldn't it be sensible to sail north with him for free? I'm sure the bus trip to Reykjavík costs an awful lot of money." Then they looked at Auður. The answers always came from her.

"The mother tubers have had it," said Auður, holding out one of the seed potatoes to show them. "Yes, and so it will go for all of us women, eventually." She got up and went back to digging, and the others followed suit. They carried on talking about the size and shape of the potatoes, and Karitas told them that her mother had once been digging up potatoes when she gave birth, and Bjarghildur had poked up between the potato plants. She told them the story as she herself had heard it, as well as the story of her own birth, and they listened attentively, having never heard the like; apparently, that's how things could be in the Westfjords—but suddenly, in the middle of it all, Karitas simply stopped. As if she were seeing the stories in a new light. "Can it be," she said slowly, "that Mama just made it all up? She rarely told stories, but the ones that she did tell were so strange, almost unbelievable."

The others hemmed and hawed. Auður cleared her throat. "No, bright heart, mothers never lie. On the other hand, life is one big lie."

But these stories, which they actually found more credible than not, had reinvigorated the women. They dug away at the potato patch as if they expected to find children under the plants, and the sweat poured from their foreheads. Karitas, on the other hand, who had just realized her mother's talent for fiction, along with so much else that she was only now seeing from a different perspective, became so pensive that she had to sit down. They let her sit in peace, it being healthy for everyone to think, but then Auður stopped digging, leaned on her shovel, and said: "Is there something bothering you? Anything with which I can help?" "No, Auður, I just started thinking about chaos." "Chaos?" the others exclaimed in unison. They wiped off the sweat and had to sit down for a moment. "When I returned home from my studies at the Academy," said Karitas, trying her best to think clearly, "I sought chaos in my art. I had learned of this from the countries down south and was fascinated by it. I wanted to interpret it with my works, but when I began painting, form gained the upper hand, contrary to what I had intended. Still, chaos slumbered inside of me, and today, at the eastern hills, as I looked at the green streaks on the mountain and the ogrish rock pillars, it reawakened—I can feel it growing inside of me, romping around like a wild foal. I've got to get back into the world of chaos."

They weren't quite sure what she meant by "chaos," but, being very familiar with the feelings awoken when viewing the works of creation, they were with her all the way when she talked about the green stripes and the rock pillars, and the inner wild foal they all knew well, although they kept it to themselves. But the mention of this sufficed to remind them of the stallion that they'd been shown at noon, and the fight that was probably taking place below the cliffs. Once again, they peered southward. The sun had disappeared, the air was cool, the clouds had lined up in a formation that boded rain. Auður said: "It's been nearly three hours since they left. They must have finished fighting long ago." Hrefna agreed: "No one can fight for so long. They must have gone down to Salthöfði to patch up the slaughterhouse, since they were practically there anyway." Karitas said doubtfully: "It's unlikely that Sigmar would join them in doing such work, let alone the foreigner." "Where is your husband?" Hallgerður then asked. "That's just it, Hallgerður. I think that my husband has left. He's inclined to disappearing without warning."

"Are they going to make me wait with the afternoon coffee, too?" said Auður wearily.

Hrefna said they could probably forget about making the planned crepes. But that was more than Hallgerður could bear—when someone said they were going to do something, they had to do it; the women should have known that. She sat down on one of the potato beds and started whimpering. "Agreed!" cried Karitas, who also wanted warm crepes. "Now you've made Hallgerður cry." The sisters looked at each other. They were in a quandary: they could hardly make crepes, they felt, if none of the men were coming for afternoon coffee. "We have crullers in the pantry," said Hrefna, but just then, they remembered the boys locked therein, and they livened up. Even though they weren't yet men, strictly speaking, they soon would be—so it was perfectly reasonable to make crepes for them. It was time to let them out, anyway; the tumult down by the cliffs was surely over by now. Hrefna walked briskly into the house, and a minute later, both boys burst out and peed in the farmyard, making steam rise from the ground. Sumarliði was close to tears; having had to hold it in for so long was torture. They were also hungry and thirsty, but hadn't dared so much as move in that white-washed sanctuary of delights, let alone open a cake tin.

Old Bergþóra had tottered down the stairs and out the door, and she turned her blind eyes toward the sea. "Do I smell blood?" "No, Bergþóra," Karitas replied gruffly, "you smell pee."

Hallgerður was first to notice the movement down at the shore. She and the others had stuffed themselves with crepes and drunk an entire pot of coffee, and the women had plucked up the courage to explain to the boys the strange behavior of some men who let themselves vanish into the blue, when Hallgerður suddenly pointed out the window and said: "Funeral." She had often seen coffins being transported from a farm to the church on horse-drawn carts, seen how people comported themselves, walking slower than usual, looking down at the ground. This must be a funeral.

They rushed to the window. Peered out, pushed each other aside, were unable to see properly, ran out into the farmyard. Then discerned three men in the distance, on horseback and pulling a cart. They appeared to be coming up out of the sea, moving as quickly as the wheels allowed, but the gloom that hung over them woke memories in Karitas. In her mind's eye, she saw a horse-drawn cart on a white mountain heath. Saw the woman with all her children and all her belongings on the cart. Remembered the silence, the hazy gray color when sky and sea grow faint just before it snows, recalled the smell of the trunk, the sacks, the wool in which she was bundled, heard the whispers that carried to her from all directions in the frigid stillness.

"Twenty-four years later and I'm still looking at a horse-drawn cart," she thought out loud.

The procession had reached the path to the farmyard before they made out whom it comprised. Hallur rode the horse pulling the cart, behind him rode Höskuldur and the foreigner, Andrea. Then those at the window knew which of the men were no longer standing. They tried not to think about the condition of those lying in the cart, whether they could still sing and speak like most people. They stood rooted to their spots until Auður said hoarsely: "Get the guest room ready." Hrefna and Hallgerður hurried in, enormously relieved to be rid of that disagreeable sight, but Auður and Karitas held the boys by the shoulders, awaiting what should be. Karitas felt as if a large fist were clenching her heart; at that moment, it became clear to her how empty her life would be without Sigmar. Even if he had never really been in it. Just then, she knew that she did not want to live if he were gone. Shortly afterward, when she saw that he was alive, her feelings did an about-face. Something similar happened with Auður. They were both filled with a kind of defiance. After halting in the farmyard, Hallur dismounted and explained that he'd had to knock the men unconscious to make them stop. "I had no choice," he said, but was clearly satisfied with his efforts. "They would have killed each other. They'd been fighting tooth and nail for over three hours, and neither would give up. I just can't understand it," he said, looking at the women and the two boys. "We aren't used to such fights here in Öræfi." The men lay in the cart with their heads against its inside wall, dazed from having been knocked out and so exhausted that they could neither speak nor move. They were bloody and wet from head to toe, covered in mud and mire, cut and torn. Skarphéðinn was unable to walk due to the back hold that his opponent had put him in, so Hallur and Höskuldur carried him between them into the house. Sigmar staggered in with the help of the foreigner. Glancing at her husband as they lumbered over the threshold, Karitas saw that he was still boiling with rage, and that sight was enough to stifle her newfound feelings for him. Hrefna whispered to her brother, Hallur, though loudly enough that most of them heard it: "Were they fighting over Karitas?" He answered that he thought it had been more about agriculture and fishing; the battle was between the farmer and the fisherman, after decades of feuding and rivalry.

The adversaries were both put in the guest room. The other men peeled off their tattered clothes and undertook to wash the muck off them themselves, as both fighters were now half-naked. In the meantime, the women stood in the doorway and looked down at the floor. Next came a hasty examination, which revealed that both men had wounds and cuts here and there, black eyes, red ears, and a few loose teeth. Auður and Hrefna immediately treated the visible wounds, applying alcohol and willow leaves and bandages, but since neither of the men could speak, it took quite some time to find out what other injuries they had suffered. By dinnertime, however, it had become clear that they were seriously injured, and that Skarphéðinn was far worse off. His back had been pulled so badly due to Sigmar's wrestling hold that he was practically immobilized. In addition, his shoulder had been dislocated, his ear and neck were so battered that he couldn't swallow, and in the heat of battle, he had bitten his own tongue. Sigmar, on the other hand, had sprained his elbow and ankle, had a sore neck and a constant buzzing in the ears from a blow to the head. Since there was still no pain medication on the farm, the women again administered the mixture used to reduce bloating and flatulence, feeling it better to give them that than nothing at all, if it could alleviate their pain even in the slightest. But the medication did little good, and their constant agonized groans could be heard throughout the house, sometimes so loud that Hallur had to shut the door to the guest room so that he could follow the progress of the war on the evening news. He found the women rather apathetic about developments abroad, and since Höskuldur had gone home for dinner, he described the situation in detail to the foreigner, using hand gestures and facial expressions for emphasis. The Germans were still in Poland; the British were conscripting every man who could bear arms. Andrea Fortunato seemed to understand what the Icelander was saying, but instead of being enthusiastic, as expected, he became silent and sad. He did, however, cheer up a bit when the women took his duvet from the guest room, led him up to the family room, pushed him onto Skarphéðinn's bed, and said that he was to sleep there now. Looking touched, he sat on the bed and ran his hand over the headboard, as if he had always dreamed of sleeping in an Icelandic family room. Down in the guest room, the men were put under guard. Nothing else would do—"For all any of us knows, they might just start up again," said the housewife, who watched over them herself and nursed them with the help of Hrefna. The boys were allowed to sit with their father until after midnight, and they stared at him with anxious eyes. Karitas made herself scarce. She came into the guest room only once, to ask if she should throw away their tattered clothes or try to rinse the dirt out of them.

Karitas

Moon over Sea 1939

Pencil drawing

Silver-white light.

In the cool of the evening, the stream winds its way down the gully, along the fields, the meadows, to the endless sea, and becomes one with it. A radiant white ball out on the horizon receives the stream, draws it into the silver light.

The moon is over the sea.

The evening is beautiful, an evening made for love.

He is sitting on the hill above the gully, leans back, looks at me. I sit by the stream, see how it winds its way toward the moon, rinse out my clothes so that everything I bring with me on the great journey over the rivers is clean. I take my dress from the wicker basket, let it dance with the rushing water in the moonlight.

I want to capture the beauty on canvas, yet don't want to paint a landscape. But as I wring my dress, I get an idea. See a new shape in my mind's eye.

A wrung dress floating in the air.

Above it, a menacing circle.

My fingers are stiff in the cold glacial water, but inside, I have a new, warm feeling. I hear a different sound, see different shapes, different colors.

I feel as though everything around me is changing.

New days have begun.

I watch the old days pass away.

They run with the stream to the sea.

With one arm in a sling, he came limping to her as she sat by the stream, and said that he wanted to talk about the journey north with the boys. Over twenty-four hours had passed since the fight down by the cliffs. She was rinsing out her clothes; in the bustle of the day, she had forgotten that she herself needed clean clothes when she left—but she also liked to sit by the stream on a moonlit autumn evening and think. So it gave her a bit of a start to see him. She hadn't expected him to be up and about so soon; Skarphéðinn was still bedridden. He stopped a short distance from her, and when she didn't say anything, he began as usual to talk about the wind, whether it might turn before nightfall, but because the wind never came down into the gully, such speculation was futile. Then he turned to other subjects, saying that his friend, Andrea Fortunato, would remain behind in Öræfi. He had made arrangements with Auður for him to stay over the winter. She was delighted that he would be staying, since she was losing the boys and then Skarphéðinn later, when the winter fishing season began. The surprised look on Karitas's face prompted Sigmar to explain the matter further: "Yes, so it goes. Andrea needs to lie low for a while. Some oafs down south want him dead, and have pursued him persistently, all over. Can you imagine a better hiding place than here in Öræfi?" She said: "No, I can't imagine any better hiding place, seeing as how it took you thirteen years to find me." "Let's not talk about that right now," he said, as if he thought it pointless to wallow in the past. "But my friend Andrea, who knows a lot about art, said that he'd gotten a fleeting look at your pictures, as I told you, and he asked what such a talented artist was doing in an isolated place like this. I told him the truth: that your stay here was at an end, and that you were on your way to Akureyri, where you would be able to devote yourself to your art in a spacious studio."

These things being said, he acted as if the matter were now settled.

"The boys will be staying with my mother, as was agreed, and I will take them with me via the southern route," she said, though not as petulantly as she had intended, because the Italian's comment had touched a sensitive string in her heart. Now Sigmar resorted to the method that had always served him so well when he wanted his own way. He sat down behind her on the rock by the river, let her feel his warmth and manhood at her back, his warm breaths that played in the locks of hair at her neck, and made her to understand in particularly well-chosen words that she was unique, different from everyone else; that art was in her blood, and that she was, therefore, superior to others, whereas he, who was just an ordinary man, had realized long ago that he couldn't hold a candle to her. But precisely because he was just an ordinary man, he wanted to be seen with their boys, let the crew of his ship see them—he had in fact told his men that he would return with his wife and sons. The boys also wanted to be seen with their father, that he knew. All boys wanted to have a strong father; it was in their nature.

And she listened to this as she shook her dress in the icy water.

When she didn't answer, he grasped her tightly by the shoulders and turned her toward him: "Karitas, my honor is at stake."

She said: "You think only of your honor. What about mine?"

Then he buried his face in her hair and whispered in her ear: "Karitas, was I thinking of my honor when I allowed you to draw me stark naked?"

These words evoked memories that only the two of them could share, and let loose feelings that neither had expected were still present, least of all so intense. Afterward, she felt as if she had had no willpower; it had clearly been the flesh that decided, not her mind. The moon hung over the sea, they drank water from the stream, and she said: "It's so strange, but in the old days when we were at this, I always thought so clearly afterward."

The ship awaited them out east in Hornafjörður.

"We'll set course for Seyðisfjörður, where we'll take two men on board, and then sail from there straight to Akureyri," the captain told Hallur when he asked for the third time how the journey would be made. It wasn't because Hallur had become hard of hearing or forgetful, he was just keeping the conversation going while folk were saying their goodbyes and the travelers mounted their horses. It was customary. Andrea said little, and the women even less. Hallgerður looked sadly at the travelers. Hrefna held her hand to her mouth, tears in her eyes. "I'm so bad at goodbyes." The housewife maintained her quiet dignity, although no one doubted that she was the one who would miss them the most. The boys and their father were now on horseback, waiting for Karitas. "Why does everything always take her so long?" But Karitas had to make numerous trips back into the house, if not to fetch something that she had supposedly forgotten, then to say goodbye to old Bergþóra and the bedridden Skarphéðinn once more. When she kissed Skarphéðinn on the cheek, he said: "He's a damned sturdy man, your husband; I wonder if I could get hired onto that ship of his?" Out front, Sigmar grew impatient, tired of Karitas's meandering. He asked if someone could go in and hurry her up. After a bit of a search, Auður found Karitas in the passageway to the cowshed. There she stood, lost in thought, staring at the bucket holding the women's sanitary belts. "I was just saying goodbye to the cows," she said, without taking her eyes off the bucket. When Auður saw that she had no intention of moving, she took her gently by the arm and led her out. "It's about time," said Sigmar. "Shall we get going, then? The river guides can't wait all day." But then it was as if Auður suddenly remembered something. She turned to the boys and said: "There is something that I have wanted to tell you, my boys. Your mother hiked with me to the highest peak in Iceland at the start of the summer. And never let up the entire way."

There was an awkward silence in the farmyard. The members of the household weren't accustomed to fabrications from the housewife, and they attributed this announcement to her strained emotions at the hour of parting. Hallur blew his nose, the boys and their father squirmed in their saddles. Then Sigmar said amiably: "I have never doubted that Karitas would reach the highest peaks. But can we leave now?"

It was then that Karitas said: "I think that I would rather take the southern route. They made me a dress, the women, so that I could be seen in it in Reykjavík. And besides, my pictures are there in the south."

It took the others a few moments to realize what she had said, but then the boys yanked at their reins as if their heart rates had suddenly shot up. They couldn't say a word; just stared in disbelief at their mother. The horses grew restless.

"I dreamed this," said Sigmar. Karitas acted as if she hadn't heard him and instead, went and stood between the two boys, grabbed their legs, and looked from one to the other. "But you go straight to your grandma when you arrive in Akureyri, because she will take care of you, see to it that you are dressed warmly, that your hair is combed properly and your fingernails are clean, and with her, you will eat at regular times and have packed lunches for school, and she will make sure that you do your homework and read the Bible, and that you always behave properly and politely toward others."

The others scratched their faces and cleared their throats. Sigmar turned toward the sea so that they couldn't see his face, but finally, the boys realized that their mother was serious. They dismounted tentatively and asked breathlessly if she would be coming north afterward—"Won't you just take the bus, Mama?"—and, of course, she said that she would come in the spring as soon as the snow melted, and then she began to kiss them and could hardly stop. And they hugged her, tried to bear up like men, told her to take something with her to throw up in as so many people got carsick, and asked her for goodness' sake to be careful crossing the rivers. "You be careful crossing the rivers," she said. Sigmar made no move to dismount. He turned to her for a moment and looked at her with his sea-green eyes. She wondered how many years might pass until she looked into them again.

They rode toward the sun, which was pulling itself up into the eastern sky. She watched them until the light blinded her. The pleasant lowing of the cows sounded from the cowshed before milking. They had no thought of leaving; they would never cross the rivers. Karitas, still wearing her traveling clothes, stuck to Auður, dogged her heels until they ended up in the cowshed. Auður stroked Fenja passionately, like a young woman caressing her prospective husband, sat down on the milking skull, laid her forehead against the cow's belly, squeezed her nipples, pulled. She had been milking for some time before she said: "That was an abrupt turnabout on your part."

"People seldom change plans once they're mounted and ready to go. I thought it better not to let them know until the last minute," Karitas said. "As if I were going to travel by sea again, just to retch and throw up! But as I said, I'm going south tomorrow morning with the summer children." Auður said that she'd known she was going to lose her. "But you get to keep the foreigner, at least," said Karitas. "He's a good man," said Auður. Karitas said, "But you can't expect him to fetch the cows for you as my boys did." Auður caressed Fenja with her cheek. "I know that, but it will be nice to have him around." Karitas thought she saw a twinkle in the woman's eye. She wasn't sure, so she proceeded cautiously, this being the housewife herself, after all, and said casually: "Isn't he twenty years younger than you?" And Auður answered just as casually: "No, eighteen."

The milk streamed down into the bucket. Karitas watched as if hypnotized, seeing her entire life in the white, warm liquid. "Bright heart?" said Auður questioningly. "It hurts so much to leave you," said Karitas. "I'm afraid that I'll never come back." Auður moved closer and hugged her. "It has been so wonderful having you here. I have to pretend as if you're returning soon; otherwise I won't be able to bear losing you. As you know, I'm not going anywhere, neither over the rivers nor to other worlds. But there is one thing that I wish to ask you while I can still hold you in my arms: try to come to my funeral; I would really appreciate it."

Karitas

Over the Rivers 1939

Pencil drawing

The rivers and the sand.

A day's journey over sandy wastes and muddy brown rivers.

The guide says the rivers are impassable following the glacial flood, so the caravan must make a detour over its source at the glacier tongue. Everyone fastens crampons onto their shoes before heading up onto the edge of the ice; the horses are shod with studded shoes. We walk across the glacier in single file, each person leading his own horse, holding on to the tail of the horse ahead. A twenty-person group: young men going south for the fishing season, young women going to work in a hospital or a factory, the summer children going home to their parents and their schools. The youngest child, a nine-year-old girl who has worked as much as an adult all summer, is ahead of me. She is very careful, knowing that one mustn't step on a crack, because it could open up. During the four-hour journey over the glacier, I keep an eye on the horses, consider what they do, observe their odd way of walking; they never step on a crack.

River horses. Powerful, calm, with a prominent whorl in the hair at their chests.

We come down from the glacier, see huge hunks of ice strewn across the expanse of sand. We remove our crampons, ride over the wastes and the river branches. Not a single blade of grass, no birds in the sky, only a deep, ominous silence. But I find it pleasant, feel as if I am free. At the refuge hut in the middle of the sands, we stop to rest, eat the food that we brought. We sit outside in decent weather, and I regard my fellow travelers, the women in windproof jackets, boots, and plus fours, the men similarly dressed, but wearing wooden clogs and peaked caps. I take a handful of raisins from my lunch bag, stick them in the little girl's pocket, and say that they're for her to munch on along the way.

A river guide comes riding toward us from the west, wet to his loins, greets the group and its guide from the east. The two guides stand next to the hut and exchange words. Neither of them is tall, but they are both agile, reliable, and courageous. Without them, we would get nowhere. They mount their horses.

River guides on their horses. Desolate sands, sea, and sky in the background.

The group packs up, the guide from the east bids farewell, rides back toward Skaftafell.

We avoided the most dangerous river by crossing the glacier, but now another river awaits us, surly, dark, and muddy. The guide leads the little girl's horse over to test the ford. He leaves the child on the sandbank on the other side while he crosses back over for the rest of us. I wonder what the little girl might be thinking, alone on the sandbank with the rushing river between her and the rest of the group. He leads the rest of us over a little farther downriver, but we still have to let the horses swim. The river swells, the horse is lifted, it's suddenly as if I'm floating freely, overwhelmed with fear and excitement, and then I feel how well the horse is swimming, become more confident, yet am exhausted when we reach the sandbank. The river horses, experienced and familiar with it all, don't even shake off the water when they emerge. We pour water out of our boots. I'm wet to my waist. With childish confidence, the little girl smiles and tells me that she ate the raisins while waiting.

It's nearing evening, the last great river lies ahead of us, and I'm bruised and battered after the ride and the exertion, thinking only of trying to stay on my horse. I look at the little girl, don't know where children get their stamina. The guide leads us over via a ford that he located that morning. The water reaches only to the horses' bellies.

We've crossed the rivers and the sands.

Over to another district.

It has grown dark. The group members separate and head to the farms where they will spend the night. I don't know anyone with whom I can stay, but the guide has made arrangements, and accompanies me and the little girl to a warmly lit farmhouse. He hasn't said a single word to me along the way, but now he turns and asks politely: "Will you be coming east again next spring?"

I give it a little thought, and then say no.

"I expect that I'll go the long way around."

ABOUT THE AUTHOR

Photo © 2016 Heida HB

Kristín Marja Baldursdóttir is one of Iceland's most acclaimed writers and the internationally bestselling author of numerous novels, including *Karitas Untitled*, a Nordic Council Literature Prize nominee; *Street of the Mothers*; *Chaos on Canvas*; and *Seagull's Laughter*, which was adapted for the stage and also into an award-winning film. She received her degree in 1991 from the University of Iceland and has also worked as a teacher and a journalist. Among Kristín Marja's many honors are the Knight's Cross of the Icelandic Order of the Falcon for her achievements in writing and her contributions to Icelandic literature, the Jónas Hallgrímsson Prize, and the *Fjöruverðlaun* Women's Literature Prize. Kristín Marja lives in Reykjavík.

ABOUT THE AUTHOR

Kristín Marja Baldursdóttir is one of Iceland's most acclaimed writers and the internationally bestselling author of numerous novels, including *Karitas Untitled*, a Nordic Council Literature Prize nominee; *Street of the Mothers*; *Chaos on Canvas*; and *Seagull's Laughter*, which was adapted for the stage and also into an award-winning film. She received her degree in 1991 from the University of Iceland and has also worked as a teacher and a journalist. Among Kristín Marja's many honors are the Knight's Cross of the Icelandic Order of the Falcon for her achievements in writing and her contributions to Icelandic literature, the Jónas Hallgrímsson Prize, and the *Fjöruverðlaun* Women's Literature Prize. Kristín Marja lives in Reykjavík.

ABOUT THE TRANSLATOR

Philip Roughton is an award-winning translator of many of Iceland's best-known authors, including Nobel laureate Halldór Laxness, Jón Kalman Stefánsson, Þórarinn Eldjárn, Bergsveinn Birgisson, and Steinunn Sigurðardóttir.